"I will pay this debt for you."

Margaret stared at Tom, her eyes wide open in shock. "Why would you do this? What could you possibly expect to gain by it?"

That was a dangerous question. Tom wasn't willing to delve too deeply into the question of why—not with her, or even with himself. "I'm trying to *help* you. I'm the only hope you have right now. Why won't you admit it?"

He could see pride battling with fear. "I will accept your offer," she said shakily. "And I will offer collateral. I have a stable of fine racehorses."

He shook his head. "Horses are not good collateral. Not long term."

She turned to face him. "What do you want from me?" she asked, her voice plaintive.

What *did* he want? At the moment, Tom wanted nothing more than just to stand here and look at her. Even now, in the midst of her distress, she was perfectly beautiful. She was fiery and determined and brave.

"I want to marry you," he blurted out.

Praise for
An Heiress at Heart

"Engrossing and heartbreaking...*An Heiress at Heart* is poignant, profound, and lovely."
—*USA Today*'s Happy Ever After blog

"This is a wonderful love story...not your usual English stuffiness; there is something for everyone."
—*RT Book Reviews*

"[A] clever historical and subtly inspirational romance... filled with emotion and sexual energy...The classic historical plot will appeal to many readers."
—*Booklist*

"Extremely well written, well plotted, and historically detailed...I definitely will read every book Jennifer Delamere writes."
—BooksLikeBreathing.blogspot.com

"The romantic tension between Lizzie and Geoffrey is ever-present, but graphic love scenes are entirely absent, which will delight those historical romance fans who prefer a more delicate approach."
—*Publishers Weekly*

"A pretty good read."
—ReadingwithStyle.blogspot.com

"Fantastic...I loved this book."
—ReadingwithAnalysis.wordpress.com

"Jennifer Delamere sets a new standard in Victorian romance, with characters who shine and a plot that'll keep you guessing."

—Abby Gaines, author of *The Earl's Mistaken Bride*

"A sweetly rendered tale of discovery and forgiveness with a refreshing touch of innocence."

—Cindy Holby, bestselling author of *Angel's End*

Also by Jennifer Delamere

An Heiress at Heart

A Lady Most Lovely

Jennifer Delamere

FOREVER

NEW YORK   BOSTON

Forever
Hachette Book Group
237 Park Avenue
New York, NY 10017

www.HachetteBookGroup.com

Printed in the United States of America

First Edition: September 2013
10 9 8 7 6 5 4 3 2 1

OPM

Forever is an imprint of Grand Central Publishing.
The Forever name and logo are trademarks of Hachette Book Group, Inc.

The Hachette Speakers Bureau provides a wide range of authors for speaking events. To find out more, go to www.hachettespeakersbureau.com or call (866) 376-6591.

The publisher is not responsible for websites (or their content) that are not owned by the publisher.

For Jim

Two are better than one; because they have a good reward for their labour...

And if one prevail against him, two shall withstand him; and a threefold cord is not quickly broken.

ECCLESIASTES 4:9 AND 11

A Lady Most Lovely

Chapter 1

London, August 1852

"Aren't you the man who rode a horse twenty miles to shore after a shipwreck?"

Tom Poole grimaced in irritation. This had to be the twentieth time tonight that he'd been forced to answer some inane question. He turned to see who had addressed him.

The man looked about the same age as Tom, but he was much shorter and a good deal more rotund. His weak, watery eyes were focused on Tom with complete fascination. Apparently everyone in London had heard his story—or some wild, exaggerated version of it. Tom had been answering questions like this all evening, trying to set the record straight for dozens of questioners who had been buzzing around him like mosquitoes. "It was only seven miles," Tom told him pointedly. "And I didn't *ride* the horse."

With a vain hope that this would satisfy his inquisitor,

Tom turned away. He no longer cared if his answers were too brusque. He'd done more than his share of socializing tonight, and in any case his real attention was elsewhere—held captive by the most beautiful woman he'd ever seen.

She was breathtaking—tall and stately, with every feature that Tom had always found desirous in a woman: gleaming dark brown hair, high cheekbones, and a full, sensuous mouth. A generous portion of her smooth, ivory skin was displayed to great advantage by the low-cut neckline of her emerald-green gown. Tom had spotted her the moment he'd come in. Although he'd been introduced to just about every other person in this overcrowded ballroom, somehow she had remained far away—unreachable, like a star or a distant planet.

Since no introductions had been forthcoming, Tom had decided to ask James Simpson who she was. James, who was the cousin of Tom's half sister Lizzie, was an affable roué who seemed to know everyone in London. Tom had been just about to ask him about the woman when they'd been interrupted.

James now looked askance at the man. "Carter, hasn't anyone told you to obtain an introduction before butting into a conversation?"

"Oh, I beg your pardon," Carter returned in an exaggerated tone, not looking the least bit contrite. He gave Tom a showy bow. "Bartholomew Carter, at your service."

Tom replied with a brief nod. Carter's lack of protocol revealed he was just like so many men Tom had met at this party: self-indulgent, self-important gentlemen who would not have given him the time of day before he'd left England. Now that good fortune in the Australian gold fields had elevated Tom from a poor farmhand to a wealthy man, he was suddenly on everyone's list of people worth knowing.

His sister Lizzie's social status had also risen dramatically. Last year she'd married a baron, and now she was Lady Somerville, a member of London's elite social circle. For her sake Tom had done his best to endure the lessons on deportment and all these irritating interactions that passed for conversation with the upper classes. He knew it was an unavoidable duty, given his new station in life, but his patience was growing short. Especially tonight. Tonight he wanted only to meet the woman who had kept him spellbound.

Once more Tom's gaze strayed in her direction. She'd spent much of the past hour speaking with a very slender, rather shy-looking young lady—one who might have been pretty, but whose features seemed to fade into her pale, peach-colored gown. On the surface these two women could not have appeared more different, yet they were chatting with the air of close friends. For some reason Tom found this intriguing. He'd seen plenty of so-called friendships that were nothing but two people pretending to like each other in order to gain some social advantage. Tom wondered if perhaps this one was genuine.

"You mean, you didn't ride to shore on a wild stallion?"

Wild stallion? With great effort, Tom turned back to Carter. "It's a *Thoroughbred*. A champion racehorse. Took first place three times at Homebush."

"That's not the way I heard it," Carter persisted. "I

heard he could barely be contained in his stall during the voyage to England."

Tom frowned. "The horse is, understandably, leery of ships."

That wasn't the half of it, of course. It was a wonder the creature had survived the voyage at all, given its constant restlessness that verged on panic whenever the seas were rough. But now that the stallion was on dry land, it was easily controlled by any competent rider. But this information would be lost on Carter. No doubt the only time he got near a horse was when he placed his generous rump into a finely appointed carriage.

Irresistibly, Tom glanced at the woman again. She looked so poised, so cool and collected, as though she didn't realize that the horde of people in the room had sucked all the air out of it.

It was hot, and Tom's collar chafed. Every part of his attire, from his elaborately knotted cravat to his trim-fitting coat and trousers, was too confining. He was still adjusting to the sheer volume of clothing that custom dictated for gentlemen. In his humbler days he'd rarely needed more than a simple shirt and trousers. He tugged at his cravat in an attempt to loosen it, even though he could imagine the look of disapproval this would bring from his new valet. Stephens was not just a servant but a mentor. He was teaching Tom how to dress and how to allow others to do dozens of things for him that any man should be able to do for himself. Being waited on hand and foot chafed Tom even more than the cravat. He would never forget that hard work alone brought his success. He would never become like the buffoon who was still questioning him.

"What was it like to be captured by savages?" Carter prompted.

"The Aborigines didn't *capture* me," Tom said sharply. "They *found* me washed up on the beach, half dead. They took me to their camp and helped me recover."

This drew a look of disbelief from Carter. He evidently preferred to visualize Tom pinned down by the point of a spear. That alone illustrated the vast difference between them. Tom had lived for weeks among the Aborigines, but it was only now he'd returned to England that he found himself among a truly different race. He had been excited about returning to London—he'd always loved the energy of its noisy, foggy, bustling streets. But he was seeing a new side of the city now. He'd been dirt-poor when he'd left for Australia seven years ago. He had lived in parts of London that nobody in this room was aware even existed. Or at least, they did not acknowledge it if they did. He'd only seen these grand homes from the outside, only observed their inhabitants from a distance. Now he was one of them. Well, not exactly *one of them*. Perhaps *among them* would be a better way to describe it.

Despite his joy at being reunited with his sister, Tom had begun to question whether coming back had been a good idea. Only now, as he watched the statuesque brunette gracing the room with her sweeping gaze, did he think all his pains had been worth it. It had been a very long time since a woman had taken such complete hold of his attention. Longer than he could remember. He *had* to get James to introduce him. "James," he said, "who is that woman?"

James looked toward the place where Tom was indicating, but Carter cut him off before he could answer.

"Tell me, Poole, is it true the Aborigine women walk around all day without a stitch of clothing?" His mouth widened into an ugly leer. "I should like to see that."

This remark swept away the last shred of Tom's patience. He took hold of Carter's coat, bringing the smug idiot close enough to sense his anger. "Do you think they are no better than animals? There are far worse savages in England, I assure you."

Carter's mouth actually fell open in shock. But then he collected himself and shook free of Tom's grasp, sputtering, "How dare you handle me like that, sir!" His right arm came up, as though he was foolishly considering taking Tom on—something that Tom, God help him, would have relished. His fists clenched, and he might actually have taken a swing if James had not stepped in and smoothly steered the man several steps away.

"Carter, you've plied Tom with quite enough questions," he admonished. "Why don't you go find the billiard room or something."

Carter straightened his coat. After throwing an icy glare at Tom, he turned and stalked off.

"Thank you for rescuing me from that fool," Tom said.

"I had the impression I was rescuing Carter from *you*," James countered with a smirk. "I could see you were ready to throttle him. Not that I would have blamed you. He is an insufferable bore."

Tom waved away James's well-meaning words. "No. It was my fault. I should not have allowed him to anger me. I should not have used force against him." He shook his head ruefully. "I keep forgetting all those things Lizzie has been trying to teach me. Not to mention—" He cut himself short.

James lifted an eyebrow. "Not to mention what?"

Again, Tom waved him off. "Never mind." There was no point trying to explain; James probably would not understand. Despite the multitude of resolutions Tom had made over the past year, there were still far too many times when he lost his temper. Why was it so hard for him to act with the patience he was supposed to have if he was truly a Christian?

"Forget about Carter," James said. "As far as I'm concerned, you acted admirably. I'm sure everyone else thinks so, too."

Startled, Tom looked around and realized what James was referring to. The gentlemen and ladies who had been standing nearby had apparently noticed his little run-in with Carter. Many were still staring at Tom, their expressions ranging from alarm to undisguised amusement. He had made a spectacle of himself.

Had *she* seen it? What would she think of him?

Tom looked quickly over to her. She may have been watching him, but it was impossible to tell. Her attention seemed to be focused on an old man with enormous whiskers who was kissing her hand. "James," he said, though his eyes never left the woman, "who is she?"

"I see you are determined to meet her," James said with an exaggerated sigh of resignation. "Well, come on then." He dove into the crowd, and Tom quickly fell in step with him. All around them, people moved aside and pretended to go back to their own conversations, although Tom still sensed that they were watching him.

"I'm surprised you should be interested in her," James remarked as they went.

"Really? Why shouldn't I?"

"Well, don't misunderstand me...Miss Cardington is a very respectable young lady to be sure, but she's a bit...bland. Sad to say, she's probably on a direct route to spinsterhood."

"Are you daft?" Tom exclaimed. "She's the most beautiful woman in the room!"

James paused, looked at Tom, and then followed his gaze back to the two women. "Oh, I beg your pardon. Were you referring to the lady in green?"

"Of course!" Tom replied, amazed that someone as astute as James could have misunderstood.

"Ah," said James. "Of course." He shook his head and gave an odd little smile, as though amused by some private joke. He started forward once more. "I told you about her before we arrived," James said as they skirted a small group of boisterous men who were on their way to the card room. "Miss Margaret Vaughn is the reason we're at this gathering. Well, half the reason. She's engaged to Paul Denault. Our host, the Duke of Edgerton, is Denault's uncle. He's throwing this party in their honor."

"Engaged?" Tom repeated.

The word came out as a gasp, and James gave him a curious glance. "She's quite beautiful, as you have noticed. She's also the wealthiest heiress in London. Inherited mountains of money when her father died two years ago. Denault is one happy man."

"Who is this Denault?" Tom demanded. "Surely not that old man!" he added in dismay, pointing to the old man with the prodigious whiskers who was still speaking with her.

"Oh, dear Lord, no," James said with a laugh. "Although

he wishes he *was* her fiancé, I'm sure. That's Mr. Plimpton—a pillar of London society, and he'll be the first to tell you so."

"Where is Denault, then?" Tom said impatiently. During the past hour, he'd seen Miss Vaughn chat with scores of people, including those he pegged as would-be suitors. But he could have sworn she had not bestowed particular attention on any one man.

"Let me see…" James scanned the room. "He's usually in the smoking rooms chatting up the barons of industry, unless he's entertaining the—ah! There he is." He pointed to a tall, sandy-haired man, impeccably dressed, who had a cohort of young ladies clustered around him.

"He has many admirers," Tom said drily.

"Oh, yes," James agreed. "Both Denault and the ladies agree that he is a very handsome man indeed."

But why wasn't he with Miss Vaughn? How could he possibly find other ladies more appealing? Remembering James's remark that she was an heiress he said, "Denault's marrying her for her money, then."

James shrugged. "I doubt it. He has plenty of his own."

"Inherited?" Tom figured that as the nephew of a duke, Denault was in that privileged class whose money was handed to them at birth. Tom was beginning to loathe that sort of man, for the simple fact that they all now loathed him.

"Not at all," James said, surprising him. "Denault's branch of the family is well connected, but not as wealthy as it once was. He made his fortune on investments in America. He is, as the Americans would say, 'a self-made man.' I suppose that's something you two have in common."

At that moment, Denault finally deigned to send a glance in Miss Vaughn's direction. As their eyes met, Denault gave her a smile and a look that seemed to say, *All the world knows that I am yours—and you are mine.* When Miss Vaughn serenely returned her fiancé's smile, an irrational jealousy wrapped itself around Tom's heart. He and Denault shared something much greater than business sense, that was certain.

"Do you still wish to meet her?" James asked.

"Yes," Tom said resolutely. Even knowing she was engaged could not curb his desire to speak to her.

She had taken note of their approach. Tom was sure of it. He could tell by a subtle shift in her posture, an extra alertness in his direction, even as she kept her eyes fixed on Plimpton. He felt a surge of excitement at this realization. Suddenly he was far too conscious of his tight collar, his heavily starched shirt, and his overpolished boots. In fact, everything he had on was foreign to him. He told himself this must be the reason why he felt as though he were moving through heavy sand.

They were stopped by Denault, who broke away from his little group of admirers and strode over to intercept them. "Simpson!" he said warmly, holding out his hand.

While James returned the greeting, Tom watched as Miss Vaughn excused herself from Miss Cardington and Mr. Plimpton and came to join her fiancé. Now that she was so close, Tom found he could hardly breathe. He marveled at her flawless features. Her eyes were deep green—nearly the same shade as her gown—and rimmed in the center with yellow gold. They studied him with cool interest.

"I'd like to introduce you to my cousin," James said. "This is Mr. Thomas Poole."

"Tom," he corrected. "Just Tom."

One of Miss Vaughn's delicate eyebrows lifted a fraction, but she said nothing.

"Tom Poole?" Denault repeated. "The man who made a fortune in the gold mines?"

News traveled fast among London's elite. Faster than the wildfires in Victoria. "You've heard of me."

"Heard?" Denault echoed. "You might buy and sell the Crown now; that's what I've heard. You're a lucky man."

There was admiration in his eyes—and avarice as well. Tom had seen it in plenty of people, from the poor ex-convict gold miners in Australia to the highborn folk in England. That look always put Tom on his guard. He'd seen how dangerous men could be when driven by greed. He also knew what hypocrisy it bred. The upper classes might abuse him behind his back for his lowly origins, but to his face they could only compliment him for having so much money. "It was a lot of work," Tom pointed out. "The gold don't mine itself."

"Of course," Denault said, waving off Tom's remarks. He turned to his fiancée. "Miss Margaret Vaughn, may I present—"

She cut him off as she extended her hand and said, "How do you do, *just* Tom?"

Tom didn't miss the hint of derision in her words. Most everyone he'd met tonight had approached him either with awe or as some kind of phenomenon to be marveled at. Yet the woman he'd been admiring all evening was actually speaking to him with condescension! It was a challenge he could not ignore. Calling him as she did by his Christian name, even in jest, she might have been speaking to an errand boy or a servant. This thought, ironically, cued something his sister had taught him to say during introductions. He grasped her hand and said with gentlemanly dignity, "Your servant, madam."

Her hand was cool but it sent a curious warmth through him. Her stunning eyes widened, as though she, too, were startled at the sensation. Tom's lessons in etiquette completely left him and he forgot what he was supposed to do with her hand. So he continued to hold it, savoring the opportunity it gave him to be close to this woman. He was fascinated by the strength and fire in her gaze.

"Will you be in London long, Just Tom?" She sounded a bit breathless.

"I..." he faltered like an idiot. Suddenly he felt as unsteady as if he were back on the stormy seas. *Keep your wits about you, man,* he told himself, and released her hand. "I will be in England for the indefinite future."

"How wonderful." Her gaze held his. "We shall be glad to get to know you better."

"Indeed we shall," Denault broke in briskly. "Mr. Poole, perhaps you would like to be my guest for lunch tomorrow at my club? I've a business proposition for you."

Denault's offer jerked Tom back to his senses. He should have expected this, even from a man as rich as Denault. Everyone, it seemed, wanted to discuss business ventures with him. So far, he'd deflected or turned down all such proposals. He could have found some reason to avoid Denault, too, but he found himself agreeing to the appointment instead. He had an unreasonable urge to find out what kind of man Miss Vaughn had agreed to marry. "Will Miss Vaughn be joining us as well?" he asked.

Denault threw a condescending look at his bride-to-be. "Heavens, no," he said with a laugh. "Women aren't allowed at the club. And in any case, she has no head for business, poor thing."

Something like annoyance or anger flashed across Miss Vaughn's face. It was brief, and she quickly suppressed it, but it did not escape Tom. As an heiress in her own right, surely she was capable of handling business affairs. Why didn't she correct him? Tom was aware of the adage that when a man and woman were married they became *"one person, and that person is the husband."* Even so, he could not imagine Miss Vaughn in the role of a meek wife.

"I could not possibly join you in any case," she said lightly. "I am far too busy. The wedding is days away, and there are a thousand details to arrange."

At the mention of their wedding, Miss Vaughn and Denault exchanged a look so amorous that Tom wondered if he'd been mistaken about her apparent irritation. She must love Denault. Once more Tom felt himself awash in jealousy, even though he had not the slightest right to be. Miss Vaughn was betrothed to another man, and it was evidently a propitious match. Certainly there was nothing he could do about it.

She turned her attention back to Tom. "Will you also marry soon, Mr. Poole?"

Steeped as he was in thoughts of Miss Vaughn, this

question took Tom utterly by surprise. He could only look at her blankly.

"I thought perhaps you were searching for a wife," she said. "I saw how intently you were studying each lady in the room."

So she *had* been watching him, just as he had been watching her. Tom found this knowledge incredibly intoxicating. He would gladly have explored this mutual attraction, if not for the unwelcome fact that she was already taken.

No, he was not considering marriage to any of the other ladies he'd met tonight. They seemed too vacant, too pliable. Tom wanted a woman who was spirited and strong. He wanted what the Bible called a *helpmeet*—a true companion, not a mere accessory. He'd thought Miss Vaughn might possess those qualities, but now that he'd seen her with Denault he wasn't so sure. He shook his head in answer to her question. "I might have to return to Australia for that. The ladies there have more backbone."

Her eyes narrowed. "Do they?" She rose up a little taller, and her gaze swept over him from head to foot. He gladly withstood her scrutiny, pleased to have drawn a spark from her again. "Everyone in Australia seems quite...resourceful," she said. "Including you. I should like to hear more about your famous shipwreck. It seems a fantastical tale."

For the first time this evening, the mention of the shipwreck did not annoy Tom. He did not try to analyze why. "I'd be more than happy to tell you about it. At times I have trouble believing it myself."

"Paul, dear," Miss Vaughn said without even looking

at her fiancé, "I am dying of thirst." She thrust her empty champagne glass in Denault's direction.

Denault looked at it in surprise, clearly taken off guard.

"That's an excellent idea," James interposed. "Don't worry, Denault. We'll entertain Miss Vaughn while you're gone."

Denault looked mistrustfully from his fiancée to Tom. Could he possibly feel threatened by him? The thought was more than a little appealing.

"I have a better idea," Denault said. "I am sure you are famished, Margaret. Why don't we both go to the supper room?" He took hold of her elbow, as if to lead her away. With a nod to Tom and James he added, "If you gentlemen will excuse us."

Miss Vaughn gently extricated herself from his grip. "I only asked for something to drink," she said, her voice edged with irritation.

"Yes, my darling, but you've eaten nothing this evening. We cannot have you fainting away from lack of food." His annoyed tone left no doubt this was an order rather than an expression of concern. She answered him with a frosty look.

Yes, there was trouble beneath those apparently smooth waters. Miss Vaughn and Denault were not as madly in love as they wished to portray. Of course, being *in love* was no requirement for marriage, certainly not among the upper classes. Even a commoner like Tom knew that. Why, then, should they pretend?

He could see her wavering, undecided. If he were a betting man, Tom would have wagered half his gold that Miss Vaughn did not have it in her nature to be docile.

He'd just as gladly give away the other half just to find out what was going on in that head of hers. He was hoping for a good display of fireworks.

To his disappointment, Miss Vaughn relented. She gave Denault a crisp nod of assent before turning back to Tom. "I do hope we shall meet again, Just Tom."

Something flickered in her eyes that gave Tom the wild hope that her words were more than mere formality. Tom kept his gaze fastened on hers. "I should like that very, very much."

Her lips parted in surprise, and he knew his meaning had reached her. She swallowed and looked away. Denault took her elbow again, and this time she did not demur.

As Tom watched her retreating form, he was captivated by a stray curl that had made its way down the back of her long, elegant neck.

And he knew with dangerous certainty that he must see her again.

Chapter 2

Margaret kept her hand on Paul's arm as they made their way to the corner where the refreshment table was located. They nodded to acquaintances as they passed, but Margaret was glad that Paul seemed as unwilling as she to stop and make conversation. She thought it wise to put as much distance between herself and Tom Poole as possible. She could feel his gaze on her back. That he had been watching her for so much of the evening had not surprised her. Since her arrival in London a few short months ago, she had found it easy to attract men's attention.

What had surprised her was her reaction to him. Her behavior had bordered on rudeness.

Why had she felt compelled to challenge him? Even now she was at a loss to explain it. She was proud, yes, but she had never thought unkindness to be among her faults. Perhaps the story of his sudden rise to wealth—which had been the topic of conversation *everywhere* these days—had stirred some trace of resentment. Or perhaps it had been the shocking way he'd roughed up Mr. Carter right here in the duke's grand ballroom. He'd proven that his pose as a "gentleman" was just a veneer; there was a rougher man hidden—though not very well—beneath that well-dressed surface.

Then he had the audacity to imply that Margaret did not have as much strength and pluck as the women in Australia. She wanted to laugh out loud. He didn't know the half of it. She might never have hauled her own firewood or cleared brush or whatever it was they did in that wild country, but her survival had required just as much stamina and a lot more intellect.

She was nobody's fool.

Tonight the duke's mansion was filled with an astonishing assembly of London's elite—and they were all gathered in *her* honor. They were here to celebrate her forthcoming nuptials with the highborn, handsome, and very rich Paul Denault. She had made the catch of the season.

Many of her rivals had been as pretty as she was, and most were younger. Margaret herself was nearing the ripe old age of five and twenty. She'd been delayed from entering the marriage market by a father who had been unwilling to let her into society, and then by two years of mourning after his death. But with her age had come wisdom. She knew how to play the game more efficaciously than they did. She had succeeded where they had failed. What those ladies would never know—nor would anyone else, including Tom Poole—was that Margaret had not been merely playing the marriage game. She'd been secretly fighting for her survival, and it had taken every ounce of her intelligence and cunning.

She was publicly acknowledged as one of the wealthiest heiresses in England. When her father had died unexpectedly, the grand estate held by the Vaughns for generations had passed to her as well. What the public did *not* know was that her father had left the family finances in shambles. Most of her inheritance had gone toward paying off his debts from gambling, mismanagement, and failed investments. With the aid of her father's solicitors, which she had also inherited, Margaret had only just succeeded in keeping her financial status unknown to the prying eyes and ears of society gossips. If anyone had learned the truth, Margaret would have been defenseless against an onslaught of bill collectors and others who would have stolen her home and lands—her very lifeblood—from underneath her. Protecting herself had required hard choices and nerves of steel. Yes, she had far more backbone than Tom Poole could ever guess at.

Paul patted her arm lightly, bringing her out of her thoughts. "Margaret, my dear, will you excuse me for a few moments?"

He flashed his most charming smile, the one that generally reduced the women to putty in his hands. Even now, after he was officially betrothed, they were all simpering and making eyes at him over their hand-painted fans. And while Margaret did not react to him in that way exactly, she had to admit his handsome countenance went a long way toward soothing her irritation over the way he had spoken to her—and *of* her to Tom Poole.

But it would not be wise to show Paul her agitation. There were certain things she must keep hidden for now.

Once they were married, she would make sure he never again spoke to her in such a patronizing way. But for now, she would play the doting fiancée. She returned his smile with nearly genuine sincerity and said she would be more than happy to wait for him.

Paul lifted her hand from his arm and brought it to his mouth for a kiss. It was a move calculated to enchant all those around them. It succeeded. From the corner of her eye, Margaret could see a cluster of debutantes sighing with undisguised envy. She knew they were thinking, *Surely they are both too rich and too handsome. They might have spread this bounty among two families, rather than to keep it all to themselves.*

Paul sauntered over to two business associates who were standing a short distance away. He could not put away work even at a social event. His Midas touch in business was, above all of his other qualities, the one Margaret admired the most.

Paul was unaware of Margaret's financial straits. She had worried he might not marry her if he knew, or else demand that the marriage settlement give him greater control over her estate. But Margaret was not about to cede power over Moreton Hall to anyone. Her very fine lawyers were seeing to that. She told herself that ultimately there would be no harm to her deception. Paul's fabulous wealth would easily make up the shortfall and with plenty to spare. He would be gaining a beautiful wife with an impeccable pedigree who brought with her the venerable Moreton Hall and all its farmlands. He was, she had decided, getting the better part of the bargain.

She took a moment to savor looking at him, admiring his trim form and tapered waist. She even enjoyed the view from behind, although she supposed this was very naughty. His backside and strong legs were indeed worthy of admiration. His sandy-blond hair and blue eyes were features so typical of English nobility. He was not actually in line for a title, but this was unimportant to Margaret. She had lands and he had money. That was all that mattered.

He turned and caught Margaret looking at him. She blushed, not from any real embarrassment, but because she saw the glint of pleasure in his eyes when she did so. Happily, Paul had been as determined as she was to arrange a quick marriage. Margaret flattered herself that the reason for his haste was the one usual to the male sex. He was in love with her, or, at the very least, he lusted after her. She had allowed him a good many personal attentions in order to pique his interest—kisses in darkened corners, intimate caresses. But she was, quite properly, holding back the best for their wedding night. There were times, such as this, when Margaret did feel a tiny spark of attraction to him. In her position she had known she might not be able to marry for love, but at least she had been spared from settling for someone who was old or odious. Marriage to this man could be very agreeable, and although in other circumstances she might have wished for more, she could not regret her choice.

"Miss Vaughn, how do you do?"

Margaret turned to see the crusty old face of Mr. Hawthorne, her primary solicitor and chief keeper of secrets. She was mildly surprised to see him here. Although he was generally invited to participate at such gatherings, she had seldom known him to do so. A widower of many years, he generally kept to himself, preferring, as he put it, "a quiet room, a glass of brandy, and a pipe" over the intrigues of society. This was the precise reason why he had been her most trusted adviser during the two years since her father had departed this earthly realm.

Margaret offered her hand, and he made a deferential bow over it. "Everything is proceeding according to plan, I trust?" Margaret was growing irritated at the amount of time it had taken to finalize the details of the marriage settlement. Lawyers for both sides seemed to be dragging their feet. She supposed this was the normal way they justified their exorbitant fees.

On the other hand, there was a need for the utmost discretion as they blended her properties with his money. Mr. Hawthorne's job was to arrange matters so that Paul would not know the full state of her financial affairs until *after* they were married. They soon discovered, however, that Paul had a team of solicitors that were just as loyal to his interests. She had the impression that there had been quite a lot of legal maneuvering going on during the past few weeks.

A shadow passed over Hawthorne's face. "I'm afraid there have been a few, ah, ruts in the road that we may not have anticipated. The carriage might not travel forward as smoothly as one might have desired."

Margaret generally took a secret delight in Hawthorne's tendency to speak in code, as though he were still back in his glory days as a young spy for Wellington's army. Tonight, however, there was something in his tone that did not bode well. "How much do they suspect?" she asked, dropping her voice. She continued to scan the crowd as she spoke, keeping a pleasant smile on her face so as not to betray the seriousness of their conversation to any casual onlooker.

Almost without effort, her eye found Tom Poole. He was a tall man, and his deeply tanned face stood out among the sea of pale gentlemen. He had the physique of a working man, his broad shoulders filling out his coat impressively. He had no need for the vain padding she had seen other men use.

His eyes met hers, and held. Now that they had been introduced, he did not even try to hide his bold interest in her. Her breath caught in a gasp as she recalled the way his warm hands had sent a bolt of electricity through her. How was it that even now, from this distance, he was having the same unsettling effect?

Mr. Hawthorne cleared his throat, in what may have been an effort to regain Margaret's attention. "I'm afraid, Miss Vaughn, that it's not so much a question of what *they* have found, as it is what *we* have discovered."

She gave herself a mental shake, tearing her attention away from Tom Poole and settling it on the wrinkled countenance of Mr. Hawthorne. "What *you* have discovered? Why—what have you found?"

Hawthorne ran a hand through his silvery hair, which was still thick despite his advanced age. "It's not something I would care to discuss here," he said. "Perhaps I may call upon you in the morning?"

"That would be most inconvenient," Margaret answered, still trying to push Tom Poole from her mind. "I have a dress fitting in the morning, and then a meeting with the owner of the banqueting hall, who is almost beside himself with arranging such a feast on short notice."

"I apologize for the intrusion into your schedule," Hawthorne said. "However, it is of vital importance."

The somberness of his expression could not be

ignored. Margaret recognized this look; it was usually the harbinger of bad news. She said with resignation, "Will half past eleven do?"

He nodded. "Very good, Miss Vaughn." He bowed and left her, quietly slipping away and leaving her to ruminate on his ominous words. Whatever the problem was, she would overcome it, as she had everything else. The important thing was not to delay. She would not wait any longer to have a settlement to her affairs that had been in a surreptitious upheaval for more than two years. There was far too much at stake.

What man could ever comprehend the pressures a woman faced who was at risk of losing everything? She had heard all about Tom Poole's story, how he'd risen from a poor shop clerk to a man of wealth and business. Having begun poor and worked his way up, he could have no idea what it would be like to find oneself on the brink of losing lands and properties that had been part of her heritage for hundreds of years. Paul, too, being born with a good family name but little money, had the advantage of a man in being able to go off and earn his fortune. A man could grasp hold of any occupation and strike it rich, while a woman had to rely upon her wiles.

Margaret had spent most of her life in the company of men. Her mother had died when Margaret was just twelve. She had been a dutiful wife, and seemed to have no greater ambition than to live for her husband's pleasure. But Margaret had been raised to a greater purpose. Upon her mother's death, her grandfather had taken on the task of Margaret's education. He had seen to it that the entail on the estate was broken so that she would be able to inherit it. He had drilled into her that this was a sacred trust, and that he had every confidence she would carry out her duties.

Her father had been of a different mind. More than once, when he was deep in his cups, he had told her point-blank she would probably lose everything within a generation. The devils that drove him to drink and gambling must have been determined to make it so. But she would prove him wrong. She would recover Moreton Hall from debt and return it to its former glory. No matter what it took to do it.

Chapter 3

The carriage rattled along the cobblestone streets, rolling in and out of pools of lamplight that did little to diminish the heavy fog. Tom spared few glances out the window, however. He was thinking about Margaret Vaughn.

What a beauty she was. Tall and regal, with pale, smooth skin that reminded him of the marble statues he'd seen in some Mayfair gardens. And her eyes. Her striking green eyes had held a particular gleam when she called him "Just Tom." The implied slight only intrigued rather than repelled him. Tom had seen many society beauties since returning to London, but none had captured his attention so completely. There was fire under her arch coolness; he was sure of it. The only question was, why did he wish so badly to find out?

"Are you planning to stay here all night?" James asked in a bemused tone.

Tom pulled himself out of his reverie. "I beg your pardon?"

"We have arrived." James made a tsking sound. "You were so caught up in your thoughts you never even noticed."

Tom looked again out the window, this time with seeing eyes. They were at the door of the Somervilles' town house.

"You didn't hear a word I said all the way home," James chided. "How annoying."

A footman opened the door, and Tom stepped down from the carriage. Seeing that James made no move to follow, he said, "Aren't you coming?"

James shook his head. "I thought I'd just pop round to the club."

"To drink a glass of brandy and gather up a card game, no doubt." After spending weeks in James's company, Tom had become familiar with his habits.

"I make no promises," James said. "But the probability is high."

"Lizzie will be disappointed. She expressly asked to see you this evening."

"Did she? How kind. However, it's late now. She probably won't even be awake."

"Don't be too sure. If I know Lizzie, she'll be waiting up."

James sighed. "All right." He exited the carriage. To the driver he said, "Wait here. I won't be long." Turning to Tom he explained, "I love my cousin dearly, but given her delicate condition, I have no intention of keeping her up until the wee hours."

"You're so thoughtful, James," Tom said, unable to keep amusement from his voice. He had no doubt that James cared for his cousin, but he also knew that he usually preferred to spend his evenings somewhere other than in quiet parlors of family members.

The door was opened for them by the butler. "Where are they, Carville? In the parlor, I presume?" James did not give the man a chance to answer, but breezed past him to the front parlor.

A look of irritation passed over the butler's face. Tom had learned enough of high society to know that James ought to have waited. Of course James *was* family, even if he was a guest in this home. So perhaps it didn't matter? Still, there was that look of Carville's. Tom would ask Lizzie about this later. He knew he had a lot to learn about London society, and he wanted to learn it as quickly as possible. He thought again about Miss Vaughn. He wanted to impress her.

Lizzie's light laughter floated out from the other room. With a brief nod of thanks to the butler, he followed James into the parlor.

James was just planting a kiss on Lizzie's cheek. "Don't you look ravishing tonight, dear cousin."

She set down the book she had been reading. "James, you always say the most complimentary things. I'm so glad you dropped by."

"You must blame Tom for the intrusion," James said, as though his cousin had not just said she was happy to see him. "He seemed convinced that you had your heart set on seeing me this evening." Crossing the room to shake Geoffrey's hand, he added, "Why she feels this way, I have no idea."

"Neither do I," Geoffrey said with a smile.

"And in any case," James said, turning back to Lizzie, "should you really be receiving guests at all hours in your interesting condition? Why are you not hidden away in some country estate awaiting the happy arrival?"

Lizzie put a hand gently on her stomach, which showed the roundness of a growing baby. How well she looked, how deeply contented. During all those torturous years she and Tom had spent together in Australia, he'd never thought to see her so happy again.

"The birth is still a good three months away," Lizzie said. "Surely you don't expect me to seclude myself the entire time?"

James shrugged. "That seems to be what most women do."

"Perhaps it is simply their way to be rid of the bothersome menfolk for a while," she teased.

"That's what I love about you, cousin," James said, laughing. "You're always so brutally honest."

"Am I bothersome to you?" Geoffrey asked, walking over to her. He gently lifted her hand and kissed it.

Tom saw her take in a slight breath, as though Geoffrey's simple action had stirred her deeply—as though they were still in the blush of first courtship.

"I ought to send you away, it's true," she said, lifting a hand to caress his cheek. "For are you not the reason for my troubles?"

Her voice faltered a little, even though she had tried to match the teasing tones that James had used. Lizzie was in love. So much so that she couldn't even pretend to be out of sorts with her husband. She positively glowed. Geoffrey returned her loving gaze with such warmth that they might have lit a bonfire.

Something squeezed in Tom's heart. So far, the kind of love Lizzie and Geoffrey shared had eluded him. For years he'd been so caught up in other problems that he'd put away any thoughts of finding a wife. Add to that the heartbreak of seeing his best friend killed, and the heart-wrenching sorrow his widow went through. They had risked all for love, and lost everything. And yet, here were Lizzie and Geoffrey, happy, prosperous, and contented. Now he was beginning to consider it again. Lizzie and Geoffrey were a true example of what a marriage should be—the melding of two lives together, built on a firm foundation of faith in God. Might he not find such a match? Who could tell for certain which way the future would lead?

Tom had liked his new brother-in-law immediately. Geoffrey had lived up to Lizzie's gushing descriptions in her letters. It was clear he was a quiet man of integrity, and he was fiercely devoted to his wife.

Their tenderness toward each other had not gone unnoticed by James. "Really, you two," he quipped. "I believe you should *both* retire to the country." Despite the frivolity of his words, his face wore an uneasy expression. It hadn't escaped Tom that although James enjoyed playing the matchmaker, he was not entirely comfortable around couples who were actually married.

James scooped up his gloves from the table. "Since it's clear you both have every intention of staying in town, perhaps it is I who must be going."

Geoffrey reached out and stopped him. "Don't go. You've only just arrived."

"He's right," Lizzie declared. "You can't leave yet. Please stay. I'll have some fresh tea brought up." She picked up a bell from the table and rang for the butler.

With an exaggerated roll of his eyes James said, "Tea. That is exactly what I wish to imbibe at this hour."

"Don't you like my tea?" Lizzie gave a playful pout.

"My dear, I love your tea almost as much as I love you. However, I am quite serious about you getting your rest. You know what the doctor told you about taking it easy."

"I'm resting here, and that is good enough," she countered, indicating the soft pillows that surrounded her, as well as the padded footstool where her feet were propped.

The butler entered, and Lizzie directed him to have tea brought up. "And some of those lemon tea cakes," she added. "I know the cook has some specially prepared."

"Lemon tea cakes?" James said, brightening. "Well, I suppose I might stay a while longer."

How perfectly Lizzie fit into the role of a baroness, Tom thought. He was tempted to chuckle as he remembered Lizzie riding her horse astride across wide-open plains, laughing with joyful abandon. Or how she had worked her fingers to the bone without ever once complaining. Now here she was, so elegant, so perfectly at ease overseeing servants and running a large house, no one would have guessed she hadn't been raised among the upper classes. No matter what she was doing, she always made Tom immensely proud.

She patted the chair next to hers. "You must make yourself comfortable, James, and tell us all about the party. You are my eyes and ears now. I want to hear everything."

"Everything?" James repeated, his eyes glimmering with mirth.

"Everything," Lizzie affirmed with a smile.

James took the chair she'd indicated. "The party was delightful, and the quality of the brandy was particularly satisfying. Best of all, the guest of honor was the very epitome of loveliness. Isn't that right, Tom?"

Tom looked at James, pretending to misunderstand him. "You're asking me? What do I know of fine brandy?"

"I was referring to Miss Vaughn, you sly devil," James returned. "You were quite taken by her—don't try to deny it."

Quite taken by her. Tom conjured up a memory of her, which left him as winded as though he'd just run up a flight of steps. *Quite taken.*

"So Miss Vaughn really is as lovely as they say she is?" Lizzie asked.

"I found nothing remarkable in her," James said in an offhand manner. "A pleasant enough English rose. Tom, however, couldn't keep his eyes off her." He pretended to look scandalized. "Terribly shocking the way he was staring at her, especially considering she is to be married in a fortnight."

"Pay no attention to James," Tom told Lizzie. "You know how he exaggerates."

Lizzie pretended to swat James in reproof. "You always want to see things between other people. You are quite the little matchmaker."

"Nonsense. I leave those duties to old Mrs. Paddington." He chuckled. "Not that she's having any success with it, poor lady. This season has been lacking in stellar matches. Except for Miss Vaughn and Denault, of course, but that's a different matter altogether."

The mention of Denault sent an uneasy chill down Tom's spine. The man was annoyingly self-absorbed, it was true, but even so, how could he act with such casual indifference toward the stellar woman who was his fiancée? "Who is this Denault?" Tom demanded. "What's his background?"

James must have caught the intensity behind Tom's question, but he merely shrugged. "Only a descendant of one of the oldest families in England. They came over with the Norman Conquest, I think."

"Surely you are exaggerating again," Lizzie remonstrated.

"Not by much," Geoffrey said. "His uncle holds one of the oldest dukedoms in England. Trouble is, no one in that family will allow you to forget it. I have had reason to work with him from time to time in the House of Lords." He grimaced. "I'm convinced there isn't a more pompous and self-important man in all of England."

"You say you have worked with him. Does that mean he takes an interest in your charitable societies?" Lizzie asked.

Geoffrey made a derisive sound. "Hardly. He is concerned with more important matters, such as whether the hallways in the House of Lords are polished to acceptable standards."

"Denault is every bit as self-aggrandizing as his uncle," James declared. "There is one difference, though. He has a splash of the hubris that comes with actually having made one's money rather than simply inheriting it."

"What terribly bad taste that is," Lizzie said, pulling a wry face.

Tom frowned. "Is it so bad to have worked hard for wealth? Why is it that one must simply *have* money, without having done a single thing to procure it?"

"Tom is right," Geoffrey agreed. "In today's world, that definition of a 'gentleman' is rapidly becoming obsolete."

"Therefore I am sure Tom and Denault will get along famously," James put in.

"How did he earn his money, exactly?" Tom asked.

"Something to do with the railways in America. I don't know the particulars."

"Really?" Tom mulled this over. "Lizzie, did you know they are going to build a railway from Sydney to Parramatta?"

She sat up a little. "Are they really? How wonderfully modern Australia is becoming."

"Why did you wish to know about Denault?" Geoffrey asked.

"He wants to meet with me tomorrow about some sort of business venture."

"How interesting," Lizzie said.

"Yes, isn't it?" James said, propping up Lizzie's pillow. "Of course Tom asked whether the captivating Miss Vaughn would be joining them."

"And will she?"

"Sadly, the club does not allow women. And what a pity that is."

Tom didn't know whether James was in earnest or simply needling him, but the man was dangerously close to the truth. Perhaps if Tom had arrived in London sooner, he might have attempted to win Margaret for himself. He gave himself a small shake. Who was he kidding? He was doing his best to live up to his new station in life—a position afforded to him by his gold and by his sister's marriage to a peer. Yet a woman like Miss

Vaughn would probably not see past his humble origins. Hadn't she chosen a man who was both rich *and* from a distinguished lineage? Everyone told Tom that money brought power, but he knew there were still plenty of things beyond his control.

His hands fisted at his side, a too-familiar reaction for him. He made a conscious effort to relax them. His discomfort did not get past Lizzie, however. She gave him a sympathetic glance before saying, "James, you are skirting the real issue here."

James pretended to look surprised. "Am I? And what would that be?"

Lizzie set her expression into her best *lady-wants-gossip* look and said, "Who did *you* dance with? Did anyone catch *your* eye?"

"Oh, I see," said James with a smirk. "I've been skirting the issue of the skirts."

Lizzie playfully hit him with one of the pillows. "How scandalous, James. I hope you do not talk like that around the ladies."

"You know perfectly well that's *exactly* how I talk around the ladies," he said, snatching the pillow from her hand and holding it close to his heart. "That is why they love me so. Except for Miss Vaughn—"

"James." Lizzie's voice held a warning tone.

"Oh, all right," James relented. "Let me see…" He tapped a finger to his chin as if thinking very hard. "I danced with Miss Hardwicke, Miss Shaw, Miss Cardington—"

"Which Miss Cardington?" Lizzie asked. The persistence in her tone was finally becoming clear to Tom, even through the fog of his thoughts—which were still centered around Miss Vaughn.

James stood up and helped himself to a tea cake from the tray that a maid was just bringing in the room. "I'm speaking of Miss Emily, of course. Lucinda has two left feet. It's no wonder she isn't married."

"Surely the ability to dance is not the primary requirement for making a match," Geoffrey said.

"Perhaps not. In any case, I am glad she isn't married."

"And why would that be?" Lizzie asked.

"Since Lucinda is the eldest, Emily cannot get married until Lucinda does. Their father is absolutely immovable on that point. It's positively draconian." He popped the little tea cake into his mouth with a satisfied air.

"How convenient," Lizzie observed. "You may flirt with Emily all you like and nothing more is expected from you."

"It is a state of affairs in which I thrive," he agreed. "But it is good for Miss Emily, too. It affords her the opportunity to enjoy a season or two as the toast of the town before she must marry and turn her mind to the nasty business of becoming a *matron*."

He shuddered so dramatically that Lizzie laughed. Even Tom found it difficult to suppress a smile.

"A society matron? Like me, you mean?" Lizzie asked with a grin. She patted her large stomach.

"No," James protested. He returned to her chair and fell down on one knee, taking hold of her hand. "You will never be like those women. You are a paragon of kindness."

"Now see here, James," Geoffrey said, pulling him to his feet and pretending to look affronted. "Shouldn't *I* be the one to spout such lovely sentiments to my wife?"

"Geoffrey, you haven't a jealous bone in your body," James declared. He threw a sidelong glance at Tom. "Now Denault, on the other hand—"

"Good Lord," Tom said, throwing up his hands in exasperation. "We're back to that."

"Denault was determined to win Miss Vaughn from the moment she set aside her mourning clothes and attended her first London ball," James continued, blithely sidestepping Tom, who wanted to reach out and strangle him. "He would positively circle around her, like a guard dog." He demonstrated by making creeping motions around Lizzie's chair and letting out a few small growls. "No one else stood a chance."

Lizzie laughed at James's comical motions, but then let out a small sigh. "I wish I could have been with you at the party," she said to Tom. She rested a hand abstractedly on her stomach.

"That's all right, cousin," James assured her, giving her shoulder a gentle pat. "He's got me. And let me see now…" He considered for a moment. "The next really good soiree will be three nights from now." He gave Tom an appraising look. "You did fine this evening, but you've still got a few things to learn. Next time, I'm sure we'll get you a dance with Miss Vaughn."

"Isn't she about to get married?" Tom said, trying to ignore the sudden thrill that ran through him at the thought of Miss Vaughn in his arms. "Don't newlyweds generally go off to the Continent or some such place?"

"Oh, that's not for several more weeks. Now that I think about it, there's no need to wait until the soiree to see her. You're liable to run across her tomorrow, anyway."

Tom advanced toward him. "I told you, the meeting is between me and Denault—"

James retreated behind Lizzie's chair and put up a hand. "I meant that you may see her in that charming square outside. I believe she goes for a walk there in the mornings."

"She does? Why would she go there?" Tom didn't think there was anything remarkable in the little patch of grass and oak-lined paths around which the town houses were clustered. Surely Hyde Park would be a more interesting destination.

"She lives right across the square at number fifteen."

Tom looked at him dumbfounded. "She does?"

"Yes," James said, the glint returning to his eye. "Isn't that convenient?"

*

Tom stood at the window of his darkened bedchamber, staring into the night. The fog lay heavy on the city, although a soft breeze broke it into patches here and there and gently rustled the leaves in the trees. A half-moon shone brightly overhead, slicing through the fog and adding its light to the street lamps below, sending the park into an intriguing play of light and shadow.

Tom had been bred in this city, but his years in Australia had made him appreciative of the special kind of peace found only in the countryside. In a few weeks the "season" here would be over, and he and Geoffrey would ride out to inspect the harvest at the Somerville estate in Kent. It would be a welcome break from the smoke and noise of the streets—not to mention the stuffy confines of overly elaborate drawing rooms.

Lizzie would go, too, if she was able. They were taking every precaution. No one said it aloud, but everyone was thinking of the terrible things her half sister Ria had endured during childbirth. In the end, both Ria and her baby had died. The possibility that Lizzie might have inherited the same physical weakness was weighing heavily on her mind. She had tried not to show this, but Tom knew. He'd done all he could to reassure Lizzie, to remind her that Ria had a different mother, and that Lizzie and Tom's mother had been quite hearty in childbearing. And yet, in his innermost heart Tom could not deny that he was worried, too. Lizzie was the dearest thing in the world to him. She was all he had now.

Clouds moved across the moon, darkening the city below. Tom thought of Margaret, on the other side of this very square. He knew which house it was from the way James had described it. It was not the most elegant town house on the square, but it was well kept. It probably was no match for the more fashionable homes in Belgravia, the neighborhood to the southwest where, as James had explained to him, the most elite were moving to, leaving Mayfair with an air of being just a bit "last season." He smiled at the thought. How well versed he was becoming in society's outlook. And yet how far he still had to go.

He could not see number 15 from here, due to the angle of the homes around the small oval park and the oak trees that stood between them. But he could imagine Margaret as clearly as if he were looking at her. He envisioned her standing at the window of her bedchamber, gazing out at the same bit of fog-laced green that Tom was looking at. He pictured her in a thin white nightdress, which covered but did not hide the shape of her curves.

Or perhaps she had pulled on a satin dressing gown to protect her from the chill of the foggy night air. Her hair would be loose, curling down around her shoulders, long and full, the rich brown strands glistening in the moonlight. Perhaps he and Margaret were looking at each other right now and didn't realize it. Everything in him ached with desire at that thought.

He laughed at himself and shook his head. "Tom, you're a crazy bas—" He cut himself off. Swearing was one thing he had been trying very hard to curb. It was not the mark of a gentleman or, more important, of a Christian. Sometimes Tom doubted he would ever be successful at being either of those things. He wanted his words to always be seasoned with salt, as the Bible said, and speak only things that would edify. It was a tall order.

He returned to his bed, stretching out and savoring the excellent feather mattress. It was, he thought wryly, one of the few comforts he found in London.

No matter what he did, he could not manage to quell his uneasiness at being back in England. The things he had done before he'd left here—his duel with Freddie Hightower among them—still seemed to haunt him. It was foolish, of course. Freddie was dead, and there was no one outside the family who knew of this part of his past. And yet, being back in the city brought so many bad memories to the forefront of his mind.

He missed Edward and Ria, and the life he and Lizzie had built with them at McCrae's sheep station. At times his heart ached for those simpler days, for although they worked hard, day in and day out, they had so many simple pleasures. Ria and Edward were blissfully happy, and Tom and Lizzie were content. It had all been destroyed the day bushrangers had killed Edward. But he had to remember that those terrible days had been the catalyst for bringing Lizzie to London, and for her ultimately finding such deep happiness with Geoffrey.

He was living between two worlds, really. He had not made up his mind to stay in England permanently—he'd wanted only to see Lizzie again—to be sure that she was happily settled. Beyond that, his plans were uncertain.

And yet, what need had he to return to Australia? The business he and Sullivan had started was prospering, and Sullivan was an able manager. They had already quadrupled the earnings from the gold they had dug out by their own hard labor. He had no wish to go back to mining. He was through with that rough, unforgiving life. But neither did he wish to live the indolent life of a "gentleman."

"Lord, what am I to do?" He spoke softly, sending up the words as a prayer, even as he lay flat on his back in the bed with his arms behind his head, staring at the ceiling. He'd never felt the need to go down on his knees when he prayed—he figured the Lord could hear him in any posture he happened to be in.

He wanted a life that gave him purpose. Many assumed he was content, given his newfound wealth. But something was missing. Something was still just out of reach. And for some unaccountable reason, the woman he'd been picturing across the fog-shrouded square made him more aware of it than ever.

Chapter 4

Denault rose from his seat at a large table, upon which several large rolls of paper were spread about. He shook Tom's hand warmly. "Thank you for coming." He motioned to the other chair. "Please, have a seat."

Tom remained standing. "Perhaps you might first tell me exactly what this meeting is about."

His curt words did not seem to put off Denault in the least. "I see you are not one to waste time," he said approvingly. "Trust me. I'm just as eager as you are to get to the heart of the matter. Very well then, I'll give it to you in one word: railways."

Railways? "You're not serious," Tom said.

"Deadly serious." Denault's earnest expression matched his words.

"I've been out of the country and missed most of what they called the 'railway mania,'" Tom said. "But I read the papers. I know more people went broke than actually made money. And in any case, the prime years for investing in the railroads are past."

"In England, maybe," Denault conceded. "There are already six thousand miles of track crisscrossing this small island. It is just about played out. But in other countries the building boom is just beginning."

"You are thinking of Australia, perhaps?" Tom knew that there weren't yet any railways in Australia, save for a few precarious tracks in Van Diemen's Land where the carriages were actually drawn by convict labor. Tom had never even seen a train up close, much less ridden on one.

"There is great need, no doubt," Denault said with a dismissive wave of his hand. "Perhaps that might be a focus of a future project. However, for the moment I am speaking about America."

"America?" Tom repeated. "I thought you just completed a rail line there."

"America is a vast place, my friend," Denault said, spreading his arms in an expansive gesture. "It is infinitely larger than Britain, and much further behind on railways. They've only just managed to reach the Mississippi River, the center of their big country. The next big push will be from Saint Louis to California. I'm telling you, the place is ripe for expansion."

Tom's knowledge of American geography was sketchy, at best. "Granted, the tracks have not been built. But why build them? And why now?"

"Good heavens, man! Haven't you heard? There is gold in California, and rumors of silver in Nevada."

"I'm well aware of the gold in California," Tom said drily. "It was the unsuccessful prospectors from California who first came looking for gold in Australia."

"And they found it! See what an advantage that was to you!" Denault exclaimed, pouncing on his words with enthusiasm. "Now you have a chance to invest it and turn your hard-earned gold into more money than you ever dreamed of. People are absolutely desperate to reach the West, and there is just no good way to get there. It takes months by wagon train, and the dangers are immense. The only other route is to go around Cape Horn, and you know how harrowing that is."

Tom considered this. Denault was right about Cape Horn—the passage across the violent icy seas at the tip of South America was just about the worst thing Tom had ever endured. It was the only time in his life he'd actually been seasick. He knew full well why people would avoid traveling that way if they could.

Denault continued to speak excitedly. "We will be bringing more than just the railway. We will be giving employment to thousands of people, establishing towns, and enabling civilization to take root in that wild place."

"Are there really thousands of people available to build it? Does that much labor exist in America?"

Denault shrugged. "Think of your own experience in Australia. How many people flooded into Melbourne and Ballarat when they learned there was important money to be made there?"

Denault had a point, although to Tom's way of thinking the chaos brought by all the newcomers had not necessarily been a good thing. "How many miles are we talking about? And aren't there mountains somewhere between Saint Louis and California?" Tom thought of the steep cliffs and box canyons of the Blue Mountains, of how they'd only just managed to build a road through there with the endless labor of convict gangs. He could not even imagine trying to build a railway through it. He had no idea what the terrain of the Sierra Nevada was like, but a mountain was a mountain, after all.

"There is a pass through the mountains," Denault assured him. "We have a cracking good engineer who has figured out all those technical details."

"Are those the plans?" Tom asked, pointing to the table.

"Yes, indeed." Denault unrolled one of the large papers. "It's drawn to scale, one inch per one hundred miles."

"One hundred!" Tom exclaimed. He looked at the map and tried to do a quick calculation in his head. "You are talking about thousands of miles."

"Just under two thousand."

"And what kind of land is it?" He knew England had many different kinds of terrain, including hills, valleys, moors, and bogs. Was America like that? Or was it more like the Bathurst Plains in Australia, which were wide and flat as far as the eye could see? He studied the map. "There are no geographical relief markings."

Denault gave him an impressed look. "You seem to be proficient at reading maps."

"I had to be," Tom said. "Mining for gold will give a person experience in that kind of thing."

"You needn't concern yourself with those details for this project," Denault said with a patronizing air. "We have a team of engineering and cartography experts who are overseeing the project."

If Denault felt he had all the organizational power he needed, that meant he was coming after Tom for something else. And now they were getting to the crux of the issue. Like so many others Tom had met, Denault was only after one thing. "All you want from me is my money."

Denault shrugged and raised his hands. "What's so

bad about that? It makes your role that much easier. All you need to do is fund this project, and then enjoy yourself while the earnings pile up. You won't need to do any of the work."

"You say that as if it were a good thing," Tom said with irritation.

"Isn't it?"

"Everyone seems to want to get something for nothing. They think that's what happened to me. It's not. I worked hard for that money, and I intend to be very careful in how I spend it."

"But it's not *spending*," Denault insisted. "It's *investing*."

Tom let out a snort of derision. These high-society people were so good at using fancy words to make anything sound better—to put a gloss on it, like shining up a worn boot. Whenever a man started talking that way, it was a signal for Tom to run in the opposite direction. Just now he was seriously considering picking up his hat and walking out without a backward glance. He owed this man nothing, after all. He'd done him a favor just by showing up.

In the end, it was thoughts of Margaret that kept him from leaving immediately. She was about to be tied to Denault by marriage, and Tom still wanted to find out everything he could about this man. Today he was speaking like many a charlatan he'd seen in Sydney and Melbourne—men who were always coming up with schemes to separate people from their hard-earned money. Was Denault such a man? If so, did Margaret have any inkling of it?

He could not simply walk away, knowing Margaret was about to place her life in the power of a man who might be disreputable in his business dealings. Of course,

he owed nothing to her, and she certainly was not looking for anything from him. This was a solid fact, and yet
to Tom it weighed nothing when placed in the balance.
He dropped his hat on the table and sat down. "All right,
suppose we go over your plans. In detail."

Denault grinned and took the other chair. "I thought
you'd never ask."

*

Margaret breezed into her study. Hawthorne was standing near the window, observing the traffic below and not
looking at all perturbed that she'd kept him waiting for
more than a quarter of an hour. She was surprised to see
that he was joined by Mr. Clarke, one of the partners in
the firm.

"I apologize for the delay," Margaret said. "The seam-
stress had me ridiculously pinned up and I was only just
able to free myself. I hope you were able to take some
refreshment while you were waiting."

"Indeed, Miss Vaughn, that was most kind," Hawthorne replied.

But a quick glance showed Margaret that the tea tray
was untouched. The two men wore solemn expressions
that were unusual even for them, given that an overly grave
aspect was a solicitor's stock in trade. "Is this visit really so
serious that it requires two of you?" She spoke lightly, but
the expressions on the men's faces did not waver. Something was definitely amiss. "What's happened?" she asked
warily. "Are Paul's lawyers still giving you trouble?"

The two men looked at each other. Mr. Clarke went
over to a table and picked up a portfolio filled with
papers. Mr. Hawthorne said, "If you would be so kind

as to sit down, Miss Vaughn, we have some information we'd like to go over with you."

Margaret walked to a large desk and moved aside the correspondence that littered it. She sat down and motioned to two chairs on the opposite side of the desk for the men. "Will this do?" she asked.

Hawthorne nodded, and Mr. Clarke pulled the papers from the portfolio and set them down in front of her.

A quick perusal of the first page showed her this was not the marriage settlement. "What is this?"

Mr. Hawthorne sat down in one of the chairs, facing Margaret. "This is all the information that we have been able to glean about the Saint Louis and Western Railroad."

"The project that Mr. Denault is spearheading in America?" Margaret said in surprise. "I thought you had been over all that already."

"Something about the financial statements appeared not quite right." With a gesture toward Mr. Clarke, who was standing deferentially off to one side, he added, "Clarke suggested we have our own men look into the matter."

"And?"

"The Saint Louis and Western is not in the robust health that Mr. Denault has led everyone to believe. In fact, it is in dire need of a large influx of cash in order to keep it afloat."

"Are you quite sure? The company's prospectus—"

"It was, I'm afraid, rather too optimistic."

Hawthorne's solemn pronouncement set Margaret's heart pounding in alarm. "Surely you are mistaken," she insisted. "Paul has more offers of backing than he can even handle. The current shareholders are practically insisting that he not sell any more, to keep their own profits high. He told me so himself."

"I have no doubt that he presented it to you in such a way," Hawthorne said, ever the diplomat. He did not need to point out that just because Paul said it, it wasn't necessarily true.

Margaret thought back to her conversations with Paul on this subject, and she had to admit that he had not been very forthcoming with concrete details. He also had an annoying habit of trying to change the subject whenever she pressed him on it. "What exactly have you found out? Who are your sources?"

"There is a man newly arrived in London—a Mr. Seton," Hawthorne said. "He is in the country to transact some business for the First Bank of New York. Mr. Clarke was fortunate enough to make his acquaintance."

Hawthorne said this last part with a tiny smile of approval, and Margaret was sure that meeting Mr. Seton had not been mere coincidence. Hawthorne's network of contacts in the city was extensive. Another legacy of his days as a spy.

"The Bank of New York has organized funding for a number of railway projects in America," Mr. Clarke explained. "Mr. Seton is quite knowledgeable in this area. His bank has been investigating complaints that the Saint Louis and Western is not being honest with its shareholders. There is a possibility that money taken from new investors is merely used to pay 'dividends' to the prior investors, giving them a false sense that the company is prospering."

"But what is the point of that?" Margaret asked, confused. "How can such a company continue to operate?"

"It can go on like that indefinitely," Mr. Clarke told her. "That is, until the influx of money runs dry. Mr. Seton is of the opinion that Mr. Denault has stolen or spent most of the capital and needs immediate cash to stave off the threat of being discovered. Mind you, we are making no accusations at this point."

"Could there possibly be a mistake?" Margaret asked. "Could Mr. Seton's information be incorrect?"

Clarke spread his hands in the universal gesture of uncertainty. "We are leaving open that possibility, for now."

"However, I feel I should tell you," Hawthorne added, "that Mr. Denault's solicitors have been asking very particular questions about the state of ready cash in your estate."

"But that's absurd!" Margaret burst out. "We can't *both* be marrying each other for money!" The idea sent terror through her.

"I'm afraid we must consider the possibility," Hawthorne said solemnly.

Margaret sat back in her chair and rubbed her eyes, pushing back the tears that threatened to come. Her finely laid plans were unraveling, and it took every ounce of will to fight the panic. But now was not the time to show weakness. She would find a way out of this. How appropriate that Mr. Hawthorne had once been a spy, she thought. This meeting was beginning to feel exactly like a council of war. She took a deep breath, straightened in her chair, and met the gaze of the two men who were now studying her with concern. "All right, gentlemen, I assume you have already considered our options. What do you propose we should do?"

Thirty minutes later, the two men took their leave.

Margaret sat down at her desk and pulled out a sheet of paper. She stabbed, rather than dipped, her pen into the inkstand. Her initial shock had been completely overtaken by cold fury. How dare he lead her on, giving her such fine stories and acting as though he were in love—or at least, in lust—when all he wanted, like every other potential suitor in London, was her *money?* It was maddening. And, if she dared admit it, embarrassing. She'd been taken in like a fool. This had been the most galling blow to her pride.

She looked down at the paper.

Dear Paul...

Dear? How laughable the term seemed to her now. She threw the paper into the fire, allowing her emotions to seethe and crackle like the parchment. Paul would be coming over this evening, and there was no point in asking him to come earlier. She would take the afternoon to compose herself. For as long as she could remember, she had faced obstacles with calm and control. Today would be no different. She would confront him face-to-face, and she would wrangle the truth out of him.

She looked over at the papers she had set aside earlier. Most of them involved plans for the wedding, but would it even take place? If her lawyers were correct and Paul had no ready cash—or worse, had been stealing money from others—what would she do? Her creditors were pressing in on her, becoming more insistent, threatening exposure. Even if she were able to disengage herself from Paul without a scandal, how was she to come up with the money she needed? She could not find another rich man to marry in so short a space of time. The idea was ludicrous.

She rose and began to pace the room, clenching her

hands so tightly that her fingernails began to dig into her palms. She welcomed the pain—anything to clear her head, to keep her wits about her.

Perhaps there really *was* a mistake, she thought desperately. Even her excellent lawyers were not infallible. They had thought this Mr. Seton was credible, but who could be sure? Paul might be able to prove that his financial status was exactly as he had led her to believe. Tonight she would tell him exactly where she stood. If he was as rich as he claimed to be, surely he would not balk at marrying her anyway. In the meantime, she could not—would not—allow herself to dwell on the possibility of anything else.

Margaret threw open the study door and strode briskly toward the stairs. As she passed the footman, she said, "Send word to the groom to saddle my horse. I'm going riding."

The footman left to discharge his errand, and Margaret took the stairs to her room. There she found her maid Bessie straightening the wardrobe. "My riding costume, if you please," Margaret ordered. Bessie was surprised by this request, but she quickly helped Margaret change.

As Bessie buttoned up the back of the comfortable blue riding habit, Margaret began to feel a certain sense of calm returning to her. She had been nearly a week without riding, too caught up in all the details of wedding planning and the multitude of other business pressing down on her. She needed open space and fresh air.

The groom stood ready with the horse at the base of the town house steps. "Will you be needing an escort, miss?" he asked as he helped her to mount.

"No." With a light touch of her riding crop she set the horse moving. "I'm going alone."

Chapter 5

It felt good to escape the house. As long as she was riding her favorite mare on a lovely late summer day in Hyde Park, it was easy to act and feel as though all were right with the world. As if it were not all threatening to crumble around her.

Although the season was nearing its end, plenty of people were still in town. Today most were on foot or in finely appointed carriages, so Margaret had ample room on the green stretch of grass reserved for those on horseback. She rode at an easy pace, savoring the birdsong and the sunshine, which was a balm to her troubled soul.

Farther ahead, another rider caught her eye. She realized with an odd jolt that it was Tom Poole. He was riding a jet-black Thoroughbred—probably the one that had survived the shipwreck with him. She allowed her gaze to linger on him, admiring the way he cantered his horse across the green with confident ease.

"Margaret, how lovely to see you." A man's voice

startled her from her thoughts. She'd been so busy staring at Tom Poole that she hadn't heard anyone approach.

She turned, unpleasantly surprised to find herself looking at her cousin, Richard Spencer. He'd given her more than enough cause to continue the forty-year rift that existed between their two branches of the family, and his departure for America two years ago had been welcome news.

She hadn't spoken to him in nearly a decade, and she saw in an instant that he hadn't aged well. He had always been a large man, bulky in an athletic kind of way and tall enough to successfully carry his extra weight. He must have been indulging in too much food and drink in the years since their last meeting; his once muscular frame now strained the seams of his riding coat. Drops of sweat trickled down his face and he was breathing heavily, a probable sign he was no longer used to vigorous exercise. He would have been better off in a carriage instead of on horseback.

"Richard! I didn't know you were back in the country." She didn't bother to hide the displeasure from her voice.

"Just got back a week ago," he said brightly, not put off by her cold reception. "How fortunate that we should meet."

"Is it?" She eyed him warily.

He shook his head like a disapproving parent. "Come now. Don't you think we should lay aside our grievances? Extend the olive branch, and all that?"

"Are *you* willing to lay aside your grievances?" she challenged. To her mind, that meant he would no longer claim he should have inherited Moreton Hall instead of her. She thought that was as likely as the sun rising in the west tomorrow.

But he merely shrugged and said, "Let us not speak

of unpleasant things just now. I must offer you my hearty felicitations. I hear you are getting married soon."

If he was angling for an invitation, he was out of luck. He was the last person she'd want at the wedding. Assuming it even took place. Today's meeting with Hawthorne had left her with a queasy uncertainty on that subject.

Richard continued to watch her with that aggravating, self-satisfied smirk that she remembered too well. Why should he look pleased at the news of her marriage? It would mean the possibility of a male heir, and any claims he would want to lay against Moreton Hall would be extinguished for good.

She'd come to the park to think, to clear her head. The very last thing she needed was to have Richard Spencer insinuating himself back into her life. "I thank you for your felicitations," she said stiffly, adding pointedly, "please, don't let me keep you."

Richard laughed, as though she'd told him a pleasant joke instead of giving him the brush-off. "Yes, I'm sure you have a lot to do, what with planning your trousseau, or writing notices to the *Times*, or whatever it is ladies do before a wedding." He lifted his hat. "Until the next time, then."

He turned his horse around, leaving the green and taking the road toward the park gates. It was a pleasure to see the back of him, but she did not stare after him long. She urged her horse into a canter, wanting only to ride far and fast, as though she could gain a distance from her troubles. It wasn't until she saw Tom Poole up ahead that she realized she'd been looking for him.

He had stopped to rest in the shade of a tree, but when he saw her, he immediately began riding in her direction. She slowed to a halt and waited for him to reach her.

What a treat it was to watch a man who could ride well—especially after the revolting spectacle Richard had made. Both men were tall, but the comparison ended there. Tom was all lean muscle, and his trim riding clothes accentuated his broad shoulders and long, powerful legs. He moved smoothly with the animal's rhythm, seated with as much ease as a man relaxing in his favorite chair. Her admiration swelled as he brought the horse effortlessly to a neat stop a few feet away. He tipped his hat. "Good afternoon, Miss Vaughn."

"Hello, Mr. Poole."

Something in his eyes glinted, and his mouth widened in a tiny, almost sardonic smile. Was he remembering the last time they'd met, when she'd greeted him as "Just Tom"? Curious that she should think of that. And yet it seemed that every minute of that meeting was engraved in her memory.

Embarrassed to realize she was staring at him, she urged her horse to a walk. Suddenly she was aware of how warm the day had become. It felt good to get a breeze from movement, however slight. Immediately Tom's horse fell into step beside hers. She had heard the stallion had a bad temperament, yet Tom controlled it with minimal outward signs of direction. There were few men she knew who had that kind of impressive rapport with their mounts. She was about to say something to that effect, but Tom spoke first, sending her thoughts in a completely different direction. "I just came from a meeting with your fiancé," he said.

The words were simple, but they held a chill that reawakened Margaret's worries. "Oh?" she said, trying to keep her voice neutral. "So, what do you think? Paul tells me there are many investors who are eager to join his venture."

"Yes, everyone's jumping at the chance. Act now, or the opportunity will be lost." He spoke in a tone so dry it bordered on sarcasm. "However, I have learned that it's precisely those times when I feel rushed to do something that I must stop, step back, and assess the situation carefully. So I told him I would be happy to consider it, but I could make no commitment at the present time."

"I see," Margaret said. She did not know which direction this conversation was taking, but she was sure that wherever it led would be dangerous territory. She could not talk about Paul with anyone right now. Not until she had confronted him personally and gotten to the bottom of the allegations that Hawthorne had raised against him. With forced brightness she said, "Mr. Poole, I came out here to do some riding."

"Isn't that what we're doing?" He looked down as if to reassure himself that he was indeed on horseback.

"I mean some *real* riding. I assume that superb beast knows how to do more than walk slowly enough for an old lady to keep up?"

He gave her an amused grin. "I thought the purpose of coming to Rotten Row was simply to see and be seen."

"Well, then, let's show them something."

What had gotten into her? She had no idea. The words were out of her mouth before she could think—a truly unusual thing for her.

He looked down the green. "To that elm tree, then."

She followed his gaze to a line of a dozen or more trees. All elms. "Which elm tree?"

But her words were lost in the pounding of hoofbeats

as he raced away. So it was going to be like that with "Just Tom," was it? With a surge of excitement that temporarily eased the troubles weighing on her, she sent her mare into a gallop and chased after him.

*

What was he doing? He shouldn't be racing, and certainly not out here. He'd picked a straight and clear path, but anyone could wander into the way unexpectedly. He'd seen that on his previous rides here—including yesterday, when he'd nearly run down a careless slip of a man who was busy preening for two ladies in a passing carriage.

He listened for the sound of her horse behind him. She was there all right; she'd caught up to him with no trouble. He had not let out his horse to full speed, but he was going fast. Miss Vaughn must be a good horsewoman. That she was keeping up with him while riding sidesaddle raised his admiration even more. He thought it a stupidly dangerous custom, but she seemed to have mastered it. Even so, he slowed his pace. He did not want to endanger her. If the horse should stumble...

She passed him, her face glowing with excitement, the silk scarf from her hat flying in the breeze.

What spirit the woman had! He had not been lying when he said he'd learned the hard way not to rush into anything. Yet she made him want to throw all caution to the wind.

He was glad she had passed him. Now he could watch her as she raced down the green. Her form showed years of real practice, not just the minimal lessons required of any society miss. She must love riding as much as he did.

He began to have visions of the two of them riding alone together in an open field, with Margaret in a much simpler dress, not the voluminous riding habit she was wearing now. Her hat would be gone, and her long brown hair would tumble down, accentuating the luscious curves of her hips—

Dear Lord, not only was he racing, but also he was now having unhealthy thoughts about another man's intended bride. She came to a stop near one of the elms, then turned to face him.

Still berating himself, he brought his horse to a halt next to hers.

Her face was flushed and her green eyes flashed like the glimmer of the hot sun on the Indian Ocean. "Is this the elm tree you were talking about?"

"Yes," he said, his heart beating wildly. "I reckon it was."

She smiled triumphantly. "I seem to have won this race. What a shame we had not placed a wager."

"I think we got that attention you were after." Tom indicated the pedestrian path, where a group of people had gathered to watch their gallop across the green. "Doesn't that worry you?"

"Why should it?" She gave a brief toss of her head. "I attract attention wherever I go."

"I can see that," Tom returned with amusement. He could not help but admire her evident pride, which he thought stemmed from her justifiable self-confidence, and not mere vanity.

They both began to move again as if by one consent, keeping to a walk, allowing their horses to cool down properly.

"The crowd is thinning out," she observed. "No doubt they are disappointed neither of us fell off or did something else equally horrifying. They will have to find other, more fascinating topics to fill their time."

Her mockery displayed the hard edge Tom had seen on the night they met. He wondered if she truly was irked at the ways of society, or whether it was mere affectation. Plenty of people spoke as if they abhorred the rules of upper-class living, and yet seemed perfectly happy to abide by them.

"In any case," Margaret continued, "there is nothing untoward in having a relaxing ride in Hyde Park."

Relaxing? Tom was still breathing heavily, his shirt lined with sweat. Checking his stallion's speed had been no easy task. The horses, too, glistened from their exertions. Miss Vaughn's face, though flushed, was alight with pleasure. "I can see you enjoy riding," he said truthfully, and added without thinking, "you have an excellent seat."

She arched one delicate eyebrow, and he realized with dismay that his remark may have been taken as having a double meaning. "I hope that is the correct term," he said apologetically. "I only meant to say you ride well."

"Thank you." She patted her horse's neck. "I do indeed ride often. I've adored it ever since I was a child, and it's a mainstay for me at Moreton Hall—that's my home in Lincolnshire."

"Lincolnshire—that's to the north, isn't it?"

"Have you never been?"

He shook his head. "Never left London. Except for Australia."

She laughed. "Two very different places."

Tom loved her laugh, which was light and smooth,

effortlessly elegant, just as she was. "I want to see more of England, now that I have time and the means to do so. Should I begin with Lincolnshire? I assume there is much to recommend it?"

"Oh, yes. Wide-open spaces, not just a small patch of green hemmed in by buildings and people." She indicated the park around them. "My favorite place is a path that runs along a stream. It's really more of a narrow river, quite deep and rushing over large boulders. The wind rustling through the leafy trees overhead is like nature's poetry." She stopped herself with another smooth laugh. "I seem to have gotten carried away with my description. I must be boring you."

"Not at all." In fact, he had been entranced, watching the joy light up her face as she described her home.

"That is a beautiful horse," Margaret said. "I would have thought him too large for racing, but clearly he has speed. We have more than two dozen horses at Moreton Hall, including some Thoroughbreds that we intend to sell for racing. Are you perchance in the market for another racehorse, now that your horse is retired?"

He shook his head. "I have sworn off racing, as well as all forms of gambling."

She looked at him in surprise. "Have you? It cannot be due to debts, surely?"

"No, or rather—yes. It's due to a debt I owe the Lord. You see, I no longer feel it is fitting to indulge in professional racing. It is called a 'gentleman's sport,' but I see it as a form of gambling."

"You needn't bet on the horses. One might go to the races simply for the love of the sport, mightn't they?"

She was beginning to look distinctly uncomfortable.

Tom marveled at how many people would say they were Christians, and yet dislike talking about the things of God. He, too, had once been that kind of person. But his experiences in Australia had changed that. God had worked in his life and given him a peace he had not found anywhere else.

He also knew from experience not to press the issue. "Yes, indeed," he conceded. "And perhaps I will." He added that mostly to appease her, though he doubted it would happen. "I am interested in breeding horses for other uses. Saddle horses, for example."

"Will you convert Thoroughbreds to riding, as you did with this horse?"

He looked down fondly at his stallion. It was prancing a little as it walked, signaling that it was itching to run. Their race down the green had not even begun to tap its energy. Only Tom's careful handling of the reins and using pressure with his legs when needed kept the horse at a measured pace. But Tom never tired of the extra effort required. "Castor is a special case. He and I have come through a lot together. He is a handful, though. I think most gentlemen and ladies would prefer a more docile ride."

She made a small sound of derision. "Yes, I suppose most people would."

Clearly, thought Tom, she did not number herself among them.

She paused when they reached a path that led back to the eastern gate near Mayfair. "Thank you, Mr. Poole. It has been a pleasure."

Tom couldn't let her go. Not yet. She had seemed unwilling to talk about Denault earlier, but he had to try again. Something about the man worried him. What if he was a fraud? Did Miss Vaughn know what she was getting into? This might be his only chance to talk to her before it was too late, and he couldn't let it slip away. "May I escort you to the gate?" he offered.

She looked hesitant, but after a moment she nodded. "How kind."

They started down the path together. The gate was not far, so Tom wasted no time getting to his concerns. "Tell me, how much do you know about your fiancé's business affairs?"

She stiffened, her mask of cool reserve dropping back into place. "Why do you ask?"

"Clearly he's told you about his company's prospects. But are you sure he's telling you the whole truth?"

She met his gaze without hesitation, but her answer was evasive. "Do you have reason to doubt him?"

"I have nothing specific as yet, but still I don't trust him. Do you?" His question was direct and harsh, but there was no time to mince words.

Something flashed across her eyes—doubt? worry?—before her mouth flattened to an angry line. "Mr. Poole, you are speaking of my fiancé! What gives you the right—"

"I know all about men like Denault," Tom cut in. "They are constantly on the prowl for money. You are a clever woman, Miss Vaughn. I assume you know what you're doing. But even so I feel compelled to warn you." He paused deliberately. He'd already insulted her, and what he was about to say would probably hurt her, too. But if she was half as strong as he guessed she was, she could handle it.

"Warn me about *what?*" she demanded.

"You should make absolutely certain he's not just marrying you for your money."

"My money!" She laughed, but there was no mirth in it. "Yes, the Vaughn fortune is famous from here to the ends of the Empire. But one thing perhaps you may not know, being new to it yourself, is that with wealth comes an army of men to protect it for you—lawyers, bankers, financial advisers. So you may rest assured on that account. Do you think I have no other virtues that might attract a husband?"

"Far from it." He reached out and took hold of her riding crop, bringing them as close together as he could, forcing her undivided attention. "I should think my admiration of you had been evident from the beginning."

This disarmed her. Tom could see that. Her bottom lip quivered as her chest rose and fell rapidly. Her eyes searched his for just a fraction too long before she turned away, fighting, it would seem, to regain her composure. "Thank you for the pleasant ride and the conversation, Mr. Poole. There is no need to accompany me further." With a smart tap of her riding crop she sent her horse into a trot and rode away, her head held high, her back rigid.

Why had nothing he said gotten through to her? Was she really in such command of her destiny? Or was she a prideful fool? The arrogance that had amused him earlier now infuriated him. It served him right, he thought, to have his unsolicited advice met with contempt.

Tom wanted to curse. He wanted to pound a wall or do anything to vent his frustration. Instead he did the only thing he could. He sent his stallion once more down the green, heedless of his speed. Anyone else had better look sharp and stay out of his path.

Chapter 6

Margaret's agitation heightened with each step of her horse back to her town house. Tom Poole had angered her, but not for his impertinence, as she'd implied. It was the way he seemed to be corroborating what Hawthorne had told her. It simply couldn't be true. In a few more hours, she'd know for sure.

The day had grown warmer as the afternoon had progressed, and it was now unbearably hot. She was overheated as well as tired and out of sorts. She was eagerly anticipating a long, cool bath and changing into a comfortable tea gown.

The butler met her at the door. "Mr. Denault is here, miss."

"What? He's not due here for hours yet."

She was not ready to talk to him. She needed time to change, to refresh, to prepare.

"I informed him you were out, but he insisted on waiting for you."

"Well, he can keep on waiting. I need to change first."

That would buy her a half hour at least, and Paul could just cool his heels during that time. "You may go ahead and bring tea to the parlor for Mr. Denault."

"Mr. Denault is in the study, miss."

She paused on the stairs. "The study? You know I have standing instructions to place guests in the upstairs parlor."

"Yes, ma'am, and I do beg your pardon, but Mr. Denault was quite particular about asking for the study. He insisted it was more comfortable and he wished to pass the time with a good book."

Margaret was pretty sure the real draw was her best brandy, which she kept in a ready decanter on the sideboard. It was already half past four, not too early in the day for those who indulged in those things. But she was more worried about what else was in that room. She remembered with disturbing clarity that the papers Hawthorne and Clarke had given her were still laid out on the large desk. If Paul should go rooting around in those papers, he would know they suspected him of deceit. Perhaps even now he was dreaming up a lie to rebuff their accusations. She could not allow that to happen. She didn't want him to be prepared; she wanted to take him utterly by surprise. That was surely the only way to get the truth from him.

Realizing she was holding tightly to the railing, she let go and took a calming breath. "Very well. Have tea brought to the study, then."

There would be no bath, no time to prepare. No time to clear out the memory of Tom Poole, who was filling her thoughts the way light fills every corner of a room. One thing she was certain about Tom Poole: he was not a liar. Honesty radiated from him. His rough frankness was worlds apart from Paul's brand of charm, which was beginning to reveal itself as calculating and sly. Margaret had rebuffed Tom's warning, but it echoed ominously in her heart as she opened the study door.

Paul was exactly where she had suspected she would find him: seated at her desk. Infuriatingly, he had his feet propped up on it as he perused several papers in his hand. She could tell at a glance it was the dossier Mr. Hawthorne had given her.

Paul looked up. Seeing her, he tossed the papers onto the desk.

She spoke without preamble. "Those are my private papers." She unpinned her hat and removed it, tossing it and her gloves onto a chair. That provided some relief from the heat, as the breeze from the open window cooled the damp hair on the back of her neck.

Unperturbed, Paul rose. "Hello, darling." He spoke as if she had just wished him a pleasant greeting. He sauntered over and gently grasped one of her hands. His own hand was cool. He was always cool, she reflected as he placed a soft, lingering kiss on her cheek. Normally such an action would give her pleasure, but at the moment it produced a far different sensation—revulsion, almost.

She drew back. "You had no right to read my private papers."

"No right?" He spoke gently, but his blue eyes were hard and unyielding. "I am your fiancé. Soon I'll be your husband. I'd say that gives me every right."

"We are not married yet," she countered, "and this is still my home. What are you doing here so early?"

"Have I caught you at a bad time? How inconsiderate of me. I assumed you'd be home attending to the details of our wedding like a proper bride-to-be, not out taking a pleasure jaunt in Hyde Park."

Margaret caught her breath. He was attempting to chastise *her!* For weeks she'd endured the way he patronized and belittled her. She'd stifled her objections out of desperation, willing to do anything to make this marriage happen. But she refused to tolerate it anymore. "I asked why you were reading my papers, Paul."

"And I believe I gave you an answer." He attempted to brush back a strand of hair from her face, but sweat had plastered it to her forehead. "What a sight you are. Why don't you go and change? I'll wait."

She swatted his hand away. "It's time we laid everything out on the table, don't you think? You told me your business had made a hefty profit in America. You've let it be understood both here and abroad that you are rich."

His cajoling smile evaporated. "And that cursed Hawthorne has gone and proven otherwise, has he?" In two strides Paul returned to the desk. With an angry swipe he sent the papers tumbling to the carpet. "Curse the man for putting his nose where it doesn't belong."

"Stop it!" She advanced on him. "You blame someone else because you were caught in a lie, but I'm glad for those men. I'm grateful I have lawyers who will ferret out—"

"Lawyers?" he cut in. "Spies, you mean. They're too old for foreign intrigues, so they take satisfaction in ruining their own countrymen. They are stirring up things that ought to have been left alone."

"It's true then, isn't it?" She grabbed a handful of papers from the floor and waved them in his face. "How could you woo me under such false pretenses? How could you lead me on?"

He pushed her hands away, his face ugly with fury. He looked ready to strike her. Margaret drew back, preparing to defend herself. For several tense heartbeats, she could almost see his mind at work, calculating his next move. Then, slowly and deliberately, he relaxed his clenched fists. "Let's stop and consider this calmly," he said in a conciliatory tone. "In the end, what difference does it make? We belong together, and you are rich enough for us both, are you not?"

Margaret stared at him aghast. "You have not the slightest bit of conscience, do you?"

The anger flashed again, and again she saw him carefully suppress it. "Let me tell you something," Paul said fiercely. "It is an age-old fact that in this world in order to make money you have to *have* money. It's the constant conundrum. The rich get richer, and the poor haven't got a chance. You will not regret marrying me. In time I can increase your wealth beyond your wildest dreams."

"Time," said Margaret coldly, "is something we do not have."

"But we have your money."

She broke free and threw her hands in the air. "I have no money!" She drew herself up, staring right back into his stunned expression. "My father left debts. Serious debts. He managed to gamble away or otherwise squander nearly everything."

"But your lands are extensive. The rents, the income…"

"—have been steadily decreasing. The tenants are

moving away to the cities, where they can find better-paying jobs. It seems that slaving away in the Manchester factories is more appealing than raising crops."

"I can't believe you lied to me!" Paul actually had the effrontery to look wounded.

"You lied to *me!*" she shot back. "I believe there is a saying about the pot calling the kettle black."

"Yes," he agreed, turning her accusation back upon her. "I believe there is."

"At least I haven't been boasting about triumphs that never happened." It was true. If anything, hers had been lies of omission only, not correcting those who assumed she was rich. "I haven't been attempting to lure innocent investors into a shaky scheme."

"Haven't you, though? You lured me into this engagement."

"Lured!" Margaret fairly stuttered from the insult of it. "Lured!"

"Be quiet!" he snapped. He turned away from her and began to pace the room, his arms crossed, thinking aloud. "Perhaps we are both being too hasty. There might still be a way we can salvage this situation. But how…"

His question hung in the air, unanswered. Margaret stared at him, her heart pounding furiously from anger and frustration, unable to accept this quagmire they'd driven each other into.

"We must use your land," Paul said at last, turning back to her. "We'll sell a portion. The Northern and Eastern Railway wants a tract for a line to Lincoln—"

"No!" she said vehemently. "The estate has been intact for more than two hundred years, and I intend to keep it that way." She looked at him suspiciously. "How did you know the railway wanted my land?"

He shrugged. "I'm in the railway business. I ought to know these things."

"But you must have *some* money," she pressed. "Can you not liquidate *your* assets? If we can just make some farming improvements, we can get the land profitable again. You can start a new company once the debts are paid."

"I do not think we can pay off your debts with my debts." He gave a coarse laugh. "If we could figure out how to do that, we could build an empire."

"You mean, you really have *nothing?*"

"My money was swindled from me!" The anger and frustration in his voice showed how deeply it pained him to admit it. "I did not lie when I said my previous investment was an unparalleled success. Unfortunately, the other partners cheated me out of my share." He gave her a look of defiance. "And that's the God's honest truth. Are you happy now?"

That was it, then. There really was no money. Margaret stood still, unable to move, her mind reeling from the cruel irony of her situation. Her anger was gone now, swept away by a tidal wave of self-recrimination. She'd thought she'd been so clever, congratulated herself for maintaining the upper hand. All the while, she and Paul had each been playing the other for a fool.

There was a light tap at the door, and the maid entered with a silver tea tray.

"Just set it down there," Margaret said, indicating a table, dismayed to see her hand was trembling. "We will serve ourselves."

Paul laughed. "Seems to me that we've been serving ourselves for quite some time now."

After giving them both a puzzled glance, the maid set down the tray and left the room. Margaret closed the door behind her. She stood for a moment with her forehead pressed against the smooth oak, searching for strength.

Behind her, Paul said, "You realize this changes everything."

"Yes," she said with a shudder. "I do."

She turned to face him, bracing herself against the door. "We must call off the engagement."

Paul's expression was stony, resigned. He did not answer.

"What a pair of fools we have been!" Margaret cried bitterly. "Leading each other on, making protestations of love. But it was never about love, was it?"

He approached her. "My attraction to you was genuine." He ran his hands lightly up and down her arms, and she shivered from his touch. He'd always had that effect on her. Seeing her react to him now, he drew closer. "Don't deny that you felt it, too," he said gently in her ear. "You felt something when we were close." He trailed soft kisses from her ear to her mouth. "If we must part, let us do it on amicable terms…"

His lips came down on hers, kissing her ferociously. He pressed her into the door, covering every part of her body with his own. The heat she had felt outside earlier today was nothing compared to this.

Over the past weeks she'd told herself that this attraction between them must be a sign that somewhere, deep down, there was love—or at least the potential for it. Now, through the tangle of her confusion, she was begin-

ning to understand. In his lovemaking, as with everything else, simple, cold calculations lay behind all his
actions. In any situation, he knew how to manipulate
people to get what he wanted. The man had nearly ruined
them both with his lies. This was just one more way he
was using her.

Margaret fought to gather her wits, pushing him
away. "Stop it, Paul," she gasped. "It's over."

He placed his hands on either side of the door, keeping her penned up against it. His eyes were hard, piercing. "If we end our engagement, we can never reveal
why. It will go better for both of us that way. And don't
even consider suing me for breach of promise—there is
no money to be gained by it, I assure you."

She was right. Paul had never even come close to caring for her. He cared for no one but himself. "Why, you
insufferable, lying bas—"

"Now, now." He placed a finger on her lips to stop
her. "You should be glad that I am willing to watch out
for both of us, despite this unfortunate turn of events. A
lawsuit would bring only shame and embarrassment and
keep either of us from our goal."

"What goal would that be?" she said, escaping his
grasp. She crossed her arms and scowled, furious to
find she was still shaking, and determined to hide it. She
would not allow herself to show any sign of weakness.

"Why, we must both marry money, of course," he
replied. "We have both proven that we are masters at
hoodwinking others. If you and I managed to fool each
other, that proves we are cut from the same cloth. You
are beautiful, and, despite your debts, you bring an
impressive estate to your dowry. As for me, despite my

money problems, I have the strength of an old family name and highly sought-after social connections. I am also quite appealing to the ladies, although I risk going to perdition for my vanity in saying so."

Vanity was not the only thing that was going to send him to perdition, Margaret thought. "But we must give some excuse for breaking the engagement," she insisted.

"Nonsense. People will talk, of course. But so long as we—and our lawyers—remain tight-lipped on this, I see no reason for worry."

"No reason for worry," Margaret repeated sarcastically. "Can you really take all this so lightly?"

"This has been a setback; I won't deny it. I was rather looking forward to marrying you, in fact." He gave her another appreciative glance. "However, I still have prospects. I *always* have prospects. If you wish to keep *your* options open, I suggest you take my advice about staying mum on why we are not getting married."

They stared at each other across the room. Taking her silence as acquiescence, Paul gave a short nod and turned to open the study door. "Don't bother ringing for the butler. I'll let myself out."

Margaret sank into a chair, listening to the sound of his retreating footsteps. Her head pounded. She closed her eyes tightly against the pain. She was trembling violently—not just from her reaction to Paul, but from the realization that her carefully constructed world had toppled as easily as a child's building blocks.

What was she to do? Look for another rich man? How could she even consider turning her life over to anyone? She had been prepared to do it with Paul, and he had led her to the brink of disaster.

She forced herself to open her eyes, rubbing her temples in an attempt to ease the throbbing as she looked over at the scattered papers. Not all were from the dossier Hawthorne had given her; some pertained to the wedding. All that time and planning, useless now.

She rose and poured herself some tea, and was gratified to find her hands shaking less and less as she drank it. Thus fortified, she tried to review her situation with a clear head. She was still determined to hold on to her land. But how was she to buy more time from the creditors?

There was, in fact, one option left to her, she realized now. She must immediately sell all of the fine Thoroughbreds she'd been carefully raising and training. She would have made a greater profit if she could have retained them for another year, but she would have to sell them now and get what she could.

In less than a month her lenders would be demanding payment. She would have to find a buyer quickly— someone who would give her cash outright for the horses. Then she would be able to give the lenders a portion of the amount owed and hope she might persuade them to wait a little longer for the rest.

If she was frugal and very careful, it might buy her enough time. The crops were looking good; the harvest potential was above average. With any luck at all she could survive another year.

But *luck* was something that Margaret found always seemed to elude her.

Chapter 7

"Have you heard the news? It's quite astounding, really." James greeted them with this pronouncement as he entered the breakfast room, newspaper in hand. "Where's Lizzie? She will want to hear this."

"Good morning to you, too, James," Geoffrey said with mock formality. "Thanks for calling. Won't you join us?"

"Why, thank you, I believe I will," he replied with a smile, ignoring Geoffrey's reproof and dropping into the chair opposite Tom.

Clearly attuned to James's preferences, one of the footmen brought coffee forward and filled James's cup. What an odd world this was, Tom thought. He still found it unnerving that the servants were so assiduously trained that they could anticipate a person's every need and then jump to meet it.

"Lizzie is well, I hope?" James asked as he inspected the eggs and sliced beef laid down in front of him.

"She is resting," Geoffrey answered. "The doctor has

ordered her to stay in bed this morning. It seems she was too active yesterday."

James looked up from his plate. "But she is well? She needs only rest?"

A flicker of something that might have been worry showed in Geoffrey's eyes. "Of course."

"Truly?" James persisted. In spite of all his frivolity, he was always quite serious when it came to Lizzie's health. Tom could see that James cared for his cousin deeply. Tom, too, had subjected Geoffrey to this close questioning before James had arrived. And just like James, he was not entirely convinced by the doctor's words. Lizzie was the center of *all* their lives. If anything should happen to her . . .

"James, we do all we can, and trust to the Lord for the rest." The look on Geoffrey's face warned James not to pursue it further.

To his credit, James knew when to stop pressing. He gave a brief nod and said, "Please give her my love and tell her I was asking after her, won't you?"

Geoffrey relaxed. "Of course. Now what is this news you spoke of?"

James snapped his fingers, as though remembering something he had temporarily forgotten. "It is astounding news."

This brought out a chuckle from Geoffrey. "I can guess at the kind of news you would find *astounding,* James. Did someone run off with a duke's daughter? Or drive a carriage the wrong way in Hyde Park?"

But James was inured to any teasing. "Oh, no," he said earnestly, "it's far more sensational than that." He looked over at Tom with the satisfaction of a cat who has just stolen a chicken off the dinner table.

"Tell us what you have to say, James," Geoffrey said.

"Oh, all right. Since you've dragged it out of me, here it is. The engagement between Denault and Miss Vaughn has been broken off."

This news hit Tom like a thunderbolt. His butter knife slipped from his hand, dropping with a clatter onto his plate. "I beg your pardon?"

"You heard right." A slow smile pasted itself onto James's face. "Miss Vaughn is once more on the marriage market."

"How can that be?" Geoffrey asked. "And how do you know this?"

"Oh, it's all over town." James tapped the newspaper. "Hasn't hit the *Times* yet, but it will. I learned about it at the club."

Tom realized this was everything he'd been hoping for. Yet it only made him worried for Margaret. "Why are they breaking their engagement? Granted, I know nothing about society matches, but isn't that unusual?"

James nodded. "*Unusual, rare, not done*—call it any number of things. I call it astounding. Everyone knew the pair of them were dead set to get married as soon as possible. Yet, inexplicably, this happens."

"But *why?*" Tom asked impatiently. James did have a way of embellishing a subject rather than just getting to the heart of it.

James gave a nonchalant shrug. "No one knows for sure, although rumors abound. At times people can be most aggravatingly closemouthed on a subject."

"Perhaps one of them decided it was not an advantageous match," Geoffrey offered.

"If so, it must have been Miss Vaughn," James said.

"Otherwise a breach-of-promise suit would be in the works. No one in the rumor mill seems to expect that." He leaned back in his chair and tapped his chin. "Something must have caused her to change her mind. I wonder what it could be?" He sent another glance in Tom's direction.

"You can't think it has anything to do with me," Tom protested.

"Of course I do," James replied unapologetically. "I think she fell head over ears in love with you the instant she saw you, and realized she couldn't possibly marry Denault."

"That's absurd!" Tom said, a little too quickly. And too loudly. Out of the corner of his eye, he saw the footman flinch. He lowered his voice to normal tones. "What do you suppose really happened, James?"

"Well..." James sat back, took a sip of his coffee, and savored it. Clearly he had more to add, but the cursed fellow was pausing for effect.

"Well?" Tom prodded, fighting to keep his irritation in check.

James set down his cup. "Well...I've heard things about Denault's business. He may have...overestimated his net worth."

"I can't believe that," Geoffrey said. "Everyone knows Denault was hugely successful in America."

"I can believe it," Tom said. "I sensed that something was not quite right as soon as I met with him. He's a good salesman, I'll grant you that. *Too* good. Once or twice he put me in mind of those preachers at big-tent revivals. They get people all stirred up so they act out of emotion rather than common sense."

"I'll bet that tactic didn't work for you," James observed. "You're too levelheaded."

"Not always," Tom said, remembering with chagrin how he'd nearly gotten into a fight with that idiot Carter. He was still prone to fight first and ask questions later. "I'm working on it."

"How interesting that we automatically assume the problem lies with Denault," Geoffrey remarked.

"Surely you can't think Miss Vaughn is at fault!" Tom protested.

Geoffrey held up his hands. "We don't know whether *anyone* is at fault," he said reasonably.

"That argument won't work with Tom," James said. "His bias toward Miss Vaughn is unmistakable."

Great heavens, they were *both* going to needle him on this now. As if he needed any more practice holding his temper, which at the moment threatened to slip deftly from his grasp. Tom threw his napkin on the table and stood up. "If you gentlemen will excuse me," he said with forced politeness, "I am going out."

*

Tom called for his horse to be brought round, then took the stairs two at a time to his room. What a waste of time it all was, he thought as he hastily shrugged out of his fine clothes and into more sturdy riding attire. Time was when he could get dressed once in the morning and be done with it.

As he stepped out of the house, Tom took a moment to survey the patch of green that was Berkeley Square. It was deserted except for a nanny watching a young boy of six or so at play. Tom sent his gaze beyond the square to

Margaret's house, hoping to catch a glimpse of her. But no one was coming or going from the large front door. No one could be spotted at its windows.

Tom was itching to march over there and ask her straight out why she and Denault had broken off their engagement. But he was certain she would not take kindly to it. He might wish to be her friend, but she clearly wanted nothing from him. Perhaps it was better that way, he told himself. For now, he would do better to spend some time in reflection and prayer. At the moment, even if the Lord wanted to extend some guidance, there was no way Tom would be able to hear it over the multitude of anxious thoughts stampeding through his head. So with a nod of thanks to the groom, Tom mounted his horse and set off in the direction of Hyde Park. It was the only place that could give him the peace and quiet he needed.

A patchy blanket of gray clouds threatened rain, but so far had delivered only a damp sensation without actually making anything wet. Rotten Row was not yet the bustling thoroughfare that it would become later in the day if the weather held. Tom turned his horse onto a patch of grass that was fairly deserted, where stands of tall elms offered shade and solitude. He dismounted, secured his horse, and sat down to ponder. After a minute or so, a cool breeze touched his face—just enough to offer an enticing hint of autumn, and bringing a fresh, new thought to Tom: *Margaret was free.*

It was an absurd thought, and yet there it was. Why her circumstances should appear to him that way, he was not ready to explore. He only knew that it was so.

"Lord, you've seen me through bad times, worse times,

and better times," he said softly. "You've taught me to look for your hand in my affairs. Is this one of those times?"

He was not expecting an answer, of course. Nothing outright, at any rate. He'd learned that God was not quite so direct as Tom would have wished. Back in Sydney, the minister had once shown him a verse about God's "still, small voice." In Tom's experience, that soft voice was mighty hard to hear.

He closed his eyes and tried to open his heart, but memories of Margaret filled him so completely that there was no room for anything else: the self-assured way she'd moved through that crowded ballroom; that loose curl that had accentuated the elegant line of her alabaster neck; the exuberance that had lit her face when she flew past him on horseback. How many women were so completely comfortable in both outdoor pursuits and elegant soirees, so thoroughly breathtaking in any setting? Not many, he'd guess.

The breeze rustled again, stronger this time, as though the clouds, searching deep within themselves, had found some rain after all. They must have, because soon he could hear the soft patter of raindrops on the leaves above his head. "The only thing the Lord is telling you," he reprimanded himself, "is that you are mighty foolish if you plan to sit out here in the rain."

Castor began to shift restlessly and sent out a soft whinny. Changes in the weather always unsettled him. Tom would do well to get him back to a dry stall as soon as possible. He stood and stretched, speaking soothing words as he took hold of the reins and loosed them from a tree branch. "Easy, boy. We'll be home soon."

He mounted the horse and turned him back toward the

open field. Castor obeyed, but Tom could tell he wasn't happy about it. The increasing wall of gray overhead showed the potential for a soaker. Other park visitors had also begun to seek shelter. Some scurried to waiting carriages; others walked briskly toward the streets that would lead them home. Castor would have liked to hurry, too; he kept shaking his head, irritated that Tom was keeping him at a walk. But despite the rain, Tom was unwilling to leave the open space of the park. He might have stayed for hours if the weather had been favorable and his horse more amenable.

When the rain became heavy enough to send large drops sliding down the brim of Tom's hat, he finally conceded defeat and set his horse into a canter for the park gates. On the main thoroughfare he threaded his way carefully through the traffic, which the mud had reduced to a crawl. Before long he was turning into the mews behind Geoffrey's house. It would be better to deposit the horse there himself, rather than ask one of Geoffrey's servants to do it. He wanted to personally make sure that Castor was properly groomed and comfortable.

He had just led Castor into the stable when the rain started to come down in buckets. The storm lasted for nearly an hour, pounding on the roof and cracking bursts of thunder, while Tom and the stable boy saw to the horse's needs.

When it was over, Tom stepped outside and studied the sky. The light was still muted, not streaming in the bright rays that so often appear after a summer storm. He considered saddling his horse again, but finally decided against it. The morning was far gone, and Lizzie would be looking for him for luncheon.

He made his way along the muddy street, doing his best to avoid the pools of standing water. Even so, his boots were becoming filthy and would soon be in serious need of cleaning and polishing. *That,* at least, was one thing he was glad to have another person do. After his jaunt today, he might have to give his valet a pay raise.

When he reached the Somerville home, Tom paused. The little square out front was deserted, its wooden benches glistening from the rain, but Tom crossed the street to it anyway. He still had a few minutes to spare before he was needed inside. He perched on the back of one of the benches, his feet on the seat, enabling him to sit without getting his trousers soaked.

He knew why he had stopped here, of course. He studied Margaret's house, wondering for the thousandth time what she was doing. As he did so, a hansom cab pulled out of the traffic and came to a stop at Margaret's door. Two men got out of the cab. One approached the door and knocked. The second spoke briefly to the driver before joining the first man on the steps. He must have given instructions to wait, for the carriage did not pull away. Tom got off the bench and walked to the edge of the square in order to get a better look.

The first man was perhaps fifty, while the other, who was considerably younger, stood next to him, a towering hulk of a man. Both were dressed in black. There was nothing unusual in that; black was the standard dress for men in London these days. On these two men, however, it seemed to lend a sinister air. They looked like undertakers.

What did they want with Margaret?

The older man rapped on the door again. It was loud and insistent; Tom could hear it from where he stood.

When the door finally opened, it was not a butler standing there as Tom had expected, but a harried-looking young maid.

The men asked her a question, then showed their displeasure at the way she answered them. Tom couldn't hear the conversation, but it was clear from their gestures that they were insisting on entering the house. He could also see that the maid was just as unwilling to admit them. The brawny man looked ready to break the door down if necessary.

When the maid turned her head for an instant, as though trying to hear something spoken from inside the house, the men took advantage of the opportunity to force their way in. They pushed past her, opening the door wide, and Tom saw the maid protesting as she followed them. The older man strode down the hall without hesitation, as though he had been there before. Both went into a room at the far end of the hall and disappeared from view. Seeing she had no hope of removing them, the maid rushed back to close the front door.

What sort of men would dare to strong-arm their way into Margaret's house? Did they intend to harm her? In an instant, Tom was crossing the square. He might have no right to interfere, but he fully intended to do so anyway. He stalked up to the driver, who was leaning casually against a lamppost and eating an apple. "Who are those men?" he demanded, pointing toward Margaret's door.

The cabbie nonchalantly disengaged himself from the lamppost. "Beg pardon, govnah?" he said in a thick cockney accent.

"Who are the men you've just brought here?" Tom said again. "What are their names?"

The cabbie shrugged. "I don't make it my business to know the names of the persons I carry. One man's money is as good as another."

"You have no idea who they are?"

"London's a big place," he replied, tossing the apple core into the gutter. "Filled with more people than I could ever count."

"Where did you pick them up? At some place of business?"

The cabbie brought a hand to his grizzled chin, as though trying to cast his mind back—as though he didn't know exactly where he'd picked up those men and had already calculated the exact fare he was going to get from them. One thing that hadn't changed while Tom had been gone from London was the way the cabdrivers would try to wring every penny out of you.

"Somewhere along Fleet Street, I think," the cabbie finally said.

This was no help at all, since Fleet Street was one of the busiest areas in London. Finding his patience was wearing dangerously thin, Tom employed another tactic. "I assume they paid you to wait?"

"Aye," the little man answered. He grinned, showing a set of teeth with so many gaps that Tom wondered how he'd managed to eat that apple. "Three shillings for waiting, with a promise of double the total fare."

The cabbie looked at him expectantly. No doubt he'd precisely assessed Tom's financial bracket from the fine tailoring of his riding clothes. He would probably be more forthcoming if he were to find some silver in his hand.

Tom pulled a half crown from his pocket. "Where will you take them?" he asked, dropping the coin into the man's palm, which was suddenly in a convenient position to receive it.

"Well, how would I know that?" the cabbie said, galling him with a cheeky grin. "I ain't taken 'em there yet." He started to put the coin in his pocket, but Tom reached out and grabbed his hand.

"Guess," Tom said fiercely, giving his arm a wrench.

The cabbie met Tom's gaze steadily, assessing him. Plainly, in his years on the streets he'd dealt with even tougher customers than Tom. But Tom didn't back down. "I said *guess,*" he ground out again, gripping the man's hand more tightly and giving it a small twist.

The cabbie blinked, and Tom knew he'd won. "I have a notion," the little man said with a slight cough, "that it might be in the vicinity of Pedley Street."

Tom knew that place. It was a haven for moneylenders—the most vile, disreputable kind imaginable. Now that he thought about it, those two men looked exactly like the sort of despicable bastards that populated Pedley Street.

He dropped the cabbie's hand without another word and raced up the steps to Margaret's house. If she was receiving calls from moneylenders, then something was seriously wrong. A woman of her means would never consort with such people.

Would she?

He was going to find out.

Chapter 8

Tom rapped the ornate door knocker with such violence that he might have made the whole house shake. He hoped so. He was fully prepared to force his way in if necessary, just as he had seen the other men do.

However, when the door opened and Tom found himself face-to-face with the terrified young maid, he relented. He was desperate to see Margaret, but it would take just a few precious seconds to speak kindly. Those moneylenders had mistreated her, but surely he was made of better stuff. "Is Miss Vaughn at home?" He tried to sound like a gentleman paying a social call.

"I'm terribly sorry, sir," the maid said weakly. "My mistress is not at home at present."

She darted a glance behind her as she said this, just as she had done earlier. She looked back at Tom, taking in his appearance. Not with the cynically appraising glance that the cabbie had used, but perhaps to gauge whether she might appeal to him for help. "Would you care to leave a card?" she asked hopefully.

It took a moment for this to register. The practice of handing out calling cards was still new to him. But he hurriedly fished in his pockets and came up with a card, glad now that Lizzie had badgered him into getting some. He gave it to the maid.

Her eyes widened when she read the card. Tom could see that she recognized the name. For once, he was glad of his notoriety. Even the servants knew his story. She raised her eyes, staring at him with awe.

"Might I ask your name?" Tom inquired, doing all he could to keep his tone friendly despite his pressing worry.

"Bessie," she said breathlessly, and belatedly added, "sir."

"Well, Bessie, I'll be honest with you." Tom was not merely feigning confidentiality; he'd always felt a kinship with the lower classes. Perhaps because he'd been only a half step above them for most of his life. "I know your mistress is at home, and I would prefer to gain access in a polite fashion, rather than bullying my way in as those two men did earlier."

She opened her mouth to protest, but was stopped by the sound of shouting coming from the room down the hall. Tom stepped closer to the door, fighting to hold on to his patience. If those men laid even the slightest hand on Margaret, he would murder them.

Doubt and fear paraded across Bessie's face. "But I have orders to allow nobody into the house," she whispered.

"I have often been called a nobody," Tom said. "Perhaps that is what she meant?"

He was gratified to see his words tease a small smile

out of Bessie, but he looked anxiously over her shoulder down the hall. "Let me in, Bessie," he urged. "I can help."

Voices raised in argument were now clearly audible, and this seemed to help Bessie make up her mind. She stood back, and instantly Tom raced in.

At the end of the hall he paused when he heard Margaret's voice. She was speaking in a commanding tone, which told him that although they were arguing, she must not be in any immediate physical danger. He reached for the handle and tested it. It was well oiled and turned soundlessly. He opened the door a crack in order to hear what they were saying.

"Mr. Mortimer, you agreed that I had until next month." Margaret's words were clear now. "Even you would not stoop so low as to revise the terms without warning." Her voice was angry and filled with disdain. Tom could easily picture her standing tall and haughty, as she had proven she could do so well.

"Things have changed," a deep-set voice replied. It was surely the voice of the elder man. "You are no longer engaged to Mr. Denault. Our understanding was that payment was delayed until you had married him and gained access to his money."

His words astounded Tom, as had everything about this situation. Why should Margaret need Denault's money?

He was aware of Bessie coming up behind him. He glanced back and saw her wringing her hands, her face distorted with anxiety.

"Mr. Denault was never my sole source of funding," Margaret said. "I had hoped to wait until our marriage, to be sure, in order to merge our resources, but—"

"Come now, Miss Vaughn," Mortimer interrupted. "If you really had other sources of money, you would never have darkened our door."

There was a chuckle, which must have come from the other man. "Ain't that the truth."

"I do regret that I ever 'darkened your door,' as you so poetically put it," she said with undisguised contempt. "Clearly I was in error. I had been told that you were the most honorable among your cohort of thieves."

"Thieves!" a voice exploded. It must have belonged to Brawn. "Don't be insultin' my employer like that."

"You stand back!" Margaret shrieked.

That was all he needed. Tom flung open the door. It gave a satisfying bang as it slammed against the wall. "What's going on here?" he demanded.

Margaret was standing behind a large desk, her face flushed, staring daggers at the two men. Brawn looked ready to advance on her, although the elder man's hand was on his arm as though he'd been reaching out to stop him. All three turned and stared at Tom, frozen in surprise. They looked like one of those tableau scenes he'd seen acted out by guests at a dinner party he'd attended. Not that any of those refined ladies and gentlemen would be acting out *this* tableau. "Young Lady Threatened by Moneylenders" was probably not in their repertoire.

"What is the meaning of this?" she said imperiously. "Why are you barging into my house?"

Her anger surprised him. He would have thought she'd be glad to see him. His own heart was pounding out of his chest, relieved that he'd arrived in time. He stood his ground. "I was admitted by the maid," Tom said. "Unlike these two"—he jerked a thumb at the moneylenders—"who forced their way in." To Brawn he said pointedly, "If you even go near her, I will make sure you heartily regret it."

Brawn bristled. Tom kept his eyes locked on him, knowing from experience that this kind of thug would quickly take advantage of any lapse in his opponent's attention.

"Are you mad?" Margaret exclaimed.

"Probably," Tom conceded. He was no stranger to fisticuffs, but up close Brawn looked a lot bigger—and a lot meaner—than he had from a distance.

"I assure you, no one is going to lay a hand on anyone," Mortimer said. "We are merely having a business meeting. You, sir, were not invited."

Tom did not move even a muscle. "If this is just a *business meeting,* then why don't you call off your dog."

Brawn tensed and made a threatening motion. Tom raised his fists in reply, showing he was more than willing to back up his words with action.

"Go stand by the window, Jake," Mortimer commanded. "You're making everybody nervous."

Jake glowered at Tom, but did as he was told.

Tom saw some of the tension leave Margaret's body as the distance between her and Jake increased, but she was still very agitated. She took a deep breath. "Mr. Poole, this is a private matter. I thank you for your concern, but—"

"That's right, I am concerned," Tom cut in. "When I see two men forcing their way into a proper lady's house, I get concerned." He strode over to Margaret, wanting to shield her from these men. He knew he was giving in to his impulsiveness again, but this time he felt justified. "Do you owe these men money? If so, tell me the amount, and I'll pay it."

He glanced over at Mortimer as he said this, and saw a gleam light up the older man's eye. He probably did not care where the money came from, so long as he was paid.

Margaret straightened. She really was tall for a woman. When she drew herself up to her full height like this, she and Tom stood nearly eye to eye. Golden flecks lit up her green eyes like sparks of fire. "Mr. Poole, we hardly know each other."

"That is something I believe we should remedy." He tipped his head in the direction of the moneylenders. "After we have gotten these two leeches out of your life."

Over by the window, Jake was still scowling at him, looking like a chained attack dog. But Mortimer was a smoother fellow. "I do not take umbrage, sir," he said mildly. "Men in my profession are often thus insulted in return for the valuable services we provide. It is one of the great injustices to which I have resigned myself." To Margaret he said, "What I *do* take umbrage at is not being paid for my services. I must again insist that we receive the full amount by tomorrow noon. Otherwise, this becomes a matter for the courts."

"The courts!" Tom repeated in surprise. "How can you possibly take this woman to court?"

"At the time of our initial loan, Miss Vaughn signed a declaration that she had never before raised money on the same security from anybody else. It was a mere formality, of course. However, the laws of our noble land do state that anyone who makes such a declaration falsely is liable, upon conviction, to a *long term of imprisonment*."

Margaret bristled. Or perhaps it was a shudder at the

prospect of prison. If Jake was looking like a chained attack dog, Margaret was looking like a cornered fox.

Tom knew exactly what Mortimer was doing. He was jumping on the chance for money when he saw it, pressing Margaret to accept Tom's offer.

Margaret knew it, too, but her pride was greater than any attempt at intimidation. "How dare you threaten me?" she said fiercely. "You miserable, loathsome, grasping—"

"Careful, Miss Vaughn," Mortimer advised. "You may call me anything you like, *after* our business is concluded."

"What does she owe you?" Tom said. He was tired of talk when the problem could be easily solved by action.

Mortimer considered him thoughtfully. "Mr. . . . Poole, is it?"

"Yes. Tom Poole." Seeing the moneylender's face wrinkle to admit a smile, Tom added sarcastically, "Yes, *that* Tom Poole. Nouveau riche, gold mine–owning Tom Poole."

"Are you really prepared to pay her debts?"

There was that look again—the one Tom had seen too often in other men. Mortimer had caught the scent of money like a hound after game. "I will pay you what she owes, and not a farthing more."

"You'll do no such thing," Margaret said indignantly. "I'll have you remember, gentlemen, that this is my house. I will not have you going on about my affairs as though I am not even here."

Her defiance was genuine. It was also, Tom thought with a flash of surprise, undeniably appealing. He knew this woman had fire in her the first moment he'd laid eyes on her. But he also had to admit she had a point. He was taking liberties, and she deserved to be better treated.

"Miss Vaughn, perhaps you and I might have a word?" He turned to Mortimer and added pointedly, "In private."

Margaret glanced from him to Mortimer. His eyebrows lifted a fraction, but then he gave a small nod of his head. He must have quickly calculated which moves would give him the best odds of getting his money. "We'll just wait in the hall while you two sort this out."

Reluctantly, and with another malevolent look at Tom, Jake followed his employer out the door. When the door closed behind them, Tom turned back to Margaret. He expected her to drop her guard a little now that Mortimer was out of the room. Perhaps show Tom some measure of gratitude or relief.

Instead, she turned her fury on Tom. "Mr. Poole, I bitterly resent you coming in here and acting in such a high-handed fashion. I'll have you know that I am perfectly able to handle my own affairs."

"Are you?" Tom said sharply. Her attitude was stoking his own anger. He could only admire her strength if it did not lead her to foolish actions. "Your engagement to Denault is broken and the moneylenders are threatening you with prison. Do you call *that* being in control of your affairs?"

She flinched at his words, but held her ground. "My engagement has nothing to do with it."

"Apparently it does," he contradicted.

She glowered at him. "Were you eavesdropping before barging in here?" Her voice was caustic and brittle. "What a gentleman you are."

"I have done plenty of things for which I might not be called a gentleman," Tom conceded. "However, I would hope that trying to help a lady isn't one of them."

She continued to glare at him. "I've already told you I have no need of your assistance."

"I've observed that people rarely tell the truth about themselves," Tom pointed out. "In fact, I'm learning that this becomes more necessary the higher one goes in society. Greater rank requires greater deception."

"You have no idea what you're talking about," Margaret retorted.

"Don't I?" Dear Lord, what was it going to take to get her honest? He wanted to help her, but he couldn't do it unless he could get past her defenses. If he had to be brutally frank in order to do so, he would. "Let's talk about Paul Denault. Off he goes to America, and comes back a supposedly rich man. Then he gets himself engaged to the richest heiress in London, who for some reason has a secret need for moneylenders. I'm guessing he was nothing but a fortune hunter—only he discovered there was no fortune to hunt. Is that what happened, Miss Vaughn? Was he taken by an even greater charlatan than he is?"

This struck home. Margaret took several steps back, her face contorted in anguish. She bumped up against the desk and put out a hand to steady herself. Her other hand went to her forehead, and Tom thought he detected the faintest tremor. Suddenly he was desperate to cross the room, to take her in his arms and comfort her. But he forced himself not to move. There was only one way to topple Margaret's stubborn pride, and that was to confront her, unflinchingly, with the hard truth.

She, however, was not ready to yield, although Tom could see what it was costing her. Pain shot across her face once more. Several long seconds ticked off the clock on the mantelpiece. She looked frail and vulnerable; perhaps Mortimer's threats of prison were beginning to sink in. She rallied, however, and straightening once more into a posture of defiance she said, "What about *you,* Mr. Poole? Are *you* as rich as you say you are?"

Tom spread his hands wide, in a gesture of innocence. "My gold bullion in the Bank of London speaks loud enough, as any clerk there can testify." She nodded, and Tom thought that at last his words were beginning to pierce through her walls. "Now, shall you be honest with me?" he pressed. "How much do you owe those men?"

She took a deep, shuddering breath, but said nothing. *This is it,* Tom thought. *Now we are going to get honest.* He allowed the silence to stretch, waiting for her answer.

When she spoke, every word was slow and strained. "Ten thousand pounds," she said quietly.

She met his gaze, watching for his shocked expression, which Tom had no doubt he was supplying. This was beyond anything he'd imagined. "Ten *thousand?*" he asked incredulously. "How could you possibly have amassed so much debt?"

"The debt is not mine!" she exclaimed. "My father left me saddled with twenty thousand pounds of debt when he died." She lifted her head proudly. "I have already managed to pay off half of it."

Tom shook his head, still unable to believe what he was hearing. "Everyone believes you are rich. How have you managed to hide this?"

"I don't wish to discuss it," she said curtly. She strode over to the door and reached for the handle. "I can see you already regret your rash offer, and so I will bid you good day." Her words sounded fearless, but Tom saw that her hand was trembling.

He went to the door and leaned against it. She pulled her hand away and took a few steps back to avoid making contact with him.

"I regret nothing," Tom told her.

It was true—despite the fact that ten thousand pounds represented a good portion of the gold he'd brought to England. Much of his money was still in Australia, providing the working capital Sullivan needed for the business. Tom could not be flippant about parting with such a large sum. But neither would he change his answer. "I will pay this debt for you."

She stared at him, her eyes wide. "Why would you do this? What could you possibly expect to gain by it?"

"For God's sake!" Tom bellowed, causing her to flinch. "I'm trying to *help* you. I'm trying to keep you away from the courts, out of prison, and safeguard your reputation. I'm guessing I'm the only hope you have right now. Why won't you admit it?"

His words shook her. Tom could see it in her stricken face, in the way she crossed her arms, hugging herself as if trying to shore up her strength. He could see pride battling with fear, trying to prevent her from reaching out for this lifeline.

He had a sudden recollection of a mournful voice he'd thought he'd heard on the night of that terrible gale, as the winds were howling and the passengers were rushing to and fro screaming and the ship was breaking apart. *"Come over into Macedonia and help us,"* the voice had said. He'd known it was from the Bible, the same plea that Saint Paul had once received in a vision. Later, when he'd had time to reflect on it, Tom thought the Lord was trying to send him a message about Lizzie. Now he realized, with a sharp jolt of his heart, that the muted and throaty voice he'd heard sounded startlingly like Margaret's. *Do it, Margaret,* he urged silently as he watched her. *Let me help you.*

She lifted her eyes to his. "Very well," she said shakily. "I will accept your offer. And I will offer collateral."

Tom knew that last part was purely due to the remnants of her pride, but he would not fault her for it. She had been pressed to give up so much of it already. Tom knew as well as anyone that change was very hard indeed— even if it was for the better. The important thing was she had said yes. He felt a burden lift—as though he'd been the one receiving aid rather than extending it. "Very well."

"I have a stable of fine racehorses. In another year they will be ready to sell. That will go a long way toward repaying the loan."

He shook his head. "Horses are not good collateral. Not long term. Too many things could happen to them." Happy as he was to be helping her, he sensed she was still withholding something. "That can't be what you offered Mortimer."

"That's none of your concern!" she burst out. No, she had not lost all her defiance, Tom thought wryly.

"It is most definitely my concern," he insisted. "If I am to help you, you must be honest with me." She stared at him mutely, so he folded his arms and leaned against the door. Surprising, really, what a patient man he could be at times. "Someone outside is pacing rather restlessly in the hallway," he observed. "Jake, probably. But he and Mortimer can wait for as long as it takes for us to reach an agreement."

He almost felt guilty bringing up the specter of Mortimer and his threats. But it paid off. Margaret threw a brief, worried glance at the door and finally answered his question. "I have been receiving offers from the railway. They want to run a direct line to Lincoln, and they need a good piece of my eastern boundary to do it. But I have no intentions of selling that land—not to anyone. Not under any circumstances."

"And yet you put it at risk with Mortimer."

"I was desperate!" she shot back. "And besides, it was only temporary. Only until—" She bit back her words and turned away.

"Only until your marriage," Tom supplied.

Her shoulders sagged ever so slightly, but she did not answer.

"I admire your desire to keep your land," Tom told her. "You had to risk it in order to save it. I understand that. You had to make difficult and courageous decisions. As you do now."

He could see the strain of weeks and months—perhaps even years—written in her expression. "What do you want from me?" she asked, her voice plaintive.

What *did* he want? At the moment, Tom wanted nothing more than just to stand here and look at her. Even now, in the midst of her distress, she was perfectly beautiful. She was fiery and determined and brave.

"I want to marry you," he blurted out.

The words slipped out of their own volition—more proof that Tom was still dangerously reckless. Margaret's appeal was undeniable. But was marriage truly what he wanted? His own life was so unsettled. He was striving to be a better man, but he still had plenty of shortcomings. By marrying now he would only subject a wife to every one of them.

Margaret's mouth actually fell open in surprise. Quickly she closed it. Her expression became absolute stone. She began to scrutinize him. As her gaze traveled from his face all the way down to his boots, Tom realized he was still damp and disheveled from his morning's activities. He also noted with chagrin that dried mud was flaking off his boots and onto the thick Persian carpet. More consequences of his hasty actions.

"Perhaps you think you might buy my affections?" Margaret said at last. "You think I'd be so *grateful* to you for coming to my rescue? Is that how they do things in Australia? Do men buy their wives there?"

"They don't have to," Tom said evenly. He was not about to be put on the defensive, no matter how untoward his proposal had been. "They go willingly."

"I'll have you know that I no longer wish to get married. Not to anyone. I had a close call, and thank God I escaped." She nodded her head toward the door. "Good day, sir."

He crossed his arms, standing his ground. "And what will you do if I walk out? Will you sell your land?"

She faced him, just as bold, just as decisive. "I will do whatever it takes to survive."

She was putting up a good front, but Tom could see through it now. He took a step back, as if in retreat, testing her reaction. She paled a little, and her lower lip trembled ever so slightly, but she did not try to stop him.

Tom knew enough about bargaining to recognize he'd gotten as far with her today as he was going to. However, he was not going to leave her at the mercy of men like Mortimer, despite her brave show. "All right, here's what I propose we do. I will offer you the loan. And I will accept your horses as collateral."

Her eyes closed briefly, and he knew she was doing all she could to hide her relief. When she opened them again, her expression became stern and businesslike, erasing the vulnerability he'd seen earlier.

"Excellent." She crossed the room to her desk, sat down, and arranged some paper. "I'm sure we can come to terms regarding repayment."

Heaven help him. Margaret was still acting as though *she* were the one in charge. *That* he would not allow. Not after what he had done for her today. She was affecting him in ways he did not fully understand, ways she could not even be aware that she was doing. He was not going to simply give her the money and walk away. As her hand reached out to dip pen in ink, Tom took hold of her wrist to stop it. "I will accept your terms. But I have one more to add."

He could feel her pulse racing underneath his fingers, belying the illusion of calm that she always stood behind like a shield. Her gaze met his. "And that would be...?"

And the Fates bedevil him if Tom couldn't keep a smile from coming to his lips. "You must dine with me tomorrow night."

Chapter 9

Margaret stood at the window, watching as Tom Poole left in the carriage with Mortimer. She saw with no small measure of satisfaction that since the carriage could only accommodate two passengers, Mortimer's appalling henchman was forced to find his own way back to wherever it was he'd come from. From hell, most probably.

Finding her legs threatening to collapse, she sank down on a nearby chair. She had come terrifyingly close to complete and utter disaster. What would have happened if Tom hadn't arrived? It was too terrible to even contemplate. She had always been a woman of strong constitution, but at the moment she didn't even have enough strength to reach for the bell. She pulled out a handkerchief and wiped her face, which was beaded with perspiration. "Bessie!" she called out. "Are you there?"

She heard the maid's swift steps coming up the hall. After taking one look at Margaret, she rushed to her side. "Are you ill, miss?" she said in alarm. "Shall I call a doctor?"

"That won't be necessary." Margaret tried to sound composed, but her voice was weak.

Bessie was wringing her hands. "I'm sorry those men upset you, miss. Truly, I did my best to keep them out, but—"

"I know you did. I'm sorry you had to go through that."

But Bessie still seemed determined to clear herself. "Those men—the first two, I mean—they forced their way in. And quite rudely, too. The shoved me aside! But Mr. Poole, he was a perfect gentleman. He told me…" She looked abashed at Margaret. "He told me he was here to help you."

Margaret sighed. "It's all right, Bessie. You did right to admit Mr. Poole."

Bessie's face lit up. "Did I? Was he able to help you?"

There was far too much impertinence in that question, but Margaret could hardly blame her. Bessie was concerned about the state of the household, and rightly so. Despite all Margaret had done to hide her financial distress, the servants must have some inkling of it. They'd seen her carefully trimming the staff. No doubt others worried they could be next—even though in every case Margaret had worked hard to find new positions for those she'd had to let go. And they were only too well aware of the hundred other ways she'd cut the household expenditures. But she doubted they knew the full extent to which she'd been pushed by her circumstances, and she was determined to keep it that way. Tom Poole may have pulled her back from the brink, but she did not need her maid to know that. "Mr. Poole was able to render me some good service today," Margaret said, doing her best to answer in a nonchalant way. She stood up, grateful the strength had returned to her legs. "Now, Bessie, the morning is far gone. Will you go down and ask the cook to serve luncheon?"

Food was the last thing Margaret cared to face right now, but it was good to keep the servants at their tasks. It kept them from asking too many questions. Her request also seemed to reassure Bessie that things were returning to normal. She brightened. "Right away, miss." With a quick curtsy, she left the room.

Margaret walked over to the desk, still trying to make some sense out of Tom Poole's sudden appearance and the way he had so swiftly become vital to her survival. It had begun the moment he'd sparred with her at the engagement party, all but daring her not to bend to her fiancé's whims. Then there had been that chance meeting in the park—the exhilarating race, the infuriating questions. Accusations about Paul, which turned out to be so timely and true. And how was it that he had burst into her house at the very moment when Mortimer was threatening the worst? It was incomprehensible. And yet, if he hadn't been there...

She refused to dwell on it. Deliberately she gathered up everything pertaining to the wedding preparations and tucked them away in a drawer. She sifted through a few of the papers her lawyers had brought over, but found there was nothing that couldn't wait another day.

Finally, she picked up the agreement that she had signed with Tom Poole. He was going to deliver ten thousand pounds to Mortimer in exchange for collateral of the horses. They were not worth nearly that much, but he'd accepted them, sight unseen. Was he a fool? Or was she? Nervously, she perused the last line, which he'd insisted upon: "In failure of providing the money within the time agreed upon, the contract will be renegotiated to the satisfaction of the undersigned." She wasn't sure she liked the sound of that one bit.

What the note did not contain was the verbal commitment Tom had required from her before signing it. Tom told her his sister would send over a dinner invitation, and Margaret had agreed to accept it. She was surprised at the trepidation this gave her. It was only dinner, after all. Surely he was not trying to woo her. He would not be renewing his offer of marriage. Margaret was sure of this; the expression on his face right after he proposed spoke plainly enough. He didn't want to be married any more than she did. She ought to be relieved about this—not feeling something so foolish as disappointment.

It's just one evening, she told herself. *Nothing more.* She went upstairs to freshen up before luncheon. She poured water into a basin and splashed it onto her face, allowing its coolness to rejuvenate her thoughts as she considered what she should do next. Without a doubt, the most important thing was to return to Lincolnshire and retrench. Every day she remained here, the town house bled away money she didn't have. The season was nearly over anyway, and with her wedding canceled Margaret was painfully aware that she no longer had any real reason to be in London.

Margaret went to the window and looked out over the little park. A refreshing breeze played along her damp face as she considered the man who lived on the other side of that square. She could not think what to make of him. Tom Poole did not fit into any mold. His accent and certain aspects of his conduct betrayed his working-class origins, but he was neither coarse nor ignorant. Far from it. He was a clever man who could walk into unknown surroundings and quickly grasp what was expected of him. More troubling, perhaps, was how swiftly he had penetrated her defenses and laid bare her weaknesses.

Margaret turned from the window. She could not afford to spend time reflecting on Tom Poole or anyone else. Their arrangement had made him a temporary benefactor of sorts. But he would never be anything more. She would never give up her self-reliance.

It was with a bittersweet sense of pride that she went to the dining room to take her soup and cold meat alone. Perhaps when she was out of debt she might be able to take a bigger house in Belgravia and host her own soirees. But always, *always,* she would be in control, living within her means. Any other path was for those who were weak or foolish. And she, Margaret thought with grim satisfaction, was neither. She was going to be free from the manacle of her debts and never again be beholden to any man. Certainly not the tall, persuasive, and unsettling stranger from Australia.

*

Tom and Mortimer walked out of the Bank of London and onto the busy sidewalk. The hansom was still there, the cabbie chatting with another driver as they waited for their fares to conclude their business.

"It's been a pleasure doing business with you," Mortimer said, shaking Tom's hand. Before he let go, he added, "Are you sure you know what you're doing?"

Tom tried to give him a wry smile, which was probably more of a grimace. "What do you care?"

Mortimer nodded in agreement. "Indeed." He briefly patted his coat pocket, in which was the deed of transfer between Tom's account and his own. "I trust, sir, that if you are ever in need of funds, you will feel free to contact me."

"So you can loan my money back to me with interest? I'll keep that in mind."

Mortimer's eyes showed a hint of amusement. He entered the carriage. "Shall I drop you somewhere?" he asked.

"No, thank you."

Tom watched as the cab lurched into the traffic and was soon lost in the busy thoroughfare. Then he turned and began to walk back toward Mayfair. He walked slowly, barely taking heed of the bustle around him. Mortimer's question still echoed in his ears. Of course, the man had only asked it *after* the money had been safely and irrevocably transferred. Mortimer was not the sort to allow any scruples to interfere with a profitable transaction.

Even though he had just parted with an alarming sum of money, Tom had no regrets. As he reflected on the morning's events, a new thought struck him. If the rain hadn't caused him to leave Hyde Park early, he'd never have seen the moneylenders forcing their way into Margaret's house. He'd never have known there was a serious problem at number 15. Had that somehow been the work of the Lord? Tom was too new a Christian to know for sure. And yet, it was a fact that his prayer had been immediately followed by the rain. Perhaps the Lord worked in odd ways indeed. Did that also mean he had some plan for Margaret? If so, Tom thought wryly, the

Lord was going to have to work mighty hard to get that woman's attention.

"Poole!"

The voice stopped Tom in midstep. He turned to see Denault standing at the door of a tavern. Fighting the urge to pound the man senseless for what he'd done to Margaret, he stood stock-still and gave Denault a cold glare. "What do you want?"

He could tell from Denault's demeanor that his hostility hadn't gone unnoticed. But Denault must have decided to ignore it. He motioned toward the tavern. "I was hoping you'd have time for a drink."

Tom would have declined, but he wanted to find out what kind of explanation Denault would give for the broken engagement. Denault was likely to hound him more about the railway, too, but nothing he could do or say would get Tom to buy in now.

Denault took a seat behind his half-eaten lunch and a tankard of ale. Tom grabbed the chair opposite and sat down as the barmaid sauntered up. "What'll you have, sir?"

Tom gestured to the ale in front of Paul. "The same."

"Anything to eat?"

In truth, Tom was hungry. The tantalizing aroma of roasting meat wafted out from the back kitchen, and Tom's stomach growled in protest. But Lizzie was expecting him for luncheon. He shook his head. "Just the ale."

"Right then—the poor man's lunch today," the barmaid said, throwing him a disparaging look before going off to fetch his drink.

Tom pulled out his watch and checked the time. "I can't stay long," he told Denault.

"Well, then, let's get right to it," Denault said cheerfully. "At our last meeting, you said you wanted to take some time to consider the company's prospectus. I assume you've done so?"

"I heard the wedding between you and Miss Vaughn was called off," Tom said.

At first this abrupt change of subject took Denault off guard. Then he laughed—a dry, bitter sound. "You and everyone else in London."

"Care to enlighten me as to why?"

"Well, just between us…" Denault pushed his plate aside and leaned forward, speaking with an air of confidentiality. "It was a mutual decision, and entirely amicable. It should not be taken to reflect badly on Miss Vaughn."

Tom snorted. He couldn't help it. "How does it reflect on *you?*"

Denault waved that question away. "Poole, you're a man of sense. You should know that what does or does not take place on London's social calendar has no bearing on the business at hand. Let's talk about the Saint Louis and Western, shall we? Are you with us? The banks are still open. I suggest we go there today."

Tom might have laughed at the man's gall, if he wasn't so appalled. "Can you really dismiss a wedding to Miss Vaughn as a mere hiccup on the social calendar?"

"I don't see why it should concern you," Denault countered. A gleam came to his eye. "Unless you have some *particular* interest in Miss Vaughn. Some connection perhaps?"

Tom refused to rise to the bait. There were better ways to fight back. So he said in a deliberately offhand manner, "As for the railway, I regret that I'm not in a position to invest in it just now. Something has arisen that requires the use of my funds elsewhere." Tom had learned all the right business jargon from Sullivan, and he took a malicious pleasure in spouting it to a dealmaker like Denault. "It's a long-term project, which, although risky, might yield appealing dividends." Tom pushed back from the table and stood up to signal that the conversation was over.

Denault quickly rose and stepped in Tom's path. "Has that little charmer been spreading lies about me? She was supposed to keep her mouth shut. We agreed—"

Tom took hold of him and pushed him against the wall. "Agreed to what?"

Denault made no move to get away. "Perhaps I ought to warn you about something, my friend," he said caustically. "Margaret is drowning in debt. You're a fool if you think she wants anything but your money."

"What Margaret does is no longer your affair. Nor do I need your advice." With one more shove, Tom dropped his hold on Denault and stalked to the door.

Behind him, Denault shouted, "You'll regret this, Poole!"

As Tom turned his head to throw back a scathing reply, he bumped into another man who was walking in his direction. The man was tall and about as broad as the door. No wonder Tom had run into him.

He shoved Tom aside with a rude, "Watch where you're going," and pushed past.

Tom was sorely tempted to give the man a taste of his fist. *Just let it go,* he told himself. *It's not worth a fight.*

It was only after Tom was outside that he realized the other man had been heading in the direction of Denault's table. Was this another potential investor? It would serve him right if he was, Tom thought. Let Denault fleece whomever he could; Tom was glad to stay out of it. And yet the stranger had seemed vaguely familiar. Probably one of the dozens of pompous idiots he'd been introduced to. Tom hadn't gotten a good enough look at the man's face to be sure.

Tom shrugged it off, resuming his walk back up the broad avenue toward Mayfair. He was glad he'd had an opportunity to close out his dealings with Denault. Now he could concentrate on Margaret—and in truth, he did not want his thoughts anywhere else. He and Margaret were bound now—by the loan, at least. But Tom wanted more. He knew that now. His impulsive proposal had been a shock to them both, and yet Tom knew it had been taking root in his soul from the moment she'd raced him down the green at Hyde Park. Probably even sooner than that.

He picked up his pace, nimbly dodging the carts, vendors, and street sweepers as he went. A strange joy surged through him. He had the sense that all the upheavals of the past few years had been nothing compared to the way his life was about to change.

Lord, he thought, *if this is Your will, lead me on.*

He could hardly wait to see what was going to happen next.

Chapter 10

G ood evening, Miss Vaughn."

Tom Poole must have been practicing the bow; Margaret was certain the formality did not come naturally to him. It was without a doubt an entirely different entrance than he had made yesterday, when he had thrown the door open and filled the room with his presence, looking ready to take on all comers like a boxer in a ring.

Everything about him was more reserved tonight. Gone were the disheveled riding costume and muddy boots. Now he wore a stiff black suit and an expertly knotted cravat, looking every inch the gentleman as he held his top hat in his gloved hands. An odd thought strayed across her mind, that somehow he looked more handsome in his rumpled brown riding coat. Odd, too, that she should find him handsome at all, but he was—in a rugged sort of way. Normally, she would never give such a man a second glance. But he had deliberately placed himself into her life. Even now he caused competing thoughts of gratitude and resentment to wrestle within her, combining to form some other emotion she had no name for.

He offered up his arm to escort her outside, and a tiny, alarming sensation raced across her stomach as she laid her hand on his arm. She was not—could not be—attracted to this man. When the debt was paid, they would go their separate ways. It was a hope she clung to. Her finances, and by extension her reputation and social standing, were precariously dependent on this virtual stranger. She was desperate to regain a firm hold on her own life.

He led her out to the steps of the town house. "Where is your carriage?" she asked, seeing none waiting in the street.

"Carriage?" Tom said, sounding genuinely surprised.

"Yes," Margaret said. "Surely you don't expect us to walk across the park?"

He did, it seemed. "Why, I never thought we'd need a carriage. A child could throw a rock and hit the Somervilles' house from here."

"Really, Mr. Poole. It's most impolite to expect a lady to walk across mud and grass in her evening clothes." She may be in debt, but she still had her dignity. "I shall go back inside and order a carriage."

"It is only a very short way," he insisted, stepping between her and the door. "It seemed unnecessary to go through all the trouble of hitching up the horses and bringing them out just to ride around the square."

"You really don't see the impropriety in escorting me on foot, do you?" she said.

"You're right," he returned crustily, not sounding the

least bit apologetic. "Clearly I don't know enough about the 'proper' way to do things. Because of this gap in my knowledge, I've had to fall back on common sense instead."

Margaret stared at him, unable to believe her ears. He truly expected her to walk through mud and traffic, like some servant on an errand.

Her mutinous glare did not seem to ruffle him at all. He reached out to place her arm once more on his. "Shall we?" he said.

As before, his touch was warm, his grasp gentle but irresistible. Margaret had a sudden, unsettling impression that whatever this man reached for, he got. And so, with a curt murmur of acquiescence, she allowed him to lead her on. If he wanted Margaret to stain his sister's carpet with mud the way he had done with hers, then she would not be responsible for it.

They walked across the square in the fading light. An afternoon shower had left the shrubs moist and green, and the scent of lilacs hung in the air. The moon had risen early and was already visible through the scattered clouds. It might almost have been romantic—if she were not being led in such an embarrassing fashion to a dinner party she had no desire to attend. She kept her face turned away from the street, hoping no one in the passing carriages would recognize her.

Why was he bringing her to the Somervilles' tonight? If there was one thing she'd learned over the years, it was that everyone had an ulterior motive for their actions. Especially men. Her uncle, her father, her former fiancé—all had pursued their own selfish aims without the least consideration of what harm they might cause to others. Whatever Tom's motive was, it would surely be revealed soon enough. In any case, she would remain vigilant.

With these dark thoughts swirling through her head, she was completely taken aback when Tom said, "Miss Vaughn, I must apologize."

She blinked. "I beg your pardon?"

"My sister has been trying to instill some of the finer arts of etiquette into me, but I admit I'm not the best student. Now I see I have committed a gross faux pas."

"Faux pas?" she repeated, bemused to hear this phrase coming from him.

He gave her a sheepish smile. "It's French, I think."

Disarmed, Margaret could only say, "Well, yes. Thank you."

They began walking again. When they reached a spot where the little path branched, Tom led her to the right instead of taking the more direct route. "This way has drained better and there are no puddles," he explained. "You will not soil your shoes."

"How do you know?" Margaret asked in surprise. "Did you inspect all the paths?"

"Of course," he replied without hesitation.

What an odd contradiction he was. He had not brought a carriage, and yet he had taken the time to examine the pathways between their houses with her in mind. Margaret could not decide whether he was truly daft or had just rendered an unusual act of kindness.

True to his word, he led her expertly along the dry paths to the opposite side of the square. Her shoes and dress were still reasonably unscathed when they reached the Somerville home.

Margaret's wariness returned as the butler led them to the parlor. She had no idea what to expect from Lady Somerville, a woman who was the illegitimate daughter of the late Sir Herbert Thornborough, and yet now was married to a peer of the realm. The official story was that she'd received a blow to the head that made her think she was her long-lost half sister Victoria. Apparently the resemblance was so strong that everyone else, including the family matriarch, Lady Thornborough, had believed it, too. Then, somehow Lizzie had regained her senses and remembered who she really was. Her husband, Lord Somerville, had been a clergyman in a very poor parish before he had unexpectedly inherited a barony. He had passed up more advantageous marriage connections and chosen Lizzie Poole instead. It was a wildly improbable tale, to be sure, and one that Margaret found nearly impossible to believe. And yet her brother had his own amazing tale, which was irrefutable. Margaret could only conclude that no one in this family did things in an ordinary way.

As they entered the parlor, Margaret saw immediately that the lady was quite beautiful, with pale blond hair and delicate features. She was also—to Margaret's shock—very pregnant. That would explain why she had made no appearances in society this summer. Her husband, Lord Somerville, stood beside her. He was every bit as handsome as the gossips had said he was. They were indeed a striking couple.

Lady Somerville looked expectantly at her brother and said softly, "You must introduce us, Tom."

"Forgive me," Tom said. "I forgot." He paused. Margaret could almost see him mentally reviewing the rules of etiquette before he said, "Lord and Lady Somerville, may I present Miss Margaret Vaughn."

"How do you do," Margaret said.

Her attempt at formality was lost on Lady Somerville. She took Margaret's hands into her own and regarded her warmly with eyes that were a very intense shade of blue. Violet, almost. "Thank you so much for coming. How wonderful that we should meet at last!"

Margaret threw a quick glance at Tom to verify that his eyes were deep brown, as she had remembered. Clearly, he and his half sister had inherited their physical traits from their different fathers.

"Won't you sit down?" Lady Somerville said, motioning to a sofa.

Margaret took a seat, and Lady Somerville gently eased herself into a chair. A tiny sigh of relief escaped her as she did so.

"It is kind of you to host a dinner party in your condition," Margaret said. "These things can be so complicated and very stressful." What she really wanted to do was chastise the woman for even contemplating such a thing. Surely it was dangerous to her health.

"This isn't really a dinner party," Lady Somerville said. "It's just the four of us tonight."

They had invited her to a *family* dinner? The implied intimacy of this gesture was unnerving. Margaret had been expecting a larger party; she would have been more comfortable with the easy, shallow conversations at such events. On the other hand, perhaps it was a good thing no others were present. Her newly broken-off engagement could have subjected her to embarrassing questions from those who were seeking grist for the gossip mill.

"How odd to be living so close to one another and never to have met!" Lord Somerville observed. "Especially since London is the smallest city in the world when it comes to its social circle." He reached out to give a gentle pat on Tom's back. "We are fortunate that Tom has made your acquaintance for us."

It was the kind of polite compliment that Margaret had heard before, but he sounded truly sincere. They were doing all they could to make her feel welcome, and by the time they all went down to dinner Margaret's qualms about spending the evening here had diminished.

She was impressed by the effortless protocol they followed during dinner, which was served flawlessly by a well-trained staff. Even Tom acquitted himself well, although Margaret noticed he kept a close watch on his sister in order to follow her lead as the various courses were served. He seemed content to let the Somervilles do most of the talking.

Although they discussed mutual acquaintances and recent society events, nobody mentioned Paul or her broken engagement. It was not until they had reconvened in the parlor after dinner that Margaret had a brief moment of discomfort. Lady Somerville said, "Miss Vaughn, Tom has told us something very interesting about you."

"Has he?" Margaret sent a worried glance at Tom. He had promised he would tell no one about their arrangement—their *business* arrangement, she reminded herself forcefully. Had he broken his word? Tom shook his head, as if to refute her unspoken allegation.

"I understand you rode together in Hyde Park." Lady Somerville's eyes sparkled. "He says your horse gave Castor quite a good run."

"I enjoyed that race very much," Margaret said, relieved not to be talking about Paul or her debts. "There are not too many gentlemen who are willing to race a lady flat out like that."

"Happily," interjected Tom, "I am not a gentleman."

He said this with a self-deprecating smile that made her regret her earlier harsh words. "But you *are* a gentleman," she contradicted, drawing a quizzical look from him. "You allowed me to win."

His smile grew wider, causing his eyes to crinkle around the edges. He did not try to defend himself against the accusation; in fact, his impish grin seemed to slyly admit the truth of it. It also caused her heart to give an odd little jump. Here among his family members, Tom seemed a different man altogether. The agitated scowl he had worn so often on previous occasions had made no appearance tonight. "So tell me," Margaret said, "are those fantastical stories they tell about you true? Were you really taken in by Aborigines?"

He nodded. "They found me unconscious on the beach, with Castor nuzzling me as though he were trying to wake me. They took me to their camp, where their medicine man performed all sorts of healing incantations. I'm grateful for this, of course, although I suspect it was the fresh water they kept forcing down my throat that finally brought me around."

"How odd that must have been," Margaret mused, trying to imagine the scene. "It must have been like waking up in another world."

"Indeed it was," Tom agreed.

"So what happened after that? How long did you stay with them?"

"It took me about three weeks to regain enough strength to travel. In the meantime, they treated me very hospitably. I ate their food, met their people, learned a bit of their language. But I set off for Melbourne as soon as I could. I knew Lizzie would be sick with grief, thinking I had died. I had to get word to her that I had survived."

"Those were hard times," Lady Somerville acknowledged with a sad sigh.

"For us both, dear sister." He gave her a tender smile, which she returned, her eyes growing misty.

At times Margaret had wondered how her life might have been different if she'd had siblings. But it was only now, as she saw the affection between Tom and his sister, that she felt the lack so intensely.

"On top of everything else," Tom continued, "the weather had been oppressively hot. In the summer, those gum trees can ignite faster than dry tinder. I was still some distance from Melbourne when the entire countryside caught fire around me. Tens of thousands of acres were burning, not to mention the lonely outposts of sheep and cattle. It was... well, words cannot describe it." His hand gripped his teacup so tightly that Margaret feared he might crush it.

Lady Somerville was seated next to Tom on the sofa, and she gently took his cup. "Thank God you survived," she said softly. "Even after you risked your own life to save others."

"Oh?" said Margaret, interested to hear more.

But Tom shook his head. For the first time this evening, his face darkened into that familiar scowl. "That is a story for another time," he said, his voice suddenly gruff.

Clearly his sister had touched a nerve. It was easy to imagine that Tom had no desire to relive such an awful scene, but Margaret wondered if there might be more to it. However, since they had kindly refrained from questioning Margaret about her broken engagement, she would return the favor by not pressing Tom on a subject that distressed him. To shift the conversation, she said, "Why is your horse named Castor? It seems an unusual choice."

This was the right thing to ask. He relaxed a little, and seemed to shake himself free from the heaviness that had fallen on him. "It's an interesting story, actually. I took the name from Castor and Pollux, who were twin sons of Zeus."

"You named your horse for a Greek god?" Margaret looked at him in surprise. "How is it that you went to Greek mythology for inspiration?"

"Oh, heavens, now here's a story!" Lady Somerville exclaimed. "Prepare for an earful, Miss Vaughn." But Margaret saw only genuine pleasure in her face. She was no doubt relieved to see her brother at ease again.

Tom said, "Castor and Pollux were among the Argonauts who accompanied Jason on his quest for the Golden Fleece. During the voyage, a terrible storm arose, and Orpheus—he was another of the Argonauts—played on his harp and prayed vigorously to the gods. He was a very talented musician, you see." Tom gave a flourish to indicate playing a harp. "And so the storm ceased." He paused, allowing the resulting quiet in the room to illustrate the calm after the storm. "Then, for some reason that I'm not quite sure of, these stars appeared on the heads of Castor and Pollux, and because of that they became the patron deities of seamen and voyagers."

How on earth could a man with Tom's poor upbringing know such tales from ancient Greece? Margaret could think of no polite way to ask, so she said simply, "I suppose you were drawn to the story because of the part about the ship in the storm?"

"In a way. I first became curious about Castor and Pollux when I read their names in the New Testament."

"Really?" Margaret said, truly surprised now. "They are in the Bible?"

Tom nodded. "After Saint Paul and the others survived a terrible shipwreck, they later got on another ship that took them the rest of the way to Rome. The sign, or figurehead, on that ship was Castor and Pollux. So that's where I got the idea for Castor's name. It seemed perfect, considering what me and that horse have been through together."

"So it is," Margaret agreed, still astounded at the different facets of this man she was seeing tonight.

Lord Somerville had been listening to Tom's story with an expression of mild amusement. Like his wife, he must have heard it before. He added, "It's interesting to note that Castor was also famous for taming horses. Often in ancient Greek art the twins are depicted on horses."

"So Tom has a horse named after a god that tamed horses," Lady Somerville summed up with a chuckle. "How appropriate, given our family's love of all things equestrian."

"Do you also ride?" Margaret asked.

"She's a natural," Tom said. "She rides like the wind."

"Geoffrey is an excellent rider, too," Lady Somerville said. "Over the years, all of the Somerville men have been known for their horsemanship." She sighed. "How I do miss it." She placed a hand distractedly on her round belly.

"Patience, my love," Lord Somerville said. "You'll be riding again by spring."

"Then we can all go together," Tom suggested. "What a jolly time that will be."

He looked at Margaret as he said this, including her in the family circle. The implication made her distinctly uncomfortable. The happy and carefree life they enjoyed was a far cry from the realities of Margaret's life. Tonight had been a pleasant interlude, but tomorrow she would return to fighting for her livelihood, facing her problems alone. She could not allow Tom to think there was anything more between them than the financial bargain they had made.

She stood up. "Thank you all so much for the lovely evening. I'm afraid I must take my leave. I depart early tomorrow for Lincolnshire."

As they said their good-byes, Lady Somerville grasped Margaret's hands as she had done earlier. "What a shame you are leaving town. It would have been nice to see you again."

"Thank you," Margaret said, oddly touched by the genuine warmth in the other woman's eyes. "However, I think you will soon have other, more important things to occupy your time."

Lady Somerville's hand strayed to her expansive belly. "Indeed I shall." A brief spasm of something like pain or sadness crossed her face, but she quickly forced it into a smile.

When Tom led Margaret outside, she saw that an open

carriage decorated with the Somerville coat of arms was standing at the curb. "What's this?" she asked.

"A landau to take you home, of course," Tom said. "I gave the order before Geoffrey and I rejoined you ladies after dinner."

Margaret felt a pang of guilt as he helped her into the ornate carriage, with its driver and two liveried footmen standing at the ready, just to take her around the square. "I may have spoken too harshly to you earlier," she said.

Tom took the seat opposite her, his expression hard to make out in the dim light. "I'm glad you spoke up," he said. "I like to know when I'm doing wrong. I always work hard to make it right."

The absurdly short trip was accomplished in no time. He escorted her up the steps. When they reached the door, he said, "Thank you for coming. I know my sister was glad for your company. It was very kind of you."

Kind? Margaret could have pointed out that she'd done no more than keep the bargain he'd extracted from her. Yet he was smiling at her with such heartfelt gratitude that she could only murmur, "It was . . . my pleasure. Lady Somerville is charming."

"She is, isn't she?" he said with pride. He paused. His gaze dropped to her lips, then met her eyes again with a quiet intensity. "In that respect I have been twice blessed this evening."

She stared back, her mouth slightly agape. His desire for her was unmasked and unmistakable. A carriage rattled by in the street, and Margaret took a step back, although there was already a respectable distance between her and Tom. Realizing she had not yet responded to his compliment, she said automatically, "You are very kind."

Her face flushed, and she felt like a fool. "Good night," she added hastily, and went inside.

It was a good thing she was leaving London, Margaret reflected once the door was firmly shut behind her. She could not afford to be kept off-balance as she had been tonight. She would be far better off once she had returned home to Moreton Hall.

Chapter 11

T he draft forced its way through the cracks in the windows, the mere glass being no match for the rushing wind as the train streamed past meadows and hedgerows. The train rocked and swayed with vigor, its much-touted "smooth" ride being to Margaret's mind nonexistent. She shifted uncomfortably in her seat. It might be old-fashioned but she still preferred a coach. The only good thing about railway travel was the speed. She would be home that much sooner.

Margaret turned her eyes to the window, trying to shake off the oppression that lay heavy upon her. All her efforts over the long months in London had largely failed. Her idea of marrying for money had proved to be a spectacular mistake, and her finances were still in a precarious position. The loan from Tom Poole had eased the pressure somewhat, but did nothing to assuage her fears. For the bitter truth was that even if she recovered financially, she would still have to marry. At the moment, the thought of becoming an old maid, growing old with the freedom to do as she liked and run her own life as she saw fit, was extremely tempting. But then she would be left with an even greater dilemma.

She needed children. Her grandfather had been able to break the entail on Moreton Hall, keeping it out of the hands of a distant relation who was not distant enough for her liking: Richard Spencer. A shiver ran through her that had nothing to do with the draft from the window. But without heirs, the Vaughn family heritage would pass away, dying out after two hundred years. She could not allow that to happen. She loved this land—it was a part of her very soul—but it would drive her to desperate measures.

Perhaps she could marry someone old—someone who would leave her a widow while she still had much of her own life remaining. She certainly was not the first woman to contemplate such a thing, and she surely would not be the last. But could an older man give her the children she needed? How could she be sure?

A younger man, on the other hand, a man in the prime of his life...The memory of Tom Poole invaded her thoughts. However, his undisguised look of relief when she had turned him down made it clear that marrying him wasn't really an option. He would be too dangerous, at any rate. A man such as that would consume her life, and her cherished independence would be lost.

"Is everything all right, miss?" Bessie asked, studying her with concern.

Margaret realized she had been clutching her reticule so tightly she was crushing its delicate velvet fabric. She carefully loosened her hold on it. "Just tired. The train wears me out."

"It does seem unnatural traveling so fast, doesn't it?" Bessie agreed with a nod. "Do you suppose God really intended for people to shoot over the countryside at forty-five miles per hour?" She made a tsking sound, answering her own rhetorical question. "It cannot be healthy."

The whistle shrieked and the brakes screeched and shuddered as they pulled into the station. "Well, now," said Bessie, "I shall be happy to get to Moreton Hall and shake off all this dirt. I don't know which is worse—the soot from living in London or the soot we collected during this train ride."

Margaret was also glad to be home. She could hardly wait to be standing in an open pasture and breathing in the scent of the late summer blooms and the freshly cut grass. Perhaps there she could find some measure of peace.

About two dozen people were milling about on the platform, either waiting to board or come to meet the arrivals. Margaret spotted Kevin, their groomsman, right away. Although he was a welcome sight, she had been expecting to see Mr. Williams, her land steward. "Are you here alone?" she asked him.

Kevin shook his head. "I've brought two footmen. They're seeing to your baggage." He pointed to the far end of the platform, where trunks and bags were being offloaded from the train onto carts.

"I was speaking of Mr. Williams," Margaret clarified. "Did he not come with you?"

"Beggin' your pardon, miss, but Mr. Williams asked me to send his apologies. He is much occupied at present and couldn't get away. He said he will meet you at Moreton Hall."

"Occupied?" Margaret repeated with irritation. "What was so important that he could not meet me here?"

A strange look crossed Kevin's face just then, but Margaret could hot decipher it. "He promises he will provide a proper explanation when you get home, miss."

This wasn't the first time Williams had disobeyed her request, Margaret reflected in frustration. At times she worried that he was pushing too far with the authority she'd given him. She would have to reemphasize those boundaries when next she saw him. But it would do no good to display her irritation in front of the other servants. "Very well."

Her footmen loaded the trunks with swift efficiency, and within minutes they were driving away from the station. She leaned back into the soft comfort of her carriage, closing her eyes and concentrating on the rhythmic sound of the horses' hooves as they traveled the last few miles to Moreton Hall.

She must have dozed. The oppression that had plagued her earlier returned, filling her dreams with dark whisperings of dread. She awoke with a start. Bessie was sitting across from her, placidly watching the landscape roll past.

Margaret straightened and took deep breaths in an effort to clear her thoughts. She looked out the window and saw they were approaching the boundaries of her estate. Fields of grain, tall and golden, flanked the road. They promised a bountiful harvest, something Margaret and her tenants desperately needed. Attempting to put away her previous forebodings, she took heart that this, at least, was going in her favor. Soon she would prove beyond all doubt that her grandfather had been right in breaking the entail and ensuring the estate went to her. Her father's ruinous ways had savagely wounded but not destroyed her. She would triumph.

Soon they would approach the meadow where the horses grazed. Margaret eagerly anticipated seeing her gelding Dante. Tomorrow she would take a long ride, traversing all the paths and fields that gave her such joy. The wildflowers would still be in bloom, especially along the lane that led from the small stone bridge by the brook. She and Dante would have a good run across the fields that led into Moreton Village, and for those precious hours she would forget she had any troubles at all.

She'd been so caught up in this reverie that it was several minutes before she realized that the horse pastures were empty. All appeared peaceful and serene, but there was not a single horse in sight. "How strange," she murmured. She slid across the seat and looked out the opposite window. The smaller field was rarely used, but it was shadier. Perhaps Garvey, her head stableman, had put the horses there to give them respite from the summer sun. But that field, too, was empty.

Where were the horses? If Garvey was keeping them penned up on such a day, she would give him a sound piece of her mind. Had all her staff planned a mutiny while she was gone? "Stop the carriage!" Margaret ordered.

Bessie looked at her, startled. "Beggin' your pardon, miss?"

Margaret took hold of an umbrella lying on the seat and banged on the carriage roof to get the driver's attention. When the carriage did not slow down, Bessie opened one of the windows. "Kevin, Mistress wants you to stop!" she shouted.

At last, the carriage rolled slowly to a stop, almost as if Kevin had been reluctant to do it. Margaret threw open the door, waiting impatiently for one of the footmen to set down the steps. When he had done so, Margaret got out and stalked to the front of the carriage.

Kevin finished securing the reins and jumped down from the driver's seat. He doffed his cap. "Is something wrong, miss?"

Margaret looked beyond him and noticed, for the first time, that the four horses in the harness were unfamiliar to her. She'd paid them no attention at the station, since her mind had been preoccupied with other things. Now she pushed past Kevin and inspected them more closely. "These are not from our stable."

"You are correct, miss," he said, lowering his head with a guilty air, as though he'd been caught doing something wrong.

"Where are our coach horses? And where are the others?" She waved a hand, indicating the empty fields. "Where's Dante?"

To her consternation, Kevin remained silent. It was unlike him not to answer a question.

"Come on, Kevin," Bessie prompted softly. "Answer Miss Vaughn."

Reluctantly, Kevin lifted his head. "I'm afraid I can't say, miss, and I do beg your pardon." His voice was low and filled with entreaty. He gave a quick glance to the footmen, who also wore strangely guilty expressions.

These men had been with her for years, staying on even when their pay had been spotty at best. It was not like them to disobey her. Something must be seriously wrong. "Kevin, take me to the stables immediately."

"Please, miss," Kevin implored. "Mr. Williams asked us to bring you directly to the house."

"I should think my orders carry more weight than my land steward's. I want to know what is going on."

A look passed between Kevin and the footmen. Margaret could tell, clear as if they'd spoken aloud, that they were trying to decide between themselves what to do.

Finally, Kevin spoke. "We can't take you to the stables. That is—" Kevin looked strained, as though every word cost him. "It isn't safe."

These words, and the stricken look on her men's faces, reawakened the sense of dread she'd been fighting earlier. If something had made the barn unfit for humans, then the horses must be endangered, too. "What's happened? Tell me!"

"Mr. Williams wanted to explain it to you himself," Kevin said, speaking in a rush now. "He wanted to wait until you were home. He made us swear not to tell you—"

"No!" she shouted, not to the men, but toward the deceitfully peaceful-looking meadow, which now seemed to taunt her with its emptiness.

Bessie took her gently by the elbow. "Won't you please get in the carriage, miss?" she urged. "Surely it would be better to wait and see what Mr. Williams has to say."

Margaret took a deep breath. The pain on her servants' faces did not escape her, and she reminded herself that her trust in Mr. Williams had always been justified. She would wait, and allow him to explain himself. "All right. Take me home. But do not waste one minute."

For the rest of the journey home, Margaret turned

over a million scenarios in her mind for what could be happening at the barn. None of them were good.

At last she heard the crunch of gravel under the carriage wheels and knew they were on the drive to Moreton Hall. Once they had pulled up to the front door and the footman had helped her down, Margaret went straight inside to the library and threw open the door. Her steward, John Williams, was seated in one of the chairs. He stood up as she entered.

"What is it, Williams?" Margaret said at once. "What's happened to the horses?"

He began walking toward her. "Won't you sit down? You must be worn out from your journey."

"Tell me!" she demanded. "I did not force Kevin to break his word to you, but I will not wait one more minute to find out what's going on."

Although Williams's demeanor was generally warm and affable, today he met her gaze with somber concern. But he knew Margaret well, and he was not the sort to prevaricate if there was a distasteful subject to be discussed. "It's glanders," he said simply.

Despite steeling herself for bad news, Margaret was stung by shock. Glanders was fatal to horses. It could spread throughout a stable and even to people, leaving a wake of destruction. "How could this happen?" she protested. "Our stable was clean!"

"There is always the possibility it arose from some weakness in the horses themselves—"

"Rubbish!" Margaret scoffed. "Some have tried to say it's not a communicable disease, but they are wrong. Somebody brought it here. Have you hired any new stable boys? Anyone from Moreton Village or London?"

He shook his head. "I've been over this with Garvey. He feels it may have been brought here by Mr. Denault's groom."

"Mr. Denault!" Was that possible? Numbly, she tried to cast her mind back over the events of the past few weeks. Paul had visited Moreton Hall shortly after their engagement was announced. He had been anxious to acquaint himself with the place and the staff.

"Garvey says Mr. Denault's groom was laid low with fever and chest pains. Garvey found out about it because our men were complaining about the extra work it caused. They thought it was an ague of some kind. No one suspected glanders. Not until one of our horses began to develop symptoms."

"What happened to the groom?"

"I've sent someone to London to inquire. Since you and Mr. Denault..." He paused and let out a short cough. "That is to say, since there is no formal connection between him and you now, we thought it best to look into the matter on our own." He shook his head sadly. "I'm reasonably certain our man will return with news that the groom has died."

"How many are gone?" she demanded, her words sharp as rage began to course through her. If Paul had brought this horse plague to her, he must have been keeping his own horses in the cheapest lodging available, the kind of stable that was a breeding ground for such a disease. His criminal carelessness had brought destruction to her house. She honestly believed if Paul was standing here right now she would have physically attacked him and wrung his neck.

"All but two have died," Williams answered grimly.

"We've quarantined the last two and are watching them carefully, but I do not hold out much hope."

"And Dante?" Her heart lurched in pain as she imagined her beautiful and spirited horse, her best and most faithful companion, in the midst of such horror. But if two horses were still alive, perhaps there was hope...

Williams gave her a sympathetic smile, as one might try to use to comfort a bereaved person. "I'm afraid he was among the first. It seems Denault's groom was much admiring of the animal and was often seen near him."

And with those words, the last of Margaret's hopes were laid to rest. Choking back a sob, she turned away from Williams and hurried out the French doors to the back terrace, unwilling for anyone to see the tears that she could no longer contain.

Margaret raced across the open field, not caring that her tears blurred her vision, not stopping until she had reached a little bridge far from the house. She leaned on the stone wall, gasping for breath, watching the brook flowing below her, its waters pushing leaves and twigs that were helpless against its current. Tom Poole's words came back to her: "Horses aren't good collateral. Too much could happen." What would he do when he discovered the "collateral" was lost?

She was out of options now. Her jewels, plate, and whatever movables she could spare had all been sold. The final blow had been this loss of her horses—especially Dante. She slammed her fist down on the rough stone. Why hadn't she taken Dante to London? She hadn't wanted to pay exorbitant stable fees and, most ironically, had not wanted to put him at risk. Even stables without disease were still suceptible to calamities such as theft or fire.

Slowly her heart rate returned to normal, and she wiped away the last of her tears. There was nothing to be gained by crying. It was time to set aside sorrow—as she had time and time again—and face her problem with cold rationality. She had pushed valiantly to keep her land safe and intact. No one could have done better than she had when faced with such odds. And yet, it hadn't been enough. She was very likely to lose Moreton Hall, either in part or in whole. But it wasn't gone yet. Whatever happened, to her last breath she would never, ever give up trying.

Chapter 12

Tom needed air—the kind he couldn't find in London. He was eager to leave behind the city's tall buildings and the narrow streets laced with smoke and fog. Although he'd traveled hundreds of miles within Australia, he'd never seen anything of England beyond the confines of London. His years away had made him homesick, and he longed to acquaint himself with his native land. A foreign critic had disparaged England as a "nation of shopkeepers," and yet it was a description that made Tom proud. He was himself an example of where hard work and industry could take a man.

There would be no point in going by train. His goal was to see the country, and he had heard that trains moved too quickly for the passengers to really see the land. Now that Castor was fully recovered from the voyage, he would provide the method of travel. Tom would journey at his own pace, stay at modest inns, and get to know this land he'd left in haste so long ago.

Tom had been invited to visit Rosewood, the country

home of James and Lizzie's grandmother, Lady Thornborough. The grand estate would provide Tom with plenty of opportunities for riding, to be sure. But Tom was too restless to consider that plan. He'd heard that parties of the bon ton might visit these country houses for weeks at a time, leading Tom to envision an extension of the precise society nonsense he was trying to escape.

He'd lost some sense of his own identity in London. He'd been trussed up like a goose and paraded before people who once would never have acknowledged his existence. He'd had no work to do besides handling occasional missives from Sullivan, and no real friends outside of his family. Despite Tom's best efforts, the few people he'd known before leaving London were now uneasy—embarrassed, almost—whenever he came to visit them. His new wealth and status had created a divide that Tom could not seem to bridge. Perhaps this time alone would give him what he needed to settle his heart and mind and see the country on his own terms.

Above all, he could not stop thinking about Margaret Vaughn. The moment he'd paid her debts, she'd left London for her home in Lincolnshire. If she harbored any gratitude at all, it was effectively hidden behind her adamant vows to repay him. Tom was just another creditor, no different in her eyes than Mortimer.

These hard truths provided no reason—and *every* reason—for his decision to take the northbound road. Yes, he wanted time to acquaint himself with his native land. But more than anything else, he wanted to see Margaret again. Although her beauty had first attracted him to her, he saw now that she wore it almost as a veil, hiding the real treasure beneath. Under that outward mask of cool poise was a woman of fire and strength. But what Tom found most tantalizing of all were the glimpses of vulnerability that she fought so hard to hide. He'd seen it in that first moment when he'd burst in on her and the moneylenders, and once again when she'd said good night to him after Lizzie's dinner party. Tom felt if he could only reach that part of her, he might at last gain her trust, rather than merely her gratitude. If there *was* any way at all into her heart, he was determined to find it.

*

"I don't think we've seen you here before." The old bartender settled his watery gaze on Tom. "Here on business, or just passing through?"

Tom lifted his tankard of ale and took a long draught before replying. He knew the man had seen him arrive and was aware the innkeeper had given Tom the best suite of rooms. He was fishing for more information, and this suited Tom just fine. He had nothing to hide, and if the barkeep was talkative, he might give Tom useful information about the little village of Moreton and the people who lived here—including its most important resident. "Tomorrow I plan to call on Miss Vaughn."

The bartender drew in his breath, pausing his task of wiping down the counter in order to give Tom his full attention. "You planning to ride that Thoroughbred of yours to Moreton Hall?"

"I am." Detecting something odd in the bartender's demeanor he added, "Is there a particular reason why I shouldn't?"

"Haven't you heard? The place isn't safe."

Tom stared at the barkeep in surprise. He had no idea

whether Margaret was liked or disliked by the locals, so he'd been prepared for any number of things he might hear about her. But this certainly was not one of them. "How in the world can it not be safe?"

"It's unsafe for your horse," the bartender clarified. "Though I've heard men get it, too."

"Get what, exactly?"

"Glanders." He spoke the word softly, checking over his shoulder first, looking worried that he might bring the disease into the inn if he spoke too loudly.

Tom set down his mug with such force that some of its contents sloshed onto the bar. "You can't be serious."

The bartender nodded solemnly. "It's true. Wiped out the entire barn."

Tom resisted the urge to groan out loud. He was sure Margaret loved them all, and he knew she was counting on the money she'd make from them. When she had offered them up as collateral, he had sensed that they were shoring up whatever had remained of her pride. With a sorrowful grimace Tom remembered a verse that Sullivan had often quoted to him from Psalms: *A horse is a vain thing for safety: neither shall he deliver any by his great strength.*

He stood up and put his payment for the ale on the bar. "Did you say everything was gone? Including all of her Thoroughbreds?"

"Yes, sir." The bartender finished wiping the counter. "Such a shame that she lost her favorite saddle horse. She loved that creature. Used to ride it into town, looking so tall and proud." He smiled in remembrance. "Often you'd see her crossing the fields, too, usually on her way to visit the tenant farmers."

"She is a good landowner, then?" Tom asked.

"Indeed she is. Takes more interest in the land than her father did, rest his soul." He shook his head again. "Too bad so many folks has already moved away."

"Why did they go?"

The bartender shrugged. "Drawn away by the promise of better pay in the factories, thinking they'll earn a better life." He motioned toward the open door and the beautiful rolling hills that lay beyond. "But I ask you, how could any life be better than this?"

*

The afternoon was far advanced. Threatening storm clouds hovered in the distance, moving in Tom's direction as he rode Castor at a slow walk along the road that edged the Vaughn estate. He ought to be getting back to the inn, to have Castor groomed and fed and to seek out his own supper as well. And yet he rode on, not ready to turn back. He rode another half mile or so to a spot where the road crested a hill. He'd been told that Moreton Hall could be seen from there. He wanted only a glimpse of it tonight. Tomorrow he'd go back and pay a proper call.

The bartender was right, Tom mused. Out here in the country, things always seemed better. God's voice was just a little easier to hear than it was in the noise and bustle of town. Today he had a dire need to hear that voice. He'd wanted only to help Margaret, and yet ten thousand pounds was not a sum to be handed over lightly, so he had accepted her terms. Now that the horses were gone, this tentative alliance they'd forged was on shaky ground, and Tom had no idea how to proceed. "Lord, what should I do?" He spoke the words aloud as he and Castor slowly advanced along the road. "Why—" He stopped himself short with a chuckle. "Never ask God *why*," Sully would often tell Tom. "The Lord has his own reasons that we are not always privy to. Instead we must ask *what*. That is, *what is to be done? How can I serve?*"

Tom brought his horse to a stop and took in the view. The land fell away on all sides, breathtaking in its late summer glory. The fields of wheat were turning to delicate golden hues, while the trees were still lush and green. Only the slate-gray clouds marred the perfect landscape, although even they brought a certain wild beauty to the place. Yes, one could certainly sense the presence of God here.

He stretcheth out the heavens as a curtain, and spreads them out as a tent to dwell in.

Off in the distance, Moreton Hall stood majestically, an august building of stone, laced here and there with ivy and topped with a slate roof and dozens of chimneys. It presided over a bucolic landscape of green pastures and woodlands, alternating with rows of golden wheat and the fields that lay fallow this year, awaiting their turn to contribute to the harvest.

As Tom's gaze took all this in, he noticed a solitary figure perched on the wooden steps that straddled a low stone wall. She sat motionless, staring out at the fields, toward the west where the sun would be disappearing soon.

Without a moment's hesitation, he nudged his horse forward, turning off the road and into the meadow.

Chapter 13

She was not likely to welcome his arrival, he knew. She might very well be angry that he had followed her all the way up to Lincolnshire. She might consider this an unwanted intrusion. But Tom considered that Sully's advice was right on the mark—especially today. Tom had his own reasons for being here, to be sure, but he believed God had a hand in it, too.

Margaret turned at his approach. "Mr. Poole," she said crisply, standing up. "What a surprise."

Tom stopped several yards away and dismounted. Thunder rolled in the distance, a dim rumble that made Castor toss his head in agitation. "Easy, boy," he soothed, scratching the horse's withers. It seemed to calm the creature, although his ears continued to flick back and forth, evidence of his anxiety.

Margaret was even more beautiful today. A fitful breeze tugged at the folds of her walking dress, shaping it to her body's natural curves and rendering it more alluring than the low-cut dinner gown he'd last seen her in.

"Forgive me for showing up uninvited," he said. "A man in town told me what happened."

She took a step back, watching him with a guarded wariness. "Did you come to say *I told you so*? You said it was a bad investment, and you were right." Her face twisted in pain. "Years of careful breeding and nothing but the best of care—all wiped out in the blink of an eye." She lifted her chin. "But I will get you the money somehow. I always repay my debts."

"The money," he said with deliberate care, "is not why I came to Lincolnshire."

Something flared in her eyes—that brief show of vulnerability, and Tom wondered if there was perhaps a chance that she was softening toward him. It was gone in a flash, however, replaced by the impenetrable coolness he was coming to know too well. She turned away as though he had not spoken, gesturing toward the gently rolling fields that lay between them and the town. "I've just come up here to give it a final look. It will go on sale soon."

"You can't mean you plan to sell your estate," Tom said incredulously.

"Not all of it. The railroad company wants to buy a large tract near town to build a new line. It will make the journey to Lincoln shorter and more efficient." Her eyes squeezed shut for a moment. "It will also be noisy and intrusive and eat up the very best of my farmland."

She began to knead the back of her neck, as though trying to relieve the tension built up there. Tom thought he detected a glimmer of a tear in her eye. He wanted to reach out, to place his hands where hers were and massage away the pain. But such actions were improper in her world, no matter how badly they might be needed. He would not push past her defenses; he would look for a way to draw her to him. As he stood there, forcing himself to keep his hands at his sides, he felt a few drops of rain hit his face. The storm was very nearly upon them.

Castor snorted and reared up a little. There was another crack of thunder, this time loud and impossible to ignore. A flash of lightning streaked across the sky.

"We need to get you home," Tom said. "I wouldn't want you to get soaked. Also, my horse gets nervous in heavy storms."

Margaret looked up at the gathering clouds. "There's no time to get back to the main house, and in any case it isn't safe to cross the field in a lightning storm. However, there is an abandoned cottage not too far from here." She pointed to a nearby wood.

It was a good plan. Tom nodded. "Come on then." He mounted his horse, then reached down to offer Margaret a hand.

"What are you doing?" she asked sharply.

"Put your foot in the stirrup and I'll pull you up. I can control the horse better if I'm riding him, and we'll get to the cottage faster."

She hesitated as Castor pranced with agitation.

"He's restless because the weather is changing," Tom assured her. "He'll settle down once the rain arrives. I promise you'll be safe." He reached out his hand again. "Please. Trust me."

Thunder cracked again, and the rain began to fall in earnest. Still looking dubious, Margaret lifted her skirt just enough to enable her foot to reach the stirrup. She extended a hand toward Tom and pushed herself up as

Tom pulled. Once she was on the horse, Tom settled her sideways in front of him, cradling her back with one arm. When he was certain she was secure, they set off.

Margaret wrapped her arms around his waist, holding on tightly and placing her head against his chest. Castor needed little urging, and in no time they were approaching the woods. Margaret kept her head down—a defense against the rain, no doubt—but Tom thought he detected a small sigh escaping from her. He savored her touch. It was heaven to have her so near to him, dependent on him—if only for these few moments. Tom kept the horse moving swiftly, even though he wished this ride might never end. Never before had a woman felt so right in his arms. Surely she belonged nowhere else.

They were soaked by the time they reached the cottage. As soon as Tom brought the horse to a stop, Margaret loosened her grip and slid to the ground, running the last few steps to the cottage door. It opened easily, and in a moment she was inside.

Tom dismounted and led Castor to a small open-sided shed. He tied the horse securely, giving it room to move but not enough leverage to break the ropes. "Easy, boy," he said, patting the horse once more. "You'll be fine." Castor eyed him as if to say he was not at all sure about that. Tom said a quick prayer as he ran across the small yard to the cottage.

Margaret had been observing his actions through a small window. "Will your horse be all right, do you think?" she asked anxiously. "I heard terrible stories about what he was like aboard the ship from Australia."

"The voyage was rough," Tom acknowledged. "Horses have a long memory when it comes to bad experiences. But I trust to the Lord to keep him safe."

Margaret made a small noise that seemed to indicate derision or disbelief, but said nothing. She was hugging herself tightly. Water slid down her face in tiny rivulets and dripped from the hem of her dress. He would gladly have tried to warm her by wrapping his arms around her again. It would have been a delicious feeling, but now that they were here, alone in a cabin, he did not want to appear to press his advantage. He contented himself by gently wiping away the raindrops on her cheek. He felt her shiver, but whether from the cold or his touch, he could not be sure. "We must get you dry," he murmured, "or you will catch a chill."

He did a quick survey of the cabin. It was empty except for a large plank table and a bench. But there was also a small stack of firewood. Sending up a silent prayer of thanksgiving, Tom knelt before the hearth and set about arranging a fire.

He could feel her eyes on his back, watching him as he worked. It took him no time at all to arrange the wood; building fires came as naturally to him now as breathing.

"We have no way to light it," Margaret said.

"Ah, but we do." Tom pulled a knife and a small piece of flint from his coat pocket, and within a few minutes he had coaxed a nice little blaze. "There you go," he said, standing back and motioning her to the hearth. "Cozy as you please."

*

The fire seemed to immediately fill the little cabin with light and warmth. Margaret's sodden dress clung to her, cold and heavy, and she put out her hands gratefully to catch the heat from the flames. She sent a sidelong glance at Tom, who remained close by, admiring his handiwork. "Do you always carry fire-starting devices with you?" she asked.

"Had to be self-sufficient in Australia." He smiled and shrugged. "I suppose some habits are hard to break."

Something in his smile caught and tugged at her, unaccountably lifting her spirits. He pushed back a lock of hair from his forehead with unconscious grace. *He has no pretense, no guile*, she thought. *In all his actions, he is as he seems.* What would it be like to live that way? A flash of envy raced through her. Embarrassed at this sudden rush of feeling, she turned her gaze back to the flames.

Tom pulled the bench to the hearth. "For you, my lady," he said with a small bow.

She took a seat at one end of the bench, wondering if he would join her, and half-wishing that he would. Tom began to shrug out of his coat but then paused in mid motion. "May I?" he said deferentially. "I believe I shall dry faster without this on."

She nodded, not trusting herself to speak and unable to turn her gaze away as he stripped off his coat and laid it across the table. His damp shirt clung to his broad chest and muscular arms, and suddenly the tiny cottage felt *too* cozy, too intimate. Tom gave the fire a poke with a bit of unused firewood, releasing a fresh burst of flames and heat. He looked around the little room with satisfaction. "I like it here," he said.

"You do?"

"It's welcoming and simple. Not like those enormous mansions in London, where a person can get lost between the front door and the parlor."

It was an apt description, and Margaret couldn't help but laugh. "I see that wealth hasn't turned your head."

"No," he said. "I hope it never does."

Watching as Tom set more wood on the fire, Margaret was struck by how he filled this humble space with dignity. The firelight played along his square jaw and strong hands. He certainly was not like any gentleman she'd known, but neither was he merely some rough laborer. He fell into a category she could not define. What sort of a man was it who could survive shipwrecks, love his family tenderly, and profess himself a Christian and yet have no qualms about getting into physical fights when threatened? Could one man truly be all those things? It was a rare mixture, to be sure.

"What happened to the people who lived here?" Tom asked.

His question drew her thoughts back to the troubles at hand. She sighed. "They're off to the factories, like so many others. It's just as well the railway company wants to buy it. No one wants to farm the land anymore."

The rain pounded against the roof. In the far corner of the room, water began to drip from the ceiling and form a tiny pool on the floor. It seemed a metaphor for her life. No matter how hard she tried to shore up against the storms, they had a way of battering through her last defenses. The futility of it echoed in her heart, louder than the deluge on the roof.

She clenched her fists, fighting to keep from showing her bitter frustration. She had learned long ago never to show her true feelings. To bare one's heart was to give someone else the upper hand, to open oneself to even worse trouble and ultimately to regret it.

Tom came over and sat next to her on the bench, gently loosening her fist with his touch. "Margaret, do not sell your land."

Warmth radiated from his body, so close to hers, tempting her to draw closer as he kept caressing her hand. His gaze, too, was warm with compassion. But his words had sparked what little pride she had left. She must make her own decisions, and fight her own battles. She drew her hand back. "I don't see that it is any of your concern."

"But it *is* my concern. You would be selling the land to repay me. Don't do it."

"It is my land," Margaret said stoutly. "I shall do what I think best."

"Margaret, listen to me." He took hold of her shoulders. "If you sell your best farmland, it will only hurt you in the long run. Your gain will be only temporary; you'll lose the future profits from harvests and rents. In a few years you may find yourself even worse off than you are now. I have a better solution."

His words, though meant to be kind, only grated her already raw emotions. She shook herself free and stood up. She had to put distance between them. She could not afford to be lured into his way of thinking. He was a man who could always snatch victory from even the most dire of circumstances. Naturally he would assume he could solve her problems. But he was wrong. Perhaps his life had been blessed, but hers had taken a decidedly different tack. One that she must navigate alone. "Oh?" Margaret said scornfully, her heart gripped with pain. "And just what, exactly, would you have me do?"

"Marry me," he said.

Chapter 14

Gauging by her expression, Margaret found his second proposal as unpalatable as the first. And yet, Tom saw confusion in her eyes, too, and this he welcomed. It was evidence that he had put at least a tiny crack into her fortress walls.

He got up from the bench and closed the gap between them. "I can help you, Margaret."

She held up her hands as if to ward him off. "Mr. Poole, this is neither the time nor the place—"

"I mean *really* help you," he said, cutting off her protest. She was trying to retreat again behind her pride, and Tom was determined not to let her do it. He took her hands and drew her toward him, willing her to meet his eyes. "We are no longer talking about some short loan just to get creditors of your hair. There is far, far more at stake now."

She stared at him for a long moment. Her silence sparked Tom's hope. But then she dropped her gaze. "You don't know what you're asking," she said, her voice strained.

"I'm asking you to marry me," Tom insisted. The memory of her involuntary sigh as she had leaned against him on Castor returned to his mind, giving him confidence that she *could* find a way to love him, if only she would give her heart the chance. Gently he tilted her chin up. "Believe me on this, Margaret. Together, we can make Moreton Hall prosperous again."

She shook her head. "Too much depends on circumstances beyond our control. Crop failures, drought, the economy. No one knows what the future holds."

"You're wrong about that."

She lifted an eyebrow. "Are you a fortune-teller, then? Some kind of prophet?"

"I'm not talking about me. The Lord holds tomorrow. We must allow Him to work, and trust His ways."

"God?" she said with a scoff.

"Haven't you ever wondered if the Lord had some plan in mind for you—some special purpose for your life?"

She walked over to the window, staring out at the streaming rain. "I haven't had time for philosophical questions. I've been too busy running this estate and digging out from under the mountain of debt my father left behind. Not to mention keeping pretenders at bay."

"Pretenders?" Tom said curiously. "You make it sound like the throne of a kingdom."

"The problem is the same," Margaret declared. "Moreton Hall was entailed, as these things often are, to firstborn sons. When it became clear that I would be my father's only child, my grandfather moved heaven and earth—and the necessary parliamentary powers—to break the entail so that I could inherit. If he had not done so, the estate would have passed to my cousin when my father died."

"You called him a 'pretender.' Does that mean he still feels entitled to this inheritance?"

She clenched her fists. "Richard Spencer will never, *ever,* own this estate," she said fiercely. "I will do whatever it takes to prevent it."

Tom now understood why Margaret was so dead set on keeping Moreton Hall at all costs. She was in the middle of a family feud, and she was determined to win it. "So you do have a purpose in life," he pointed out drily.

Her eyes flashed. "You may call it what you like. I call it fighting for my family honor. And what about you?" she challenged. "What is your *purpose* in life?"

What drive and determination she had, Tom thought. What strength and resourcefulness. Yet somehow she did not see the obvious solution to her problems, although it was right here, right in front of her. It was time to show her.

*

Tom swiftly crossed the room. Margaret was so taken by surprise that she did not think to resist as he took her into his arms. He drew her close, and she was met with the intoxicating scent of rain and soap and starched linen. She found herself inhaling, remaining in his arms, feeling the heat of his chest through his still-damp shirt. "There is one thing that I am very sure I must do," he murmured in her ear. He cradled her face with one hand and brought his lips to hers.

He kissed intently, as though wanting to draw Margaret out of herself and into him. And suddenly, she found she wanted to go there, wanted to lose herself in the heady emotions he was arousing. She delighted in the feel of being pressed against his broad chest as his strong arms wrapped tightly around her. He seemed to radiate more heat than the fire. He kept kissing her, exploring her mouth with confident sensuality.

At last he moved to kiss her cheek, to nuzzle her neck. He murmured something very softly, so low Margaret could hardly make out the words. Then she realized he was not talking to her. "Thank you, Lord," he whispered.

A flash of lightning lit up the cottage, followed by a crack of thunder so deafening they both jumped. Margaret was grateful for the interruption. This was not right; she could not be falling for this man. She went to the fireplace, feigning a need to warm her hands, although she would have done better to step outside and allow the pelting rain to cool her body, which was alive with the flames of desire.

"*That,*" said Tom from behind her, "was what the etiquette books call a frightful breach of protocol." But he spoke without a trace of remorse. In fact, Margaret thought with hot embarrassment, he sounded rather pleased with himself. She kept her eyes glued to the crackling hearth, trying to still her wildly beating heart.

He came up behind her, and she could feel him standing just inches away. His mere presence called out for her to turn and melt back into his arms. "Come now, Maggie," he whispered. "Didn't you like that just a little?"

Grabbing on to what presence of mind she had left, she turned to face him. "My name is *Margaret,*" she said, dredging up all the chilly authority she could muster.

He laughed, not the least bit put off by her rebuff. "I think *Maggie* suits you much better."

He had to be toying with her. No one had ever called her anything but Margaret, not even members of her family. Coming from Tom it sounded too tantalizingly familiar, like the memory of his kiss that still burned on her lips.

"How beautiful you are," Tom observed. "You have such a lovely blush on your face just now."

His words only fueled the flame in her cheeks. "It is from anger!" she protested. "You took ungentlemanly advantage." Thunder shook the house once more. "Hah!" she said disparagingly. "Perhaps God does not approve either."

But nothing she said rattled him. He only laughed again. "Why do people think thunderstorms are a sign that God is angry? Perhaps, Maggie, it means He is up in the heavens jumping up and down and shouting for joy."

He seemed determined to keep her off-balance. "Why would God be jumping for joy because you kissed me? And I told you, my name is—"

"Hear me out," he interrupted. "And let us consider the question logically."

His dark eyes regarded her steadily from under full brows. The firelight played on the late-day growth of stubble on his jaw, illuminating the roughness she had felt against her cheeks just moments ago. She ought to step away, tell him to leave at once. And yet her feet refused to move, even as her eyes refused to quit his gaze. "What can possibly be logical about this?" she said, her voice a small gasp. Even now, she was embarrassed at her reactions to his kiss, and how easily she had lost control.

"It's simple, really," Tom said. "You are in need of money. I have money."

"Money is not the only issue," she protested.

"I realize that," he said doggedly. "You are concerned

about your family honor. You think I am beneath you, perhaps. I don't have some lofty lineage that goes back to William the Conqueror." There was an edge to his voice now. "But allow me to remind you of one very important fact, Maggie: you were about to marry into such a family, but you would have been forever bound to a man who is a liar and a cheat."

Tom's words struck home. His unvarnished honesty sliced through her objections like a knife, but they cut her bitterly in the process. Margaret looked away, chafing at his words but unable to refute them.

"Now let's talk about my family," Tom continued. "Lord Somerville is one of the most respected men in the House of Lords. Lizzie is the kindest and truest soul, and the venerable Thornboroughs have accepted her without hesitation. You could do far worse than to marry into such a family."

Margaret still did not answer. She refused to accept the rosy picture that Tom was painting. There had been no bastards in Paul's family tree—no scandal at all, only staid respectability. If only he had lived up to his honorable heritage! Then Margaret would not be forced to stand here, alone in this cottage, having a soul-baring conversation with a man who would not leave her in peace.

When at last she spared him a glance, she saw that he was watching her intently. "Have you thought beyond your own lifetime?" he asked. "You fight to keep your inheritance intact, but who will inherit if you don't have children?"

"Enough!" she cried, pushed to her limit by his unrelenting arguments. "It is no reason to rush into marriage. I am young; I have time."

"I would not delay even a year," he said. "The land won't wait."

His insistent urging kept pushing her to places she didn't want to go. "What can you possibly know about it?" she accused. "What makes you such an expert?"

"Was Paul an expert?" he shot back.

Margaret gasped. "Paul was a *gentleman!*" she sputtered. "Naturally he would leave the day-to-day management to a land steward, but—"

"I *know* farming," Tom cut in. "I'm also an expert with the care and training of horses, and—unlike some men—I've proved I can properly handle great sums of money." It was a dig at Paul, and by implication everything Margaret had tried to do on her own. He paused, and when he spoke again, his voice was calm and gentle. "But there's something even more important than all of those things, Maggie. I will be a good husband to you. And how much is that worth?"

Margret trembled as he ran a light hand across her cheek, sending shock waves of unwanted pleasure through her. The vision he painted was so enticing. How easy it would be to give in, to believe he could make good on all his promises. But she had already learned the hard way that when something sounded too good to be true, it was. She fought to clear her mind of the fog that seemed to envelop it. She couldn't think straight when he was near. He threw every one of her emotions into disarray. Did she really want to place herself under the power of such a man? *No.* She was on the verge of losing all she held dear; she could not add the risk of losing the deepest part of her heart as well.

If he would not accept her refusal, then she would

simply have to get him to rescind his offer. "Very well, Mr. Poole."

Her abrupt change in tactic seemed to take him momentarily by surprise. "Very well?" he repeated with a questioning lilt. "Are you accepting my proposal, then?"

Margaret allowed herself a crisp nod of her head. "A fortunate choice of words. For it is a proposal, is it not? A *business* proposal. If I marry you, I gain financial security and some advantage in society. If you marry me, you gain important real estate."

"If you wish to discuss marriage as a profit-and-loss statement, allow me to add an item. I would also gain a wife whom I find very appealing. So far, I see only advantages." He gave her a look filled with admiration and, more unnervingly, desire. Heat consumed her face once again. Before she met Tom Poole she could have counted on one hand the times she had truly blushed. Now that he had awakened this ability in her, her body seemed to be attempting to make up for lost time.

"Yes, well...," she stammered. With great effort, she regained her breath. She could not allow emotion to cloud her reason. She could not afford to lose her control. "I should point out that if I were to marry you, there would be an important caveat."

He blinked.

"That means there are conditions," she clarified.

"I know what it means," Tom said brusquely. "You do not have to condescend to me." He crossed his arms and gave her a wary look. "Suppose you tell me exactly what those conditions would be."

"I have been running the affairs of this estate from the

time I was eighteen. That was about the time that my grand-father died and my father became too fond of his liquor."

There, she thought. *Now it is out in the open.* He would know that her father was not only a wastrel but also an unrepentant drunkard. Perhaps that would be enough to scare away Tom Poole. Everyone knew alco-holism ran in families, after all. Would he want to risk it? She watched his face for his reaction. His eyebrows lifted, but he did not look at all shocked, which was why she could not resist adding, "I do hope you have not fallen prey to this vice after years of living among convicts."

This got a reaction out of him. He lifted his hands, and Margaret took an involuntary step back, wondering if he was going to hit her. Surely he wouldn't? But his hands froze in midair, then rose again as Tom ran them through his hair as though that had been his intention all along. Or perhaps he was trying to calm his frustration. "You seem to be deliberately trying to goad me," he said. "Why don't you just save yourself the trouble and tell me your *caveat.*"

Margaret let out a breath, realizing she had been fool-ish to provoke a man who expressed his feelings in such physical ways. "Very well, then," she said, trying to speak with businesslike calm. "As I was saying, I have managed my own affairs for many years. I do not intend to relinquish my authority to a husband or to anyone else. If we are to be married, then I must be allowed to continue running the estate as I see fit. To guarantee this, I shall have my solicitor put it in writing."

This was exactly the plan she had been about to carry out with Paul. He had been willing to acquiesce, but now she knew why. He'd had no interest in the management of the estate; he'd merely been desperate to get his hands on the money he *thought* she had. She was sure that Tom would never agree to such a thing. It was the only tack she knew that might get him to change his mind about wanting to marry her.

Sure enough, Tom was looking at her as if she'd lost her mind. "I think you are unaware of simple marriage law. When a woman marries, everything she owns comes under the control of her husband."

"There are ways around that," Margaret declared. "Money or lands that are set aside and remain under the wife's power. Dower property, and such. I have very competent lawyers."

"You just said if I marry you I gain this land. Now you are saying I'll have no control over any of it? Which is it?"

"It is as I have just stated," Margaret replied.

"I'm sorry, but that's unacceptable. And in any case, you are in no position to dictate terms. You are already heavily in my debt."

"Then I shall find a way to pay off that debt—without marrying you."

Tom rubbed his chin with the air of a person deep in thought. Behind her, Margaret heard the pop and fizzle of wet firewood as it ignited. The rain hammered down, and the drip in the corner kept up its slow *plop, plop*. Tom remained silent. Margaret began to grow uncomfortable. Now that she had gotten him to reject the idea of marriage, where did that leave her? She was in the same straits as before. She would have to sell land to the railroad, or find some other way out.

"Let me point out something about marriage," Tom said, breaking the silence at last. "It is a sacred bond.

And yes, it is a contract. But every marriage is unique. Every husband and wife must decide between themselves which arrangements are right and proper for their lives. No one else can determine these things for them."

"*Both* of them decide? But you just said that according to law and custom, the husband has all the power. Don't you know that is a heretical statement?"

"Is it? I got it from Geoffrey, and since he is a minister, I figure he ought to know."

Margaret could not believe the turn this conversation was taking. She had tried to push him away from marriage with her demands, and yet here he was still talking about it. "And what sort of 'arrangement' would you consider 'right and proper'?" she asked warily.

"You and I will take *joint* responsibility for the estate. As you pointed out, you have been running your own affairs for a long time. Considering the circumstances and the heavy burdens placed upon you, you have done a laudable job. But I would argue that you have not always pursued the best possible path."

She bristled. "How easy it is to judge another person's mistakes."

"I am not your judge. But I am willing to be your partner. Two are better than one, Maggie. If you are truly the capable woman that you claim to be, you will listen to any sound and reasonable suggestions." His mouth tilted into a hint of a smile. "Even if they happen to come from your husband. That, by the way, is how it should work in any true marriage."

"Do you really believe that?" Once again, it sounded too good to be true.

He took hold of both her hands. "I do." He gently

traced her ring finger—the place where her wedding band would be, if she carried out this bizarre plan.

Think this through logically, she told herself. *Emotions cannot enter into it.*

She cleared her throat. "I am amenable to the idea of the two of us managing the estate together. However, there is more to consider than simply the financial matters."

This statement actually seemed to amuse him. "Is there?" he said. "I am surprised to hear you say it. And what, pray tell, might those other matters be?"

"Well…there is our place in society to consider. We must spend the season in London, of course, and hold house parties at Moreton Hall at other times of the year, as appropriate. Doing these things properly requires a certain amount of decorum and finesse."

"Are you afraid I am too uncouth for these endeavors?"

"Well, it certainly means no fisticuffs at formal gatherings, or at gatherings of any kind, for that matter. You must learn to control those behaviors, to learn proper deportment. I cannot have a savage for a husband."

She had been too sure of herself, gone too far. He grabbed her by the arms and pulled her roughly to him. "I shoved a man at a party," he said, his voice low and gruff. "Trust me, the irritating bastard deserved far worse."

"Mr. Poole, your language—"

"In fact, I believe I was behaving quite honorably. But we will leave that for now. Suffice it to say that you will have nothing to fear about my *deportment*." He said the word as though it were as distasteful as she found his swearing to be. "These public trappings are all very well; however, in private I want *you* to act as my wife."

She swallowed. "Of course I know there are certain things you wish of me. You are a man, after all." She wished her voice did not sound so raspy. Frightened, almost. She took a deep breath and tried to inject more certainty, more assuredness into her voice. "I shall not shirk my duties in that regard."

He pulled her closer, so close that she fancied she could feel the beat of his heart. "Your duties may involve more than you think."

She tried to find her calm, not to allow wild fears to grow about what he meant by *more.* She had heard of men whose appetites ran in strange directions, requiring things of their wives that were unnatural. She'd once found a book of pornography among her father's possessions that had made this fact quite clear to her.

Tom placed his cheek next to hers, so close they were within a fraction of touching. "Oh, Maggie," he whispered into her ear. "There is so much you have to learn."

Dear heavens, she thought wildly. He *was* talking about those things, those unnatural acts. Her heart began hammering wildly as she considered all the things a man could do to a woman—and that he could force a woman to do to *him*—things that had been described in graphic detail in her father's book. "When I said *duties,* I meant only that which is normal and customary. We have a duty after all to produce children—"

"Oh my God," he said with genuine surprise. "You are speaking of sex, aren't you?"

"Of c-c-course," she stammered. "Aren't you?"

He brought one hand up to stroke her cheek, a whisper-soft caress. "I have never forced myself on a woman," he said gently. "When we come together, it will be because you want it. Because we *both* want it."

She blinked. "Then what did you mean about me acting as your wife?"

"The Bible says that a man is to love his wife, and that a wife is to reverence her husband. I don't know why the Lord states it that way, but I hope in time to find out. Until then, I plan simply to believe it, and live it."

"So my duty is to 'worship' you?" Margaret was now more confused than ever. This biblical talk only seemed to complicate matters. Why could they not simply keep this a straight contract between two parties, the way everyone knew marriages were supposed to be?

He shook his head. "Not 'worship.' It says 'reverence.' That means respect. You must respect me. To my mind this means, for example, that you are not to disparage me in public, or even in private among your friends. If you take issue with anything I do or say, you must tell me so *privately*. I am willing to do many things for you, Maggie, but in return I expect a few things from you. Surely this is not asking too much. I will not back down on it in any case."

"So I am to 'reverence' you," she said cautiously. "And you will 'love' me in return?"

He laughed. "Yes, although I can't help but wonder just how difficult you will make that task for me. So how about it, Maggie? Are we engaged?"

"Yes," she said, hardly believing she was saying it. "I suppose we are."

Chapter 15

The rain had ended, leaving a steamy mist in the clearing. To Tom's mind the mist only added to the feeling of unreality, that he had entered some strange new world. And he was being led into it by the woman now walking beside him. Her cool reticence had returned, but Tom had hope. He cherished the memory of those moments when she had returned his kisses without reservation.

Castor was calm now that the storm had passed. "He really is beautiful," Margaret said wistfully as she watched Tom lead him from the little makeshift stall.

Tom's heart was squeezed by the pinch of sadness he saw in Margaret's eyes as she reached out to pat the stallion's neck. He remembered how, during their ride in Hyde Park, she had described her gelding Dante with such pride and love. "We shall find you another," Tom promised. "We will build a new stable and fill it with fine horses. Just as soon as we return from our honeymoon."

Her hand jerked away from the horse. "Honeymoon!"

Tom was tempted to laugh at the way she looked at him, aghast. "Isn't that normal for a newlywed couple?"

"Well, yes, but—"

He motioned to the tiny cottage. "Perhaps you would like to honeymoon here? It is rather a cozy spot."

She made a wry face. "We'd have to fix that leak first."

Tom pretended to think it over. "Too much trouble," he said. "I have a better idea. Let's go up to Scotland. I read in the paper that the queen and Prince Albert spend a lot of time there. It must be spectacular. We'll go in the fall, after the harvest is over. The weather will be lovely and cool, and we can ride to our heart's content."

A tiny smile broke through her chilly reserve. "That would be wonderful."

Tom mounted the horse and reached his hand down to Margaret, just as he'd done earlier. Once more she found the stirrup with her foot and took his hand. In a moment she was on the horse, landing smoothly as though they'd been doing this for years. As he settled his arm around her waist to steady her, he thought again how right this felt. He wanted nothing more than to hold her like this always, and now that she had agreed to be his wife he would be able to do just that. He took a deep breath. It seemed to him that the air had never smelled so fresh, nor the rain-kissed leaves looked so green.

They left the woods and crossed the open fields at a leisurely pace. Tom kept the horse at a walk to avoid the risk of it stumbling on the soft, wet ground. This also provided a wonderful excuse to make this ride last as long as possible, allowing Tom to savor the glorious feeling of Margaret's body against his own.

When they reached the house, the front door opened

and the butler came out, followed by a maid. Margaret slipped down easily off the horse, and the maid ran to her, offering her a towel. "Oh, Miss Vaughn, we knew you must be caught out in the rain, and we were ever so worried."

"Shall I get someone to attend to your horse, sir?" the butler asked Tom deferentially.

"That won't be necessary," Tom answered. "In fact, I would like to leave him over there." Tom pointed to the side of the house, where the grass, although well manicured, was tall enough for a horse to graze. "Could you call for one of the servants to bring out a tub of water for him?"

The butler looked over to Margaret, seeking confirmation for this strange request.

"Do as Mr. Poole requests, Mitchell," Margaret directed. "He does not want to risk putting his horse in our stable."

"I assure you there is no cause for concern," said a voice behind them. "The area has been thoroughly cleaned, and none of our hands show any signs of illness."

Tom turned to see who had contradicted the orders of the lady of the house. He found himself looking at a tall man with receding hair and a prominent nose, whose long neck rose above two stiffly starched collar points and a neatly tied black cravat. "And you are...?" Tom asked pointedly.

Margaret said, "Mr. Poole, this is Mr. Williams, my land steward."

The land steward. That would explain a lot, Tom thought. A land steward was akin to a lawyer or some other professional man. He would not be Margaret's equal on the social scale, but neither would he have any qualms about stating his opinions.

Williams was sizing up Tom, too. After a ride through the rain and the mud, Tom doubted he was making a good first impression. He wondered if Williams would accept Tom's new authority at Moreton Hall. Judging from the man's expression, Tom guessed it might take some doing. "The place ought to be quarantined for several weeks, at least," Tom said. "Just to be certain."

Williams waved a dismissive hand. "That's nonsense. The barn has been thoroughly cleaned and the danger is past."

"The issue is not under discussion," Margaret said crisply. "Mr. Poole has made a request, and we will honor it."

Williams's eyebrows rose a fraction, but he gave an acquiescent nod. "As you wish, Miss Vaughn."

"Mitchell," Margaret said to the butler, "while you are seeing to the water for the horse, please tell Cook there will be a guest for dinner."

"Right away, Miss Vaughn," the butler said, and hurried away. Tom thought he looked relieved to be sent on these errands and escape the little battle of wills between his mistress and the land steward. Perhaps he had been caught in their cross fire before.

Margaret turned her attention back to her land steward. "Mr. Williams, will you take a few moments to acquaint Mr. Poole with the house? I must go and change."

"It would be my pleasure," Williams replied. His words were polite, but the chill of irritation was impossible to miss.

Tom watched as Margaret went up the broad stone steps and into the house. When next he saw her, she'd be once more in prim and proper clothes. He wanted to remember her as she appeared now, with her damp dress clinging to her body, her bonnet hanging from its ribbons, and stray locks of hair falling from the loosened bun at her neck. Then he realized, with even greater pleasure, that he would soon have plenty of opportunities to see her in such a casual state. A picture burst onto his mind's eye of the two of them alone, and Tom pulling the pins from her hair and running his fingers through her long tresses...

Williams cleared his throat to regain Tom's attention. "Is this your first visit to Moreton Hall, Mr. Poole?"

With an effort, Tom turned his eyes from the house. "It is." But he did not add the happy news that this visit was just the beginning. Margaret wanted to inform the staff herself, and Tom would honor her request.

When they reached the spot that Tom deemed adequate for his horse, he took a stake from a small pouch attached to the saddle. He plunged it into the ground, which was still soft from the rain, and secured Castor's reins to it.

"I see you come prepared," Williams remarked.

Tom nodded. "Never know when it will come in handy."

A young kitchen maid came from the back of the house. She was carrying a large wooden tub, struggling under its weight as water sloshed over the sides. Tom hastily crossed the lawn to meet her. "Thank you," he said, relieving her of her burden. "You're very kind."

"'Twas no trouble, sir," she murmured, looking surprised at the compliment. Belatedly she remembered to drop a small curtsy, then turned and hurried back to the house.

Williams was still studying Tom with curiosity. To prevent any more questions about himself, Tom began to ask Williams questions about Moreton Hall.

"It's a fine old place, as you can see," Williams said with undisguised pride as they made their way to the front drive for a better view. "The original part of the house was built nearly two hundred years ago." He pointed to what was now one wing of the mansion. "The section that now forms the main part of the house is Georgian."

"It's a charming place," Tom said, although he thought the roof looked like it could use repair in a few spots, and one wing of the house was nearly swallowed by ivy. "And how many acres of land?"

Williams immediately launched into details about the amount of arable land, the number of tenants, and the projected crop sizes.

"Those are impressive figures," Tom said.

"I like to think the estate has benefited in some small measure from my oversight." Williams's self-satisfied smile belied the modest words. "Of course, Miss Vaughn would be the best judge of that."

"Undoubtedly," Tom said.

Williams caught the reproof behind Tom's answer. "Will you be staying here long, Mr. Poole?" he asked, his frosty tone suggesting he hoped the answer was no.

Tom simply shrugged. "Perhaps."

The two men eyed each other, and Tom was satisfied when Williams looked away first. With a nod toward the house Williams said, "I see Mitchell is waiting to show you inside. I must be going, as there are matters that require my immediate attention. I trust you'll have a pleasant visit, Mr. Poole."

Tom watched as Williams strode away. He had no doubt Williams would be pressing Margaret for information about Tom as soon as he could. Tom saw trouble ahead; he distrusted this man's headstrong attitude. But he'd faced worse problems, and he could deal with Williams when the time came.

He went up the steps and allowed the butler to usher him inside. As Tom surveyed the front hall, he saw easily that, like the outside of the house, the stately interior was showing signs of neglect. Tom paused to inspect a thin crack in the wall and found it was a symptom of a larger problem. "The plaster is damp," he said, placing a hand on it. "There is a leak there that will need to be fixed. It's probably where the portico meets the wall over the door."

The butler looked at him quizzically. It would seem odd, Tom realized, for a stranger to come in and begin making orders about household repairs. He shrugged it off. Mitchell would find out the reason soon enough.

Mitchell led him down the hall to the library, an enormous room lined with shelves and containing more books than Tom had ever seen. Arrangements of chairs, sofas, and tables created comfortable seating areas designed for reading and reflection. Immediately Tom drifted toward a large leather chair near the fireplace. He could imagine spending many comfortable hours there. But this room, too, had a faded air, as though it had seen better days. Tom wondered how long it had been since someone had polished the wood or beaten out the rug. Margaret must have let most of her staff go in order to save money. Tom would see to it that they hired more.

Seeing a set of French doors, Tom stepped outside to orient himself. A long terrace ran along the back of the house, dropping down in tiers lined with huge flowerpots. An immense lawn sloped gently down to a quaint stone bridge over a stream. From the bridge, a path wound its way into a peaceful wood. Tom shook his head, amazed to think all this would belong to him. No, it would not be *his,* but *theirs.* He would share this house with Margaret. He smiled at the thought, once more allowing his mind to fill with pictures of the two of them together.

He was aware, however, that he was probably painting too idyllic a vision. Margaret could still change her mind. Tom was not naïve enough to think he had won her over completely. Perhaps even now she was thinking it would be better to lose her estate than be forever linked to a shopkeeper–farmer–gold miner who was trying— and not always successfully—to live as a gentleman. She would have good cause to think so, he thought, remembering how close he had come to fisticuffs with Carter in the midst of an elegant party. Tom scrubbed a hand through his hair and focused once more on the peaceful landscape. He was fully aware of one other trait he had in abundance, and that was stubbornness. Margaret was meant to be his. His elation when she was in his arms, her lips pressed against his, had told him so in no uncertain terms. If Margaret refused to marry him, he would just keep on pursuing her until she said yes.

*

Margaret paused at the door of the library, taking a moment to look at Tom before making her presence known. He stood with one arm against the door frame, his broad shoulders outlined in sharp silhouette by the late-day sun. He looked at ease standing there. *Too much at ease,* she thought as a prickly sense of worry walked down her spine.

She'd been turning over the day's events in her mind, her indecision growing. Could she really marry someone she hardly knew, someone so different from the kind of man she had always envisioned for a husband? She had tried to tell herself the other alternatives were far worse. Yet now, as she watched Tom surveying the grounds as though he already owned the place, all her fears rose up again tenfold. Perhaps he was already planning what he would do once he was in control of Moreton Hall.

Well, he won't be, she thought, stepping determinedly into the room. He had promised her a partnership. Maybe that was just a pretense to win her over, but she would make sure he lived up to it. He might bully some men around—she had seen him do it with her own eyes—but he would *not* bully her. "Enjoying the view?" she said caustically.

He turned. His face was in shadow, but she felt him looking her over from head to foot. "It's not nearly so lovely as you are," he said as he walked over and kissed her hand. "May I say you look ravishing this evening, Miss Vaughn."

An unwarranted heat washed over her, which she tried to cool with a light laugh. "Such fancy language. Is that something you were taught during your etiquette lessons?"

"Actually, I learned that one from James Simpson," he admitted with a genial smile.

"Mr. Simpson is a shameless ladies' man and full of empty flattery," Margaret said pointedly, uncomfortably aware that Tom's warm hand still held hers.

His gaze held her, too. "Happily for me, I have no need of empty flattery."

Margaret pulled her hand from his. "Shall we go into dinner?"

She turned toward the door, but Tom stopped her, holding up his arm. "I believe I should escort you. Isn't that the proper thing to do?"

His words gave Margaret pause. In truth, the two of them dining alone was most improper. She ought to have invited additional people—Williams and his daughter, perhaps, or the rector and his wife. But the unforeseen events of the day had set her thoughts in such an uproar that she'd not given any real thought to dinner at all. Of course, if she married Tom, there could be no damage to her reputation—

"Humor me, I beg you," Tom said, cutting into her thoughts. "I want to practice so that I will not embarrass you in public when the time comes."

The irony in his tone worried Margaret. He was the kind of man who probably did not place much stock in the opinions of others. But he proffered his arm once more, and since he was standing between her and the door, she took hold of it and allowed him to lead her into dinner.

Once the soup had been served, and the servers had retired to a more comfortable distance, Tom said, "So tell me about Mr. Williams. He seems to think he's been a valuable asset to you. Would you call that an accurate assessment?"

"Of course," Margaret replied, irked that his question seemed designed to put her on the defensive. "After my father... Well, when I began to look after the affairs of the estate, Mr. Williams took me under his wing, so to speak. He taught me many things about the workings of such a large property. I was very young when he began to work for us, after we had to…that is, after Mr. Browne, the previous land steward, had to retire due to ill health."

Margaret took a long sip from her water goblet. She did not wish to mention that it was her father's drunkenness and compulsive gambling that had made him unfit to manage his affairs, nor did she wish to speak of Mr. Browne's near-criminal ineptitude. But both were gone now, and Mr. Williams had been helping her to bring the estate around. He was far too aware of his value, to be sure, and his arrogance often led him to challenge her authority. But the progress they had made had been worth the occasional battle.

"He seemed ill-informed about the proper treatment of the horses."

She set down her goblet so hard it clunked as it hit the table. "He's a land steward, not a veterinarian," she said frostily. "And in any case, you know nothing about the particulars." Too late she realized how loudly she spoke. She ought to have kept her voice more moderate, especially with the footman in the room.

"You are right," Tom said evenly. "I don't know nearly enough. But I intend to learn." He picked up his soup spoon, but he was still looking at her with a determined expression. "I meant what I said about being involved in everything."

"I would appreciate it if we could discuss this later," Margaret said softly. With a slight motion of her head she indicated the footman, who was arranging something on the sideboard. "When we can be alone."

"As you wish." Tom went back to his soup, and they ate in silence. When Tom reached the bottom of the bowl, he tipped it toward him in order to get the last of the soup onto the spoon.

"Mr. Poole," Margaret said archly, "you must remember to tip the bowl *away* from you, not toward you."

He set down the bowl with a little thud and the spoon followed it with a clank. "Thank you, Miss Vaughn. I had forgotten." He might have been addressing a schoolmarm. Then he added, with a hint of mischief in his eye, "You should have seen the way I used to finish off the soup."

This, thought Margaret with embarrassment, was what she had to look forward to.

When the footman had taken away the soup and set the fish course in front of them, Tom made a show of looking over the variety of forks in front of him. "Let me see... it's this one, isn't it?" He lifted a fork.

Margaret nodded stiffly. She was aware that his playful manner was intended to lighten the mood, but it only irked her.

"I think," Tom said, cutting into his fish, "that you should give me etiquette lessons, just to be sure I have everything right for our wedding breakfast."

There was a clank of metal from the direction of the sideboard, as though something had slipped from the footman's grasp. Margaret looked at him sharply. He'd been trained not to listen, of course. Or at least, not to appear to listen. But she did not doubt he'd heard Tom's mention of the wedding. "Mr. Poole," Margaret hissed, "you *promised*."

"So I did." But he gave her only an apologetic shrug.

Somehow, they kept to more neutral topics during the rest of dinner, whenever they spoke at all. The advancing darkness was evident through the dining room windows by the time they had finished eating. Margaret was relieved when Tom refused to linger over coffee, saying he needed to get Castor back to his stall and a good rubdown.

"Will you walk with me outside?" he asked when they reached the front hall. "There's one more thing I'd like to say to you, out of earshot of the servants."

Margaret studied him warily. His ways were far too unconventional. "You know a gentleman would not ask this of a lady."

"Just to the edge of the drive," he pressed. "The grass is still wet from the rain, and we must be mindful of your shoes."

It was an oblique reference to the dinner party at the Somervilles', when Tom had ultimately shown himself more than willing to see to her needs. He spoke with such cheerful deference that she found herself grudgingly agreeing to his request.

"What did you wish to say to me?" Margaret asked when they had reached the edge of the gravel drive.

Tom drew her a few steps farther down the drive, until they had stepped out of the light streaming from the mansion windows and were bathed only in moonlight. He took her face in his hands, an intimate gesture that set her pulse racing. She could just make out his features as he gently brushed her cheek. "Your skin is so soft," he murmured. "So delicate for such a robust and determined lady."

She tried to think of some retort, but her mind was

stupidly a blank. She was aware only of the lovely sensations he was drawing with his touch.

He drew his thumb gently across her lower lip. "I propose that we should end every night with a good-night kiss," he murmured. "And that we should begin tonight. What are your thoughts on the matter?"

Margaret's heart hammered wildly. "Well, I…" She tried to remind herself of his nosy questions, his barely civilized manners, the way he threatened the very foundations of her self-sufficiency. But she could trap none of these things in her mind—they flitted through her brain and were gone, like the moths in the night.

Her mouth went dry. Without thinking, she licked her lips. Taking this as a sign of assent, Tom bent his head and touched his lips to hers. It was not a deep, passionate kiss, but light and gentle, unbearably tender and teasing, making her want more. Breathless with anticipation, she waited for him to pull her close.

Instead, he pulled away, and a small sigh escaped him. "Good night, Maggie."

He turned to go.

Wait! she wanted to cry out. But she was speechless, unable to move, the echoing whispers of his kiss still playing across her lips. She stood breathless for quite some time, watching until he was long out of sight.

Chapter 16

The mutton chop is excellent, is it not?" Margaret said. "I do enjoy coming here." She knew her voice had an unnatural sprightliness. She was trying to hide her lingering discomfort over what she was about to divulge to her luncheon companion.

Margaret's unease was lost on Miss Lucinda Cardington, however. She was looking distinctly uncomfortable for reasons of her own. She glanced around the small restaurant, scrutinizing the patrons for what had to be the dozenth time. Joining Margaret for luncheon here at Verey's restaurant on Hanover Street had been for Lucinda an act of unqualified courage.

"Are you worried that someone will accost us?" Margaret asked. "I assure you it's perfectly safe. Women are dining without escorts much more than they used to. Soon it will be quite the thing."

"Oh, I'm sure it's safe. It's just that Mama is so terribly old-fashioned. If she finds out I've come here, she'll be livid. She thinks I'm shopping on Regent Street."

"Well, then, everything depends on the loyalty of your footman, doesn't it?" Margaret nodded toward the window, where they could see Lucinda's footman standing outside, waiting like a sentry keeping watch.

"Yes, he's very discreet," Lucinda confirmed. "He's had to accompany me on some journeys to the darker parts of London, where I've been working to help the poor. Places that would make Mama faint dead away in horror."

"Well, this is hardly such a place. And since we're only two steps from Regent Street, you can pick up a new set of gloves or a shawl on your way home, and your alibi will be intact."

"In fact, it's the proximity to Regent Street that has me worried," Lucinda said with another nervous glance out the window. "Someone might recognize my footman and realize I'm inside."

"*Someone* as in your little sister, perhaps?" Margaret teased.

"Exactly. She's no longer little, unfortunately. Now that she is fully out in society, she's had plenty of opportunities to observe my actions. More than once she's tattled on me for some supposed offense."

"Then she is still *little*," Margaret averred. "Infantile."

"I feel I should not comment on that remark," Lucinda said sagely, although she brought her napkin to her lips to hide a tiny smile. "However, there is nothing here that Mama could find objectionable. The place is clean and orderly, and the clientele quite respectable. Governesses, and the like. And old maids." Seeing Margaret's eyebrows raise, she added hastily, "I'm speaking of myself, of course. Not you. Even though your engagement to

Mr. Denault has ended, you will find someone else. You're beautiful."

Lucinda said this with such sincerity that Margaret felt a sting of tears in her eyes. When she came to London, Margaret had been introduced to countless members of society, but she had been careful to keep a formal distance from everyone. There were too many things about her situation that she had to hide. But one night she'd found herself chatting with Lucinda at a dinner party. It hadn't taken long for Lucinda to win her over with her sensible conversation, so different from the vacuous drivel being spouted by the other society misses.

"It takes more than beauty to find a husband," Margaret said. "And I don't believe for a moment that you will end up an old maid. Times are changing, and quite rapidly. Even our visit to this restaurant is proof of that. You're different from all the other vapid society ladies. Someday, someone will realize what a catch you are and scoop you up and marry you."

"You must also believe in fairy tales," Lucinda said robustly. But she gave Margaret a grateful smile and went back to her mutton and potatoes.

This was as good an opening as any. "Actually, Lucinda, the subject of marriage is why I asked you here. I...have some news."

"Oh?" Lucinda looked up. "Is it good news?"

"I believe so," Margaret responded hesitantly.

"You're engaged again—how wonderful!" Lucinda exclaimed, immediately coming to the obvious conclusion. "Who is this most fortunate gentleman?"

Margaret's smile faded at Lucinda's use of the word *gentleman*. Tom Poole was so different from the kind of man she had expected to marry. Was she really making the right decision?

"Don't tell me it's Mr. Plimpton," Lucinda said, misinterpreting Margaret's uneasiness. "He's far too old, even if he is rich."

"No, it's not Mr. Plimpton," Margaret said, unable to repress a shiver at the thought. A widower twice over, despite his riches, Mr. Plimpton was considered one of London's most *in*eligible bachelors—by the ladies, at least. Even if their grasping mothers did not agree.

"Thank heaven. Well, then, who is it?" Lucinda prompted.

Margaret hesitated, taking a deep breath and another sip of ale. This was the first time she would be telling this to anyone, apart from her solicitors. "I'm going to marry Mr. Tom Poole."

"Truly?" Lucinda's eyes danced with happy astonishment. "How brilliant!"

"Do you really think so?" Margaret said in surprise. "So you know him?"

"Of course. His brother-in-law is Lord Somerville—such an excellent man." She sighed, and her face reddened.

"I'm sorry—is this a painful subject?" Margaret said apologetically. She had heard that at one time many people thought Lord Somerville was going to marry Lucinda.

"No, no." Lucinda waved away Margaret's worry. "There was never any actual understanding between Lord Somerville and me. He would have been too honorable to break off an official engagement."

"What sort of man is he, really?" Margaret asked. "Mr. Poole, I mean."

"He's handsome and rich. What more do you need?" Lucinda giggled, an uncharacteristic sound for her. "Oh dear, I sound like Emily now, don't I?" She gave Margaret a reassuring smile. "I have had occasion to speak with Mr. Poole several times. Our family even dined at their home, although my mother—" She cut herself off, shaking her head.

"Go on," Margaret said. "What about your mother?" Most probably the lofty Lady Cardington did not approve of this nouveau riche man among the more rarefied folk.

"Well, never mind about that," Lucinda said. "The point is that Mr. Poole seems a most honest and kind gentleman. I think at times he feels awkward at society events, but I do not consider that a fatal flaw."

"Some say he lacks manners because of his humble origins," Margaret pointed out. "They say he will never fit in."

"Are you really so concerned about fitting in?" Lucinda asked with a chiding grin. "I think you're too intelligent for that. And besides, I've been born and bred in society, and I don't feel comfortable at formal gatherings, either. I'm always making some faux pas or other and driving my mother to her wits' end."

"What a diplomat you would make," Margaret said, amused by Lucinda's unique way of looking at problems. "If only women were allowed to hold such positions."

Lucinda smiled at this remark, but merely said, "I think Mr. Poole is a man of principle. Surely that's what's important, isn't it?"

Again, with the soul of a diplomat, Lucinda had discerned the heart of the matter. Lucinda had blamed Paul's lack of scruples for the broken engagement, even though Margaret had never been able to tell her the whole story. Margaret was painfully aware of her own role in the near disaster, but she was grateful for Lucinda's fierce loyalty.

"I suppose you will want me to act as your bridesmaid," Lucinda said with resignation. "Even though I am terrified about standing up in front of all those people. Who will be standing up with Mr. Poole?"

"I believe he is going to ask Mr. James Simpson to be the best man."

"Mr. Simpson!"

Another flush turned Lucinda's face to a fiery red. Margaret thought she couldn't look any more dismayed. "Are you embarrassed to stand up in church with him? I know he has a reputation for being somewhat of a rogue—"

"It's fine," Lucinda broke in. "It just seems odd to picture him as a groomsman. Especially since he is always saying he will never get married himself." She hastily finished the last of her ale. "Shall we settle the bill? It's getting late and Mama really will suspect something if I don't return soon."

As they walked out into the street a few minutes later, Lucinda said, "I confess I will miss having another single lady to commiserate with. I've enjoyed our brief time together. On the other hand, perhaps I might now accompany you when you are out and about. Married ladies have so much more freedom."

"I wouldn't be too sure of that," Margaret cautioned. Although she had a legal document giving her joint power over her estate, Margaret still had concerns. Was a person really free when they were yoked to another? What if her heart truly became entwined with this man?

If her heart gave up its independence, surely the rest would follow all too easily.

*

"You're doing *what?*" Lizzie exclaimed.

Tom stood in the parlor, patiently awash in the astounded exclamations of his sister and brother-in-law. He had expected this, of course. It was one of the reasons he'd put off telling them. That, plus he wanted to make sure the marriage was actually going to happen.

"I'm going to marry Miss Vaughn," he repeated. The papers had been signed, and he and Margaret had come to an agreement on how the land should be settled. The lawyers had been amazed, of course. That Mr. Hawthorne, especially. But he'd nearly managed to hide it under the usual sanguine expression that was the stock in trade for solicitors.

Lizzie's reaction was much more vibrant. "Oh, my dear brother!" She held out her arms and he obligingly knelt down by the chair so she could hug him. "I thought some plan was on your mind when you brought her to dinner." She grinned and pinched his cheek. "I saw the way you looked at her. I had no doubt you were smitten."

"Was it really that evident?" Tom said, smiling.

"Oh, I shall be so happy to have a sister-in-law!" Lizzie continued brightly. "And I'm ecstatic because it means you'll be staying in England. Just think—you'll be a proper member of the gentry! When is the wedding? Next spring?"

"In fact, we have planned it for three weeks from tomorrow."

"Oh! So soon!" Lizzie's face fell. "That means I won't be able to attend, I'm afraid."

Tom hated to see regret dampening her excitement. He adjusted one of the cushions in her chair. "I know how badly you wanted to see me get married. You've been telling me so for years," he teased. "I'm sorry you won't be there, but I'll find a way to make it up to you."

"Marriage is an awfully big step," Geoffrey said. "Why the rush?"

"Well, there is a need for haste."

Geoffrey's eyebrows rose. Lizzie fanned herself. "Merciful heavens," she giggled.

"I don't mean it in *that* way," Tom amended quickly. "Everything between us has been perfectly proper. But she has some legal and financial affairs that need attending to right away. As her husband I will be in a better position to help her."

Geoffrey shook his head, still unconvinced. "Are you sure you've thought this through completely?"

"He's right," Lizzie said reluctantly. "You do have a tendency to leap rather swiftly into action."

Tom paced to the fireplace, then paused when he realized he was illustrating what Lizzie had just said. It was true; he preferred action. But he wanted to assure them he was no longer as reckless as he had once been. "Trust me, we've been over everything carefully. The lawyers have drawn up all the papers—"

"I'm speaking of more than legalities," Geoffrey said. "What I mean is, how well do you really know her?"

"Know her?" At times Tom felt he knew her like his own soul. At other times, she was a complete mystery. In Tom's mind, the real question was whether he wanted to know *more,* and the answer to that was unequivocally yes. But he did not think that answer would alleviate

Geoffrey's concerns, so he said instead, "You know her story. She comes from an old and well-respected family. Her father's death two years ago left her with no immediate relatives." He saw no need to mention Margaret's cousins, since they had been cut out of her life.

"Perhaps the more important question is what does she know of *our* family?" Geoffrey said. "How much have you told her about your past? Or about Lizzie? About why the two of you went to Australia?"

It was an issue that could not be ignored. Years before, Lizzie had fallen in love with a wealthy young man named Freddie Hightower. Seducing her with promises of marriage, Hightower had taken her to Europe only to abandon her there. Tom had shot him in a duel and then fled to Australia, taking Lizzie with him. No one outside their immediate family knew this part of her past. They knew only that Lizzie had been living in Australia when she'd learned of her connection to the Thornboroughs and decided to return to England.

Lizzie grasped a cushion and held it tightly, her forehead creased with worry. "I hadn't thought of that! Tom, will she keep our secret? If anyone else should discover my scandal...that would be disastrous..."

Tom swiftly returned to her side. "Don't worry, Lizzie. You and I made a pact long ago never to speak of those events. There will be no need for Margaret to keep that secret, because she will never know it."

"It is not a good start to a marriage to be keeping things from your wife," Geoffrey said with concern. "Marriage ought to be based on full openness and trust."

"But doesn't it say in Psalms that God forgives our sins and remembers them no more?" Tom asked earnestly. "Shouldn't we also live that way, and not bring up past mistakes that the Lord has already forgiven us for?"

"You are turning into quite the Bible scholar, Tom," Lizzie said, but her voice held gentle reproof. "Don't forget Geoffrey is an ordained clergyman. He has great knowledge in these matters."

"I beg your pardon, Geoffrey," Tom said. "I meant no disrespect. However, I believe we must keep this matter private."

A long silence followed this pronouncement, while Geoffrey considered Tom's words and Lizzie looked at them both anxiously. At last Geoffrey sighed and said, "As you wish. I have had my say, but you must do as you see fit."

Tom knew it was the right answer. Lizzie let out a great sigh, her eyes misting with tears as she told Geoffrey, "I must confess I am relieved."

Geoffrey still looked troubled but he simply said, "We will take things one day at a time."

Lizzie gave him a grateful smile, then turned back to Tom. "And now, dear brother, I have one more thing to ask you."

"Anything," Tom said.

"Well . . . to be honest . . . when you returned to London I had worried that you would be beset by fortune hunters. But instead, you are engaged to someone who is rich already!" She beamed. "Does this mean Margaret understands what a treasure *you* are? I can see how much you love her, but tell me—does she return your love?"

This was a question with no simple answer. Margaret *did* need his money. But never, ever would he think of her as a fortune hunter. After all, he had pursued *her*, hadn't he? Not the other way around. All he knew for sure as he looked into his sister's clear, wide eyes, so full of love and completely without guile, was that he could not lie to her. So he simply said with a hint of self-deprecation, "Margaret is willing to marry me. Does not love make fools of us all?"

Chapter 17

The morning fog was dense, slowing the pace of Margaret's carriage as it brought her to the ceremony that would change her life forever. So many details of this day were exactly as she had laid them out weeks before. She was dressed in a fine white dress and lace veil, and would be married in a large church in front of hundreds of well-wishers. She and the groom would host a wedding breakfast so grand that they had to hire a banquet hall, as there was not enough room in her hired house to hold all the guests. Then they would return to Lincolnshire and begin the task of revitalizing Moreton Hall.

There was just one, vitally significant difference: the groom.

Margaret twisted her hands in her lap, toying with a delicately embroidered handkerchief. Was today proof that she could meet disaster and still come out victorious, or was she the butt of a very elaborate joke planned by the Fates? She had done all she could to be sure it was the former. The lawyers had drawn up everything to her satisfaction, amazed at the concessions Tom had willingly made.

Yet still she felt uneasy. Once they were married, any number of things might turn out to be beyond her control. Her lawyers had confirmed Tom's financial status through a variety of reliable sources, and yet Tom's choice of a business partner worried her. Sullivan was an ex-convict. He'd been sent down to Australia for murder and theft. Although the murder charge had been commuted, could a man such as that really be trusted?

And what about Tom himself? Everyone was of the opinion that Tom was an honorable man, but many had been fooled by Paul, too. She could not be totally sure the legal agreements were safe from challenge. Tom might well be able to get them overturned in a court of law if he put his mind and resources to it. Lord Somerville had vouched for him—surely she should trust the word of a clergyman? She gave a small, hollow laugh. She'd never known a man of the cloth to be reliable simply because of a title the church chose to give him.

"I'm glad to hear you laugh, miss," Bessie said. "'Tis your wedding day, after all, and you seem far too sad about it." She gave Margaret a sunny smile. "This is the beginning of brighter days, is it not? The mourning has turned to singing."

Margaret sighed, twisting the handkerchief tighter, wishing she had Bessie's simple optimism.

The carriage came to a stop. Dozens of carriages lined the street, evidence of the number of people who had come to the ceremony. Lord Somerville stood waiting at the church door. He helped Margaret descend from the carriage. Behind her, Bessie took hold of the back of her gown to enable it to flow unhindered behind her as she stepped down.

"Everyone is ready," Lord Somerville said with a smile. "All that is needed is the bride."

Suddenly, Margaret had a wild urge to flee, to climb back into the carriage and ride off as swiftly as she could. Why could she not settle in her heart that she was doing the right thing?

Lord Somerville patted her hand, which she realized was gripping his arm tightly. "Don't worry, Miss Vaughn; it's natural to get jitters on your wedding day. I will tell you quite confidentially that Tom has been unable to speak a coherent word all morning."

He was trying to set her at ease, but his words only added to Margaret's qualms. Was Tom having regrets? It still seemed unreal to Margaret that they were all here, that this wedding was going forward. But as Lord Somerville began to lead her toward the church door, she had to face the fact that this was indeed very real. Taking a deep breath, Margaret tried to relax the worry wrinkles in her forehead, but that did nothing to ease her inner trepidation.

Lord Somerville's keen dark eyes were watching her with compassion. "*Believe* that the Lord has brought you to this day, Margaret. Put your trust in Him."

Believe. Trust.

It was a large thing to ask of a God she knew little about.

*

Tom stood at the altar, listening as the church bells struck the hour. He was astounded at the number of people here.

The law required that all weddings be open for anyone who wished to attend, and clearly there were plenty who wanted to see this one. Ushers had carefully weeded out the crowd, allowing invited guests to sit in the front pews while the mere onlookers sat or stood in the back.

Tom was too nervous to look at the congregation directly. He kept his eyes fixed on the altar, with occasional glances at the clergyman standing placidly in front of him. Once or twice Tom had looked toward the wide church door at the opposite end of the church, searching for Margaret. This had been a useless endeavor, as his vision was blocked by a sea of bonnets and top hats. On the clergyman's right side stood Margaret's bridesmaid, Miss Lucinda Cardington. She tried to bolster Tom with an encouraging smile, but her cheeks were awash with red and the bouquet she held was trembling.

Only James looked perfectly at ease, not at all concerned that hundreds of eyes were fastened on them. "Let's hope the bride arrives on time," he said as the final stroke of the bell vibrated through the church. "I'm famished, and I want to get to that wedding breakfast."

"Is that all you can think about?" Tom asked. "The food?"

"Well, the champagne is on my mind, too, of course," he said with a wink. "But that goes without saying."

Lucinda gave a small gasp at this remark, but Tom wasn't surprised. He knew James would always find something humorous to say, no matter what the situation.

The soft murmurs of the crowd began to fade, replaced by a rustling as everyone stood up. Margaret and Geoffrey must be making their entrance. Tom held his breath, waiting for the first glimpse of his bride.

And there she was. The worries that had besieged Tom all morning fell away as he stared at her in wonder. Her silvery dress was decorated at the throat and waist with orange blossoms, as was the wreath of flowers in her hair.

His heart stuttered as he watched her walk up the aisle on Geoffrey's arm, moving in solemn, measured strides with that elegant grace of hers. A veil of sheer lace cascaded down the length of her back, fluttering as she walked. She looked straight ahead, as though unaware of the hundreds of people crowding both sides of the aisle. Her face was unmoving, like a fine marble statue. She was regal, unearthly. A vision of beauty. And very soon, she would be his. It was a sacred trust that he would honor with all that was in him.

The knot in his throat made him wish his valet had not tied his cravat so tightly. *Dear Lord,* he thought, overcome with the magnitude of his joy. *Dear Lord.*

"She is lovely, isn't she?" James whispered. "Congratulations, old man."

At last, Margaret and Geoffrey reached the altar. Tom fancied that he could smell the tart scent of the orange blossoms decorating her hair and dress. She stood, perfectly poised, not quite meeting his gaze.

The minister motioned for the guests to sit down. Once the rustling had ceased, he began. "Dearly beloved, we are gathered together here in the sight of God, and in the face of this congregation, to join together this man and this woman in holy matrimony, which is an honorable estate, instituted of God..."

As the minister continued in slow, measured tones, Tom stole a glance at Margaret. Her face, still perfectly composed, gave no indication of what she was thinking. Did she love him? Sadly, Tom knew the answer to that question already. But *could* she love him? Would she grow to love him in time?

"It is not to be taken in hand unadvisedly, lightly, or wantonly, but reverently, discreetly, advisedly, soberly, and in the fear of God."

Tom believed these words. He believed them with his whole heart. And he would keep praying that his own reverence for God would someday grow to be hers as well. *Lord, I will love her, protect and cherish her. Please allow her heart to open, and cause her love to grow.*

With this prayer, peace settled upon him. His restless anticipation had not left him, but the worry had. This marriage—and all that would come—was in the Lord's hands now.

*

Margaret kept her gaze fixed on a spot just beyond the minister's left shoulder. She feared that if she looked at Tom, all her uncertainties would burst forth and bring her, trembling, to collapse.

"Tom Poole, wilt thou have this woman to be thy wedded wife, to live together after God's ordinance in the holy estate of matrimony? Wilt thou love her, comfort her, honor and keep her in sickness and in health, and, forsaking all others, keep thee only unto her, so long as ye both shall live?"

She felt Tom's eyes upon her, felt the heat of his gaze. "I will." He spoke with utter assurance.

"Margaret Vaughn, wilt thou have this man to be thy

wedded husband, to live together after God's ordinance in the holy estate of matrimony? Wilt thou obey him, and serve him, love, honor, and keep him in sickness and in health, and, forsaking all others, keep thee only unto him, so long as ye both shall live?"

Obey. Serve. Love.

Margaret had been to many weddings; she had heard these words before. But never had she truly considered their significance. Now she realized how unprepared she was. She'd been raised to see the wedding as a mere ritual to be gotten through so that the real business of marriage—the sharing of wealth, the elevation in society—could begin. But she had heard Tom's firm answer, and she had had time enough over these few weeks to see his unshakable trust in God. He would not take the wedding vows lightly, and he would expect no less from her. She closed her mouth and swallowed hard, her throat too dry to allow speech.

The silence lengthened. There was a nervous rustling in the congregation, and one or two people coughed. The minister looked at her questioningly. Lucinda gave her a tremulous smile, although her eyes were clouded with concern. But still, Margaret could not speak.

She tried to tell herself that perhaps these *were* mere words. After all, Tom had spoken of their partnership, of the ways this marriage would benefit them both. He had not spoken directly of love—although when he had kissed her, when he had called her Maggie . . . she gasped as the memory of it lit a fire of need that threatened, even now, to consume her.

I should not be marrying this man, she thought wildly. *I should not marry someone who can weaken my resolve so easily.* For that was the crux of it—Margaret had lost herself too readily in Tom's arms. It was above all things what she feared the most. She had always stood alone, dependent upon no one else, for that was the only way to keep the demons and the hurt at bay. To trust others brought only disappointment and bitter sorrow. Hadn't that been proven to her time and time again?

And yet, she was committed to marry this man, and it was far too late to turn back now. Margaret reached down for the inner strength that had always been her mainstay. She reminded herself that she must save Moreton Hall—save her inheritance and the only home she had ever known. And no matter what happened, she would never, ever let down the guard around her heart. When she finally found her voice, it was clearly audible and unwavering. "I will."

A collective sigh of relief echoed through the church.

The minister smoothly continued on to the next part, but Margaret was barely conscious of what was happening. She had the sense that she was being pulled across a vast chasm to a place entirely unknown, like the old maps in her father's library that marked such places *terra incognita.* The minister placed Tom's right hand in hers, and Tom recited his vows perfectly. Margaret had to rely on soft prompts from the minister, and stumbled more than once over the words.

Her resolve to be strong, to not allow herself to be carried away by emotion, nearly crumbled when Tom placed the gold band upon her finger and said, "With this ring I thee wed." Something in his voice irresistibly called to her, and at last—at last—she was brave enough to raise her eyes to meet his. "With my body I thee worship," he continued, stunning her with the intensity of his gaze. "And with all my worldly goods I thee endow."

She could only stare at him, her heart lodged in her throat.

The minister gently set a hand on their shoulders, indicating for them to kneel. Margaret sank down easily, still reeling. From somewhere above them, the minister said, "Let us pray."

As the minister prayed aloud, Margaret's heart filled, uncharacteristically, with a prayer of its own. *Lord, if it's true that you hear our innermost prayers, I beg that you hear mine. Please let this man be all he says he is. And please, help me...*

It was surely not the right thing to pray, but it was the best she could do.

When the prayer was over, Tom helped Margaret to rise, his hand firm and reassuring beneath her elbow. The minister took their right hands, placed them together, and announced, "Those whom God hath joined together let no man put asunder."

Lucinda was crying tears of joy, and even James Simpson seemed moved. Lord Somerville's expression was more contemplative.

As the minister presented them to the congregation, Margaret looked into a sea of smiling faces. Perhaps the worst was past, she thought with a twinge of hope. But she suddenly felt Tom tense beside her. She followed his gaze to see what had startled him. There, in the back row of the church, stood Paul Denault.

Her stomach gave a sickening lurch. Why had he come? Had morbid curiosity brought him here? Was he wondering what this day would have been like had *he* been standing in the groom's place? Or was he thanking his lucky stars for his narrow escape?

Tom's joyous expression had changed to one of near murder. "What is it?" Margaret asked. "Does Paul's presence here upset you?"

"Denault can go to hell as far as I'm concerned. I'd even give him train fare to go there."

"Then what—"

Her question was cut short by the minister, who was instructing them to follow him into the church office to sign the wedding registry. With great reluctance, it seemed, Tom turned, preparing to follow him. Margaret, still clinging to his arm, did the same.

"Who is the man standing next to Denault?" Tom hissed under his breath.

Margaret twisted to look back, getting a quick look over her shoulder before her view was cut off by James, Lucinda, and Geoffrey, who were following them to the church office. Now it was her turn to start in surprise. Her cousin, Richard Spencer, was standing next to Paul. Why had she not noticed him before?

Surely it was mere coincidence that they should be standing together. She did not think they could know each other. She managed one more quick glance before they were ushered into the church office and the door closed behind them. Richard was speaking into Paul's ear, and Paul was listening with a self-satisfied grin.

"Who is that man?" Tom said fiercely.

"It's Richard Spencer. My cousin."

"Your cousin!"

He said this with such alarm that the minister paused, lifting his pen.

"I beg your pardon, sir," Tom said, moderating his voice.

The minister proffered the pen to Margaret. "Be sure to sign the register with your maiden name," he reminded her.

As she accepted the pen, Tom said softly, "Let me get this clear. The man in the gray coat and waistcoat, the one on Denault's left, that is your cousin?"

Margaret's hands were unaccountably shaky as she dipped the pen into the inkwell. "Yes, he is my cousin, but we are...well, estranged." She signed her name, *Margaret Louise Vaughn,* for one last time. She looked at it and sighed, but there was no time to dwell on it. She was Mrs. Tom Poole, and the sooner she got used to it the better. She straightened and handed the pen to Tom.

"Estranged?" Tom repeated, his voice sharp although he was keeping it low.

"Yes, I told you before. Our families had a falling out some years ago, and we've had little to do with one another since."

Tom's face darkened. "Do you mean to tell me that is the man who thinks he should own Moreton Hall?"

"Yes."

Tom gripped the pen with grim determination as he bent down to sign his name with sure, quick strokes and said, "I have a very bad feeling we'll be seeing much more of him in the future."

Chapter 18

"Is everything all right?" James asked Tom.

James and Lucinda had finished adding their names to the register as witnesses, and they were all filing out of the church office. The congregation would be waiting to cheer their exit, throwing rice and shouting well wishes.

"Nothing to concern yourself over," Tom said tersely. Tom had not recognized Spencer when he'd briefly run into him at the tavern after meeting with Denault. But today as he saw him in the church, Tom realized who he was, and a whole host of bad memories rushed to the forefront of his mind. Spencer had been present when Tom shot Freddie Hightower seven years ago. He'd acted as an impromptu second when Tom had pulled Hightower from a tavern and challenged him then and there to a duel. Tom could still hear Spencer's shouts as he'd gripped his bleeding friend, promising retribution.

Tom had not known his name at the time, but he did now. What was worse, he had just married into the man's family. Judging from the way Spencer was looking at him, he had recognized Tom, too. It wouldn't take long for him to figure out that Lizzie was the woman Hightower had seduced and abandoned all those years ago. Lizzie was a respectable married woman now, but if Spencer began to spread word about her past, her reputation would be ruined. Tom had to find a way to stop that from happening. He had a grim foreboding that it wasn't going to be easy.

"If nothing is wrong, you might want to stop glowering," James admonished. "You've just gotten married, you know. You're supposed to look happy. Lord knows I'd be wearing your look if *I* had just gotten married, but that's a different matter."

"Do you know Richard?" Margaret asked worriedly.

"We'll talk about it later," Tom said harshly.

She started back as though she'd been stung, and Tom immediately regretted his tone. He did not want to hurt her, no matter what he was going through. He brought her hand up to kiss it. "Right now, I have a date at a wedding breakfast with my beautiful bride."

This seemed to appease her. She gave him a tiny smile that wavered a little, the first crack he'd seen today in her normally impenetrable exterior. Tom caressed her cheek with the back of his hand. "I love it when you smile like that," he said gently. "Perhaps in the future we can find more of them." Certainly he had wanted nothing more than to give her reasons to smile. Spencer, however, worried him.

Ahead of them, the minister addressed the crowd. "Ladies and gentlemen, may I present Mr. and Mrs. Tom Poole."

There were cheers and applause as Tom and Margaret made their way down the aisle. They were nearly to the door when Tom saw Denault and Spencer again.

"Welcome to the family," Spencer said drily.

The way the man looked at him—practically sneering—made Tom want to punch him right then and there. Only the pressure of the crowd behind them, who were now in a great hurry to leave the church, kept him from saying more than, "We must talk."

"Oh, we'll talk," Spencer replied. "You can be sure of that." He looked to Margaret and added, "My heartiest felicitations to you, dear cousin."

"Hello, Richard." Her voice was cool.

Margaret squeezed Tom's arm gently. Clearly she did not wish to linger, and neither did he. This was neither the time nor the place to settle old scores. That would have to wait. Tom leveled a flat, unfriendly smile at Spencer, then led Margaret out the door. Later he would find out exactly what had transpired between the Vaughns and the Spencers. He was beginning to understand why Margaret had been so vehement that the Spencers would never own Moreton Hall.

The open carriage awaited them just outside the church door, gaily festooned with flowers and ribbons. The sight of it brought Tom once more back to the reason he was here. Pushing aside his worries about Spencer, Tom shielded Margaret as they hurried through a pelting rain of rice. They were both breathless when they reached the carriage. Tom helped her in and was about to signal to the driver to move forward when an object came hurtling into the carriage. It fell with a *thunk* at their feet. He bent down to pick it up. "A shoe?" he asked, bewildered.

"For good luck," Margaret said, taking the shoe. "Who threw it, I wonder?" She turned to look back at the crowd. Her lady's maid, Bessie, was standing some distance away, well behind the upper-crust well-wishers but within throwing distance of the carriage. She waved vigorously, a broad grin on her face. Margaret gave her a tiny wave of acknowledgment. "I should have known it would be Bessie. She never forgets any of those old country customs."

Soon they were traveling at a brisk pace down the street, leaving the crowd behind. Tom savored the joy of having Margaret—his wife—next to him. She was his now, *to have and to hold*. He could not deny that he was looking forward to holding her. He wanted to do that right now, in fact. He wanted to kiss her thoroughly right here in the carriage, so anxious was he to taste her soft lips again and to feel her body pressed against his.

She would not thank him for it, he knew. They were in an open carriage in bright daylight, and there was a certain level of propriety to uphold. He contented himself by once more kissing her hand, inhaling the soft scent of her skin. "At last we are alone, and I can tell you how lovely you look today," he said. He turned her hand over and kissed the inside of her wrist. "And tonight, when we are truly alone, I plan to shower you with many more compliments."

To his surprise, his words had the opposite effect of what he'd intended. Margaret stiffened, and the gaiety he had seen in her face just moments ago faded. She reached up to adjust her veil, which had been displaced by the breeze. "I have Bessie to thank for the fine job she did with my dress and hair. And how amazing that she thought to throw a shoe for good luck! She really is invaluable. You know, it's so difficult to find good help, someone who is both loyal and talented."

She spoke in a rush, her voice oddly high-pitched. Tom guessed what was going on. For all of her bravado and the capable way she'd handled business affairs, there were many things she had not yet done, areas of life in which she was completely inexperienced. "Are you afraid?" he asked gently.

"Afraid?" she repeated. She licked her lips. "However do you mean?"

"I think you know." He took hold of her hand once again, this time entwining his fingers through hers. He found this thrilled him in a way that made the simple gesture seem far more intimate. She sucked in a breath. Seeing she really was afraid, he hastened to reassure her. "I won't...that is, we won't..." He stumbled over the words. "What I mean is, I can wait until you are ready."

Margaret's green eyes were unfathomable, like the ocean itself. "Thank you," she said softly.

Her words sent a bolt of disappointment through him. He'd been hoping against hope that waiting would not be necessary, that she would come to him tonight, without hesitation. But that was not likely to be the case. *You had best cool your ardor,* he told himself. *You may have a longer wait than you realize.*

Margaret cleared her throat, and Tom saw with a pang of regret that her usual cool self-possession was returning. "What was going on back there with you and Richard?" she asked. "Have you two met before?"

Tom leaned back and sighed, running a hand through his hair. There was no escaping the fact that Spencer had thrown a pall over what should have been a much happier day. "We met once. It was years ago, before I left for Australia. He was friends with a man I knew. Freddie Hightower." Despite his best efforts, he spoke the name with a bitterness that Margaret did not miss.

"Hightower? The man who died at the Thornborough estate last year?"

"Yes—how did you know about that?"

"The gossip mill. It was one of many pieces of information I picked up after I came to London and began to make my way in society." She looked at him thoughtfully. "Does this animosity between you and Richard have something to do with Mr. Hightower's death?"

"It's a long story, and we are almost at the banquet hall. We'll talk more this evening." In truth, Tom needed more time to think through what he would tell Margaret. How could he explain his connection with Spencer and yet still keep Lizzie's secret? He would have to use care. Tom gave a sigh of resignation. Of all the things he had hoped to do on his wedding night, discussing Spencer had certainly not been on the list.

*

Tom sorely wished they'd opted for a traditional wedding breakfast at home, with only close friends and family attending. Instead, they'd rented this large banquet hall for an ostentatious feast. Margaret had insisted that this was the newest trend, and Tom had seen no reason to argue. He knew that suffering through an interminable wedding feast would be a trial, but he figured it was a small price to pay to make Margaret happy.

Two hours had passed since the guests had arrived

and been served. Somehow Tom had made it through dozens of toasts and the many assurances (from people who barely knew them) that theirs was bound to be a long and felicitous marriage.

Throughout it all, Tom had done his best *not* to think about Spencer. He was glad now that Lizzie's delicate condition had prevented her from attending the wedding. He did not want Spencer anywhere near her until Tom had been able to warn her and Geoffrey about the hazard he presented.

Champagne was flowing freely although it was only two o'clock in the afternoon, and everyone had eaten their fill of beef, chicken, sweetbreads, and puddings. Tom did not mind the expense, but he marveled at how much a hundred people could consume, especially when someone else was paying for it. At last, the food having been devoured and the wedding cake served, most of the guests rose from their tables and began milling about, greeting one another with champagne-induced friendliness, making sure they were seeing and being seen by every other attendee, the mark of their social status that they had been invited to this grand event.

"Will you excuse me?" Margaret murmured after she and Tom had finished greeting yet another in the endless stream of well-wishers. "I must go find the ladies' retiring room."

"Shall I escort you?" Tom asked. For the first time he noticed small circles under her eyes, signs of fatigue that she had been doing her best to hide. The strain of the day was beginning to wear on her.

"That won't be necessary." She disengaged herself from his arm. "I'll be back shortly."

Tom watched her thread her way through the crowd. He could not help but be reminded of the night he had met her, how he'd watched her much as he was doing now. How much had changed since then. The best change was that Margaret was no longer on another man's arm. She was his now, in name at least. He was determined to do all he could to capture her heart as well, even if it took the rest of his life to do it.

A dozen conversations buzzed around him. Tom's hearing was excellent, having been well honed during his time in the Australian wilderness, where he'd learned to pick out the sounds of animals and bird calls. Many times being alert that a dangerous animal was nearby had saved his life. This luxurious banquet hall was far different, but Tom had the sense that plenty of dangers lurked here, too.

He had no sooner had this thought than he heard a voice say quietly, "Tom Poole. How fortunate that we should meet again."

Tom turned to see Spencer leaning nonchalantly against the wall near a potted plant. "Were you invited?" he said coldly.

Spencer held up his hands. "Shockingly bad taste, I know, to turn up where one isn't invited. But of course, you'd know all about that." He paused to let his insult sink in. "However, I only wanted to offer my personal good wishes to my cousin Margaret. She did tell you that we are cousins, didn't she?"

"She doesn't want you here."

"Neither do you, I'll wager." He moved away from the wall. "You have played this game well, Tom Poole. Now you have married her, and gained Moreton Hall in the bargain."

Tom took a warning step forward, his hands clenching

to fists. "What happens to Moreton Hall will never be any business of yours."

Spencer leveled a hateful glare. "That property should have come to me, and I'll be damned if I'll let you keep your filthy murderous hands on it."

"You don't have any say in the matter."

"Don't I? Suppose I notify the authorities about a certain illegal action you were involved in back in forty-five? Suppose I get you brought before a tribunal for attempted murder?"

Spencer's large and menacing physique was at odds with his university-educated speech. He looked like one of those brute beasts who guard the doors to gambling dens, throwing troublemakers out on their ears. But Tom had faced down worse men, and he wasn't about to cower now. He took another step forward. "I don't have any idea what you're talking about."

Spencer laughed. "You're more cagey than you used to be, aren't you? You used to be all boldness and bluster, barging in like a bull in a china shop. You act so fine and genteel now. But I'll wager it wouldn't take much for your criminal nature to reveal itself."

Rage was rising inside Tom—too familiar, too hard to stop once it broke free. But Tom would not allow it. He had to keep it at bay. For Margaret's sake, he had to avoid an altercation here if at all possible. "If you have something to say, then say it," he said through clenched teeth. "Then get out."

He expected Spencer to say more about the duel. Instead, Spencer said, "Your sister is married to Lord Somerville, isn't she? How in the world did *she* manage to marry a man who is an ordained clergyman?"

Tom fought for self-control. He could not allow this man to manipulate him. "Do not speak ill of my sister," he ordered. "She is a good woman."

"Oh, she's a model of virtue," Spencer replied sarcastically. "But perhaps you heard about the incident that happened last year at the Thornborough estate in Kent? A man died there. A mutual acquaintance of ours. His name was Freddie Hightower."

At the sound of Hightower's name, the murmur of nearby conversations ceased. These people were nothing if not excellent eavesdroppers. Tom had to keep the conversation away from dangerous territory. "Hightower died of natural causes. It's in the coroner's report. It's public knowledge."

Spencer made a scoffing noise. "When has there ever been any correlation between an official report and the truth? Hightower was there for a little assignation with Lizzie—"

Tom grabbed him by the collar and shoved him against the wall. "She is Lady Somerville to you," he ground out.

Spencer delivered a swift, surprising blow to Tom's gut, forcing him to take a step back, gasping. "You are the last person to tell me what to do," he said. "In fact, you'd better heed *my* instructions, unless you want certain information about your sister to get out."

Tom straightened, finding his breath. "If you say anything to slander Lizzie, I will make sure you regret it."

"What will you do? Attack me?" He looked Tom up and down with disdain. "I'd like to see you try."

The last of Tom's resolve snapped, rage twisting his soul and rising so quickly that he was barely conscious of what happened next. His fist connected with Spencer's jaw, sending him backward, knocking over a potted plant as he tried to regain his balance. He recovered quickly, though, in a move that was surprisingly agile. He lunged at Tom, tackling him and sending them both colliding into a nearby table. It collapsed amid the crash of silverware and breaking glass, the force of the fall making him temporarily breathless. But he didn't stop to think. He pushed Spencer off of him and rolled him over on his back against the remnants of the table, hitting Spencer's mouth repeatedly, this time drawing blood.

After that, it was a complete blur. There was nothing except Spencer, the man who threatened everything Tom held dear—the man he wanted to pummel into extinction right here in this banquet hall. All his anger over Hightower's treatment of Lizzie came pouring out into each satisfying punch. But Spencer was a tough foe and he knew how to fight, landing vicious blows of his own.

Through the haze of the fighting he heard Margaret's voice. "Stop! Tom! What are you doing!" But Tom was not about to stop. He was gaining the upper hand; he could see Spencer's strength was flagging. He pulled Spencer to his feet and gave him one last, final shove, sending him over another table and crashing to the floor along with its contents—plates, glasses, and an enormous silver urn. Tom stepped around the pile of debris and looked down to assure himself that Spencer was not going to get up for more. He was out cold, bloody from the fighting and from landing face-first in shards of glass.

The roaring that had filled Tom's ears during the fight was now replaced by an eerie silence. As he stared down at what was left of Spencer, Tom felt, rather than saw, the shocked expressions of everyone in the room.

"Tom Poole!" Margaret's voice broke the silence. She rushed forward and bent down over Spencer, then looked up at Tom with anger. "What have you done?"

Tom clenched his fists, trying to rebottle his rage, trying to regain his equilibrium along with his breath. A quick glance confirmed that their fight had made a shambles of the banqueting hall. But he'd be damned if he was going to show any remorse. "He came here uninvited," he said, as though that explained everything.

Chapter 19

Three hours.

Three hours it had taken to sort out the mess, to clear the guests from the hall as graciously as she could, and to settle with the owner for the damage. It would take far longer to recover from the blow to her good name. Tom Poole had humiliated her publicly. He had shown the world that he was nothing but an ill-bred, lower-class hooligan with no regard for common decency. He had turned their wedding breakfast into a brawl.

It had taken four men to carry Richard out of the hall. Tom had beaten him so viciously it was a miracle he'd not been killed. Even now, the memory of the look on Tom's face during the fight sent chills down Margaret's spine. Even though she had seen him threaten a man before, she had not fully comprehended how dangerously volatile he was. Now that she was his wife, how was she to deal with this dark aspect of his nature?

Margaret paced up and down in the suite of rooms Tom had rented for them in the hotel. She felt trapped in these unfamiliar surroundings, wishing she had not already closed down the town house. Coming here after the wedding breakfast had been her only option. All of her clothes and immediate necessities had been brought here.

"Shall I find some tea, madam?" Bessie asked. "Perhaps some chamomile to help soothe the nerves?" She was sitting in a corner of the room, working on some darning and keeping Margaret company until Tom arrived.

Where was Tom, anyway? He'd left with the men carrying Richard out of the hall, and he'd arranged to get the man home and under a doctor's care. Then he had left, saying grimly that he had something else to attend to. But he had not told her what it was. Nor had he offered any apologies. "Tea won't be necessary," she told Bessie, ignoring her maid's concerned expression. Nothing would calm her until she had given Tom a good piece of her mind.

Margaret whirled from the window as the door opened and Tom walked in. Whatever he'd been up to since they had parted, he'd done nothing to repair his disheveled appearance. His cravat was loose, his shirt collar smudged with dirt and blood, his coat sleeve torn. Her heart leaped into her throat when she saw the dried blood crusted along his right eye and hairline. She told herself it was anger she felt. What kind of man fought like this, heedless of danger to himself? "Where have you been?" she demanded.

Tom shot her a look, but didn't answer. He set down his hat and looked at Bessie. "Leave us, please. I need to change."

"Then we shall both leave," Margaret countered,

motioning for Bessie to follow her to the door. "Where is your valet?"

Tom put out a hand to stop her. "My valet has the night off. You will help me."

"Me?" Margaret said, astounded.

"You are my wife."

"Precisely. I am your wife, not your valet."

He took a step toward Margaret, hands outstretched. "I had hoped I could count on my wife to help tend my wounds."

Margaret took an involuntary step back. What did he think she'd do after the mortification he'd caused her today? Run into his arms? He was a fool if he thought so.

Disappointment crossed his face, but he made no move to close the gap. Instead, he surprised Margaret by walking past her, pulling off his coat as he did so, and tossing it onto a table. He began tugging furiously at his cravat. *Good heavens, he's serious,* Margaret thought. *He's going to undress right here in front of me. In front of the maid.*

Bessie flushed, turning her eyes away in embarrassment, and Margaret had to take pity on her. This was Margaret's problem now. She would have to face her husband alone sometime, and the sooner they had things out between them, the better. "That will be all, Bessie. I will send for you if I need you."

"Yes, madam," Bessie said with unmistakable relief. She hastened to the door and let herself out.

The cravat came off, and Tom tossed it onto the coat. His shirt fell open, exposing the base of his throat and upper portion of his chest. He slipped the braces off his shoulders.

Margaret stood, unable to move, her anger displaced by the shocking novelty of seeing a man undressing. Her heart began to pound wildly, so much so that she thought he must be able to hear it. She tried to hold on to her resentment at all that had happened today, at how his actions had embarrassed and humiliated her. But it was difficult not to be distracted by the outline of his broad chest under the white shirt, at the way his trousers dropped lower on his hips without the braces to hold them up.

He looked up and caught her looking at him, and Margaret thought she detected a particular glint in his eye. He had promised her he would wait, but here he was, half-undressed, and today he had proven himself a man of uncontrollable passions. What if he decided to take her now, even if she was unwilling?

But he made no move to unbutton his trousers. Instead, he dropped into a chair by the fireplace. He lifted one foot and began to tug at his boot. After a moment he seemed to think better of it and allowed his foot, still shod, to fall back to the floor. He rubbed his hands over his face but then stopped, wincing, as he found a tender spot—a cut that was probably the result of his tumble into the broken glass. With a groan he leaned back in the chair and closed his eyes. "God, I'm tired," he said.

Seeing that there was no immediate threat to her person, Margaret found her righteous anger returning. She crossed her arms and regarded him coldly. "I should think you would be tired." Her voice was crusty and hard, as she intended it to be. "It takes a lot of energy to get married and destroy a banquet hall in one day."

He merely opened one eye and looked at her. "Are you going to stand there all night?"

"What would you have me do?"

"For God's sake, Margaret," he said with bitter irritation. "Do you plan to fight me on everything? Please, sit down."

Margaret took the other chair, watching him warily. At the moment there was no sign of that animal brutality with which he'd attacked Richard. He simply looked exhausted. He sat with his head against the back of the chair, unmoving, his eyes shut, one cheekbone tinged with purple. Clearly, he'd received as good as he'd given. Margaret had no idea her cousin could fight that way. It had been no easy matter for Tom to best him. Tom shifted in the chair, but winced at the pain this movement caused him. He might be more injured than Margaret had initially realized. He was probably suffering from a bruised rib or two.

"Are you all right?" she found herself asking.

He opened his eyes, studying her as intently as she'd been studying him. It made her uneasy, but she did not look away. "A wet towel would be nice." He indicated the cut above his eye. "It hurts like the devil."

"I'll get you something." Margaret went into the bedchamber that adjoined the sitting room. She skirted the bed, steadfastly avoiding looking at it. Reaching the washstand, she poured water from the pitcher into the bowl and moistened a small towel. Tom was still in the chair when she returned. "Here," she said, and began to carefully wipe away the dried blood.

He winced at the first contact, but relaxed once the

area around the cut was clean. His hand reached up and covered hers. "Thank you," he said quietly.

An unexpected pang shot through Margaret's heart, unsettling her. She slipped her hand away and returned to the chair.

"Maggie," Tom said, "I'm very sorry for what happened today."

"What did happen, exactly? How could you possibly feel justified in attacking him?"

"I don't." He held up a hand. "Wait. Yes, I do." He sighed. "I'm not saying I believe the fight was a good thing. But he was threatening you. Threatening *us*. That I could not allow."

The fight was to protect her? It didn't seem possible. Margaret fingered the gold band on her left hand. It still felt strange there. Uncomfortably heavy. "I don't understand. How is Richard a threat?"

"That is what I need to find out. First, I need you to tell me what caused the rift in your family. Why was your grandfather so determined to keep Moreton Hall away from the Spencers?"

"Does it really matter?" Margaret asked, irritated.

"Yes," Tom insisted, returning her defiant look. "It matters very much."

Margaret sighed. If it was true that Richard posed some kind of threat, perhaps Tom did have a need to know—even if it meant revealing things her family had never discussed with anyone. "All right, I will tell you. My grandfather and Richard's grandfather were brothers. The trouble started when my uncle—my father's younger brother—died in 1815, in France."

"He was a soldier?"

Margaret shook her head. "He worked for the war office. He may even have been a spy. We are not really sure what he did, nor even exactly how he died. What we do know is that Richard's father was also out of the country at the same time. He claimed he was in Holland, but he may have been in France. My grandfather was convinced that he was actually a counterspy, working for Napoleon, and that some piece of intelligence that he'd passed on to the French led to my uncle's death."

"Why would he do such a traitorous thing? Why would he work for the enemy and cause his own cousin's death?"

"What motivates anyone?" Margaret answered caustically. "Money, of course. His wife was descended from the French nobility. Perhaps Napoleon promised to return money or lands they had lost during the Revolution."

Tom took a moment to consider this. "That would certainly be a powerful reason to cut Richard's family out of the inheritance. But if it's true that Richard's father was a traitor, surely under the laws of England he'd not be eligible to inherit anyway?"

"Nothing was ever proven. Richard has always asserted his father's innocence. He said his father was blackmailed, that he was forced to agree to break the entail or else be hung as a traitor. But I have no doubt of their guilt. They are all traitors, murderers, and liars."

"I see." Tom tossed aside the cloth and leaned back once more in the chair.

"I've answered your questions," Margaret pointed out. "Now I expect the same in return. Why was Richard able to goad you into a fight so quickly? What does he know about *your* past?"

"My past?" Tom said defensively. "What could he know about my past?"

"You said you'd met him before. And there are rumors…"

He tensed. "What kind of rumors?"

"Some say you killed a man. With your bare hands." After today's spectacle, Margaret could believe it.

Tom grimaced. "Like any rumor, it comes nowhere near the truth."

"I disagree. A rumor is usually based on *some* shred of truth. Does this have anything to do with Freddie Hightower?"

He lifted his head sharply. "Who told you that?"

"Your argument was overheard by at least a dozen people. Someone told me afterward that you were talking about Hightower. Did you have something to do with his death?"

"How could I?" Tom exploded. "I was in Australia when it happened!"

"But you *were* talking about Mr. Hightower, weren't you?" Margaret pressed. "Why?"

"I can't tell you," he said. "It involves other people, innocent people who were unjustly harmed. There are certain events that they understandably wish to keep private."

"Do you not trust me? And if it involves Richard, don't I have a right to know? He is my cousin, after all. And you are my—" She stopped herself.

"Yes?" he challenged.

She lifted her chin. "Husband." The word lingered in the air, suspended in a thick silence.

"I'm glad you are willing to acknowledge it." Tom

stood up, taking in a painful breath as he straightened. He walked to the window and leaned heavily on the sill, looking out at the growing dusk. "I don't doubt you, Margaret. It's just that the secret is not mine to tell. I would be breaking a promise I gave to someone else."

Someone else. Someone he evidently believed was more important than she was. "It's about the Thornboroughs, isn't it? After all, Mr. Hightower died at their home, didn't he?" Tom grimaced again, and this time Margaret was sure it had nothing to do with his injuries. She had hit the heart of the matter. "You have no problem protecting your family. But what about me? Don't I have a stake in this?"

He slammed a hand on the windowsill. "Margaret, I just need time. Time to sort out what all this means and figure out what to do."

"Do about *what?*" Margaret exclaimed, rising from her chair. "You have told me nothing. From where I stand, it seems the problem is not with Richard but with *you*." She could see her words hurt him, but she continued on. "Your actions today demonstrated how far you are from being a true gentleman. A well-bred man would never lose control like that."

Tom turned from the window and came to her in two strides, taking her by the arms. "Do *not* accuse me of lack of control," he said roughly. "Trust me, Margaret: self-control was the only thing that kept me from killing that man."

His voice was sharp as a knife, sending a stab of fear through her. "Will you attack me, too?" she accused, covering her fright with a show of strength. "Is that always how you show your anger?"

Tom's grip loosened. "I'm sorry," he said quietly. "At times my anger still gets the better of me, and that's wrong—no matter what the circumstances. I have already gone to the Lord tonight in penance." He slid his hands down her arms, caressing her. "But you do not need to fear me, Maggie. I am your husband. To *cherish*, remember?"

He pulled her to him, wrapping his arms around her. It was a tender, comforting hug, but it sent powerful sensations through her. She told herself she ought to withdraw, but her legs refused to move. "I..." she murmured against his chest. Words died in her throat.

"I'm sorry for the pain I caused you today, Maggie. It's not the way I envisioned the start of our lives as man and wife. The Bible says we are to be as one flesh." His hand lightly caressed her hair. "I can't tell you how much I want that."

His touch was exquisitely tender, coaxing from deep within her a need so powerful it terrified her. How could this be the same man who had been fighting so viciously just hours ago? She could not reconcile it. She tensed. "Please," she whispered. "I can't—"

He loosed her so that he could look into her face. "I was speaking of the figurative meaning, Maggie. I hate that there are things I cannot tell you. I'm asking you to trust me."

The appeal in his eyes was so strong, she could only nod her assent. Her heart was beating swiftly, but everything else had frozen, as though her legs had been caught in a trap. He brought his lips close to hers and said softly, "Tonight, I ask only for what you promised me on the day we became engaged. A good-night kiss."

His lips brushed hers, and Margaret found herself

leaning into him. When his lips settled on hers for a proper kiss, he filled her senses so completely that everything else faded.

After long, luscious moments, he pulled away. "Here is more of that self-control you berated me for not having," he said. "You ought to go to bed now." He motioned toward the other room. "You may take the bed. I'll sleep out here."

She looked at him, still dazed. "You want me to go?" Her question came out embarrassingly plaintive.

"I could live for a lifetime off the look you gave me just now," Tom said, giving a little laugh that only made him wince and press a hand to his ribs. "But yes, I think it's for the best."

A curious mixture of relief and disappointment filled her as she left the room, leaving her feeling oddly forlorn as she shut the door behind her.

Chapter 20

Tom woke early to the light tapping on the door. He stretched, catching himself as pain shot through his side. Several ribs were cracked, for sure. Spencer's fist had been too adept at finding his rib cage. Sleeping on the hard floor had done nothing to help matters, but his only other option had been the small sofa, which would only have held about half of him.

The knock on the door was repeated, heavier this time. Tom was about to call out that he was coming, but he checked himself and went silently instead. Early dawn was barely lighting the sky. There was a good chance Margaret was still asleep, and Tom didn't want to wake her. He hoped that one of them had gotten some rest, anyway.

He riffled his hands through his hair and tucked his shirt into his trousers so that he would look somewhat presentable, although he suspected it was probably just a servant at the door. He was right. He unbolted the door and looked out to see his valet, John Stephens. "I apologize for disturbing you so early, sir." He extended a note.

"This just came for you, and I thought you would want to see it right away."

Tom took the note and read the return address. "Good Lord," he muttered. He opened the door. "Come in, Stephens."

Stephens entered, and Tom saw him take note of the sofa cushion on the floor, the boots set to one side of the stuffed chair, and other evidence that Tom had made his bed in here last night. But his valet said nothing. He also kept his face turned away from the bedroom door— probably in case the new Mrs. Poole should step out in her nightclothes without warning. Stephens was the soul of tact.

Tom tore open the note.

Sir,

Please do me the honor of calling on my house at your earliest convenience. There are important matters we ought to discuss—things that cannot wait until after your felicitous honeymoon.

Your servant,
Richard Spencer

Tom made a sound of contempt. Spencer was issuing orders to him. It may be phrased as a request, but it would be foolish of Tom not to heed it. He'd do whatever was necessary to keep Spencer quiet about Lizzie's past.

The train to Lincolnshire left at half past one, and Tom and Margaret planned to be on it. There was still time for him to see Spencer first. The problem was, he needed to change his clothes, and everything was in the room where Margaret was sleeping.

He crumpled the paper and tossed it in the fireplace. The banked coals were warm enough to ignite the paper, and Tom watched while it burned. "Wait here," he told Stephens. He went to the bedchamber door, put his ear to it, and listened. There was no sound within, no rustling noises to indicate she was up and about. His hand hovered above the door handle while he considered the propriety of going inside. *She's your wife,* he told himself. *You have every right to go in there.* Even so, he felt like an intruder as he carefully opened the door and peered inside.

She lay on her side with her back toward the door. Instantly the sight of her sent a visceral jolt of need through him. He stood, watching her for several moments, drinking in the sight of her. The blankets rose and fell with regular rhythm, showing the steady breathing of sleep.

Quietly Tom crossed the room to the wardrobe. From this vantage point he could see Margaret's face. She looked unbelievably angelic, her usual guarded expression relaxed by sleep and lit by the soft glow of the banked fire. Tom found he had to work hard to steady his own, irregular breathing. He turned back to the task at hand.

The wardrobe opened soundlessly on well-oiled hinges, and Tom pulled out a coat and a clean shirt. That would have to do for now. As he stepped aside to close the wardrobe door, he accidentally brushed against a pair of boots standing next to it. One boot fell over with a thud. Margaret's eyes flew open, and she instinctively drew the blankets to her chin.

"I'm sorry to have awakened you," Tom said. "I've

only come in for a few things." He held up the clothes in his hand as proof.

She pushed back a lock of hair, her eyes still heavy with sleep. "Are you going out?"

"Only for an hour or so." In reality, he had no idea how long this errand would take.

Margaret sat up. She was careful to keep the blanket pulled up high, although her modesty was already protected by a nightdress that covered everything, including her arms and her lovely neck. Her dark braid fell forward on her chest. Tom found the sight of her indescribably alluring, even though she was primly surrounded by the counterpane and pillows and miles of nightdress. "I don't think I can sleep anymore," she said. "Will you send Bessie to me when you leave?"

"Of course." He dragged his eyes from where her braid lay against her soft breasts in order to meet her gaze. Suddenly the room felt far too warm. He slipped out the door and closed it behind him before she could ask any more questions.

Within an hour Tom was standing on the steps of Spencer's town house. The bell of a nearby church was just striking eight as Tom rapped on the door. While waiting for someone to answer, he distracted himself by watching the comings and goings on the street. There were already plenty of people about—up and down the street, butchers, grocers, and dairy maids were delivering their goods to waiting recipients below stairs.

It was too early for callers, of course. Even so, Tom did not have to wait long before the door opened and a butler stood looking at him without any sense of surprise. "May I help you, sir?"

"I'm here to see Mr. Spencer. He is expecting me."

The butler held out a silver tray to receive Tom's calling card. Tom stared at the tray in irritation. The butler had to know very well who was going to be calling at this hour; Spencer would have told him. Swallowing a caustic comment to this effect, Tom reached into his pocket for a card—only to realize he had none with him. Stifling an urge to throttle the butler, who was still appraising him coolly, he said, "Please tell Mr. Spencer that Tom Poole is calling."

"Of course, sir." The butler opened the door wide and ushered Tom into the front hall.

Tom waited while the man disappeared up the stairs under the pretense of seeing "whether Mr. Spencer was at home." It would all be laughable if it wasn't so deadly serious. From somewhere down the hall he could hear a clock idly ticking the seconds by while Tom tried to imagine once more how this interview might go.

At last the butler reappeared, descending the stairs with stately gravity. "If you will follow me, sir," he announced.

Two flights of stairs later, the butler paused at a door that was flanked by two tall footmen. As though Spencer felt he needed personal protection from him. Well, thought Tom, perhaps he did.

"Come!" said a voice from inside, in response to the butler's light knock.

Spencer's bedchamber was large and ornate, with heavily gilded wallpaper and velvet window curtains that were probably as thick as the exterior walls. Spencer lay in the middle of the four-poster bed. He turned a cold glare on Tom, despite the quantity of bandages that covered his head and nose. Evidence of a physician's ministrations stood on the night table in the form of several bottles and small vials of potion.

"Mr. Poole, how nice of you to visit," he said, his voice heavy with sarcasm. He ended the sentence with a small, painful-sounding cough. "I expect you are here to ask after my health."

"If you thought that, you wouldn't have posted two guards outside the door."

"One can never be too careful." He lifted a hand, which was bandaged around the knuckles. "Won't you have a seat?"

Tom took the chair indicated. He was willing to play Spencer's games up to a point, but no further. "Why did you ask me to come here?" He deliberately phrased the question that way, refusing to admit that Spencer's note was tantamount to an order.

"I feel we got off on the wrong foot yesterday. Don't you?"

"You should not have come to the wedding breakfast."

"Well, you made that abundantly clear," Spencer replied, touching the bandage on his nose and grimacing.

Tom wanted to add, *You should not have insulted my sister,* but he held his tongue. He wanted Spencer to make the first move.

"Why do you suppose that I, Margaret's nearest living relative, was not invited to the wedding?" Spencer asked. "I suspect she told you some untruths about our family history."

"She told me your father forfeited any right to Moreton Hall."

"It was stolen from him!" Once more Spencer's words

disintegrated into a fit of coughing, and it took several moments for him to find his breath. "Her grandfather manufactured all kinds of so-called evidence against my father, which he bribed the authorities into accepting without question. They forced him to agree to break the entail."

"That sounds preposterous to me."

Spencer snorted. "*Life* is preposterous, Poole. For example, imagine my surprise when I entered that church yesterday to see what kind of man my cousin was marrying, only to find out it was the blackguard who had tried to murder my best friend." He turned to pick up one of the bottles on the bedside table. Laudanum, probably, Tom thought, or some other painkiller. Spencer drained the contents into his mouth, then carelessly dropped the bottle back on the table. It rattled back and forth a half-dozen times on its rounded edge until finally coming to a stop. Spencer wiped his mouth and leaned heavily back on the pillows. "As I reflect on the matter, however, I see that this marriage is actually a good thing. It can enable us to forge a truce."

"What kind of 'truce'?" Tom said suspiciously.

"Margaret's grandfather brought misfortune to my family with his lies. I, on the other hand, could use the truth to bring misfortune to you." He lifted his bandaged hand and pointed to Tom. "I could have you arrested."

"Don't be ridiculous. Plenty of people saw us—it was a fair fight. I might just as well have *you* arrested for causing it."

Spencer gave a short laugh. "I'm not talking about yesterday. I'm talking about your attempt to kill Freddie Hightower."

"Hightower died last year of natural causes. I wasn't even in the country."

"But you tried to kill him first, back in forty-five. You were dueling—and duels had been outlawed by then. I could have you prosecuted."

"Go ahead," Tom challenged. "No court of law will care about that now."

"Perhaps," Spencer replied. "But there are plenty of other people who will be interested in the question of *why* you were fighting that duel. Or rather, I should say, *who* was the reason for it."

Here is was, then. The real reason Spencer had called him here. Lizzie.

"As soon as I saw you at the wedding, I began to put two and two together," Spencer continued. "Freddie dueled with the brother of a woman whom he'd supposedly wronged. That man was you. You have only one sister, and she is married to a baron. A baron who is also a clergyman. That's a rather high reputation to uphold, isn't it? You might be willing to send yourself to the devil, but what about the lofty Lady Somerville? If word got out about her unsavory character—"

"You wouldn't dare." Tom gripped the chair, primarily to keep himself from lunging at Spencer's throat. Hightower had seduced Lizzie with false promises of marriage, then abandoned her like so much worthless rubbish. Tom had worked for years to help her recover from this blot on her past, and she'd finally achieved it with her acceptance by the Thornboroughs and her marriage to Geoffrey. Now her life could be ruined because Tom had been fool enough to marry a woman he'd barely known. He'd selfishly returned to England to see Lizzie, thinking the danger was past because Hightower was dead. He'd never dreamed the other man present at that duel could end up wishing him ill for more reasons than what had transpired on that November morning seven years ago.

Spencer looked at him smugly, knowing he had Tom in a corner.

"You want money in exchange for your silence," Tom said flatly.

"You really are a coarse bastard," Spencer retorted. "You think money is the important thing."

"What does that mean? That you're too good for it? That it doesn't matter?"

"Of course it matters," Spencer said impatiently. "But what the nouveaux riches like you don't realize is that the upper class isn't about wealth. It's about breeding, titles, and land. You will never be my equal."

"Your ideas are outdated, Spencer. Plenty of men are rising up in industry and business, gaining wealth— and social position—by hard work rather than having it handed to them like it's their God-given right."

Spencer actually smiled at this. "Trust me, my eyes are wide open to what is going on today. As a matter of fact, your little polemic about industry leads me to the reason we are having this conversation. I know of a company owned by a man who has a remarkable vision for a railway line in America. It's a company you are already acquainted with."

It all came together in Tom's mind—why he had seen the two men conferring at the wedding. Together they would come after Margaret's land and Tom's money. "What have you told Denault?" Tom demanded. "If you've whispered even one word about Lizzie—"

"Relax, Poole," Spencer broke in. "I only told him I was sure I could persuade you to buy in. He does not know the particulars, nor does he care."

Of course, Spencer could easily be lying about this. "I think you're in league with Denault," Tom said. "You plotted this whole thing just to blackmail me."

"Plotted? Blackmail?" Spencer repeated with a scoff. "I would be careful at the words you throw around. I'm making you a business proposition, that's all." His malicious gaze bore into Tom. "Let me put it in words that even you can understand. I have invested in Denault's company, and I *highly encourage* you to do the same."

Chapter 21

O nce again Margaret found herself in the odious position of having to stand by and do nothing, wondering where her husband was. She paced the room, reviewing her options. Somehow Tom had won her over last night. He'd used heated caresses to confuse her thoughts and melt her cold logic. Even now, in the cool light of day, her face heated to think of it. She was equally angry with herself at how she had so easily yielded to his touch.

She could not allow herself to lose control like that again. This morning was proof of that. The little clock on the mantelpiece showed it was nearly noon. They'd been married less than a day and already he'd lied to her, saying he'd be gone only an hour. She had to make him understand that she would not tolerate being left in the dark regarding where he went and what he did.

There was a knock at the door. Since Bessie was busy packing the trunks in the next room, Margaret answered it herself. Tom's valet stood in the hallway with two hotel porters. "Where is Mr. Poole?" Margaret demanded.

Stephens gave a deferential bow. "He's asked me to escort you and your maid to the station, madam. He will meet you there."

Margaret opened the door wide, allowing the men to enter. Bessie appeared at the door of the bedchamber. "The trunks are in here," she called to the porters. "Everything's ready."

"There is a cab waiting downstairs," Stephens said. "I'll just go help the lads with those trunks." He made as if to follow the porters, but Margaret put out a hand to stop him. "You haven't answered my question, Stephens. Where is Mr. Poole?"

Stephens dropped his gaze. "I beg your pardon, madam, but Mr. Poole specifically instructed me to say only that he had urgent business to attend to, and he will explain everything once the two of you are on the train."

"I'm sorry, Stephens, but that isn't acceptable," Margaret said. "I think you should know that from now on, you will answer to me as well as to Mr. Poole. Where did he go?" she demanded again. "To Mayfair?" Margaret had an idea that Tom would go to Geoffrey for advice on how to handle the unsavory gossip that was bound to follow yesterday's events. She could almost see people tittering in their drawing rooms as they discussed the Great Wedding Breakfast Brawl.

"No, ma'am, he's not in Mayfair," Stephens answered, before he realized he shouldn't have said anything at all. "I mean, that is…"

"You cannot keep secrets from me, Stephens," Margaret said sternly. "The sooner you recognize this, the less time we will waste."

Stephens threw a quick glance at the clock. "We really

ought to be getting to the railway station, Mrs. Poole. There's a lot of traffic on the roads today, and there's no telling how long it will take us to get there."

The porters struggled out of the bedchamber, each holding an end of a large trunk upon which they'd stacked two smaller trunks. Bessie followed behind, carrying a carpetbag and a hatbox. The porters set their load down with a thump, pausing to regain their breath and looking at Margaret and Stephens for more direction. "Take those things down to the station, the three of you," Margaret instructed. "Stephens and I have an errand to run. We shall meet you there."

"Mr. Brown won't like us leaving the hotel," one of the porters said doubtfully, referring to the hotel proprietor. "There are other guests who need our services."

"You may tell Mr. Brown that I shall pay him an amount totaling triple your wages for the next two hours. At that rate he ought to be able to get along without you."

"But, madam, I don't know these men," Bessie protested.

Margaret scrutinized the porters. Both were short, wiry, and well past the bloom of youth. They were dressed in livery that had been provided for them by the hotel. "I'm sure you'll be perfectly safe," she assured Bessie. Just to be sure, Margaret reached into her reticule and pulled out two half-crown pieces, giving one to each of the porters. "That's for your trouble. And you'll each get another half crown for remaining at the station with my maid until I arrive."

This arrangement was clearly more than satisfactory for the two men. They grinned, pocketed their money, and once more hoisted the trunks, carrying them out the door. Margaret gave more money to Bessie. "Please buy our tickets when you get there and meet us on the platform." Bessie still looked uncertain, but she followed the men out into the hall. Margaret heard the sound of the men's footsteps and their occasional grunts as they worked their way down the stairs with the trunks.

She turned back to Stephens, who was by now looking distinctly uncomfortable. He'd confirmed Tom wasn't in Mayfair, so he hadn't gone to the Somervilles' home. The second possibility involved someone who did not live in Mayfair . . . It was highly unlikely, but seemed just the sort of mad thing Tom would do. "He went to Mr. Spencer's house, didn't he?"

"No!" Stephens exclaimed. But Margaret saw from his expression that she was right. She reached for her shawl, the last of her personal items still in the room. "If Tom intends to finish what he started yesterday, I'd better see if there's any chance left of stopping him."

They were out of the hotel and into the street before Stephens finally admitted, "He was at Mr. Spencer's house, but he's not there now. He's . . . he's at the bank."

"The bank!" She grilled him with her gaze. "Are you sure?"

He nodded.

Margaret turned on her heel and began walking. The bank wasn't so far away, and the streets were so heavily congested that it would be pointless to take a cab. Not hearing footsteps behind her, she paused and turned back to see Stephens still standing dumbfounded by the hotel door. "Come along," she instructed, picking up her pace. "There isn't much time."

*

Tom stood waiting impatiently at the corner, keeping his eyes on the Somervilles' house farther up the block. He was desperate to talk to Geoffrey, and the only way to do that without Lizzie getting wind of it was to wait here and catch Geoffrey during his daily walk.

While he watched the busy street, he prayed that Geoffrey and James had kept their promise not to tell Lizzie what had happened at the wedding breakfast. Tom did not want her to have even an inkling that anything was wrong. She would be devastated to learn that the terrible events they thought they'd put behind them were once again threatening their happiness. Who knew what such a shock might do to her and the baby she was carrying? He could not risk it.

Tom pulled out his pocket watch and groaned when he saw the time. Very soon he would have to be at the bank to meet Denault as Spencer had instructed him—ordered, really—to do. Tom thought it best to go along with their demands for now, if only to buy some time. He would not rest until he had found a way to beat Spencer at his game.

"Hello, Tom," said a voice behind him.

He turned to see James. "What are you doing here?" he asked in irritation. He wanted to talk to Geoffrey alone.

"I was just on my way to visit Geoffrey," James said, pointing his gold-handled cane toward the Somerville home down the street. "Aren't you? I think it would be helpful if the three of us put our heads together about this problem of what happened yesterday."

"You?" Tom asked, unable to fathom how James could be of help.

"Oh, look, he's coming this way now," James said.

Geoffrey was indeed now visible, having just passed a man who was wearing a large sandwich board advertising Holloway's Pills for curing asthma. "Are you waiting for me?" Geoffrey asked as he reached them.

"We are," James affirmed. "I think you can guess why."

Geoffrey nodded. "This is not the best place to talk, however." He indicated the people who continued to jostle past them. "Shall we go to the park?"

"There isn't time," Tom said. "I've got to be at the bank soon." He motioned for them to follow him into a narrow side street. No one was about; there were only some quiet stables farther down the lane and a small yard of chickens and geese. "We can talk here."

"I suppose you want to tell us what happened yesterday," Geoffrey said. "Why you and Spencer got into a fight. Do you know him?"

"Unfortunately, yes."

"He was at that duel you fought with Freddie Hightower, wasn't he?" James put in.

"You knew?" Tom exploded, turning on James. "You knew I was about to marry his *cousin*—and you didn't tell me?" He took hold of James's coat, barely resisting the urge to shake him. "You had to have known what trouble this would cause!"

"I didn't know for sure," James protested, trying to free himself from Tom's grip.

"Tom, please," Geoffrey said, swiftly interposing himself between the two men. "We need to discuss this rationally."

Tom fought to get hold of his frustration and anger.

Between his troubles with Margaret and the pressures Spencer was putting on him, he felt like he was walking on a knife's edge. Slowly he forced himself to let go of James. "Forgive me," he said. "My temper—"

"Perfectly understandable," James said, readjusting his coat. "I know you're upset. But I meant what I said; I didn't know for certain that Spencer had been the man with Freddie at the duel."

"But clearly you had some suspicion," Tom persisted. "Why didn't you say something?"

"Spencer has been out of the country for over a year. I didn't even know he'd returned until I saw him at your wedding. And I didn't know he was Margaret's second cousin."

"How could you not know? I thought you knew everybody!"

He gave Tom a chiding look. "Despite how it may appear, I don't keep an extensive catalog of every family in England. Margaret and her father lived, rather hermit-like, at their estate in Lincolnshire. Last night, after Spencer had been carted away, I began to make inquiries among some of the older society folk. That's when I discovered that Spencer and Margaret are related."

"Hundreds of families," Tom groaned, "and I have to marry his cousin."

"So Spencer has recognized you from the duel?" Geoffrey asked. "Is that why he approached you?"

"Yes," Tom said wearily. "Naturally, it means he's figured out that Lizzie was the woman who had run away with Hightower."

Geoffrey grimaced. "Oh, dear Lord."

"He's threatened to reveal everything," Tom said.

"He'll tell her shameful secrets to the world...he'll say you married a fallen woman—"

"Stop right there," Geoffrey said, cutting him off sharply. "I know Lizzie made mistakes, and she paid for them dearly. But those things are all *in the past*. Her slate is clean."

"Not as far as Spencer is concerned."

"But your fight was with Hightower, not Spencer," James interjected. "Why should he want to take the trouble to raise these specters from the past and besmirch Lizzie's reputation?"

"Two reasons," Tom said. "First, he hates Margaret. Now that she and Lizzie are sisters-in-law, ruining Lizzie means throwing mud on Margaret as well. The second, more damnable reason, is pure greed."

"Don't tell me that's why you're on your way to the bank," James said with concern.

Tom nodded.

"But Spencer can't get away with extortion!" Geoffrey exclaimed. "It's reprehensible."

"Let's get this straight," Tom said fiercely. "I have no intention of remaining under that man's thumb. Rest assured, I will personally see to it that he gets his due. But for the moment, I'm more concerned about Lizzie. Her health and her reputation are at stake. I don't think we should do anything right away—at least not until after the baby is born."

Geoffrey considered this. "You have a good point. For Lizzie's sake, we must be cautious. However, we may not need to wait before taking action. I know a few men in the House of Lords who are very adept at keeping a lid on personal scandals. Let me approach them and see what they advise."

"Can you be sure they'll keep the secret?" Tom asked.

"Trust me, Tom," Geoffrey said wryly. "I've been among them for nearly two years now, and I can tell you they have quieted more scandals about their own families than you or I could ever dream of."

"Society," Tom said in disgust, nearly spitting out the word.

"It's what I love about them," James remarked. "They watch out for their own, especially when it is in their best interests to do so."

"What is Spencer demanding, exactly?" Geoffrey asked.

"A thousand pounds, as payment for his medical bills, he says. For the injuries he incurred yesterday." Tom clenched and unclenched his fists, taking a grim satisfaction at the remembrance of inflicting those wounds.

"That seems a paltry sum, considering how rich you are," James said.

"That's not all he's after. He also wants me to buy into the Saint Louis and Western Railway."

"He wants you to give money to your wife's former fiancé?" James scratched his chin thoughtfully. "That seems an odd connection."

"Exactly," Tom answered. "I suspect there is something underhanded about that railway scheme. Whatever it is, they are both profiting from it." Grimly he added, "And considering the way things usually go with blackmail, I suspect their demands on me will only get higher."

Chapter 22

How had it come to this? Tom thought as he signed his name to the document the clerk had set in front of him. He'd always been shrewd in his business dealings—first at his father's dry goods shop in London, then at the shop in Sydney where he and Lizzie had worked, and later as he oversaw supplies at the sheep station in Bathurst. He'd been especially proud of how he and Sullivan had staked a claim to one of the richest veins of gold at Ballarat. When they'd finally sold out, they'd made a tidy profit that would keep both of them comfortable for a long time.

Unless one threw it away on a woman—which, Tom reflected, was a pretty good description of what he was doing. He'd fallen in love with Margaret Vaughn and paid an enormous sum to get her out of debt. Now he was funding a highly questionable venture just to keep her cousin quiet about Lizzie's past.

Denault sat across from Tom, leaning back in the chair with his arms crossed, watching as he signed the papers. "You won't regret it, Poole," he said with a self-satisfied grin.

Without a word, Tom dropped the pen into the inkstand and stood up. No, he would not regret it, but someday he'd make sure the men extorting money from him did. It rather amazed him, really, that he was finding the strength to bide his time and wait for the perfect chance to destroy their plans. Perhaps in some things he could show patience after all.

Denault accompanied him out of the small back office and through the bank's imposing lobby with its vaulted ceiling and marble floors, between two rows of stiffly suited clerks sitting on tall stools behind high counters. "Remember, I don't want word of this getting back to Margaret," Tom said. He had decided that he would have to tell her about Lizzie's past, but he wasn't going to do it until he had Lizzie's blessing. And that would have to wait until after the birth.

"I assure you, I shall be entirely discreet," Denault said, ushering Tom through the massive front door as though he owned the place. "But soon, when this venture takes off, you will be proud to tell the world you have shares in the Saint Louis and Western."

Tom paused at the top of the half-dozen or so steps that led down to the street, giving Denault a hard look. "Save the fancy speeches. Just know that I will be watching the company carefully, and requesting regular, detailed reports."

He meant this as a threat, of course. No word had passed between them about *why* Tom was suddenly so willing to be a financial backer in Denault's company. Spencer had "suggested" that Tom go to the bank right away, and Denault had been waiting there when he arrived. The papers were already drawn up. Not trusting Spencer's assurances that Denault knew nothing about Lizzie, Tom wanted to make sure the man knew exactly where they stood. "If anything is amiss, and I find any— shall we say—*reason* to report it to the authorities, I guarantee you I will."

But Denault did not seem the least bit concerned. "Understood," he said with a smile. They descended in order to make room for two other men who were coming up the steps. "I won't keep you," Denault said, tipping his hat. "I know you are in a hurry to return to your lovely bride." He walked away before Tom could answer.

Tom tried to dismiss the man from his mind. For the moment, he had other things to attend to. He pulled out his pocket watch to check the time and saw that it was later than he'd realized. He would have to find a cab quickly in order to reach the railway station on time. He began walking in the opposite direction from Denault, toward the corner where he knew a cabstand was located. After a few steps he stopped short. Margaret was standing at the corner, looking directly at him.

Had she seen him with Denault? She must have. She stalked up to him, her face red with anger. Tom's astonishment at seeing her turned to irritation when he noticed Stephens following in her wake. She'd reduced his valet to some kind of footman. "I sent instructions for you to meet me at the station," he said hotly. "Why are you here?"

"Why were you with Paul?" she retorted. "How could you meet with him and not tell me about it? And why were you at Richard's house this morning?"

Tom threw an accusing look at Stephens, who looked thoroughly guilty and completely miserable. "She forced me to tell her," his valet said glumly. "She said I was also in her employ now, seeing as how you two are married—"

"That's enough, Stephens," Margaret said, not even looking at him. She was still glaring at Tom. "What are you trying to hide?"

Tom had put up with plenty of things this morning, but he was not about to allow himself or his valet to be chastised by his wife on a public street. He took her by the elbow and turned her around, forcing her to walk with him.

"What are you doing?" she protested.

"We are going to catch a cab," he said between gritted teeth. "And you will keep your voice down and walk with me like a genteel lady. I don't need you raising a riot right here on the street. Our reputations are in enough trouble already."

"And whose fault is that?" she hissed. But as they had caught the eye of several curious onlookers, she relented and walked beside him without further protest. Stephens hurried on ahead to locate a cab.

"Don't think this is the end of it," Margaret said through a pasted-on smile. "I will get the truth out of you."

"We'll have plenty of time to talk on the train," Tom pointed out, and ushered her into the carriage.

"I believe we shall talk about it here," she contradicted, speaking as soon as the cab was under way. "Tell me why you spent the morning with the two most vile men in London."

Tom couldn't find fault with her assessment, but neither would he be pushed around by his wife. "If you will be calm, I will tell you," he said, crossing his arms and showing he was prepared to wait.

She glowered at him, unspeaking, until gradually her breathing settled. "Very well," she said at last.

"I felt it was important, after yesterday's events, that Richard and I reach some kind of truce. Also, I wanted to assure myself that I had not beaten him beyond repair."

Tom thought he detected the barest hint of a smile. Given how Margaret felt about her cousin, some part of her must surely be happy that he had been thrashed. But whatever Tom saw was quickly gone. She said, "There can be no such thing as a truce with that man. Not after all he's done."

Tom held up a hand. "Let's just say he's been mollified." That was a good stretch of the truth, but it was as far as Tom was going to go. He had promised to keep Lizzie's secret, and he would not break that promise. "As for why I was with Denault, I've decided to buy into the railway." Now that Margaret had seen them together, Tom figured there was no point in trying to hide it.

"What?" she shrieked. "You know that will be like throwing money away. How could you even consider it?"

"It's my money, Margaret," Tom cut in. "I'll do with it as I please. But don't worry, there's still plenty left for Moreton Hall."

It was still a sore point to her pride, Tom knew, that Margaret was dependent on Tom's money. He hoped his words would sting her enough to make her drop the subject. She rallied, though. "Why didn't you tell me all these things before?" she persisted. "Why should it be such a secret?"

"I think the way you are acting right now is answer enough," he said, putting harsh emphasis on the terse words. "And that's all I'm going to say on the subject."

Margaret fumed, but did not press him more as the cab made its interminable journey to Euston station. Carriages, omnibuses, pedestrians, and crossing sweepers slowed their progress at every turn. Tom heard the driver complain loudly when they were blocked by a wagon stacked twenty feet high with wooden crates and lumbering straight down the middle of the thoroughfare.

As they approached the station, the traffic slowed nearly to a standstill; the roads were choked by everyone else who was trying to get there, too. How much time would they need once they actually got to the station? Tom had never ridden on a train before. He'd have to count on Margaret to show him what to do.

Margaret sat stony-faced, watching the commotion in the streets, never once looking at him. Her hands fidgeted in her lap, her right hand occasionally tugging at her left ring finger. She was wearing gloves, but Tom had the distinct impression that the ring beneath it was chafing her, just like this marriage.

Well, the feeling was mutual. So many things he'd thought he'd be doing when he married her were now thrown into complete upheaval. What was worse, they would spend weeks in Lincolnshire overseeing the harvest when Tom wanted nothing more than to remain in London and keep tabs on the volatile situation with Spencer and Denault. So here he was, sitting in a carriage with a wife he barely knew and could hardly control.

At last they reached the gates of the station. "That'll be two shillings," the driver announced.

Tom reached in his pocket to pull out the money, but Margaret said, "Two shillings? That's ridiculous." She turned to Tom. "Give him one and sixpence."

"Now see here," the cabbie protested. "I drove you all the way from the Strand—"

"—which everyone knows is worth one and four at most. You should be grateful we're even giving you a tip, after you tried to raise the fare like that."

The driver crossed his arms and surveyed Margaret. "Well, ain't you the lady," he said, shaking his head in admonishment, "standin' there and tellin' your 'usband what he should and shouldn't do." He turned a cheeky grin to Tom. "You ain't gonna allow that, are you, govnah?"

Tom knew the cabbie was trying to goad Tom by attacking his manly pride. But Tom didn't have time to worry about it. A deafening, high-pitched train whistle shrieked from nearby. Tom looked at the coin he'd just pulled out of his pocket, considered it for a split second, then dropped it into the cabbie's hand. "There's a half crown for your trouble." Then he took the still protesting Margaret by the arm and led her to the station door.

"You gave him nearly twice what he was owed!" she sputtered.

"Which would you rather do—argue with the man or miss the train?" He paused as they entered the station, bewildered by the swirl of people moving in all directions through a broad, high-ceilinged entrance hall. "You'll have to show me what to do," he told Margaret.

Bessie hurried up to them. "I've got your tickets." She handed them to Margaret. "First-class coach. Track two."

"Excellent," said Margaret. "Come along."

She began walking swiftly along the platform with Bessie, as though she expected Tom to follow along behind like one of her servants. He took hold of her arm, slowing her down. "I said *show* me the way, Margaret. Not *lead* the way."

She looked at him, her green eyes ablaze with all kinds of fury. They may have done with Spencer and Denault, but in Tom's estimation they still had a good many things to discuss.

When they reached the first-class carriages, Tom realized there would be no opportunity to speak privately. Every carriage was nearly full. They finally found one that had two free seats facing each other. Two couples already sat in the remaining four seats. It was not ideal, but it would have to do.

Upon seeing that Tom and Margaret meant to enter the carriage, one of the gentlemen—a stout man with graying temples—stood up and moved to the single seat on the other side, leaving two that were now side by side. "Please, take these," he offered. He looked at the woman still seated there, presumably his wife, although she was far younger. "You don't mind, do you, Fanny?" he said with a wink. "New acquaintances for you, since you are always so bored with my company."

Fanny was a petite blonde, dressed in a pink gown and an elaborate bonnet that was probably considered the height of fashion. She studied Margaret and Tom. Her gaze lingered on Margaret's gown and fine silk shawl, then traveled to Tom's face, where it lingered even longer. Apparently she approved of them both, Tom thought wryly. "I shall be delighted!" she said brightly.

The other couple, who looked about the same age as Tom and Margaret, gave them a friendly smile. Margaret returned their greeting, but Tom could see she wasn't happy about the need to keep her anger penned in for the duration of the journey. Perhaps it was better this way, he thought. Perhaps by the time they were able to talk, they would be able to speak more reasonably.

Tom motioned for Margaret to take the middle seat. It seemed more polite than causing the other lady to have to sit so close to a man she did not know—although given the glances she kept throwing in his direction, Tom had the feeling she would not have minded. The whistle blew again, this time so loud and close that Tom thought it would tear out his hearing.

Bessie and Stephens hurried away to take their seats in one of the second-class carriages. The train conductor walked down the platform, stopping at each carriage to check everyone's tickets. Tom was glad to see that the man carefully secured the carriage door after he did so. Tom had read that trains went very fast—upward of forty miles per hour—and he did not want to risk falling out.

At last, with one final shriek and the hiss of steam, the train pulled away from the station. Tom watched out the window as the station disappeared behind them with astonishing speed.

Just like his old life.

Within minutes they were hurtling past derelict buildings and run-down warehouses. Tom imagined the train was attempting to free itself from London's seedy edges and find the open countryside. He would be glad to see it, too.

The sky was heavy with dark clouds. They would be passing through rain soon. Tom wondered if trains had a harder time staying on the rails when they were wet. The thought left him uneasy. He turned from the window, settled into the cushioned seat, and looked at the couple sitting opposite him.

They had a comfortable familiarity that signaled they'd been married for a while. The woman's arm was tucked into the crook of her husband's in a way that stirred a pang of envy in Tom. He wondered if he and Margaret would ever be so at ease with each other.

The man leaned forward and extended his hand across the aisle. "How do you do. The name's John Thorsten." He introduced the man who had given up his seat as his brother-in-law, Mr. Wilson.

Fanny's face brightened in recognition when Tom gave their names. "You just got married, didn't you? I read about it in the *Times*. A whirlwind courtship. How romantic."

She said this without a trace of irony. She must not have heard about the wedding breakfast.

"Our felicitations," said Mrs. Thorsten.

"Are you going to Manchester?" Tom asked.

"Yes." She sighed contentedly. "It's good to be going home."

Tom turned to Margaret, hoping this mention of *home* would stir something in her, but she merely sat with a polite smile frozen on her lips. No doubt these others would think she was the shy and retiring type. Now *there* was an irony, he thought.

"I dread going home," Fanny said. "I daresay the house will be in complete disarray." She fanned herself vigorously. "It's impossible to find good servants in Manchester," she explained to Tom. "They can make more money working in John's cotton mill."

Tom looked at Thorsten, impressed. "You own a mill?"

He nodded. "Are you also a man of business, Mr. Poole?"

"I guess you could say I've done a number of things," Tom replied, at a loss to describe himself.

"Tom Poole!" Wilson said, snapping his fingers. "Of course. I should have recognized you right away."

"Have we met?" Tom said apologetically. He'd been introduced to many people over the past few weeks, but did not think the man looked familiar. "At a party, perhaps?"

"Oh, we don't get invited to very many society events," Fanny said with a pout. "I daresay we could if my husband would try harder."

"You would have me ingratiate myself with them," Wilson replied. "Can't see the point in it."

"Nor I," agreed Tom. He felt Margaret shift in her seat, perhaps bristling at this remark.

"I've heard your name, though," Wilson said. "You're the man who made a fortune in the gold mines."

"Gold mines?" Fanny exclaimed, her eyes growing round with excitement. "We're comfortable, of course," she added. "My husband is the owner of the Manchester Bank. But a gold mine!" She turned her excited gaze to Margaret. "And here you are, married to him." With another admiring glance at Tom she added, "I'll bet it was love at first sight."

Now Margaret stiffened noticeably. "Well...," she murmured.

"It doesn't have to be love at first sight, you know, Fanny," Mrs. Thorsten said, perhaps sensing Margaret's discomfort. "You know John and I didn't even like each other when we first met."

"You're stating it too strongly, my love," Thorsten said, giving her arm a gentle squeeze. "I for one was immediately devastated by your beauty. Some part of me knew I was in love with you the first moment I saw you."

"Well, you did a good job hiding it," she teased.

He cocked his head in surprise. "Is that what you think? Perhaps you just didn't perceive it."

This little interplay intrigued Tom. Not only did Mrs. Thorsten resemble Margaret, with her rich brown hair and wide, generous mouth, but also their story seemed to echo his own. "Did she act cold to you at first?" Tom could not resist asking.

Thorsten was too diplomatic to answer this question outright. "Perhaps I should just say that true love breaks down all barriers," he replied with a laugh.

Mrs. Thorsten chuckled with him. "Indeed, my love."

Wilson was not about to be outdone by their playful banter. "I thought *this* little girl was the cutest thing I'd ever seen," he said, blowing a kiss to his young wife, although she tried to wave it off. Tom guessed she'd married Wilson for his money, and that Wilson didn't mind this one bit. He grinned at Tom. "It's their beauty that reels you in, ain't it, Poole?"

"Yes," said Tom, intensely aware that the most beautiful woman he knew was sitting so close to him, and yet so distant. "It is."

Outside the carriage window, the landscape had changed yet again. They were passing through open areas, past homes with large yards for chickens, geese, and other livestock. In a matter of hours the train would cover a stretch of land that used to take days to cross. Tom sighed. If only it were so simple to bridge the gap between him and his bride.

Chapter 23

It was nearly sunset by the time their train journey began to wind down.

Margaret sat idly fidgeting with a handkerchief. She hadn't said a word since they'd changed trains at Rugby, even though they were the only occupants in this carriage.

Tom had suspected marriage to Margaret would not be easy, but he was dismayed—appalled, actually—at just how badly it had begun. He hated that he was forced to keep secrets from her. Gaining her trust would probably be fruitless so long as she sensed he was not telling her the whole truth, but he had to try. But how to go about it?

He realized with chagrin that he had not yet prayed today. Immediately he rectified that, sending up a silent plea for help and guidance. He had to find some way to reach her. He looked out over the fields of golden wheat that they were passing at incredible speed. "Are those our fields?" he asked.

She looked up, pulled from her thoughts, and gave him a dark look. He knew that saying "*our* fields" would annoy her, but he wanted her to get used to the idea.

She gazed beyond him to study the landscape. "No," she said finally. "Our—Moreton Hall lands do not border the railways until we get beyond Melton."

"And how far are we from Melton, do you reckon?" He wanted to keep her talking. Even her short answers were better than cold silence and watching her sink into gloomy reflections.

"We'll be there in a very few minutes, I should think."

The wheat fields gave way to an open pasture dotted with cows and edged by a wide stream. Tom pulled out the Bradshaw's timetable once again and thumbed through it until he found the page that corresponded to the route they were taking. The confusing jumble of town names and rail times was slowly beginning to make sense. He checked his pocket watch, which he'd adjusted to match the large clock at the last station, and compared it to the time listed for Melton. If Margaret was right, then the timetable was accurate. How amazing it all was.

And how fast. Even after seven hours on the train he was still amazed at their speed, finding it hard to believe that people could travel like this day after day. The train pulled in to Melton, stopping for less than five minutes as travelers scurried on or off the carriages. Tom had the unsettling sensation that everything was changing in ways he could never have imagined. He looked once more at the timetable. "We'll be at Bingham in twenty-three minutes," he marveled.

"Not soon enough for me," Margaret said wearily, leaning her head back against the seat.

"But that means we are going to cover fifteen miles in less than half an hour!" Even with the multitude of concerns crowding his mind, he couldn't shake the wonder of this first train journey. "Don't you find that even the least bit miraculous?"

His enthusiasm must have finally buoyed some part of her, too. A faint smile came to her lips. "Yes, I suppose it is."

The train slowed and pulled in to Bingham, which was the closest station to Moreton Hall. Bright gaslights held the growing darkness at bay. Tom and Margaret stepped out onto the platform as Stephens and Bessie emerged from another carriage and joined them. "How did you find the ride?" Tom asked his valet.

Stephens answered with a grimace, rubbing the small of his back. "No seat cushions in second class."

"Really? I wish I had known. We might have put you in first class with us."

"That's very kind of you to say so, sir, I'm sure," Stephens said, "but it wouldn't be my place."

What a shame, Tom thought, *that class distinctions should be extended even into railway carriages.* When he was poor, he'd never thought twice about giving way to his "betters," just as Stephens was doing. But now that others were submitting to *him,* he found these barriers disquieting. Somehow, remembering his *place* seemed a lot harder to do now that he was rich.

"Williams, there you are!" Margaret said as her steward approached, followed by another servant. "You are right on time."

"As are you," Williams said. "Like clockwork, these trains are."

"Hello, Mr. Williams," Tom said, extending his hand.

Williams hesitated. Was he still holding a grudge over the incident with the stable? Once again Tom found himself thinking that this man needed to realize Tom was here to stay. He kept his hand out, his gaze expectant.

Williams finally accepted his hand, and said, "May I offer you both my heartiest felicitations." However, the warmth of the sentiment was not reflected in either his voice or his expression.

"Thank you," Tom said, keeping his voice firm along with his handshake. "That's very kind."

Bessie and Stephens went off with the other servant, who had been introduced as Kevin, to locate the luggage. Soon they were all outside the station. Williams and Kevin had brought a carriage for the travelers and a wagon to transport the baggage. Kevin began heaving the trunks onto the wagon. Despite his still-sore ribs, Tom began to help. He'd lifted several of the smaller items onto the wagon before he paused, feeling, rather than seeing, a frosty glare aimed at his back.

He turned to find that, sure enough, Margaret was frowning at him in disapproval. "Kevin can manage the task quite well," she said.

"I'm sure he can," Tom replied coolly. "He'll manage even better with my help."

"That's the last of it, sir," Kevin said, giving the final box a pat for emphasis as he placed it on the wagon. No doubt he was trying to help keep the peace.

Tom helped Margaret into the carriage that Williams had brought. He motioned for the maid and valet to join Margaret inside, and then began to shut the door.

"Aren't you coming?" Margaret asked.

"I'm going to ride outside," Tom said. "I want to be able to see the road." He shut the door to cut off her protests, then climbed onto the high bench where Kevin was already seated, holding the reins.

Williams looked highly perturbed but said nothing. He got into the wagon and prepared to drive it behind the carriage.

"Best get a move on," Tom told Kevin, who was staring at him openmouthed. "I'm sure we all want to get to our beds."

"Yes, sir," Kevin said, giving Tom a grin that said he'd caught an innuendo in that remark. Tom hadn't intended one, but he smiled anyway. He was happy for the company of someone lighthearted just now. Kevin gave the reins a good shake and the carriage lurched forward.

Soon their small procession was leaving the brightly lit train station behind. Tom stifled a yawn, glad the journey was nearly over. The events at the station had probably given Margaret something new to be angry about, but Tom had good reasons for his actions. He wanted the staff to know he was not afraid of hard work. "How long have you been at Moreton Hall, Kevin?" he asked.

Kevin glanced at him, not hiding his surprise at being addressed. "Ten years, sir. I started as a stable lad. Since then I've had all sorts of duties. Now I work at the main house, and I also run errands for Miss Vaughn—er, Mrs. Poole."

"She must place great trust in you," Tom said.

"I hope I've earned it, sir," Kevin replied modestly. "I always try my best."

Kevin did indeed seem capable; Tom was impressed at the way he handled the team he was now driving.

"Perhaps, since you are so knowledgeable, I can count on your help as I settle in to Moreton Hall?"

"*My* help, sir?"

"You can help me get acquainted with the land and the house. Help me find my way around, so to speak."

Kevin looked genuinely pleased. "Yes, sir, any way I can. It would be a privilege, sir."

As the evening settled into night, mist rose gently from the fields all around them. The slow pace of the horse-drawn vehicles was jarring after a day on the trains. It seemed an age before Moreton Hall finally came into view. The place was somber and subdued, with lights in only a few of the windows. Torches sparsely scattered along the drive provided such limited light that Tom supposed the horses must be finding their way by memory.

Despite the lateness of the hour, the servants were at the ready. They gathered near the front steps to meet the carriage as it drove up. There were about a dozen of them, from the grounds and stable men to the butler and the housekeeper. It seemed a small number for such a large place. There had been at least this many at the Somerville home. Several of the indoor servants he had met already, on the night he'd proposed to Margaret. "Great heavens," he heard one of the maids exclaim. "Mr. Poole's ridin' outside with Kevin."

Tom jumped down and helped Margaret out of the carriage. "Welcome home," he said softly in her ear. She turned tired eyes up to his, searching his face, but made no reply.

When they were facing the little group of servants, Margaret announced, "This is Mr. Poole."

"Welcome, sir," they said in unison.

Their expressions were inquisitive but friendly. Unlike Williams, they seemed glad to have a new master in the house. They must have heard, or at least suspected, that Margaret's marriage would bring an influx of cash to the estate. Perhaps they'd all been hanging on, loyally working as Kevin had done, and waited for the time when she could make good on the back wages that she owed them.

"Thank you for the welcome," Tom said. "I won't keep you long, because I'm sure you all have very full days and need your rest. But I want you to know that I also intend to work very hard, right along with you."

This brought a ripple of delight from the servants, but beside him he could almost feel Margaret's disapproval. She probably thought the place would dissolve into chaos if he did not show them who was in charge. That was a complaint he'd heard from many wealthy people in London. And so for Margaret's sake he added, "Do not misunderstand me; I shall take my duties as master of the house quite seriously. If any of you has a concern about how things are handled here, I encourage you to speak to me directly."

This remark only brought on a worried glance between the butler and the housekeeper, and so Tom had to qualify his statement yet again. "I do not intend to belittle the confidence that has been placed in the butler and housekeeper by Mrs. Poole. I do expect you all to follow their directions." This seemed to appease them.

"I'm sure we hope to live up to your trust, sir," the housekeeper said, in a manner that was perfectly correct and diffident.

"Thank you for that, Mrs. Walker," Tom said. "And now I have a question to place to you."

"Yes, sir?" she replied, startled.

"Is there perchance a supper prepared? I am starving."

"Indeed there is, sir," the cook chimed in, without waiting to be asked.

"Excellent," said Tom. "That will be all."

The servants began to disperse, with a few staying behind to help unload the luggage.

Tom waved Williams over. "Would you be so good as to meet me here tomorrow after breakfast?"

He nodded. "Of course."

Margaret looked quizzically at him, but he merely took her arm and said, "Shall we?"

He was showing more confidence than he actually felt. It was disconcerting to be walking through these doors as if he owned the place—which, in a manner of speaking, he did. He was a country gentleman now, he supposed.

"Why are you meeting with Williams?" Margaret asked as they handed their hats to the servants.

"The harvest is under way, and I want to learn all I can." Before she could ask anything more, he added, "Now where is that supper?"

The cook had laid out a tasty supper of cold chicken, boiled eggs, bread, cheeses, and fruit, and Tom was glad to finally get a proper meal. Nothing they'd found on the journey had even come close. Margaret, however, ate little and spoke less. All her fire from earlier in the day now seemed muted by fatigue. She toyed with her wineglass, and seemed to grow more disquieted as the meal progressed. Tom was pretty sure he knew why. They were both thinking of the moment when he would take her upstairs.

Well, it would do neither of them any good to remain in suspense. Tom tossed his napkin onto the table and said, "Shall we retire?"

As he escorted her up the stairs, Tom could feel how tense she was. It was a sad state of affairs, Tom thought, that they should be embarking on their second night as man and wife, and yet still this unease simmered between them.

"This way," she said, turning to the left when they reached the landing.

Tom followed her willingly. Tonight, he would allow her to lead. Tomorrow he would explore every room so that he knew the place as well as she did. This was his home now. He had bought it at a very great price. He intended to learn every part of it and give it the best possible care. And he would do the same with his wife. Tonight, Tom had no plans to sleep on the floor. He would never force himself on her by any means, but he called to mind the times he had held her, the few precious moments when she seemed to have remained willingly in his arms. Surely he could find a way to coax such a response from her again—especially if they were in the same bed, with no barriers—

Margaret threw open a large oak door. "I thought this arrangement would work well for us."

Arrangement?

Tom followed her through the door and found himself in a sitting room fitted up with comfortable furnishings and a large fireplace. But no bed. There were doors that opened off either side of the room.

Margaret pointed to the door on the left. "That is your bedchamber." Indicating the door on the right, she said, "That one is mine."

"You arranged for us to sleep in separate rooms?" he said, staring at her in disbelief.

She took a step back in surprise. "The husband and wife always have separate bedrooms," she said. "That is how it is done."

"Dear Lord," Tom said, exasperated. "How is it that there are any of the upper classes left at all?"

She colored. "I do not say that the husband and wife never share the same bed. Although in our case, you did say that we would wait…" Her voice trailed off, but in her eyes he saw a renewal of the stubborn defiance that had plagued him all day.

Tom cursed himself for this promise he'd made. How could he win her if he couldn't even get near her? "Fine," he said, struggling to restrain his disappointment. "We shall wait."

"There is much to be said for having separate rooms," Margaret pointed out. "Especially in the mornings. I could not dress in the same room if your valet was assisting you."

There was logic in that, even though Tom thought the real problem was the convoluted rituals involved just to get dressed. "All right, Margaret. If having two rooms is what you deem proper, we shall have it that way."

He opened the door to his bedchamber and looked in. The room was large and airy, handsomely furnished, the wardrobe and washstand gleaming with fresh polish. Stephens had already been here, unpacking his trunk, setting out items he would need.

He turned back to find that Margaret had not moved from the center of the sitting room. "I would like to take a bath," she said. "That is, I will be calling Bessie to help me bathe, if you don't need me anymore this evening."

Need her? Tom needed every part of her. They were alone at last and he wanted nothing more than to sweep her into his arms. He closed the distance between them so quickly that her eyes opened wide in alarm. Remembering his promise, he checked himself with great effort and settled for taking hold of her hands. They felt silky and cool. "There is one more thing I need," he said softly. "It's that good-night kiss." That had been *her* promise to *him,* and by God he was going to take it.

"All right." Her breathing quickened, but still she looked maddeningly resigned.

He cupped her face in his hands. Her eyes warily searched his. He felt a small tremor run through her. Was it fear? Exhaustion? He wanted to kiss both of them away. Gently, he touched his lips to hers.

Her response was stiff, but not unyielding. Her lips were soft and delicious, and he kept on kissing her, seeking some spark of warmth, some reaction that said she was as thrilled and breathless as he was. He wrapped his arms around her and she placed her hands against his chest, not actively trying to push him away, but he sensed that she wanted to. She was keeping her part of the bargain, and that was all. Was this heady rush entirely on his side only?

He pulled back. For the briefest of moments her lips seemed to follow his. She opened her eyes and he would swear that for an instant he saw the same fire, the same passion. She blinked, then reached her hands up as though to rearrange her hair, although he had not touched it and every lock was still firmly in place.

"Thank you," he murmured, although he felt like a fool for saying it.

She gave a sort of dazed nod, then turned and walked into her room. As the door closed softly behind her, Tom couldn't help but wonder whether she'd locked it.

Chapter 24

After a fitful night's sleep, Margaret did not welcome the coming of day. But the sun was up, and she knew she must rouse herself. She stepped out of bed and pulled on her cotton wrapper. At the bedroom door she hesitated, wondering whether Tom was on the other side. She steeled herself and opened the door.

The sitting room was empty. Seeing that the door to Tom's room stood ajar, Margaret went over to it. "Tom?" she called softly.

No answer.

She peeked in. The room was empty, although evidence of Tom's presence was everywhere. The bed was rumpled, and his clothes from yesterday were draped across a chair. His comb, brush, and other toilette items were scattered on the dressing table, as though they'd been used and set down in haste. He had evidently not called his valet for help.

The large wardrobe stood open, now filled with Tom's clothing. Stephens would have unpacked them last night while she and Tom were at dinner, as Bessie had done with Margaret's clothes. She fingered one of the shirts, and ran her hands along a wool jacket. Everything was so sturdy, so strong. Very different from her collection of silks and satin, and even her cotton walking dresses. Everything was clean and pressed, exuding some kind of sharp, crisp scent—sandalwood, perhaps?—that was utterly lacking in her own wardrobe. She lifted a shirt-sleeve and placed it against her cheek, breathing in deeply. The scent brought her back vividly to the moment she'd been pressed against his chest, her thoughts jumbled by his nearness, the urge to push him away warring with the need to pull him closer. In the end she'd done neither but had stood, frozen by conflicting sensations, until he'd let her go.

She let the sleeve drop and turned away. She found herself staring at the bed, looking at the sheets Tom had tossed aside and the depression in the feather pillow where his head had lain. True to his word, he had done no more than kiss her good night. But she had seen his desire clearly enough. Sooner or later, he would surely come to her. Would he ask permission first, or would he simply slide into her bed some night, unannounced? He could take her by force—as a husband, it was his due. And yet each time he kissed her, such a thing was harder and harder to imagine. Every kiss held unmistakable passion and a tender insistence that she open up to him. His touch, his taste, were so intensely pleasing that she responded without hesitation. Last night, if he had not stopped, she could easily have succumbed completely. She might have invited him to continue, might even have begged for it—

She turned sharply from the bed and hurried out, closing the door firmly behind her.

Bessie came quickly to her summons, and in no time Margaret was dressed and downstairs. When she reached the breakfast room, the butler informed her that Tom had already left the house, but not before he'd consumed a substantial breakfast. "He does like to eat," the butler said. "I believe his words were, 'Got a big day ahead. Got to be fortified.'"

Margaret sat down to breakfast alone, just as she had done countless times. This morning, however, the room held a kind of hollow silence she hadn't noticed before. She was oddly aware of the clink of her teaspoon against the china and the quiet rustle of the footman bringing the food. She told herself she was imagining things, and tried to concentrate instead on all the things she had to do today. After months of being away in London, she had plenty of things to catch up on.

She was still eating when she heard footsteps coming down the hall. She looked up as Tom came in. His boots were dusty and his hair disheveled from the September winds. Margaret was amazed at how easily his presence could fill a room. He bent down to kiss her cheek. "Hello, my love." His brow furrowed as he got a good look at her. "Didn't you sleep well?"

Margaret thought the dark circles under her eyes must have given her away. She had seen them, too, as she stood before the mirror dressing. But she was unwilling to discuss her lack of sleep here in front of the servants, so she said casually, "Mitchell told me you went out. Did you go for a walk?"

"Yes. I went to inspect the barn. I want to be sure

the disease is completely gone before I bring Castor up here."

"The stables are perfectly safe. Williams has seen to that already."

Tom shook his head. "I directed the stable hands to do another cleaning. I want the barn emptied completely. They are going to pull out every last bit of straw and wood shavings, and wash down every surface with soap and creolin solution."

Margaret chafed. She knew Williams would not like this directive, and she didn't like it much either. Surely it was unnecessary work. "But you saw our horses last night," she protested. "They are perfectly healthy. Are you going to second-guess all of our decisions?"

"Whoa," he said, holding up a hand. "You should be glad I'm getting involved in all the day-to-day decisions. Would you really prefer a husband who took no interest at all in how this estate is managed?"

"There is a fine line between taking an interest and meddling. You don't know this place the way Williams does."

"Your argument makes no sense," Tom rejoined. "You say I don't know enough, but you would chastise me for trying to learn more about it."

Unable to think of a reply, Margaret drained the last of the coffee from her cup.

The butler entered. "Mr. Williams is in the study," he announced.

Margaret began to rise from her chair, but Tom stopped her by placing a hand deftly on her shoulder. "No need to join us," he said. "Finish your breakfast."

"But I want to—"

He pressed harder, leaving her no choice but to remain seated. "Please. I insist." He gave her shoulder a small squeeze before releasing it.

Margaret sat, unmoving, until he had left the room. Then she forced herself to take a few more bites of food, largely for the benefit of the footman serving her. She hated to look as though she had lost control in her own house, yet indulging in a full-scale mutiny was not the way to combat this image. For now, she must look as unruffled as possible.

By the time she'd left the breakfast room, she found Tom and Williams already in the hallway putting on their hats. "We're going out," Tom informed her.

"You can't leave without telling me your plans," she protested, stepping between them and the door. "Where are you going?"

"Williams is going to show me around and acquaint me with the harvesting." He lifted his eyebrows, his look inquiring whether she was going to give up her post.

Reluctantly she moved aside. As they passed her, Williams gave her a glance that looked both apologetic and irritated, as if to say, "I'm sorry for this, but *you* have put him in this position."

"I won't be back for luncheon," Tom said over his shoulder as he and Williams descended the front steps. "I will be back for tea, however. Then we can review the finances."

Tom strode quickly across the yard to where a groom stood waiting, holding two horses that were already saddled. Williams had to hurry to keep up with Tom's long, purposeful strides. Margaret watched as Tom mounted the horse with an easy grace that bespoke years of experience. Williams took the other horse, and the two rode off at a brisk trot.

Watching him disappear down the lane, Margaret felt ungrounded, like she was suddenly a visitor in her own home. Something very important was slipping from her grasp. She looked over the wide valley. It was still hers, but it wasn't hers. A voice within her protested, *What right does he have?* But she knew the answer already. Yes, the property was still hers, but the law would certainly side with Tom, an able man and her husband, if he wished to take full control.

Margaret considered having a horse saddled and following them. But they had just four horses at the moment, and the two not being used by Tom and Williams were needed for harvest work. She would just have to occupy herself here.

Immediately she went to the study, knowing there would be a stack of correspondence requiring her attention. She would get everything organized before Tom returned to "discuss" the financial matters. Surely he could not help but be impressed at how she had managed so admirably over the years with so few resources. As soon as she entered, however, Margaret saw with irritation that Tom had already been here, too. The servants had placed the papers on her large desk just as she had trained them to do, divided into three neat stacks of bills, business correspondence, and personal letters. But to her irritation, the first two stacks had already been opened and probably read. She stood looking at the desk, feeling violated. The fact that he had not opened the letters that were clearly personal did little to appease her. Tom had wasted no time in putting his nose into affairs that, up until two days ago, were none of his concern.

It took Margaret two hours to review everything. So much had piled up in her absence. Many bills were related to the wedding preparations, and others were brought on by the running of the estate. Yet as she went over them, Margaret concluded that nothing had been in excess of what was absolutely necessary. Tom could not possibly challenge her on any of it. And yet, for all her pains, what had she achieved?

With a sigh, she dropped the last bill back in place and stood up. Looking out the large window, she could see that the clouds were gray and ominous, ready to unleash another torrent of rain. She could only hope they'd be able to get in the wheat before it rotted in the fields. Knowing they now had the benefit of Tom's riches did not assuage her concerns. She'd seen how quickly money could drain away.

Never lose the land. Her grandfather had drummed this into her ears time and time again. Well, she thought bitterly, she had done exactly what he had raised her to do. She'd succeeded in that, despite her father's declaration in his final, drunken stupor, that she would fail. And yet here she was, still dependent on another man's whims—a man who for some reason was having dealings with her greatest enemy.

If Tom's interaction with Richard had ended at the wedding breakfast, Margaret might have been more at ease. She might have believed Tom was merely reacting to Richard's rude intrusion. And, angry as she had been at the time, she admitted to herself now that she had taken some satisfaction in the fact that Richard had gotten exactly what he deserved. But she sensed that there was something deeper at work. Tom's explanation of why he had visited Richard the next day did not entirely convince her. When pieced together with his sudden desire to do business with Paul, nothing about his actions made sense.

Tom was a man of contradictions—she had known that from the beginning. He had asked her to trust him, but how could she when his actions seemed to threaten the very things she was fighting for?

She reached up to push back a stray lock from her face, and found her hand was trembling. The fears she had tried to push aside now returned sevenfold. She would use those fears as a constant reminder that she would have to remain continuously on guard to protect what was rightfully hers.

*

Tom wiped the sweat from his brow and tried to shake some of the dust loose from his clothes as he prepared to enter the building that functioned as Moreton's little post office. He envied his horse, which was presently drinking greedily from the water trough outside. Tom was thirsty, too, and dead tired. But the day had been worth it.

He'd spent the bulk of it riding over all of the Moreton Hall holdings with Williams, meeting the tenants, helping out where he could. Time and time again the clouds had been on the verge of opening wide, threatening to rain on the wheat before they could bring it in. Each time, Tom had found himself praying with all his might and pitching in as everyone redoubled their efforts. And each time, the clouds had passed.

Even now, he noticed, glancing up once more, the sky, though gray and somber, did not threaten rain. The danger had passed them by. He gave another silent prayer of thanks to God as he opened the post office door and went inside.

A bell on the door clanged as he entered. An older man, graying and stooped, turned from where he'd been sorting letters and parcels. He gave Tom a nod and a pleasant, if mostly toothless, smile and welcomed him.

"Good afternoon," Tom said. "Are you the postmaster?"

"I am. That is, if you could give such a grand name to the little tasks I perform here." He indicated the small pile of mail he'd been sorting. "I don't get a whole lot of work." He smiled self-deprecatingly. "But it gives me something to do, and my wife, Nelda, says it's good to be rid of me for a while each day."

Tom offered his hand for the man to shake. "I'm Tom Poole."

"Very glad to meet you," the old man said, returning his handshake. "I'm Jim Rawlins. I've heard a lot about you."

"Have you?"

"Don't need a telegraph—my wife is attached to all the gossip. You're the new owner of Moreton Hall."

Tom had heard pretty much the same thing from everyone else he'd met today. But there was no point in telling them that he and Margaret were sharing the ownership of the land. "Yes, I'm privileged to be there now. I look forward to becoming a part of this community."

"Well, I wish you both much happiness. Mrs. Poole is beautiful, isn't she?"

"Yes, she is."

"My Nelda was quite a beauty in her day. Still is, of course, where it counts." He gently tapped his heart, and Tom had to smile. "I'm happy to see Mrs. Poole so well married," Rawlins continued, studying Tom with appreciation.

"You do me much credit."

"Well deserved, I'm sure—based on everything else we've heard about you."

"About my time in Australia, do you mean?"

"That's right. The gold mines, the shipwreck." He grinned broadly. "What stories you have to tell, I'm sure!"

"There are plenty," Tom acknowledged.

"Mrs. Poole has had some difficult years, you know. Ever since she was a child, there has been so much uncertainty, a lot of speculation about the land. A lot of bad blood between her and her cousins."

"Do you know the Spencers?"

"I've met 'em." Rawlins's expression turned dark. "Wouldn't give tuppence for the whole lot. I'd be happy if none of them ever sets foot in Moreton again. That's why we're glad you're here." He straightened as much as his hunched back would allow, and the smile returned once more to his face. "God willing, you'll have fine young heirs, and the Vaughn line will continue—in blood, if not precisely in name."

Tom appreciated the man's frankness. If everyone felt as Rawlins did, it would explain why the tenants had greeted Tom so hospitably today. "Thank you, Mr. Rawlins. I'll do my best to live up to your high hopes." Tom would of course have to take Margaret into his bed before this much-anticipated heir could arrive. However, just as the good folks of Moreton did not need to know the details of the land ownership, they certainly did not need to know about his and Margaret's conjugal arrangements. Or lack thereof. He cleared his throat. "Mr. Rawlins, I have a favor to ask of you."

"Of course," the man replied without hesitation. "What can I do for you?"

"I may receive some correspondence that will be marked to be held here until I call for it. I would appreciate it very much if you would keep an eye out for those letters and hold them aside as directed."

To his credit, Rawlins didn't even blink. No doubt he'd handled plenty of confidential matters in his day. "You can count on me, Mr. Poole."

"Thank you," Tom said with a grateful smile. "I'd also like to add—although it goes without saying, I'm sure—that I'm counting on your absolute discretion in this matter."

"I won't breathe a word of it," Rawlins assured him. "Not to anyone."

*

Margaret sat in the parlor, with the tea growing cold, waiting for Tom. She tapped her foot impatiently while she distracted herself by gazing out the window. All day long, as she'd gone about her tasks, she'd been amazed that the looming rain never arrived. That must be why Tom was late. With the rain holding off, the workers would be taking advantage of every minute to bring in the crops. Perhaps Tom was spending the day in the fields, harvesting like some common laborer.

When the parlor door finally opened, Margaret turned, not to see Tom as she'd expected, but Williams. "Hasn't Mr. Poole come back with you?" she asked in surprise.

"No. We split up about an hour ago. He was on his way to town. Said he had some business to attend to there." He dropped into a chair, and Margaret thought she had never seen him looking so dusty and out of sorts.

"What kind of business?"

"He didn't tell me. He asked me to come to the house and tell you he'd be along 'directly.'" Williams's manner of delivering this message showed both what he thought about being an errand boy and about Tom's choice of vocabulary.

Still, Margaret could benefit from Tom's delayed arrival. It gave her a chance to speak to Williams alone and glean information she may not have gotten from Tom. She poured him a cup of tea. "Where did you two go today? Please, tell me everything."

Williams accepted the tea gratefully and took a long sip before answering. "Mr. Poole dragged me from one end of the property to the other. He wanted to meet every tenant. He talked to every one of them. In most cases, he met their families, too."

No wonder Williams looked so dusty and parched. "What did he want to talk to the tenants about?"

"Their lives, their families, how long they've been on the land."

"I could have given him all that information," Margaret said.

"Precisely," Williams answered, not hiding his scorn. "It's just the sort of things the *lady* of the manor might busy herself about."

Margaret poured more tea into his cup. "You know, we have to accept that Mr. Poole's way of doing things may be different from what we've done in the past." She spoke without conviction, however, and Williams did not offer a reply. "He told me his intention for going out with you today was to learn more about the farming."

"Oh, he did that, too, believe me," Williams said. "He just about drove me mad with his questions. By the end of the day I was beginning to think he didn't trust a single thing about how I've been managing this estate. He bedeviled the farmers with his questions, too, asking them *how* they knew to do this or that, *why* they'd made certain decisions. At one point I pulled him aside and told him—with all due respect, mind you—that some of those men have been farming for longer than he's been alive. They know full well what they're doing."

Margaret was not surprised by Williams's report, nor that he would find Tom's actions so annoying. "And how did he reply?"

"He said maybe that was part of the problem."

"Problem!" Margaret scoffed. "What problem?"

"Exactly! I told him we've been getting on quite well, thank you—insomuch as farming is always subject to the vagaries of nature."

"Like this year's rain," Margaret said, agreeing with him.

"Yes. Although it held off today, thank God. But as I pointed out to him, our bad years were often due to circumstances beyond our control."

Margaret put down her teacup and sat forward in her chair. "Mr. Williams, I'm going to be quite frank with you."

"I hope you may always feel so, madam," he said deferentially.

"When Mr. Poole and I discussed marriage, I told

him of my . . . concerns. I've worked very hard to recover from the damage wrought by my father and his worthless steward. I couldn't have done it without your help, of course."

Williams gave her a satisfied smile. "I thank you for the compliment."

"I told Mr. Poole that I was determined to stay involved in managing the estate and that I trust your judgment implicitly. He assured me that we would continue to proceed in just that way."

"But that hasn't been the case, has it?" Williams said with a sniff.

"On the other hand, it's only the first day. It could be true that he is simply trying to learn the details of what goes on here. It could be he didn't even realize he was causing you offense. As you have noted, Mr. Poole is not always well versed in the more subtle arts of conversation."

"A very astute observation," Williams said. "However, I am quite sure Mr. Poole knew *exactly* what he was doing. I believe he is trying to undermine my authority—and, by implication, yours as well."

"We cannot allow it!" Margaret said, rising to her feet. "What if he does something that jeopardizes all we've worked for?" She could not shake the specter of Richard and Paul—Tom had dealings with them that he would not explain, and both men had plenty of reason to wish Margaret ill. If Tom was in league with them, or if either had some kind of control over him, it could only spell disaster.

Williams stood and said forcefully, "He won't jeopardize Moreton Hall. I'll make sure of it."

She regarded him earnestly. "Mr. Williams, I need your help more than ever. You must be my eyes and ears; keep me informed of everything that goes on. If you have any concerns whatsoever, you must bring them to me immediately."

Williams's expression was cold and determined. "You can rely on me for that."

Chapter 25

Margaret smiled uneasily as she and Tom walked down the aisle to the pew that had always been reserved for the Vaughn family. It had been months since she'd been in this place. Everyone else knew this, from the townspeople in the pews to the Reverend Hollister, who beamed at them from the altar.

Now, after five days at home—five long days with a husband who was largely absent during the day and still leaving her undisturbed at night—it was the Sabbath and Tom had insisted they come to church. He said hello to many of them by name as he and Margaret made their way to their seats, and they returned his greeting joyfully. In just a few short days, Tom had already become part of the town. Margaret, despite her intense ties to the land and her efforts to make the area prosperous, had never experienced a truly close bond with the townspeople. There had always been a barrier between her and them, one she had ascribed to differences in station. There was no doubt that Tom's working-class background had appeal for them. But she sensed there was a greater reason for their respect. Many here were greeting him with an attitude of gratefulness and even adding "God bless you, sir." What had he done to merit this? she wondered.

The service was, as Margaret expected, a rather standard affair. She had seen Tom's intense interest in the Bible, the way he read it every evening with the dedication of a clergyman. Clearly he thought about it, ruminated on it, and took pleasure in it. Margaret had warned him that the service might not be as thrilling as someone with Tom's avid interest might wish it to be. And indeed, the sermon was short and mildly vague. But Tom listened intently, and afterward as Reverend Hollister met everyone at the church door, Tom shook his hand and thanked him heartily.

Virtually the whole congregation clustered around Tom and Margaret in the little churchyard, offering their good wishes. First to greet them were Mr. and Mrs. Rawlins. "I'd like to introduce you to my wife," Mr. Rawlins told Tom.

Tom took the old lady's hand and kissed it. "Mrs. Rawlins, what a pleasure to meet you. I have heard your beauty praised and your virtue sounded."

Margaret turned to stare at Tom in surprise. He was quoting Shakespeare! Did he realize that? He gave his most charming smile to the old lady, who blushed— probably for the first time in fifty years. "Oh, heavens!" Mrs. Rawlins warbled. "What a gentleman you are, Mr. Poole."

It was only after many more introductions and welcomes, and after Tom had invited the reverend and his wife to dinner on Sunday next, that they finally were able to get into their carriage for the journey back to Moreton Hall.

"Everyone seems quite enamored with you," Margaret observed, once they were on the road.

"It's a fine town," Tom replied. "They are kind people."

"The admiration on their faces was unmistakable," Margaret persisted, despite Tom's humble answer. "What did you do? It must have been something extraordinary."

Tom stared thoughtfully ahead, driving the team of horses with care along the rough road. "Do you really want to know?" he asked.

"Of course," she replied, startled.

"I prayed with them."

"You what?"

"Not all of them, mind you, but some of those farmers I met on the first day. They were heartily worried about their crops. I told them there was once a man in the Bible who prayed earnestly that it would not rain—and it didn't rain for two whole years."

"Two years?" Margaret said doubtfully. "How could that be?"

Tom shrugged. "There was a reason for it when it happened in the Bible, I guess. But I told our good people that God would help them in time of need, too—and they *needed* to get those crops in. So we prayed."

"It didn't rain that day," Margaret said, recalling how the dark clouds, although swollen with rain, had passed them by. "Was Mr. Williams with you when you prayed?" He had not mentioned this incident to Margaret.

"Yes, but I don't think he took any stock in it. He said something about the 'vagaries of nature,' as I recall."

"But the farmers believed in those prayers, didn't they? Country folk have always been a superstitious lot."

This brought another shrug from Tom. "I think *superstition* is a name people give to something others believe in but they don't."

There wasn't any way around that kind of logic. Margaret looked out over the fields, now shorn and brown. Whatever the cause, today the sky was bright blue. If the weather held like this, the harvest would be safe and they would have a successful year. If this made Tom a local hero, what was the harm? And yet... would it really be safe to have people idolize him? The thought worried her. "Hadn't you better leave the praying to Reverend Hollister?" she asked. "Surely it would be embarrassing if you prayed publicly for something and it didn't happen."

Tom shook his head. "Prayer never hurt a thing. Saint Paul said we should 'pray without ceasing,' so I reckon that's a good plan. Although—" Tom pulled the horses to a halt. He tied off the reins and turned to look at her. "Although there are times when the good Lord answers our prayers in ways we do not expect. Some might find *that* embarrassing, too."

He raised a hand to her cheek, much as he had done every night, the prelude to their "good-night kiss." Those kisses had become longer and more sensuous each time, and yet without fail Tom had broken it off before they could progress any further. The tension of waiting, wondering when he would press for more, was coiled up inside her, growing tighter with each passing day. His gaze traveled from her eyes to her mouth, and she knew he was not planning to wait until tonight for their next kiss. He wanted it right here, in the open road, in the light of day. On a Sunday.

And she wanted him to do it.

No, surely she didn't. It was foolish and improper. She struggled to find her breath. "Did you know that you were quoting Shakespeare to Mrs. Rawlins?"

She had merely been searching for something to say—anything that might get them back to safer ground. Her words were more effective than she'd expected. The passion in Tom's eyes faded, and he turned away. "Was I?" he said with a strained laugh. He loosed the ribbons and set the horses in motion. That moment that might have ended in a kiss was gone, and Margaret was relieved.

Wasn't she?

"It . . . was from *The Taming of the Shrew,* I think," she stammered.

"Hearing thy mildness praised in every town," Tom recited, even as he kept his eyes on the road. "Thy virtues spoke of, and thy beauty sounded—yet not so deeply as to thee belongs—myself am moved to woo thee for my wife."

"How do you know that passage?" Margaret asked.

"I learned it from Edward Somerville," Tom said. "He loved poetry."

"Edward—that was Geoffrey's brother?"

"Yes. He was a good friend. Someday I'll tell you more about him. For the moment, suffice it to say the man was an actor at heart. He kept us entertained, especially on those cold winter nights when we were all huddled around the hearth to keep warm." He chuckled. "Those lines about *mildness* and *beauty* and *virtue* were ones he loved to quote in reference to his wife, who was indeed a charming woman and completely in love with him."

"Those words had a very different meaning in the play," Margaret observed. "They were used ironically. Katherina was not exactly mild. She was a fierce woman who stood up for herself."

"Is that how you see it? Yes, I suppose you would." He threw Margaret a quick sidelong glance. "She was not so fierce by the end, though."

Margaret could not help but give a little sniff. "I feel she was coerced."

"I see." Tom gave another slap of the reins and the horses picked up their pace. "I prefer to think of it as—how did the man on the train put it?—love breaks down all barriers."

*

"There is something for you today," Mr. Rawlins said as Tom came through the door to the post office. He reached under the counter and pulled out a letter. True to his word, for the past month Rawlins had been quietly setting aside letters for Tom that had been marked "to be held until called for."

Tom frowned, thinking this was likely to be another missive from Spencer or Denault. Both had written to him every week, and he had put them off as long as he could, explaining that he could not make another trip to London until after the harvest. This had kept them at bay, but he could tell from the tone of Spencer's last letter that he was growing impatient. Tom would have to go down to London very soon. He'd already accepted that the funds he'd given Denault for the railway were lost forever, but every part of his soul rebelled against paying blackmail money to Spencer.

Tom took the letter from Rawlins. His heart lifted when he saw that this letter was from Geoffrey. Perhaps this was good news at last. "Thank you, Mr. Rawlins," he said, and hurried toward the door.

"You're welcome. Good day to you!" Rawlins called after him.

As he stepped outside, Tom tucked the letter into his coat pocket. He would wait until he had reached a place where he could read the letter undetected. As he mounted his horse, he saw Williams coming out from the butcher shop across the street. Williams waved. Tom returned the greeting, but did not stop.

He rode swiftly, with an occasional glance back to check that he wasn't being followed. He'd begun to notice that Williams had the oddest way of turning up unexpectedly. But Williams must have remained in town. The only travelers on the road were the farmers bringing in their loads from the harvest. Tom turned into a meadow and rode to the little abandoned cottage where he and Margaret had made their wedding pact. It had become his private spot for reading and replying to sensitive correspondence. As always, it stood empty. Tom eagerly tore open the letter as soon as he was inside.

Dear Tom,

    I have conferred with several people whom I can count on for their extreme discretion. Of particular help to me was Lord Ashley. He has conferred with Mr. Charles Dickens, who is a friend of his. Do you know the man—the writer? If so, you may be aware that he is exceedingly familiar with the people generally referred to as "the criminal element." He has spent a lot of time accompanying the Metropolitan Police, and has seen firsthand their ways of dealing with those who commit crimes, both minor and serious.

Dickens put Ashley in touch with a man named Inspector Field, who was the chief of the Detective Branch until he retired last year. He now works in a private capacity, helping people with matters they would prefer not to take to the police. I believe this Inspector Field can help you find the best plan for dealing with your situation. He is a most congenial and forthright sort of man. He has years of experience and is renowned for his shrewdness as well as his wide knowledge of crime and the law.

He is willing to meet with us at four o'clock on Monday next. This should give you time to come down to London for the meeting. Please write back at your earliest convenience and let me know if this will suit. This seemed a good time, since you indicated in your last letter that the harvest is nearly complete.

Lizzie sends her love. Our prayers are with you.

Yours most sincerely,
Geoffrey Somerville

P.S. Chalmers, the head groom, has done a good job of looking after Castor, but he says the horse is getting restless.

Tom read the letter through a second time, and then burned it. As he watched the flames reduce the paper to ashes, he considered what he would do. This Inspector Field sounded exactly like the sort of man who could help. What a boon that Geoffrey's connections had provided access to such a man.

When Geoffrey mentioned Castor, he had given Tom the best reason for going to London. He would tell Margaret that he was going to supervise Castor's transport to Moreton. He had intended to do this anyway, having satisfied himself that the stables no longer posed a threat.

He would have to make sure Margaret did not go along with him. If anything, she would probably be relieved that he was going away for a few days. Even so, he would not take any chances. He would make sure she did not know about any of this until he had found a way to deal with Spencer once and for all.

*

Margaret stalked into the breakfast room. "I just found Stephens packing your trunk," she said, throwing out the words as an accusation. "He says you are going to London. Why didn't you tell me?"

"Hello, my love," Tom said, rising languidly. He appeared not the least bit ruffled by her anger. In fact, he grinned. "So you went to my room. Were you looking for me?" His voice dropped to a husky whisper as he placed a light kiss on her cheek. "Had I known you wanted me, I would have stopped by your room on my way out."

Margaret took a step back and crossed her arms. She was beginning to recognize Tom's tactics. He was trying to evade her question by distracting her. "You can't just leave for London without giving me any advance notice," she insisted, her irritation still firmly in place.

He shrugged. "A business matter has arisen unexpectedly. It requires my immediate presence in London. I had every intention of telling you about it at breakfast."

"What kind of business?" she asked suspiciously. Williams had told her of Tom's frequent visits to the post office, and she was worried that events were once again slipping out of her control.

Tom gestured to the table. "My eggs are getting cold. Are you going to stand here questioning me all day, or will you sit down to breakfast?"

Margaret stood her ground. "What kind of business?" she persisted.

His eyes flashed in annoyance. "If you will recall," he said acerbically, "John Sullivan sends me regular reports. The latest dispatch has arrived, along with a fresh shipment of gold. I assume you would like for me to go and look after my money? Or should I say, *our* money," he added pointedly.

"I—" she stammered, suddenly chastened. It sounded perfectly reasonable, of course, but still she could not shake her worry. "So that's it, then? Nothing else?"

"There is one more thing I need to do, as it happens." He paused, picking up his cup from the table. She tapped her foot impatiently while he finished his coffee, knowing he was deliberately making her wait. Finally he set the cup back down with a small noise of satisfaction. "I am going to bring Castor back with me. Geoffrey says the old boy is getting lonely without me, and I don't trust anyone else to load him on one of those trains. I might even bring you back a present. Wouldn't you like a new horse, a proper mount to replace the gelding you lost?"

The warmth was back in his expression. It seemed to her that Tom was as variable as the wind. She never knew which direction he would take next. He took a gentle hold of her hands. This time she did not try to pull back, but said stoutly, "I would prefer one of my own choosing."

He laughed outright. "Oh, my dear Maggie," he said with a gleam in his eye, "didn't anyone ever tell you not to look a gift horse in the mouth?"

*

Well, he had done it. He'd convinced Margaret to stay at Moreton Hall while he went to London. He was free to meet with this Inspector Field. Already he felt one step closer to solving the problem of what to do about Spencer. Tom knew that vengeance belonged to the Lord, not to man. That would keep Tom from finishing the job he'd started at the wedding breakfast. He would not allow Spencer to provoke him again to physical violence. But that did not mean he could do nothing. The laws of England punished extortionists, and surely Tom was justified in seeking that end for Spencer. But he had to find a way to protect Lizzie, too.

It would be good to see her again. Her letters had been getting shorter, and Geoffrey's were getting longer as though trying to make up for the shortfall. This might not signify anything at all, and yet something kept tugging at Tom's consciousness. He wanted to see for himself that she was well. He'd come back to England for her sake, yet here he was living far away from her. Although the railway had reduced the distance to one day's journey, he still felt as if he'd abandoned her. It was a foolish notion, of course. Lizzie had her husband, not to mention her grandmother and her cousin. She had all the good care that she could wish for.

As he watched the fields roll by, Tom's thoughts returned to Margaret. He missed her already. He was actually growing fond of her prickly ways and her stubborn self-confidence. He only wished he had been able to find the way to her heart by now.

Every night she responded more and more to his kisses, but by day she was still resisting him. He was under no misapprehension that she loved or trusted him. Nor, he supposed, did he deserve it. Not until he could be completely honest with her.

Holding off, when he longed to take her to his bed, had been the most difficult thing he'd ever done. At times the pain of longing was so intense that not even his trials after the shipwreck could compare. But he knew in his heart that he was right to wait. Every night, as he returned to his cold bed, he prayed, believing that when the time was right he would know it, and that they would be coming together for all the right reasons.

*

Margaret was only half listening to the housekeeper's report of the state of the linens and other household goods. Ordinarily this was a task Margaret enjoyed. She had kept a sharp eye on the few items she'd been able to retain, making sure everything was accounted for and carefully maintained. Today, however, she was unable to concentrate. Her thoughts kept straying to Tom. She was troubled by his sudden departure, and far too keenly aware of the difference between his being just over the ridge or hundreds of miles away.

Slowly she became aware of a silence in the room. She looked up from the list she had been pretending to read, only to find the housekeeper waiting politely for a response. She must have just asked Margaret a question. Margaret gave her an apologetic smile. "Mrs. Walker, would you mind terribly if we continue this in an hour or so?"

"Will you be needing a bit of a rest, madam?" the housekeeper replied with mild concern. "Shall I call for your maid?"

"That won't be necessary." Margaret stood up with an air of briskness that she hoped would convey that she was perfectly well. "Will you ask the butler to come in here, please?"

The housekeeper nodded and left the room.

A few moments later, the butler entered. "You asked for me, madam?"

"Did Mr. Poole receive any correspondence today, before he left?"

"Today? No, madam."

"Yesterday, then?"

The butler shook his head. "I've seen nothing for him these past two or three days."

"Are you quite sure? Might any of the other servants have received it?"

"I doubt it, but I will be happy to check with them."

"Yes, please. If you would be so kind."

The butler left on his errand. Margaret believed he was correct, that no mail had come, but she wanted to be absolutely sure. That would mean Tom hadn't received a sudden notice about his business, as he'd implied. It was possible that he had deliberately waited until he was packed and ready to go before he told her about it, to ensure she would not go along. She found the idea disquieting.

Another possibility occurred to her. Williams had told her that Tom frequently visited the post office in Moreton. It was possible Tom was receiving correspondence directly from there. When the butler returned and confirmed that no letters for Tom had come to the house, Margaret gave instructions to have her carriage prepared. She would take a ride into town.

Chapter 26

Geoffrey personally greeted Tom in the front hall and escorted him to the parlor. As they entered, Tom was surprised to see no one there. "Where is Lizzie?" he asked.

"She must remain upstairs now, on strict bed rest."

This news sent Tom's worries to flight once more. "What's wrong with her? Is the baby all right?"

"At the moment, everything is fine," Geoffrey assured him. "However, the doctor has insisted she remain in bed until the baby arrives."

"But that's over a month from now. A long time to remain in bed." What was more troubling, it sounded too much like what Ria had gone through. Lizzie and Ria were half sisters; would this fatal trait be one thing they shared? The look on Geoffrey's face did nothing to assuage his fears. "What else did the doctor say?"

"He recommends that we avoid any subjects that would upset or worry her. To my mind, that includes telling her about our meeting with Inspector Field."

"Of course. That's been our plan all along."

"Now it seems more critical than ever. I have been careful in what correspondence I allow her to see, and what news she receives. She still has no notion of what happened at your wedding breakfast, nor of the subsequent troubles. We must keep it that way."

"Believe me, I agree with you wholeheartedly." Tom motioned to the door and added, "Can I see her now?"

Geoffrey nodded. As they made their way up the stairs, Geoffrey said, "Even James has managed to curb his tongue and not speak of it. He has restricted himself to mindless babble about the goings-on about town. But he makes her laugh, and that is a good thing."

They paused outside the door to her room, and Geoffrey said quietly, "I beg of you not to show too much dismay when you see her. If we show fear for her, it will not help her own view of the situation."

The room was dim. Lizzie lay with her eyes closed as a nurse sat in a chair near the window, placidly sewing and keeping watch over her charge. Tom thought Lizzie must be sleeping, but she opened her eyes immediately as they entered. "Tom!" she cried out joyfully, stretching out her arms in welcome.

Tom was glad Geoffrey had given him some warning. Lizzie looked very pale, and although the girth of her stomach had increased she seemed to have shrunk everywhere else. Her face was pinched and drawn. Tom bent down to kiss her cheek. "I want you to know, dear Lizzie, that I am quite affronted that you did not greet me at the door."

His attempt at humor brought out a wan smile. "You must blame Dr. Layton for that, I'm afraid. And Geoffrey, too, who I am convinced is in league with him. They seem to think I must be coddled."

"Then you must allow them to do it," Tom said. "There are not too many women I know who would complain about being waited on hand and foot. Enjoy it while you can."

"Listen to your brother," Geoffrey put in with an approving nod. "You must rest up, my dearest. Once you have given birth to that fat, pink baby, you may trot up and down those stairs all you like."

Lizzie sighed. "It's not the stairs I miss. It's the park, and the riding. I miss the company, too. No one seems to visit us anymore."

"Yes, well...perhaps that's for the best," Tom said. He could not help but throw a quick, worried glance at Geoffrey as he said this, which he regretted instantly, because Lizzie saw it.

"Why is it for the best?" she asked anxiously. "Is something wrong?"

Tom blamed himself heartily for his mistake, and hurried to cover it. He made an exaggerated tug at his cravat, which Stephens had so expertly tied for him this morning. "I have concluded that there is nothing more boring than society people, nor anything more confining than its rules. Be glad you do not have to endure such people for a while."

She did not look convinced. "Does that mean you're happy to be in the country, far away from the strictures of town life?"

"Well, my wife still has an annoying habit of making me dress for dinner." It seemed odd to say those words— *my wife*. Tom was still getting used to them, especially since she was still his wife in name only.

Lizzie sat up, her eyes how bright and eager. "And

how is married life, Tom? You are the most wretched letter writer, you know. You've hardly told me anything. Now that you are here, you must tell me all about it. Are you and Margaret getting along well?"

Very rarely in his life had Tom been able to keep anything from his sister. Especially not when she looked at him so earnestly with those vibrant, violet-blue eyes. Today would have to be one of those times. He could not tell her of his trials at Moreton Hall—the separate bedrooms, the secret correspondence, the moments when he and Margaret had been tantalizingly close, only to have something arise that brought discord yet again. Tom could not trouble Lizzie with any of these things. She looked far more ill than Geoffrey seemed willing to acknowledge.

Happily, Tom had observed James's trick of being able to say one thing and mean quite another, without exactly lying. It was a skill, indeed. And so, putting on an air of contentment to cover the irony, he said, "Oh, Lizzie, the way we are getting along would astound you."

*

Margaret walked swiftly up the street toward the livery stable where she'd left her horse and carriage, pondering the conversation she'd just had at the post office with Mr. Rawlins. No matter how Margaret had approached the subject, he'd given no hint that Tom had been collecting letters there. He'd said only how happy he was that Tom would stop by from time to time to pass the time of day with him. Margaret was still unconvinced.

As she drove her carriage toward Moreton Hall, she breathed in deeply of the fresh, cool air. Autumn was advancing rapidly; they might even have an early winter. All around her, the shorn fields lay brown, their bounty yielded up. Of all the seasons, Margaret loved the autumn best. The intense labor of summer was over, and life slowed to a more comfortable pace. The days grew shorter, but remained long enough to drive out and to pay visits to neighbors. Best of all, the weather was usually perfect for riding. Margaret longed to go riding again, to explore the meadows and woods as she used to do.

She was just approaching the little lane that branched off to the abandoned cottage, and on an impulse, Margaret turned her carriage into it. She had a sudden desire to see the place again. Upon arriving at the cottage, she was just getting down from her carriage when something unexpected caught her eye. There was horse dung near the hitching area, and it was fairly fresh—no more than a few days old at most. Someone had been here recently. Had Tom sent someone out to repair the leak? She could see no outward signs of roof work. Other than the evidence of a horse having been here, the place was undisturbed.

The interior of the cottage looked just as it had the day she and Tom had sought refuge from the rain. Memories of that day, which had wrought so many changes in her life, began to flood her mind. She ran a finger over the rough-hewn table where Tom had casually tossed his coat, and pictured him as he had stood by the hearth, his damp shirt clinging to him and his features lit by the fire he had started so deftly. Something *had* changed, though. She caught sight of a small wooden box on the floor, sitting half-hidden by a table leg. She bent down and lifted the lid. The box held pen, ink, and paper.

Margaret could think of no one else who would have placed these items here except Tom. He must have been coming here for a private place to read and write. That would explain why she had occasionally noticed ink stains on his hands, even after he'd been gone from the house all day. It would also explain those times when Williams had been unable to discover where Tom had gone or what he had been doing.

In Margaret's mind, this was all the proof she needed that he had been keeping secrets from her. She returned the lid to the box and considered taking it with her in order to confront Tom with it as soon as he returned. But she doubted even this would force him to talk. Margaret had spent the weeks since their marriage learning, to her chagrin, that Tom was every bit as stubborn as she was.

Leaving the box where it sat, she straightened and prepared to leave. She paused at the threshold and turned back for one last look, her eyes drawn to the spot where he had kissed her for the first time. Even now the memory of it brought fire to her face and sent her pulse racing. On that day, as in all the days since, Tom had never concealed his desire for her. And yet he had never taken that desire to its logical conclusion. This had confused her, but now, suddenly, she understood. Tom had held back because she had pushed him back. In this one very important thing he had been a gentleman, not willing to take her against her wishes. With this realization came the certainty of what her next step should be.

With a man like Paul it had been easy to wield those powers of persuasion known as "feminine charms." Why had she not tried this with Tom? In the depths of her soul, Margaret knew the answer. Back then, her heart had been safely aloof, invulnerable. With Tom it was infinitely more complicated. Her reactions to him had been too intense, too unsettling, and she'd kept pulling back, afraid of losing control. She had never even considered that she might use their physical attraction in a way that could be to her advantage. Perhaps she should be like the biblical Delilah, coaxing the secrets from Samson's heart.

*

"You understand, Mr. Poole, there may be repercussions from this," Inspector Field said. "You must decide if you are willing to take that risk."

Tom and Geoffrey were at Inspector Field's home, which he had assured them was ideal for privacy and confidentiality. Field's own wife sat in a chair outside the door of the little parlor where they were meeting, keeping watch to be sure they were not disturbed nor overheard by any of the servants. Since Mrs. Field was a sturdy, take-charge kind of woman, Tom had no doubt she discharged this duty quite well.

They'd only been here for a quarter of an hour, but Tom was already convinced that if anyone could help them, it was Inspector Field. He was a short man, but wide and solidly built. He kept an aggressive stance as he talked, constantly using gestures to punctuate his words. Tom could easily believe he'd kept criminals in line with his authoritative and no-nonsense manner.

Tom had explained that Richard Spencer wished to blackmail him with something he knew about Tom's past. Inspector Field had not yet asked him the particulars, but Tom sensed they were getting around to that.

"What kind of repercussions are you speaking of, Inspector?" Geoffrey asked.

"If we prove Spencer is blackmailing you, and we subsequently bring him to justice, then the information you are now paying him to conceal may yet come to light. It could come out at trial." He leaned back in his chair and steepled his fingers above his round chest, sending Tom a piercing glance. "Are you prepared for such a thing?"

Tom thought about this. "Yes." He took a breath. "And no."

This brought an inquisitive tilt of the head from Field.

"I'm not worried about myself," Tom explained. "However, the honor of a lady is at stake. She has done nothing illegal, mind you—and yet she stands to lose her good reputation."

"I see." Field's wide forehead scrunched in thought while he removed his wire-framed glasses and wiped them with a handkerchief. "Naturally, when blackmail is involved, one expects that there are sordid or embarrassing reasons for it." He resettled his spectacles on his wide nose. "I must ask for your complete candor, gentlemen. I promise you that nothing you tell me will go beyond this room."

Geoffrey cleared his throat. "Very well, then. Inspector, the lady we are speaking of is my wife."

"I see," Field said again, showing no appearance of surprise. No doubt scandals among the titled classes were not news to him. "It is no small thing to slander the wife of a peer."

"She is also my sister," Tom said. "And I will do anything to protect her."

"Is she aware of your problems with Mr. Spencer?"

"No," Geoffrey said firmly. "She is about to give birth to our first child, and she is in delicate health. She must not know anything about this until after she is fully recovered."

"I understand. The timing is vital. When is the happy event to be?"

"In just over a month."

"Never you worry, sir," Field assured him. "We'll do everything we can to keep the lady from distress. We shall proceed with the utmost care."

Chapter 27

"Whoa, there!" Tom struggled with the rope as he led his stallion off the freight carriage. Castor snorted and pranced, pulling Tom with him as he rushed down the ramp. Tom regained control once the horse was standing on solid ground. If anything, Castor's spirit set Tom's mind at ease. It was proof he had survived the journey intact, and for that Tom was immensely thankful.

The speed of the trains, not to mention the vigorous starts and stops and the piercing whistle, had been difficult enough for Tom on his first journey. Today they were doubly distressing because he had worried about their effects on his horse. Everyone had assured him that this was actually safer for the horse than tramping along rutted roads, but Tom had still been wary. They had come too far together for Tom to lose him now.

The gelding Tom had also brought was standing docilely a short distance off, held by a station hand. That horse had probably taken a train journey before, perhaps on its way to London from the farm where it had been bred. It was a tall creature, and Tom liked the way he held his head. He could easily imagine Margaret on this horse. He had known it was the right one for her as soon as he had seen how easily the horse handled, and how well it moved. The gelding had plenty of spirit, though, and Tom was sure Margaret would be pleased. He could hardly wait to present it to her.

He hired a driver to take him to Moreton Hall. The horses were tied to the back of the dogcart, easily keeping up with its slow pace.

"Them's gonna be a fine addition to any stable," the driver said with admiration. "Don't often see 'em so fine around these parts."

"It's just the beginning," Tom said. "I plan to build the best stable of horses in Lincolnshire."

"I reckon you'll be up against Mr. Innis for that honor," said the driver with a chuckle. "He's got some fine ones, he has."

"For riding?" Tom asked with interest.

The driver gave a nod of his grizzled chin. "Aye, and racehorses, too. He's made a good penny or two on several of 'em."

Seeing that Tom was inclined to listen, the driver launched into a description of Mr. Innis, who was by all accounts a conscientious and well-respected man. He was actually a tradesman, but through some distant relation he'd inherited an ailing estate. Under his oversight it was prospering, and he was even adding to his holdings. It occurred to Tom that perhaps he should make this man's acquaintance, and find out what he had done to be so successful. Maybe Tom could apply the information to the Moreton Hall farms.

The dogcart plodded steadily along the country road. Everything around Tom gave him pleasure, from the smell of wood smoke wafting through the air to the leaves rustling in the stiff breeze. Already the place felt like home. He could not recall feeling this way about anyplace in Australia. His home with Lizzie had been a happy one, to be sure, and the landscape had become comfortably familiar over time. But never had his heart given the curious little stutter it was doing now as Moreton Hall came into view. He knew why, of course. His wife was there.

He knew that he was returning to worries and cares not readily apparent behind the placid façade of the stately old mansion. But he was brimming with renewed determination. He'd seen once again that deep, irrevocable bond between Lizzie and Geoffrey. Their love, respect, and tender care for each other was a shining example of what a true marriage could be. Tom wanted that for his own life, and he was ready to redouble his efforts to win his wife.

As the wagon approached the house, Margaret stepped out the main door. She paused at the top of the wide stone steps, waving and sending him a bright smile that seemed to reach out and latch on to his heart. Had she missed him, perchance? His throat tightened, and blood began to thunder through his veins. Hope could do that to a man.

She hurried over as Tom jumped to the ground. "Welcome home," she said, drawing close to him.

Dazed by this reception, Tom drew her into a hug, savoring the soft warmth of her body pressed to his. He'd been dreaming of just this kind of tender moment. Far from avoiding his embrace, she had invited it. "Hello, Maggie," he said in her ear. "Did you miss me, then?"

"Very much," she replied, lifting her face to his. Her

green eyes danced, and her full red lips lingered tantalizingly close, beckoning for a kiss. He was about to do just that when she reached up and placed a finger on his lips. "If you please, husband, people are watching." She said it with a flirtatious smile that only made him want to kiss her more.

A thump and a soft whinny startled them. They turned to see Castor tossing his head and tugging at the rope. The driver waggled his eyebrows suggestively. "Looks like the stallion's gettin' restless."

Tom shot him a quick grin before turning back to his wife. "Come here, Margaret, I've brought someone for you to meet." He led her around to the back of the cart. The last rays of the late afternoon sun gleamed on the gelding's bay coat. Even in the fading light it was easy to see he was a magnificent animal. "Mrs. Poole, may I present Bright Star."

"He's beautiful!" Margaret gasped. Immediately she began inspecting the animal with practiced care, her hands traveling over him from head to tail. "He's perfect," she pronounced. "I can't wait to ride him!"

"We must go out first thing tomorrow," Tom agreed.

Gently she traced the star-shaped mark on the horse's forehead. "Bright Star. It's lovely." Tom could have sworn there was a tear in her eye. But it might have been a trick of the fading light. "Thank you," she said softly.

For once her smile reached her eyes, lighting her face with pure happiness, making her nearly irresistible. More than anything in the world, Tom wanted to hold her tight and kiss her senseless. Only an impatient stamp and a snort from Castor, who could sense that meal and bed were close at hand, kept Tom from carrying out this notion.

Two servants carried Tom's baggage inside while

Tom paid the driver. "Let's get the horses settled, shall we?" he said to Margaret as the driver tipped his cap and drove away.

"I'd like that." She took hold of Bright Star's lead.

A lamp at the stable door shone like a beacon, lighting their way. As they walked, Margaret spoke quietly to the horse, telling it how happy it would be here and of all the wonderful times they were going to have together. She spoke with the simple exhuberance of a child, and Tom was glad. He had hoped this gift would soften Margaret's heart, and her giddy rambling seemed proof that it had worked. Remembering the warm greeting she had given him even before she had taken note of the horses, Tom's heart lifted with thankfulness.

A stable boy who slept above the barn heard their approach and came out to meet them. Tom set him to work grooming and feeding the horses. Margaret spoke to Bright Star once more before they turned to go. "Rest up," she said, patting his neck. "You and I shall have a good long ride tomorrow."

"May I come along, too?" Tom asked with a smile as they strolled arm in arm out of the stable. He liked this new, friendlier Margaret. He hoped fervently that it would last.

"Do you think Castor can keep up with him?" she teased.

"I think they are a well-matched pair."

She looked up at him quizzically. "You speak as though they were carriage horses."

"Cannot two riding horses be well matched also? They are free to go in any direction, and yet they can move together in harmony if they choose to."

A flicker crossed her face as she caught the meaning of his words. "I suppose they can," she acknowledged.

Once again Tom was seized with the urge to pull her close and kiss her. This time, there was no reason not to. He was alone with his wife on a moonlit fall evening. Her lips parted, as though she were thinking the same thing.

He leaned in, ever so slowly, every nerve alive with anticipation. Her breath quickened, but she did not pull away. Dear Lord, she *wanted* this as much as he did. Their lips touched. Tom kept the kiss gentle, savoring it, marveling that she was so willing. Then her arms came up around his neck, pulling him closer, and he was lost.

Her lips opened to him freely, and he deepened the kiss, reveling in the taste of her. She returned the kiss with equal passion, her body pressed against his, igniting flames of desire. Tom began to loosen the pins from her hair, relishing the feel of the silky strands as he ran his fingers through them.

"Oh, dear," she murmured. "What will the servants think if I return to the house with my hair in disarray?"

"They will think I have been greeting my wife," he said, trailing kisses along her cheek. The warm vanilla scent from her skin and hair roused every one of his senses. "There's no sin in that."

She placed soft hands against his chest in gentle remonstration, murmuring between his kisses. "But we mustn't ... there should be ... propriety ..."

Tom relented, but as he stepped back he chided gently, "I'm afraid you asked for it, my dear wife." He loved how she looked just now, with her hair down around her shoulders, and her softly parted lips swollen from his kisses. "It's too late for propriety," he observed. "They'll know you've been giving me a warm welcome."

It was too dark to be sure, but Tom imagined a lovely pink blush on her fine, high cheekbones. He sincerely hoped it was there. It was more proof that she was coming alive to him. He took hold of her arm and they began to walk once more toward the house.

Tom pulled her gently to a stop before they reached the front steps. Although he wanted nothing more than to sweep her up the staircase and into his bed, he felt that simple logistics were against them. Lights poured through the open door, and the butler and footman were visible in the entry hall. Margaret had again reached up to rearrange her hair, and already she was taking on the posture of the lady of the manor. Soon her mask of propriety would be firmly in place. This moment they were sharing was a delicate thing that could be easily lost in the glare of lights and the presence of the servants. It would be swept away by the bustle of the maid and the valet and the usual business of turning in for the night. There were things Tom needed to share with her—plans she probably would not like. Perhaps she would be more amenable if they talked now. "Let's not go in just yet," he suggested. "It's a fine night. Perhaps a stroll in the back garden?"

The glow from the house bathed her face in pale light, and she relaxed into a smile. She almost looked relieved. "All right."

*

Margaret sat in the garden, waiting for Tom's return. He had gone inside briefly to release the servants for the evening. She ran her fingers along the rough stone bench, glad for these few moments to compose herself. She took in long, deep breaths, thankful for the way the night air cooled her cheeks.

She had planned to give Tom a warm greeting, to set in motion her plan of winning his confidence rather than trying to force it from him. She had not planned on the particular way her heart had jumped when she saw him, the way his presence only magnified how lonely the house had been without him. Tom's gift had touched her deeply. He had clearly chosen Bright Star with care, understanding Margaret well enough to pick a horse that was exactly right for her.

He had been gone just a week, and yet she had forgotten how easy it was to lose herself when he was near. The idea that she could remain aloof in her heart, even as she attempted to draw him physically closer, had faded. She realized she was nowhere near being able to play Delilah. She had caught a glimpse of just how intense their physical union would be, and it had shaken her soundly.

"I've brought you something." Tom slid onto the bench beside her. He was holding one of her shawls. He carefully draped it over her shoulders. "I didn't want you to catch a chill." His arms wrapped around her along with the shawl, encircling her with warmth.

"I could hold you like this forever," he murmured in her ear.

She leaned against him and sighed. Perhaps she had been mistaken. Perhaps his trip to London had been just what he'd said it was: an opportunity to handle papers that had come from Sullivan and to visit Lizzie. And yet, as the breeze sent a few dead leaves dancing at their feet, she remembered her discovery at the cabin. "Tom?" she said tentatively.

"Hmm?" He was nuzzling her ear.

"I visited the little abandoned cabin the other day."

"Oh?" The nuzzling paused.

"I found a box of writing papers. Are they yours?"

"Yes." He pulled away slightly, though his arms did not entirely leave her. "I suppose you are wondering why they are there."

"I was."

"I've been doing a bit of writing." He actually sounded sheepish, not as though he'd been caught at anything underhanded. "It's just for myself, you understand. Thoughts on things I am learning, or things God is showing me."

Margaret certainly had not been expecting this. "You mean, like a diary?"

"Of sorts. Nothing formal. Just notes. I find it helps me to write it down. And I like that cabin. It's quiet, and easy to think there."

It was a plausible enough explanation, if somewhat unusual. But she wouldn't mind seeing proof. "Will you show me your notes sometime?"

"If you like. I doubt you'll be able to decipher much of it, though." The breeze blew more stiffly, ruffling Margaret's shawl. Tom settled his arms around her again, and she had the sense that he had dismissed the writing papers from his mind. "And now, Margaret, I have something to ask of you. Would you like to spend Christmas in London this year?"

"London?" she repeated in dismay. "But that's such a dismal time to be there. The wind howls around the buildings, and the coal dust makes everything filthy."

"I know it's asking a lot, but you see, Lizzie is not well. She cannot leave her bed, and we are all deeply concerned about her health, although no one will admit it." The pained look on his face showed the depth of his worry. "She will be glad for your company, and you can help her when the baby arrives."

"Me?" Margaret had no idea how much help she would be. The thought actually gave her some trepidation. "But the baby is due well before Christmas, isn't it?"

"In early December. The fact is, I'd like to leave here in just a few weeks, if we can manage it."

"Surely you don't mean we should stay with the Somervilles all that time?"

"Will it really be such a trial?" He squeezed her gently. "I know I promised you a honeymoon in Scotland. But perhaps we can go in the spring. For now, Lizzie needs us. And isn't that what's most important?"

"Of course," Margaret replied, though without enthusiasm. She understood the need, but still she did not relish the idea of leaving Moreton Hall for weeks on end when she felt like she'd only just returned. She thought, with some small measure of resentment, that it was a hard thing to ask of her. She stood up, wrapping her shawl tightly around her. "Well, good night," she said. "I'm sure we can discuss more of the details tomorrow." He looked disappointed, but made no move to follow her as she hurried back to the house.

*

"Here we are. It's cozy, but comfortable." Mrs. Claridge, the Somervilles' housekeeper, threw open the door to the bedchamber where Tom and Margaret would be staying.

Margaret gasped. The room was small. And there was, of course, just one bed. "We are both staying here?" she whispered to Tom.

"I'm afraid so," he whispered back, looking decidedly pleased at the prospect.

Mrs. Claridge did not miss the look of dismay on Margaret's face. "We are a bit tight for space at the moment, I'm afraid. We've had to convert one of the rooms into a day room for Lady Somerville, now that she is no longer able to take the stairs. And of course, another is being prepared for the nursery." Mrs. Claridge beamed at the prospect. "But we'll do all we can to make you feel at home." She pointed to the far side of the room. "There is a small dressing room through there, to make things more convenient for you."

Margaret threw a cold look at Tom, wondering why he had not mentioned this arrangement before they'd come. He had to have known. He'd lived here all summer, so he knew full well the layout of the house.

"Thank you, Mrs. Claridge," Tom said. "I'm sure we'll be quite happy here."

As soon as the housekeeper left the room, Tom closed the door and burst out laughing.

"What's so funny?" Margaret demanded.

Tom leaned against the bedpost and gave her a cheeky grin. "Don't look so scandalized, my love. You are my wife, remember? Besides, there's one thing very convenient about this arrangement."

"Just one?" Margaret asked drily.

He walked over and lightly touched her chin. "I won't have to go very far to find my good-night kiss."

Chapter 28

At last Lizzie was asleep.

Margaret put down the book she had been reading to her, setting it gently on the small table next to the bed. She stood and stretched, careful not to allow her skirts to rustle too much, wishing most of all not to awaken Lizzie. Reading to her every afternoon had proven to be the best way to calm Lizzie's restless agitation. Margaret was glad to see her drop off at last into a doze. The room was far too hot, and Margaret was desperate to step outside for some cool air. She could not understand why it was necessary to keep the room so stuffy, with the windows tightly shut and the fire burning hot. But she knew little about these things, and she supposed the doctor knew best.

Carefully she slipped out the door and down the hall. Lizzie was likely to stay asleep for an hour or more. There would be time for Margaret to step outside and breathe. The day was fine, if cold, but Margaret would welcome its bracing effects.

As she reached the first floor, she was surprised to hear Lady Thornborough's voice coming through the open door to Geoffrey's study. "You mean you haven't told her yet?"

Margaret paused, wondering why Lady Thornborough had not come upstairs to visit her granddaughter straightaway. That had been her usual pattern on her daily visits here. In the brief time Margaret had known Lady Thornborough, she'd been rather put off by that lady's crusty and somewhat imperious manner. Margaret was debating whether to slip quietly outside and avoid seeing her when she heard Tom say, "I haven't yet gotten permission from Lizzie to tell her about it."

Who were they talking about? Was it her? She slipped back against the wall so she would not be seen. There were no servants about, so she could listen without detection.

"You don't mean to say Lizzie knows about this," Lady Thornborough said, sounding affronted. "In her condition—"

"Lizzie does *not* know," Geoffrey broke in. "We are all in agreement that she does not need any more cares thrust upon her at this time."

"But, Mr. Poole," Lady Thornborough said, "I don't understand why you have not told your wife. After all, she is part of this family now."

Margaret had to admit this remark made her like the old lady a little bit better. By the same token, it made her angry at Tom. There was something he was keeping from her. But what? And why?

"The secret is not mine to tell," Tom insisted. "I promised Lizzie that I would never speak of those events to anyone. I do not intend to break that promise until I have gotten her permission to do so. Until then, we must wait."

Tom said this with the adamant air of one who has gone over a problem many times and always arrived at the same conclusion. Margaret was all too aware by now that Tom was stubborn enough not to budge once he'd made up his mind on something.

"Aren't you afraid Margaret will get wind of this some other way and end up telling Lizzie about it by mistake?"

"I have the situation under control," Tom insisted. "Spencer is not going to do anything that will jeopardize his position."

Spencer! Shock rattled through Margaret and she leaned against the wall for support.

"I've told him that drawing up the proper documents will take some time, as will bringing Margaret around. He doesn't like it, but he has accepted it. He wants that land too badly."

Nothing in this conversation made sense to her, except for one thing: Tom was talking to Spencer. About her land.

"I still don't like it," Lady Thornborough was saying. "What you are doing is dangerous. If things turn out badly, the scandal could be ten times greater. You must be careful."

Margaret heard the tread of someone coming up the stairs from the kitchen. Probably a maid bringing tea. Margaret had no wish to be found eavesdropping by one of the servants. She hurriedly straightened, took a deep breath to calm her nerves, and walked briskly into the study. "Good afternoon, everyone," she said. "What must we be careful about?"

She didn't really think that plunging in so rudely would get them to dislodge the information, since they had just agreed on secrecy. But it was worth a try. She stood waiting, her heart pounding during the uncomfortable pause while Tom and the others exchanged glances. Then Lady Thornborough said, "Hello, dear. We were just discussing Lizzie, and how we must be careful about these final days of her lying-in."

"Were you?" Margaret said crisply.

"Yes. I was just saying that it's a common practice to bring in a nurse at this time," Lady Thornborough continued, ignoring Margaret's undisguised disbelief. "I have persuaded Lord Somerville that my servant Martha is the best person for the job. Her grandmother was a midwife, and she herself has attended many births."

"Exactly," Geoffrey said, taking Lady Thornborough's story and running with it. "I agree that it is an excellent idea. How is she, Margaret?"

"She is sleeping. I came downstairs for some fresh air." She wasn't getting it here, however.

"You will be glad for Martha's help," Tom told her, picking up the charade. "We've asked too much from you. You are looking tired, and we mustn't take advantage of your good nature."

Margaret could only stare at him, having no words. How on earth was she going to get to the bottom of this? She opened her mouth to speak, but Tom gave her hand a squeeze and dropped a quick kiss on her cheek. "Oh, look," he said as the maid and a footman entered with heavily laden trays. "Here's tea."

*

"Are you absolutely certain everything is safe?"

Margaret sat in Mr. Hawthorne's office at Lincoln's Inn Fields. She had come here as soon as she could arrange it, still worried by the conversation she had overheard at the Somervilles'.

"There is nothing untoward going on, I can assure you," Hawthorne said. "If, as you say, Mr. Poole intends a land transfer of some kind, you know he cannot proceed without coming to me first."

"And you would tell me if he had, wouldn't you?" Margaret watched him carefully as she asked, searching for even the slightest indication that her solicitor was lying to her.

He only looked saddened by her question. "How can you even suggest I would do otherwise?"

"Because the laws of our nation have never been in favor of women," Margaret pointed out. "As my husband, Tom might be able to find some way to circumvent my wishes. He might find a way to break the stipulations of the trust."

"I assure you that would be difficult, even with the bias of the law. Also, I would certainly alert you immediately if your land was in any danger."

His demeanor and deference toward Margaret were exactly as they had always been, leading Margaret to believe his assurances. But there were still too many unanswered questions. "What do you suppose that conversation meant?" she asked.

He sat back in his chair, contemplating the question. "At this point, it's difficult to say. But I shall look into the matter. Ask a few judiciously worded questions among my colleagues. There is not much I can do for the next several days, however. All work is at a standstill until the duke's funeral is over."

Margaret could believe this. The Duke of Wellington's funeral was to take place in two days, and the entire city was in upheaval from all the people who had come to town in order to pay their last respects. Even Hawthorne's chambers had been difficult for Margaret to reach, as there were teams of workmen everywhere, erecting viewing stands and barricades along the five-mile route laid out for the duke's elaborate funeral procession. She sighed. "I suppose you will also be attending the funeral?"

"Indeed I shall." Hawthorne gave a tiny, sad smile and his eyes grew misty. "There has never been a man in England as great as the old duke. We will never see his kind again."

"You served him well," Margaret said. She did not know all the details, but she was aware that Hawthorne's espionage activities had been instrumental in the effort to defeat Napoleon.

He acknowledged her compliment with a respectful nod. "That is another reason why you can have complete confidence that I will do all I can to prevent your lands from falling into the hands of anyone who did *not* serve our country well."

He did not elaborate. He did not have to. Margaret was perfectly aware that he hated Spencer's family for the very same reasons she did. "Mr. Hawthorne," Margaret begged, "you must find out why my husband is in league with a traitor."

"Is that what troubles you?" Hawthorne responded

with an enigmatic smile. "Madam, one thing I have learned over the years is that one must never rush to judgment before gleaning all the facts. That something untoward is happening seems to be undeniable. But consider this: it's possible that Mr. Poole has not entered into these negotiations willingly. I believe you said his words were 'I've told him that drawing up the proper documents will take some time…' This could be true…or perhaps he is stalling."

Margaret blinked. "Stalling?"

"Looking for a way out of Spencer's grasp."

"Tom…in Richard's grasp? But why? That would be disastrous!"

Hawthorne held up his hands in a calming gesture. "I can only counsel you to be patient and to remember that in life there is always more than meets the eye."

*

Margaret was still mulling over Hawthorne's words the next day when Geoffrey said, "I'm afraid I shall be required to attend the duke's funeral at Saint Paul's."

Margaret, Tom, and Geoffrey were seated together in Lizzie's room, keeping her company for the afternoon. Geoffrey had made his announcement with an air of chagrin, prompting Lizzie to respond, "Why do you look so glum? It's an honor to go, surely?"

"Yes, but I must leave very early in the morning and be gone for most of the day. I hate to be gone from you for so long."

Lizzie gazed at him tenderly. "You needn't be concerned on my account. I shall be fine."

He did not look convinced. "I must also tell you that

James will be escorting Lady Thornborough to the Beauchamps' home to watch the procession from their parlor windows. That will leave you with no one for company, I'm afraid."

"I'll be here," Tom put in. "And so will Margaret."

Lizzie looked at him in surprise. "Don't you two wish to see the procession? I have heard it's going to be very grand. There will be ten thousand people in the procession alone, and a million people coming out to watch it. The *Times* says there has never been anything like it."

"I have great respect for the old gentleman, to be sure. But he will have plenty of people watching out for him today." Tom reached out and took hold of his sister's hand. "*You,* dear Lizzie, are far more important to us." With his free arm he grasped Margaret around the waist. "Isn't that right, Margaret?"

On the surface, this display signaled that they were all one happy family. It was true that Margaret was growing fond of her sister-in-law. But at the moment, Margaret could only see hypocrisy in Tom's actions. How was Margaret truly a part of this family if they were keeping secrets from her?

Chapter 29

It rained steadily through the night, and an icy wind howled around the chimneys and found its way through tiny cracks edging the windows. Tom lay awake, staring at the ceiling, as he had done night after night for weeks. His worries for his sister's health were mounting, and so was the ache in his heart over all that was dividing him from the woman lying next to him.

Margaret had been acting cold and distant ever since she had walked in on his conversation with Geoffrey and Lady Thornborough. How much, if anything, had she overheard? Tom tried to tell himself that Margaret would surely have confronted him directly if she'd heard them talking about Spencer. He might even have preferred her to do so; at least that way he would know what she was thinking. But her reticence was harder to decipher. It placed Tom in a difficult position. He could not bring up the subject himself without the risk of admitting that he was keeping things from her.

Margaret lay unmoving, her eyes closed, and yet Tom

sensed she was awake. She did not have the deep, regular breathing of one who is sleeping. She turned her back toward him, indicating she had no desire to talk. Perhaps that was just as well. Tom wanted desperately to bare his soul to her, but he could not do it yet. He must have patience. Once Lizzie had gotten through childbirth and was fully recovered, Tom would be free to explain everything and somehow find a way to break through Margaret's wall of doubt and suspicion.

So much hinged also on finding a way to end these dealings with Spencer. His demands had mounted, as Tom had suspected they would. Now he was making it clear that he was after Moreton Hall itself. Tom had been able to do little besides make up excuses and drag his feet while Inspector Field tried to find a way to give them the upper hand. So far, all had been unsuccessful. There seemed no way to prevent the day coming when Tom must either allow his sister's reputation to be ruined or gain the undying hatred of his wife. Perhaps he already had the latter.

It broke his heart, day after day, to keep these secrets. He was paying dearly for it, having a wife who was so tantalizingly near and yet entirely inaccessible. He stifled a groan, feeling the surge of unrequited longing. No wonder he was unable to sleep.

He lay pondering these things until daybreak. Then he slipped quietly out of the bed, dressed quickly, and left the room. As he came down the stairs, he was surprised to see Geoffrey already in the front hall putting on his coat.

"I'm glad you're up," Geoffrey said. "I was hoping to see you before I left."

"Are you really leaving so early? I thought the service didn't begin until eleven."

Geoffrey nodded as he finished buttoning his coat. "With these crowds, getting to Saint Paul's may take hours. The muddy streets will not help matters." He paused before reaching for his hat and gloves. "Take good care of Lizzie today, Tom."

"I should think that would go without saying."

"Of course. But I'm concerned about her. She keeps insisting that she is comfortable, but I am not so sure. The look on Martha's face this morning told me otherwise. She didn't even want me to enter Lizzie's room. She claimed Lizzie was getting some much-needed rest and that I mustn't disturb her. But I hate to leave without saying good-bye."

"What a man in love you are," Tom chided. "She'll be fine. Maggie and I will see to that."

His gentle ribbing gleaned a small smile from Geoffrey. He shook Tom's hand vigorously. "Well, then, I leave it in the Lord's hands. And yours," he added, seeing that Tom was about to lodge another protest.

Tom watched as Geoffrey dashed through the rain and into the waiting carriage. He wondered how far they would get before Geoffrey would be forced to complete the trip on foot. It was a miserable day, and Tom was not sorry that he had promised to remain here.

He went to the breakfast room, but found the servants were still laying out the dishes and were not yet ready to receive him. He was considering waiting in the library, where a book might distract him from his growling stomach, when he saw Martha hurrying by. A maid followed her with a tea tray. "Martha, what news? Is Lizzie awake? Is anything wrong?"

Martha paused only briefly. "She's a bit uncomfortable, but it's just gas pains, I expect. I've made this special herb tea for her, and soon she'll be right as rain. If you'll excuse me, sir." She went up the stairs, with the maid close behind her, before Tom could ask any more questions.

Tom followed them upstairs and watched as they disappeared into Lizzie's room. It was all he could do to keep from busting the door down and demanding entrance. These women had continually been frustrating his efforts to see his sister. He'd seen so little of her in the past few days that he might just as well have been in Australia.

It occurred to him that even if he could not enter her room, they might allow Margaret to do so. He went swiftly to the bedchamber, where he found Margaret seated at the vanity table and brushing her hair. She looked pale, and dark circles under her eyes showed she had been missing sleep, even as he had. He closed the door gently behind him. "Margaret, how quickly can you get dressed? I need to know what is happening with Lizzie, and the nurse refuses to let me in."

Margaret set down her brush and stood up. "Is something wrong?"

"I don't know. That's what I need you to find out."

*

Martha started up out of her chair as Margaret opened the door, and then relaxed when she saw who it was.

Lizzie was sitting up, sipping tea. Her hands were shaking as she brought the cup to her lips. She gave Margaret a wan smile. "Good morning."

Margaret took the chair next to the bed. "How are you?" she asked, concerned by Lizzie's pallor and the thin film of sweat on her forehead.

"I have had a bit of cramping, but Martha says these herbs will help." She took another sip of tea, but a grimace shot across her face. She set down the cup with a clatter.

"Are you all right?" Margaret asked, now genuinely alarmed. Surely cramping could not be a good thing.

"It's nothing," Lizzie insisted. "I'm afraid these herbs are somewhat bitter." She turned to Martha. "Would you be so good as to have some toast brought up for me? That will help me get the rest of this tea down, I think."

Seeing Martha's hesitant expression, Margaret said, "I'll stay here with Lizzie."

"Very well," Martha said reluctantly. "I shan't be gone long."

When she was gone, Lizzie sighed deeply and said, "To tell you the truth, Margaret, I am afraid."

She said this so quietly that Margaret did not think she had heard correctly. "I beg your pardon?"

"Geoffrey and Tom refuse to acknowledge that anything could go wrong. They won't even allow me to speak of such a possibility. But you see, I've only ever attended one birth—that of my poor half sister, Ria. Her child was stillborn, and—" Her voice cracked. "Ria died a few months later."

"Surely you don't believe the same thing will happen to you?" Margaret asked.

Lizzie looked down at the blanket covering her large belly. "All I know," she said, her voice trembling, "is that I have been experiencing the very same troubles Ria had. Those final days with her…they are burned into my memory forever. It's so hard not to imagine what might happen when my time comes." She raised large, troubled eyes to Margaret, fear plainly written across her face.

"I have heard that all women go through trials at this time," Margaret stammered. In truth, she had absolutely no experience with childbirth at all, but she was searching for a comforting answer. "Not all births end in ... that is, most end well. Besides, you are getting the best possible medical care."

This last remark had the opposite effect from what Margaret intended. Lizzie's expression grew even more distressed. "Dr. Layton is giving me the very same instructions that the physician in Bathurst gave to Ria— but she died! Don't you see? Either they are wrong, or else there is nothing they can do!" She began to sob, clutching the blanket as though for dear life. She must have been holding these fears for quite a long time, desperate to unburden herself. "It's not only fears for myself," she choked out. "It's Geoffrey. And our child—"

Margaret perched on the edge of the bed and placed an arm around Lizzie's shoulders. "Everything will be fine," she soothed. "You'll see." She continued offering such words until finally, after several long minutes, Lizzie's cries subsided, and her shoulders no longer shook.

Lizzie wiped her eyes and gave another rattling sort of sigh. "I'm glad that Tom is settled, at any rate. That way, I know that he has someone, just in case something should happen to me."

"Nonsense," Margaret said, with more conviction than she felt. Lizzie's fears were beginning to settle onto her as well. "Nothing will happen you. For one thing, you know that Geoffrey would never allow it."

Lizzie sniffled and tried to smile. "Geoffrey has been petitioning the Lord quite vigorously on my behalf. He says the Bible instructs us to pray without ceasing. Do you pray, Margaret?"

Prayer might not have been Margaret's solution, but she was not surprised to hear that Geoffrey would take this approach. "Tom quotes that verse, too, and I think he does quite enough praying for us both."

"He didn't used to be that way, you know," Lizzie said. "He never was religious. He used to positively rail at God. Especially after—" She broke off as the door opened and Martha entered with the toast. "Well, I'm sure he's told you all about it," she finished quietly.

In fact, Margaret did not know. Tom had never completely shared his past with her, and Margaret had many questions. However, with Lizzie in such a fragile state, now was not the time to ask.

Lizzie took a few bites of toast, then drank some more tea. She seemed calmer now. Margaret was beginning to breathe easier herself, when suddenly Lizzie cried out, spilling the tea as she dropped the cup and clutched at her stomach. This time she fairly screamed in agony.

"What's happening?" Margaret shrieked as Martha raced over to the bed and began to pull back the blankets.

"Merciful heavens," Martha said. "She's going into labor."

"No," Lizzie protested. "I can't be. The baby's not due—aah!" She screamed again, and this time the bedroom door opened and Tom said, "What's going on?"

"Mr. Poole, don't come in, I beg you," Martha said. "It wouldn't be proper."

"Proper be damned," Tom said, rushing to his sister's

side as Martha hastily replaced the blankets. Lizzie moaned again, grabbing his arm and looking at him with terrified eyes.

"Martha says I am going into labor," she gasped. "But that can't be. It's not due for weeks yet."

"A baby comes when it decides it's ready," Martha said, "not when we think it will. Mr. Poole, will you go and fetch the doctor?"

Tom didn't answer, and Margaret could see his desire to stay with Lizzie was warring with the need to get help. "We could send a servant," Margaret offered. She was as eager as Lizzie was for Tom's presence. She did not want to be left to care for Lizzie without his support.

But Tom shook his head. "Getting the doctor will be difficult. The roads are nearly impassable due to the crowds. I can't trust anyone else to go." He took both of Lizzie's hands and looked at her earnestly. "Lizzie, I'm going for Dr. Layton. You must be brave. Margaret and Martha will be here to look after you."

Lizzie nodded, trying to stifle another cry as a spasm of pain hit her again.

"Don't you worry, sir," Martha said. "We'll keep her comfortable until the doctor comes."

"Thank you," Tom said. "I know I can count on you both."

Margaret knew this was her cue to nod and give a reassuring smile. In the end, it didn't matter that she could not, for without even glancing in her direction, Tom turned and hurried from the room.

Chapter 30

The rain was tapering off, but the streets were thick with icy mud. It was slow going. The Somerville house was located north of the route planned for the funeral procession, and the doctor's house was even farther north. This meant that Tom was traveling against the crowd of people who were walking south to find a view along the route.

The procession had already begun its long crawl from Buckingham Palace to Saint Paul's Cathedral. The beating of drums and the music of the death march was carried along on the biting wind, drawing late-arriving spectators to the sound. Tom's cab kept pressing north. It was only as they drew near the doctor's home that Tom allowed himself to even consider the possibility that Dr. Layton might not be there. He might be watching the procession or on his way to attend the service at Saint Paul's.

Tom rang the bell for several minutes, growing more worried. At last an elderly lady who identified herself as the housekeeper answered the door and informed Tom that the doctor had gone out.

"Can you tell me where he is?" Tom asked anxiously. "It's vital that I reach him right away."

"He was invited to Lord Morrissey's home in Pall Mall to watch the procession," the housekeeper said. "His lordship's home lies directly along the route."

Tom thanked her and set off once again, praying with all his might as the cab headed south, directly into the fray. He kept repeating to himself a verse from Psalms: "Our help cometh from the Lord, who made heaven and earth..."

The traffic thickened, and finally the cab was forced to a halt. "I'm sorry, sir," the cabbie told Tom. "We can't go no further."

Tom got out and paid the driver. He would have to go the rest of the way on foot.

The army regiments marched along Pall Mall, ten thousand strong and interspersed with the carriages of dignitaries. Tom could see no end to it in either direction. The streets were barricaded to hold back the people, who were everywhere—climbing lampposts and statues and any building that might offer a ledge or a foothold for a better view. But there were not the usual sounds one associates with such a crowd. Everyone was reverent and quiet. Tom asked a man if he knew which was Lord Morrissey's house.

"Indeed I do," the man said. He pointed straight ahead, past the crowds and the barricades and the never-ending stream of soldiers and royal carriages to a stately mansion on the opposite side of the avenue.

All of Tom's prayers dissolved into the frigid air as

he realized the impossibility of his situation. Dr. Layton may as well have been on the moon.

*

The room was stifling hot.

Margaret longed to throw open a window, if only for a moment, to clear her head. But that was impossible. She sat cradling Lizzie in her arms, trying to soothe her as she continued to moan in pain.

Tom had been gone for hours. Where was he? If the doctor was lost amid the teeming masses, how could Tom hope to find him? Margaret tried to clear her head of such dire thoughts. "Surely there is something we can do?" she asked Martha, who was just finishing the task of changing the bed linens out from underneath Lizzie.

Martha straightened and gave the soiled sheets to a maid, who took them away. Her brow creased as she studied Lizzie. "I do have a mind to try something. My grandmother always said the best thing to do was to get the lady up and walking."

"Walking!" Margaret said in dismay. "Surely not. Look at her."

"It does seem odd," Martha agreed. "However, my grandmother swore by it." She gently took hold of Lizzie's arm. "Are you willing to try it, Lizzie?"

"But the doctor insisted she should not leave the bed," Margaret argued. If something bad should happen...and if Tom should blame her...

Lizzie grimaced in pain from another contraction. Then she nodded her answer to Martha's question. "I...don't... believe...the doctor," she rasped. "I want to move."

They helped Lizzie rise slowly to her feet, carefully

supporting her as she took one tentative step, and then another. Margaret was sure Lizzie was still in pain, but the satisfaction she was deriving from moving was evident on her face.

"That's a girl," Martha said soothingly. "Move just as much as your body tells you to."

They continued like this for some time, stopping whenever Lizzie was overtaken with contractions, until at last she asked for the bed. She lay down gratefully, looking tired but marginally better.

Margaret sank into a chair. She watched as Martha ran her hand over Lizzie's stomach, gently probing, looking worried. She dared not ask why Martha looked so troubled. If it was bad news, it would only raise Lizzie's fears even more. Margaret thought her own fears couldn't get any higher. She had never attended a birth, and Martha's knowledge was primarily secondhand. Yet the lives of a mother and her baby might well rest in their hands. What if the baby arrived before the doctor did? What if there were complications? All sorts of gruesome scenarios suggested themselves. She gripped the chair and tried to keep from panicking. Now she understood why a person might wish to pray. Perhaps it was time she learned how.

*

Lizzie was on her hands and knees on the bed, breathing hard. Hours had passed, and still there had been no sign of Tom or the doctor. Martha had suggested Lizzie get into this position for reasons she would not explain, saying only, "I believe it will help."

"We can't possibly do this!" Margaret protested,

watching in horror as Lizzie groaned, screaming outright whenever a labor pain hit her.

Martha gave Margaret a smile that was somewhere between grim and apologetic. "I'm afraid we don't have a choice, ma'am." She nodded toward Lizzie. "Will you give her some comfort?"

Margaret had slim comfort to provide. But she set her hands on Lizzie's shoulders, trying to keep from mirroring the panic she saw on Lizzie's face. "Take heart. Everything will be fine." Unfortunately, she could not inject any certainty into her words.

"Help me," Lizzie wheezed. She twisted in Margaret's arms, and Margaret realized she was trying to return to a reclining position. She looked to Martha for approval, and the old servant gave a nod. As soon as Lizzie was on her back, she grabbed hold of Margaret's hand, still gasping from her pains and the effort of moving. With her free hand she clutched at her belly. "Something is not right. I can feel it. Will you pray for me, Margaret?"

"Of course I will," Margaret said. But as Lizzie continued to look at her expectantly, Margaret realized Lizzie wanted her to pray aloud. All morning Margaret had been sending up endless silent pleas to heaven: *Dear Lord, this woman is too good to die. Please, help her.* But those prayers would hardly reassure the patient. She inhaled and tried to speak, but could not find the words.

"Please," Lizzie begged, dangerously close to blind panic. "Geoffrey said we must pray—"

"And so we shall."

Geoffrey's calm voice filled the room, cutting through the palpable distress. Instantly Lizzie tried to sit up, crying out his name in relief. Margaret stepped back as Geoffrey rushed to his wife's side. "Oh, Geoffrey," Lizzie sobbed, clutching his neck and crying into his shoulder. He held her gently, murmuring soothing words until her grip began to relax. "I'm here, my love. I'm here."

No one was going to try to keep Geoffrey out of the room at this moment. Not even Martha. "Thank God you're here, sir," she said, her eyes shining with grateful tears.

"Is the baby coming, then?" Geoffrey asked. "Has someone gone for the doctor?"

"Tom went," Margaret told him. "But it's been ages. We're afraid he's caught in the crowds."

"Something is wrong, Geoffrey," Lizzie said, her panicked look returning. "The baby's head is not—" She cut herself off with a cry as another labor pain struck.

Geoffrey's face contorted in shock, even as he tried to comfort her. "Everything will be all right, my dearest," he said when Lizzie's pains had subsided. "At my little country parish I was called to many a home in times such as these, to offer prayer. I've seen that the Lord can and does work wonders." He smoothed back the hair from her damp face. "We will pray, and all will be well. Are you ready?"

This last question was addressed not only to his wife, but also to all in the room. Martha nodded eagerly, and Margaret, with less certainty, did the same.

"Dear Lord, we place ourselves in your hands." His head was bowed as he spoke with both solemnity and confidence. "You keep watch over the sparrows. You have numbered the very hairs of our heads. We place our trust in you. Keep watch over us, and most especially over my dear Lizzie and our child. You are love and you are light. Your will be done. Amen."

It was not the kind of prayer Margaret was used to hearing from clergymen. There was simple dignity and unfeigned believing in those words. If any prayer were to reach God, Margaret thought, it would surely be that one.

"Amen," she whispered, surprised to feel her own fears lighten. "Amen."

*

Tom had the sense that crucial time was slipping away.

He had been able to push his way through the crowd and reach the barriers, and he stood, squeezed in shoulder to shoulder with hundreds of other spectators, watching the endless line of soldiers parade past. Lizzie's screams still rang in his ears, the memory of them louder than the drums and the funeral dirge. Crossing that street was going to be nigh on impossible. And yet he knew he had to try.

The elaborately designed funeral car that held the duke's remains was now coming into view. It was enormous, being more than twenty feet long and made from wrought iron, wood, and steel. Twelve great black draft horses with black ostrich-plumed headdresses drew it slowly forward. As it reached the place where Tom was standing, the men around Tom removed their hats.

In desperation, Tom prayed. He took a deep breath, allowing the weight to drop off as he pictured placing the burden on God. All around him, he heard nothing but the drums and the marching and the sound of his own heart.

And then, the marching stopped.

Tom opened his eyes. The entire procession had come

to a halt. In a moment, Tom saw why. The funeral car was stuck in the mud. There were gasps of surprise all around. "Getting it unstuck won't be easy," said a man next to Tom. "I read in the paper that it weighs over ten tons."

The soldiers nearest to the funeral car broke ranks and began to line up around it, preparing to push it out of the mud. Then Tom saw his opportunity. While the men were scrambling, he vaulted up and over the barrier and into the group of soldiers. A few tried to stop him, but most were more concerned with the wagon than with him. Swiftly he moved through their ranks and over to the other side of the street. Taken by surprise to see Tom dashing toward them, the spectators parted as he jumped over the barrier.

He had made it.

*

The delivery was imminent; Margaret could sense it. Yet Lizzie continued to push and strain to no avail.

"Push, Lizzie! Push!" Martha coaxed, again and again.

Margaret looked on from the corner, feeling powerless and yet desperate to find some way to be of use.

After another futile attempt, Lizzie sagged back onto the bed, defeated. "I…can't…" she croaked, "…no air…can't breathe…" She was drenched in sweat, as was everyone in the room. No wonder the poor woman couldn't breathe, Margaret thought—the room was stifling. Unable to bear it any longer, she turned and threw open the window, fairly gasping as a gust of icy wind rushed past her. She waited to hear protests at her actions, but none came. She turned to see Lizzie breathing in deep gulps, a thin smile on her face. The shock had invigorated her.

A powerful realization came to Margaret just then, hitting her with more force than the fresh air. All of her worries about Tom or Moreton Hall or anything else were insignificant compared with her responsibility to help this woman bring a child safely into the world. For once, Margaret would expend all the force of her stubborn will toward a truly selfless act. Never before had she felt such unbounded joy. She rushed to Lizzie's side. "You can do this, Lizzie," she proclaimed. "You're almost there. I know it."

Lizzie sat up, energized by the absolute conviction in Margaret's words. Another contraction seized her, and she met it with renewed determination.

"That's it!" Martha cried. "Again... Bear down as hard as you can!"

Two housemaids came into the room, carrying the hot water and extra towels that Martha had requested. "Oh, my gracious," one of them exclaimed as they set down their items. "The baby's coming! I can see it!"

"Aahhh!" Lizzie moaned again, her face bright red as she pushed with all her might.

"It's the head!" Martha shouted, her voice exultant. "The baby has turned. Praise be to God."

Upon hearing these words, Lizzie pushed again, crying out—no longer in agony, but in triumph.

*

Tom heard Lizzie's long, loud cry the moment he and the doctor burst into the house. And then there was silence.

As he and Dr. Layton raced up the stairs, Tom prayed fervently that they were not too late. They turned into the hallway just in time to see Geoffrey throwing open the door to Lizzie's room. And then a new sound filled the air.

It was the sound of a baby crying.

Tom followed Geoffrey and the doctor into the room. He could not remain outside. He had to know what was going on. For propriety's sake, he tried to keep his gaze averted, looking only at Lizzie's face. Her damp hair was plastered to her head, and her cheeks were flushed. Margaret sat next to her. Tom's heart leaped for joy as he took in the sight of the two women he loved most in the whole world, tears streaming down their elated faces.

Martha held up the tiny, crying child for all to see. "It's a boy!" she announced. "A fine, lusty boy."

Chapter 31

Margaret sat at her dressing table, her hands unsteady as she loosened her hair from its pins and began to brush it. It was late, and she was utterly spent. They had all stayed up until the doctor had finished his tasks and assured them all was well. At last, mother and baby were getting some sleep, and Geoffrey had insisted that Margaret and Tom retire also.

Margaret savored these few minutes alone while Tom was in the dressing room preparing for bed. Her nerves were raw from the events of the day. She felt intensely fragile, but it was not from mere physical exhaustion.

From the time she was young, her father had instilled in her the belief that only weak people let down their guard and show their true feelings. This had been her guiding principle, and it had served her well. Until today. Today, Margaret had seen men and women with their hearts wide open, displaying every intense, unfettered emotion from darkest fear to transcendent joy. But this was not weakness. Rather, they had shown strength that Margaret was only just beginning to comprehend.

The door to Tom's dressing room opened and he came in. After weeks of sleeping next to him in the same bed, Margaret ought to be getting used to the sight of him in his nightshirt. But she wasn't. She could not help noticing the shape of his square shoulders, which were clearly visible despite the loose-fitting garment, and the movement of his powerful legs, which the nightshirt exposed from the knees down, as he approached her.

He lifted the hairbrush from her hand and began to run it gently through her hair, arousing pleasant shivers along her back. "Thank you for all you did today," he said.

"I did very little," she protested.

He continued to brush her hair in long, languorous strokes, making it difficult for Margaret to concentrate on anything else. "You were there for her, and that was the most important thing of all. Lizzie has always had a deep distrust of physicians, especially since the tragic events that happened with Ria. I think she actually had greater confidence in you and Martha than she would in any doctor." He chuckled. "I really believe my late arrival with Dr. Layton was an answer to prayer."

"You can see God at work in good circumstances or bad," Margaret observed.

"That is because he never leaves us or forsakes us. Also, he says that all things work together for good for those who love God. Therefore it is easy to see the hand of God at all times. One has only to look for it." Tom set the brush on the table and began to caress her neck and shoulders. "Do you remember something I told Denault on the night we met?"

"I—" She wanted to relax into his hands, to revel in the sensations he was awakening. "I can't say I remember much about that night—except for you."

"I told him I was fortunate enough to lay claim in the right place, but the gold don't mine itself." He paused, meeting her eyes in the mirror. "That's what it's been like with you, Margaret. I knew that beneath your haughty exterior, you had to be harboring some measure of love for me, and I was determined to find it." He bent down to kiss her neck. "Tell me it's so. Tell me you love me."

"I..."

He placed kisses on her cheek. "Say it," he said with soft urgency.

"I..." She turned to face him. "I love you," she said, exhaling as she spoke.

Tom's face lit up with pleasure. He extended his arms toward her. "You are a brave woman, Maggie."

At the sound of her name—*Maggie*—brimming with all of Tom's tenderness and wry humor, Margaret rose and in one swift movement threw herself into his arms, knocking him onto the bed and landing on top of him. "I have done many brave things today."

He lay beneath her, laughing, his chest rising and falling with each chuckle, and she felt the heat radiating from him, felt the heat of her own desires rising. He said with a hint of sly wickedness, "Is this our good-night kiss, then?"

"Yes," she breathed. She lowered her lips to his—a tender, light kiss, filled with promise. He lifted his head to press his lips harder against hers, wanting more. She readily complied.

When she finally pulled away, she saw a question

written clearly in his eyes, and her own gaze returned the answer. In one swift movement he flipped her onto her back, holding himself poised over her so as not to crush her. His eyes locked on hers again for a breathless, heart-stopping moment, then slowly drifted down to her lips. "Oh, Maggie," he said. "How I have longed…wished for…"

"Me, too," she whispered with a smile. Never had her heart been so wide open—vulnerable, yes, and yet absolutely free. She pulled his head down to hers, returning his kisses with passion and all the love that was within her. Tonight they would be one. There would be no going back. And there would be no regrets.

*

Margaret was still asleep. Tom paused to look at her as she lay curled up on her side, her dark hair contrasting with the white pillow. She had been so warm, so passionate last night. Despite their fatigue from the day's events, they had both wanted this further celebration of love and life.

Before they had drifted off to sleep she had murmured something about spending the following morning together, and he had not contradicted her. But the truth was he had another engagement this morning. One he hoped would help end his dealings with Spencer once and for all.

*

Dense morning fog surrounded Margaret as she rapped purposefully on the door of Richard's town house. She had awoken alone this morning, and her surprise and disappointment had turned quickly to worry when she'd discovered Tom had left without telling anyone where he was going. After all that had happened yesterday—and last night—she could no longer bear not knowing what was still separating her from her husband. She had given too much; her heart was too invested. If Tom was still unwilling to confide in her, she would have to find another way. And she would begin with Richard.

When the door opened, the bright light from the hallway pierced the gloom. The butler led her to a parlor and informed her that Mr. Spencer would be down shortly.

Margaret paced the floor as she waited. She was prepared to wait all day if need be. It was time to get some answers.

"I apologize for keeping you waiting, cousin," Richard said, breezing into the room. "I'm afraid you caught me just as I was preparing to go out." The overcoat he was wearing and the gloves in his hands gave evidence of his statement. He made as if to give her a kiss on the cheek, but she stepped away before he could do so. "Come now," he admonished. "Not even a friendly greeting for a kinsman?"

"I want to know what your business is with my husband," Margaret said.

Richard cocked his head to one side. "Business?"

"Don't equivocate, Richard. I know you've been talking to him about Moreton Hall. If you've been trying to convince him you have some kind of claim on my land—"

"*Your* land? My dear, you are married now. Moreton Hall is in the power of your husband."

He said it with such smugness that Margaret was

tempted to laugh at his ignorance rather than set him straight on the matter. "Is that so?" she said.

He nodded. "And, as it happens, I have indeed convinced Poole of my right to that land. Soon I will be its rightful owner."

This bald confirmation of her greatest fear hit Margaret like a blow to the chest. She took a deep breath. "Tom would never agree to give you Moreton Hall."

Again, the self-satisfied look. "We have an arrangement. Let's call it a bargain for both sides."

"I don't believe it," Margaret said flatly.

"Why don't you ask him? He's your husband, after all." He paused to reconsider that statement. "I'll wager you *have* asked him. And he has refused to tell you. Now that I think about it, he was quite adamant that this whole transaction be kept secret from you until the deal was done. Now why do you suppose that is?"

"It could not possibly be kept secret from me," Margaret said. "The land cannot be sold or transferred without my consent."

He gave a disbelieving laugh. "*Your* consent?"

She lifted her head proudly. "Apparently he hasn't told you that the land is in a joint trust. Any major decision requires two signatures—his and mine."

Richard's eyes narrowed. "You're lying."

"You are the liar, Richard. Not me."

It gave Margaret a particular satisfaction to see the anger that colored Richard's face. But his expression cooled and he said, "I had a feeling he was dragging his feet on this. Now I know why." He gave her a malevolent smile. "He's been waiting until he got you fully in his camp."

"What are you talking about?"

"I imagine Poole knows that a woman will do anything her man asks—*if* she is in love with him. He's got to win you with *gentle* persuasion."

Was Tom trying to manipulate her? Richard's suggestion was galling and yet so many of the things Tom had done since their wedding could be seen as attempts to win her over. But couldn't they also be seen as things a loving husband would do for a wife? Everything he had done could be interpreted two ways. Margaret knew better than to take anything Richard said at face value. And yet, she had heard from Tom's own mouth that they were planning something.

Still, she protested. "It makes no sense. He loves Moreton Hall. He's thrown himself into every aspect of running the place. Why would he turn around and sell it to you?"

"You are a fool if you think he cares about the land. He wanted *you;* I'll grant you that. But he told me himself he has no desire to stay in Lincolnshire. He said he'd much rather live closer to his sister. I'm sure you know how important she is to him."

Margaret did know. Her face must have revealed something, and Richard always knew when to press his advantage. "Go ahead—ask your husband where his real loyalties lie. Ask him just how much he'd be willing to do—how far he'd be willing to go—for his sister."

Margaret had every intention of asking him. Today all of her fears had been realized. But she would not back down for anyone. She advanced on him. "You will never get that land, Richard," she said forcefully. "I would die first. Or better yet, I'll see you dead."

"I would advise against making any threats, Margaret. One way or another you are going to lose that land, and it will either go to me or be seized by the Crown."

"Now who is making threats?" Margaret accused. "And empty ones at that. You're lying to me, simply to get your way."

"On the contrary. I plan to get my way by telling the truth." Abruptly he turned and walked into the front hall, pulling on his gloves as he went.

Margaret followed in his wake. "Wait! Where are you going?"

Picking up his hat from a side table, Richard trotted down the steps and up into a waiting carriage. It was a high gig, one that Margaret could not have mounted herself without help. She stood on the curb, frustrated, looking up at him. "You cannot leave!" she protested.

He picked up the reins. "I really must be going. Also, I apologize, but I seem to have sent away your cab. Don't worry; my butler will fetch another for you." With a quick slap of the reins he set the carriage in motion and was swiftly lost in the swirl of fog.

*

Spencer kept Tom waiting for nearly three-quarters of an hour. Tom knew this by the sounds of the church bell ringing the quarter hours while he sat in the little pub drinking his ale and waiting. Inspector Field was waiting, too, but he was nearly unrecognizable. If Tom hadn't known Field was the grizzled old man sitting nearby, puffing a pipe and reading the paper, he'd never have guessed it. The man's appearance was changed entirely.

Men from the Detective Branch of the police force

had taken up a post in the back of the pub, where they would not reveal themselves until they'd gotten the signal from Field. The trap had been carefully constructed.

When Spencer finally arrived, he paused at the door. He took a long look around, scrutinizing everything about the place and the few patrons in it. Behind him, dense fog obscured everything outside. His gaze rested on Field for several moments. Field looked up, gave him a disinterested look as one does to a stranger, then nodded politely before returning to his reading. This act must have convinced Spencer that there was nothing out of the ordinary. After one more darting glance, he removed his hat and gloves and strode over to the table where Tom was sitting.

"You're late," Tom said as Spencer sat down. "It's not enough that you are coercing me into giving up my land; you must now make me *wait* for the privilege?"

"I was detained," Spencer answered. His tone made it clear that he did not offer it up as an apology. "And you will kindly keep your voice down." He glanced over at Field again, as though trying to gauge whether he was listening.

But Field was just at that moment calling out to the barmaid for more gin and water, which gave the impression that he was oblivious to Tom and Spencer. He was also making it plain that he was hard of hearing, for he spoke unnaturally loud to the barmaid and asked her to repeat herself twice, saying, "What's that? Speak louder!" A masterful performance, thought Tom. Field ought to have been on the stage.

"All right," said Tom, "let's get down to business. Did you bring the document?"

Spencer nodded and tapped his breast pocket.

"Well, let's see it, then," Tom demanded. "I want proof that the information you are holding against me is as damaging as you say it is."

Spencer pulled a folded paper out of his greatcoat. Tom took the paper and began to read. Just as Spencer had told him, it was a sworn statement from Freddie, dated the day after their duel seven years ago. It clearly stated Tom and Lizzie's names, and that an altercation with Tom had been the cause of Freddie's life-threatening injury.

"Altercation!" Tom read aloud, nearly spitting out the word. He slammed the paper on the table. "It was no 'altercation.' It was a duel."

Spencer leaned back and crossed his arms. "You took hold of a man as he was coming out of a tavern in the wee hours of the morning, hauled him to a field, and put a gun in his hand. If you want to call that a duel, that's your privilege. I call it an elaborate kind of murder."

"I didn't kill him!"

"No, but you thought you did. And that was your intent. Don't deny it." He took the paper and folded it carefully, placing it back into his coat. "If you call it a duel, it changes nothing. Either way, you will lose your freedom—if not your life."

"No magistrate is going to bring me up on charges for that. Hightower recovered from that duel, and he died last year while I wasn't even in the country."

Spencer gave a wave of impatience. "So you have insisted. Dozens of times, in fact. It's been getting rather tedious. However, I have to admit that something about Hightower's death still bothered me, and it wasn't until this morning that I finally figured out what it was."

Something in Spencer's manner made Tom wary. He had a foreboding that this couldn't be good. "Out with it, then."

"Hightower died in the presence of the other person named in this document. Someone who had a vested interest in keeping him quiet. That sounds very suspicious to me. I believe the authorities will think so, too."

He was actually implying that Lizzie had committed murder. Anger surged through Tom like his blood was on fire. But he could not afford to lose control, no matter how much Spencer goaded him. Inspector Field had told him exactly what he needed to hear in order for the police to have an extortion case against Spencer. "You told me you would not take this paper to the authorities," Tom ground out, fighting to keep his anger clamped down. "You said I could buy your silence with Moreton Hall."

Spencer shook his head. "Actually, as I understand it, the purpose of this meeting was to discuss your sale of Moreton Hall and surrounding property to me. I know you have been eager to get it off your hands, but I'm afraid some information has come to light that may compel me to reject your offer of sale."

This change of tack utterly bewildered Tom. "My offer of sale! What are you talking about? It wasn't my idea."

"I'll admit your offer was tempting," Spencer said, as though Tom hadn't spoken. "However, just this morning I was informed that you are not actually at liberty to sell Moreton Hall. You can't sell it to me, or to anyone else for that matter, without your dear wife's written consent."

This was not at all how Tom had planned this meeting. Everything was going wrong, and he was beginning to suspect why. "Who gave you that information?"

"Why, Margaret, of course," Spencer answered, confirming Tom's fears.

She hadn't trusted him. She'd gone to Spencer and ruined Tom's carefully constructed plan.

"I think she wishes now that she'd been more careful in picking a husband," Richard said. "When she found out you were trying to sell off her property, she became positively livid." He laughed. "I don't envy you, my friend. You won't have a good time of it when you go home tonight."

"I don't suppose you told her you were trying to force me into giving up the land." Tom knew he was grabbing at straws, but he was desperate to prove Spencer's guilt. If he could just get Spencer to admit to the extortion, he might still have a chance.

But Spencer was too cagy. "I believe Margaret and I talked about your sister, *Lady Somerville.*" He pronounced Lizzie's title with relish. "Margaret knows you are awfully attached to your sister, of course. But I don't think she knows about Lady Somerville's sordid past. Are you afraid to tell her?"

Tom lunged across the table, grabbing Spencer by the neck as the two of them went crashing to the floor. Spencer's head hit the floor hard as they landed, leaving him stunned. The table toppled over, slamming Tom in the back before rolling off him, but Tom was unheeding. His self-control had evaporated, and he began throwing punches, wanting only to kill this man. Blind fury propelled him.

Two men grabbed Tom and pulled him to his feet, dragging him away from Spencer. It was the men from the Detective Branch. Field knelt down by Spencer and tried to revive him.

As Spencer came to and looked up at Tom with satisfaction, Tom realized he had played right into his hands. "As I was saying, Poole, I hesitate to enter into contract negotiations with a felon who is about to lose his land to the Crown. Also, as a moral matter, I find the criminal evidence against Lady Somerville to be quite disturbing."

*

No one was at Mr. Hawthorne's place of business. When her repeated knocking went unanswered, Margaret decided to walk the short distance to his lodgings. She had to find him.

Mr. Hawthorne's housekeeper informed her that he was indeed at home, but unable to receive visitors. "He was outside all day yesterday, watching the duke's funeral procession," she explained. "It seems he caught a chill after standing for hours in that nasty weather. But the doctor said there is nothing to be alarmed over. Mr. Hawthorne should be up again in a day or two."

Margaret hated to leave without seeing him, but it appeared she had no choice. There was nothing for Margaret to do now but return to the Somervilles' house. She would far rather have had Mr. Hawthorne's advice before confronting Tom, but she would just have to go ahead without it. The joys of yesterday were long gone. Emotions, as she had always known, were fleeting. The only constant in her life seemed to be that she must face her problems alone.

Chapter 32

Tom stalked up the steps to the Somerville home, still seething from the disaster. He had been unable to collect evidence of Spencer's guilt; in fact, Spencer had made it plain that he was going to proceed with all of his threats.

His plans had been ruined because of Margaret's interference.

Tom fully expected to see her when he walked through the door, and sure enough, she was standing in the front hall. She crossed her arms and glared at him. "We need to talk."

"Not here." Tom took her by the arm and led her to the study, slamming the door shut behind them. He was not about to have every servant in the house know their business.

"You were with Richard, weren't you?" she accused.

"Tell me, why would you be paying a call to a man you hate so much?"

She bristled. "I wanted answers. You would not give them to me."

"I asked you to trust me, Maggie."

"Trust you!" she scoffed. "Why should I, when you are conspiring with my enemy to separate me from my land?"

Tom knew he ought to let it go, not try to justify himself. The more she hated him, the easier this would be. Even so, her single-minded focus, knowing she cared about her land more than him, still stung. "It's always about your land, isn't it? You don't care about anything—or anyone—else. Well, then, let me ease your mind. I have, in fact, been working very hard to keep the land *out* of Spencer's hands."

Surprise—and uncertainty—shot across her face. "What do you mean?"

"Do you remember at our wedding—" He felt physical pain just bringing that day to mind. It seemed no easier for Margaret; he saw her flinch visibly. He forced himself to continue. "Do you remember what I said when we first noticed Spencer?"

She thought for a moment. "You said we'd be seeing more of him."

"Yes. And that is because Spencer knows something about my past. Something he has been holding over my head."

"Do you mean to say he's been blackmailing you? What have you done, that he has such a hold over you?" He couldn't tell whom her anger was directed at.

"Dueling, attempted murder, manslaughter." He forced himself to say the words. Yesterday she had said she loved him. Today she must be thinking she had married a monster. She must be thinking only that she had given herself to him, and he had betrayed her. He steeled himself against the pain brought on by this realization. "Margaret, you must listen to me. Very soon, the courts may bring me up on one or more of these charges. If I'm convicted, my goods and money may be forfeited to the Crown. Therefore, I have been working on a plan to revert the lands solely to you, along with a generous annuity. Also, I believe we should find a way to end the marriage."

She stared at him, openmouthed. "You do not wish to be married to me?"

It was, to judge by her face, a painful idea. Tom took some comfort in that. Perhaps she did still harbor love for him. The memory of last night was seared on his heart forever, and he would always cherish it. But it was also the very reason why he had to take these steps now. "Your land will be saved, Margaret, and you will be free to do as you wish. This is your way out, and I advise you to take it. Otherwise, you may find yourself married to a convicted felon."

She continued to stare at him without moving. "You really want me to go?" She spoke matter-of-factly, but her voice held a note of sadness.

He turned away from her. "Yes."

There was silence. She was standing there, no doubt weighing his words, making her decision. But he knew, ultimately, what she would do. She was a strong woman. She had wanted to stand on her own. At last she said with a kind of shuddering sigh, "Very well. I am going home."

He heard her footsteps retreating, the door closing behind her. His heart was breaking, but he told himself he was doing the right thing.

*

Margaret had been expecting bad news ever since she received Mr. Hawthorne's telegram notifying her he was on his way to Lincolnshire. "What has happened?" she asked as soon as the butler had ushered him into the library. "Has Tom been arrested?" This was her greatest fear.

"No, he hasn't been arrested. Nor is he likely to be. You may rest easy on that score." He set down the satchel he'd been carrying and opened the flap. "What I've come to talk to you about is the future of Moreton Hall." He began to pull out a stack of papers.

"Is it in danger, then? Tom said it could be seized by the Crown."

"Did he not also tell you he'd been taking steps to assure that never happened?"

"Well, yes, but..." So much about their last encounter was a blur to her now. There had been anger and hurt and recrimination on both sides. Tom had told her that their separation was the only way to assure the safety of her lands, and so she'd gone. But she'd been plagued with doubts and worry ever since.

Hawthorne laid out the papers on the desk. "Mr. Poole wishes to transfer complete ownership and control of Moreton Hall back to you. He will relinquish any and all claims. These documents will begin the process, although it will take some months to complete it."

Margaret looked at the papers. Such news ought to thrill her—the land would soon be safe. But whatever she was feeling, it wasn't joy. "Is he absolutely sure he wants to do this?"

"Oh, yes. Quite adamant. In fact, Mr. Poole first

approached me about this not too long after your wedding."

"You've known all this time, and you haven't told me? You let me worry that my husband was trying to give away all that I hold dear?"

"I regret that it was necessary to keep you in the dark," Hawthorne acknowledged. "But we were dealing with a very sensitive matter, and the utmost secrecy was required. As you know, Mr. Spencer's aim had been to ensure you lose Moreton Hall. He had damaging information about Mr. Poole's family that he was prepared to capitalize on in order to accomplish that goal."

"His family?" Margaret repeated in surprise. "I thought it was just Tom who was in trouble."

"A few years ago, Mr. Poole fought a duel with a Mr. Freddie Hightower. He wished to avenge the honor of his sister, whom Mr. Hightower had seduced. I'm sorry to state it so bluntly, but there it is."

"You can't be talking about Lizzie—about Lady Somerville?"

"Sadly, I am. Today her life is above reproach, but she does have what one would call a checkered past. Spencer knew about it and used it to force Mr. Poole to agree to his demands. Mr. Poole was doing all he could to keep this information from becoming public. Unfortunately, we were not able to do so." Hawthorne pulled a newspaper out of the satchel. "Here is today's paper, which I brought up with me from London." He handed it to her. "You may read it for yourself. It isn't pretty, I'm afraid. It will do serious damage to her reputation and standing in society."

Margaret had only to glance at the beginning of the

article before her heart went out to Lizzie. "They cannot just brand her as some sort of fallen woman! She's the most upright woman I know."

"She and Lord Somerville are both facing it bravely. They know the worst of the effects will lessen with time."

"But what does this have to do with Moreton Hall?" Margaret asked. "Her scandal alone would not endanger this estate."

"Mr. Poole found himself under a double vise, as it were. Spencer was going to try any means, whether by law or threats of scandal, to get what he wanted. Mr. Poole has been valiantly acting to protect the two women he cares for most."

*

"What's the news?" Lizzie demanded as soon as Tom and Geoffrey entered the room. She was alert and sitting up in her bed, but her face was pale with worry.

She was slowly recovering from the stress of childbirth, but Tom was still troubled by how frail she looked. He knew her fears for him were compounding the problem. After Margaret's departure, and with the possibility of charges being laid against him, Tom had been forced to tell Lizzie all that he had been keeping from her. He had been reluctant to do so, but there had been no way around it.

Happily, today he had good news.

"It's all right," Geoffrey assured her, leaning down to place a kiss on her forehead. "The magistrate is not going to pursue the matter further. Tom has been cleared."

"Thank God!" Lizzie beamed. "I suppose this means you will be returning soon to Moreton Hall? We will be sorry to lose you, of course. Perhaps you and Margaret can still join us on Christmas? We might get back to Kent by then, and the Somerville grounds are lovely, even in winter."

How like Lizzie to automatically assume all problems had been so easily solved. She always did have rather simplistic notions about everything. But it was time to set the record straight, although he knew they would not like what they were about to hear. He had not even told Geoffrey of his plans. He wanted to tell them both at the same time. "I am in fact planning to return to Australia. This was my original plan, after all. I believe I should stick to it."

As he had expected, this announcement brought looks of alarm from them both. "Has Margaret agreed to this?" Geoffrey asked. "It's asking quite a lot of her to leave England."

"I have not spoken to her. I plan to return alone."

"Tom, you cannot leave without your wife," Lizzie remonstrated.

Wife. The very word pained him. "Actually, I was thinking about a divorce."

"You can't be serious!" Geoffrey protested. "Aside from the very important moral issues, the legalities are next to impossible. It takes an act of Parliament to approve it."

"I am well aware of that," Tom said. "As for the approval—you are in the House of Lords; I thought perhaps you could use your influence."

"But, Tom," Geoffrey persisted, "you should be reconciled with your wife. You know that is the Christian thing to do."

"She has no desire to reconcile with me."

"Have you asked her?" Lizzie said gently.

Tom didn't answer. He could not imagine Margaret would want him back after all he had done.

Lizzie gave him a sympathetic smile. "You have spent most of your life trying to solve other people's problems. I have often been the beneficiary of your efforts, and believe me, I am grateful."

Tom grimaced. "I appreciate your kind words, but I haven't any right to them." Indeed, he thought, Lizzie ought not to be thanking him. She ought to be scolding him for all the ways he had done more harm than good.

She cocked her head a little and looked at him the way she sometimes did when she was about to deliver a lecture, so perhaps that's what she had in mind after all. "The fact is, dear brother, you tend to want to solve everyone's problems *yourself*—unilaterally, without anyone else's input or help. Through the years I have been guilty of encouraging this behavior, because I have always trusted you and followed along willingly."

Tom would love to have contested this; in fact, he opened his mouth to do so. But she gave a small shake of her head, cutting off his protests. "Please do not misunderstand me," she continued. "I know your heart has always been right. Often, I deferred to your decisions. But I am your sister, not your wife." She laughed. "I'm sure I don't need to remind you of that. The thing is, a wife is someone with whom you must have full sharing and open your heart completely. You never fully took Margaret into your confidence, did you?"

No. He had not.

"Go to her," Lizzie urged. "Speak to her. Bare your heart. Hold nothing back."

Geoffrey nodded to confirm the truth of what Lizzie was saying. "We know this from personal experience, Tom. Nothing can be truly resolved—and love certainly cannot grow—until you have taken that step."

Tom tried to imagine himself and Margaret as open and loving with one another as Geoffrey and Lizzie were. He craved it, but he knew it was a vain dream. "Everything I have done, I have done for you, Lizzie."

Even as he said this, Tom knew it was not entirely true. Yes, he had been desperate during these past weeks to save Lizzie's reputation. But his desire to protect Margaret had started his most recent troubles and been a driving factor in all he'd tried to do.

"Things are different now," Lizzie said. "For this cause shall a man leave his father and mother—and his sister," she added with a little smirk. "Geoffrey and I have each other. If people shun us because of my past mistakes, there is nothing we can do about that. We can only live today as best we can. We must place our lives in the Lord's hands, Tom. Our own are quite insufficient for the task."

Her voice broke a little as she finished, and Geoffrey came over and put his arms around her. "Oh, my dearest," he murmured, kissing her cheek.

They were the picture of harmony and contentment, their eyes brimming with tears of love for each other. When they turned their gaze on Tom, he stood up abruptly, running his hands through his hair, using the motion to hide the telltale sting of tears in his own eyes. "You are a sentimental one, Lizzie. The answers are not so easy as that."

"I did not mean to imply that they were. The best

things in life rarely come easily." She looked over at the sweet face of baby Edward sleeping in the cot next to the bed, as though to illustrate her point.

"You two were able to overcome your problems because you love each other."

"I believe that deep down she loves you, Tom," Lizzie insisted. "You have kept her at arm's length. If she has done the same, perhaps it is because she has been struggling with the very same fears that you have."

Margaret afraid? Tom could not believe this. Hard, yes. Haughty and disdainful and self-sufficient, no doubt. Lizzie's words, if they were to be believed, would set the situation in a much different light. But it could not be true.

"You are also very proud, the two of you," Lizzie proclaimed. "Heaven help you both."

Tom turned and walked to the door. His thoughts were in a jumble, and there was nothing more any of them could say that would help. As usual, talking only ever made things worse.

"Will you go to her?" Lizzie asked hopefully.

Tom shook his head. It was hard to deny his sister anything, but she was asking for too much. "I need time to think."

Chapter 33

S now blanketed the landscape, sparkling in the winter sun. Margaret sat at the window, deep in contemplation. Christmas was approaching, but Margaret had made no plans. She had politely declined several dinner invitations, all of which had been addressed to Mr. and Mrs. Poole. Her affairs were in limbo. On the outside, the pattern of her life looked no different than it had last winter——Margaret was alone, steeped in the quiet solitude of a country winter. Only the inner reality of her turbulent thoughts contradicted this. She was a far different person than she had been at this time last year.

"You've been at that window for hours, madam," Bessie said. She was seated nearby with her sewing, keeping Margaret company. She was looking at Margaret with concern. "It can't be healthy to sit and mope."

Margaret turned from the window. "I assure you I am not moping. Merely thinking."

"It's a fine line between the two, I'd say," Bessie said stoutly.

Margaret rose and smoothed the wrinkles from her gown. "As it happens, I was just thinking of taking a ride."

"In this weather?" Bessie looked at her aghast.

"You can't have it both ways, Bessie," Margaret chided. "Come and help me change into my riding clothes."

The day was fine, and the blanket of snow only an inch thick, and Bright Star had no trouble navigating the narrow lane. How utterly beautiful everything was. She remembered the times she and Tom had ridden this path together, and was struck with a pang of loneliness—a sensation that was becoming entirely too familiar.

So many things about the future were still uncertain; so many details had yet to be settled. Mr. Hawthorne had been writing frequently, keeping her abreast of all that was happening in London. Tom was determined to give everything to her, including a sizable amount of money. He was, it seemed, buying her off. Perhaps he was glad to be done with her. And who could blame him? She had not come close to being the kind of wife he would have wanted, and brought him nothing but problems as well.

She brought her horse to a stop at the crest of a hill and looked out over the gently undulating valley below. The trees were bare now, and although it was a half mile away Margaret could see the little cottage in the woods where Tom had proposed to her. Memories flooded her mind of the way he had kissed her that day, and every evening thereafter. She flushed with heat, breathing deeply of the chilly air in an attempt to counteract it. Somehow Margaret could not bring herself to fully believe those days were gone, that she would never see Tom again.

In the heat of the moment on that last terrible day before she'd left London it had been easy to agree with

Tom that they were better off parting from each other. She had been convinced that the threat to his freedom, and to Moreton Hall, had been real. And in truth, she had been afraid of him after those revelations about his past. Now that she understood everything, she knew that Tom was an honorable man who would never hurt those he loved. And now, in his absence, she truly realized how much he had come to mean to her. As she looked out over the achingly beautiful landscape, she finally allowed herself to admit how desperately she missed him.

Here, laid out before her, was all she'd fought so hard to achieve. For years her sole aim had been to keep her land and to be free of debts. She was in control of her land now, and her livelihood. But she had lost control of her heart. This was, at last, what she understood as she looked out over everything she used to hold most dear.

Slowly she turned her horse and began the trek back home. As she neared Moreton Hall, her eye was caught by a horse and rider in the distance. Her breath caught as she realized the horse was Castor, Tom's stallion. The horse had been at Moreton Hall ever since Tom had brought him here weeks before. Had Tom returned? She set Bright Star into a trot to close the gap between them.

No sooner had she done this than she realized Tom was not the man riding the stallion. It was Kevin. The disappointment hit Margaret with such force that she pulled her own horse to an ungainly stop, very nearly falling off in the process. She was breathing heavily, pushing back the tears that tried so insistently to force themselves into the open. She sat, unmoving, as Kevin approached and stopped a short distance away.

Vaguely Margaret heard him offer a polite greeting,

but she could only stare at him, stupidly caught in her vain wish that he had been Tom. "What are you doing?" she rasped.

"Mr. Poole asked me to ride Castor regularly while he was gone. He was concerned about the horse staying in shape." He patted the stallion's neck. "We're just finishing a nice workout." Castor pranced, tossing his head, clearly still full of energy. Margaret's eyes were on the horse, but for some reason she could only see Tom racing him down the green at Hyde Park.

Reacting to the apparently stricken look on Margaret's face, Kevin said apologetically, "Have I done something wrong?"

"No," she said quietly, eking out a wobbly smile. "You did nothing wrong."

She turned her horse away, largely to hide her pain. Kevin rode a polite distance behind her as they returned to the stables. While a stable boy tended to her horse, Margaret leaned on a railing and watched as Kevin removed Castor's saddle and began to brush him down. How many times had Tom done this task himself, for the sheer joy of it, tenderly caring for the animal that had meant so much to him.

Margaret found a particular comfort every time she looked at Castor. She'd been telling herself it was because he was such a beautiful animal. If she were honest with herself, the real reason was because she had been expecting Tom to return for him any day now. If Tom was serious about leaving Margaret, surely he would come here to fetch his horse. At the very least, this would give Margaret one last opportunity to see him.

The tiny spark of hope nurtured by this thought suddenly lit up when she heard a wagon approaching. Perhaps he was coming back after all. She raced out to the yard, only to see a dogcart driven by one of the local farmers and carrying a passenger she vaguely recognized. He was a young man, wearing clean work clothes. He jumped down from the cart and tipped his worn hat to Margaret. "Good afternoon, Mrs. Poole," he said, bowing his head deferentially. "I don't expect you'll remember me, but my name is John Turner. I work for Lord Somerville."

"Of course," Margaret said, trying to place him. A footman, perhaps? "All is well, I hope?"

"Oh, yes, ma'am," Turner responded. "Lady Somerville and the baby are getting on quite well, and of course Lord Somerville is ever so proud." He gave her a sheepish smile and looked embarrassed, perhaps wondering if he had spoken too freely.

"Can you tell me—" Margaret stopped short. She had wanted to ask about Tom, where he was and what his plans were. But a servant like John Turner was not likely to know that, and in any case, it would look terrible if Margaret could not claim a knowledge of her own husband's whereabouts. She did at least have that much pride, if not much more. Instead she said, "What is the purpose for your visit today?"

"I'm here at the direction of Mr. Poole," he answered. As he spoke, Margaret finally remembered where she had seen Turner—he was one of the grooms. A particular kind of dread filled her when Turner pulled a letter from his pocket and extended it toward Margaret. "Mr. Poole wants me to bring his horse back to London."

Margaret stared at the letter. "No." It could not be.

Turner's arm faltered, but he kept it extended. With

an apologetic tone and without meeting her eyes he said, "Mr. Poole told me to give you this letter as proof of his instructions—just in case you should doubt me."

As Margaret took the letter, some distant part of her brain wondered how she could stand there so stoically when the last of her hopes had fallen, shattering into countless pieces all around her. "That's quite all right, Turner," she said, her shock actually sending her into a numb calm. "I'm sure everything is exactly as it should be."

*

For nearly a week after Turner had left with Tom's horse, Margaret remained in a kind of dazed fog, unable to come to terms with the reality that Tom truly had no intention of ever returning. Over and over again she told herself this was for the best, forcing herself to rail against Tom in anger. He had been the one to lecture her about marriage, but now he was the one most anxious to bring it to an end. What right had he to use her so? She was determined to rise above it, to show Tom that she could function perfectly well on her own. She certainly had plenty of experience. She had done it for years.

She occupied herself by systematically going through every room in Moreton Hall, making list after list of the repairs and improvements to be made—from patching a drafty window to purchasing new bed furnishings. She had saved Tom's room for last. On the day she finally entered it, she tried to look at it objectively, to concentrate on mundane things such as whether the wardrobe would benefit from refinishing. Instead, she found herself sinking onto the bed, overtaken by the hollow loneliness that echoed around the room.

It was then that the answer came to her. It shot through her with such complete clarity that it left her breathless— an idea that was completely shocking and yet utterly liberating. She must have sat there for hours, turning it over in her mind, marveling that she could consider the idea at all, much less accept it so easily. But accept it she did. Tom would never return to Moreton Hall; therefore, she must leave it.

*

Margaret rode her horse through gloomy mists into town. She tied him up to the iron fence that surrounded the church graveyard, then pushed open the little gate and stepped inside. It was time to make peace with her own past once and for all.

Gray, dismal clouds sent forth a wet snow. Unheeding, Margaret continued on, taking the path to a large gravestone that marked the final resting place of her parents. There they lay, buried side by side, their names etched together on the stone, implying a greater intimacy than they had ever shared in real life. She knelt down in the snow and for several minutes did nothing more than contemplate the grave site. In time, her own tears mixed with the snowflakes lighting upon her face although her heart felt utterly sure and at peace.

"Father, I think it's time we had a little chat." After saying these words aloud, Margaret took one more glance around the graveyard to ensure that she was alone. No one was about; all were indoors seeking a warm hearth on such a day. She turned back to the grave. "I have something very important to tell you. You left me with land—and your debts—and the responsibility to save

Moreton Hall from disgrace. You didn't think I would be able to do it, but you were wrong. Moreton Hall will be well cared for, and it will never go to our enemies. But now I must confess to you, that it isn't enough for me."

She stopped to take a breath, wiping away her tears with the back of a gloved hand.

"You see, what can be more important than love?" Hearing herself ask this question of her father brought forth a humorless laugh. "You are not the person to ask that question to, I know. You and Mama had quite a different arrangement. I had planned to follow your example in that regard, too, but now that hasn't turned out quite according to plan. The plain truth is, I must leave here. I must go to him."

Forsaking all others. These words from her marriage vows had been circling in her brain for days, leading her to make the final decision.

"I know you will never understand. I only hope that in some way, you can forgive me. You see, something else that you bequeathed to me was your headstrong determination. I have made a vow, and I am determined to keep it."

*

Lizzie's words still echoed in Tom's heart. *"Go to Margaret,"* she had said. *"Speak to her. Bare your heart."*

It sounded so simple. And yet with everything that had happened, how could he even hope a reconciliation would be possible? He had fallen so far short of the man he wanted to be. When he had told Margaret she was free to go back to Moreton Hall, she had been more than willing to leave. Why would she do so, unless she was content and had no need of him?

"Perhaps she is afraid of the very same thing you are."

Tom shook his head. He didn't believe it then, and he did not believe it now. And yet...

"I beg your pardon, sir."

Tom turned away from the window to see the butler standing at the door. "Yes, what is it?"

"The groom has returned with your horse. He wishes for you to know that it is in the mews, safe and sound."

His horse. He'd forgotten that he had sent Turner for it some days ago. Here would be a friendly creature, one that had been his steadfast companion. Tom ought to have gone after him sooner.

A few minutes later Tom was in the stable, surveying Castor from head to foot. The horse whinnied softly, as though he were as content as Tom was at their reunion. "You've missed me, haven't you, fella?" Tom said, running a brush over the stallion's back. Castor's coat was still too thin for winter; it had not yet caught up to the way they had skipped the usual rotation of the seasons by their voyage up to the northern hemisphere.

Tom's heart felt as out of place as Castor's summer coat. Nothing was where it should be. "What would you say if we went back?" Tom asked the horse softly.

Castor snorted and tossed his head, and Tom took a quick step back to avoid the horse's stamping foot. He moved out of the stall and shut the gate. "You're right."

But there were a few things Tom had to do first. He hurried through the gently falling snow. Once he had regained the Somervilles' study, he found the current issue of the *Times* and turned to the shipping news.

Chapter 34

W here to, m'lady?"

Margaret looked at the cabdriver in surprise—not because of the lofty way he'd addressed her, but because he was wearing a very large and ostentatious sprig of mistletoe attached to his well-worn top hat. He must have been wearing it for weeks; it was a bit worse for wear and a few of the berries looked ready to fall off. He was a broad man; his round cheeks had a ruddy glow from too many hours out in the bitter weather.

Margaret gave him the address. "And hurry, if you please!"

"Right you are, m'lady," he replied. "I'll get you to that cozy and welcoming hearth in no time."

Margaret did not bother to contradict the man, even though she was painfully aware that the hearth that awaited her might be neither welcoming nor cozy. She only knew she had to find out.

When they finally reached the Somerville house, Margaret raced up the steps and fairly pounded on the door until someone answered. It was Mrs. Claridge, the Somervilles' housekeeper.

"Why, Mrs. Poole!" She opened the door wide, and Margaret stepped in, relieved to be out of the biting cold.

"Where is Mr. Poole?" she asked breathlessly. "I must see him."

"I'm so sorry, madam, but he's gone. They've all gone."

Now that she had caught her breath, Margaret was able to take in her surroundings. Her sudden arrival had taken more people by surprise than just Mrs. Claridge. An entire crew of servants were at work giving the house a thorough cleaning. Some were on hands and knees polishing the baseboards, others gently wiping down the plate on the large dining room table. All had unabashedly stopped their work to stare at Margaret. She was undoubtedly a sight, red-faced from the frost and windblown as she was.

"Where have they gone?" she implored.

"Lord and Lady Somerville left yesterday to spend Christmas at the Somerville house in Kent."

"And Mr. Poole? Surely he is with them, too?"

Mrs. Claridge shook her head. "I don't rightly know. He left in a separate carriage at a very early hour."

One of the men who had been cleaning the baseboards took a step forward. "If I may be of help, Mrs. Claridge?"

"Yes, Peter?"

"I heard Mr. Poole's valet telling one of our footmen that they were on their way to the docks. Said the ship for Australia was leaving at midnight with the tide, and he had to get there before it left. I can call the footman if you'd like to question him further—"

Margaret held up a hand. "No, thank you. You've been very helpful. And thank you, Mrs. Claridge."

"Mrs. Poole, if I may also add—"

But Margaret didn't wait to hear the rest. She dashed back to the cab, which was still waiting for her along with her baggage. "Do you know the way to the docks?" she asked.

"Why, of course, madam. Which pier?"

She looked at him, confused. "I don't know. I need to find a ship bound for Australia. One that's leaving tonight."

He nodded. "Right then. To the port authority."

The roads were dark now, nearly deserted. A thin layer of snow covered the streets, just enough to cause the horse to slip occasionally on the cobbles. Those who were about were hurrying as though to reach their warm hearths, whether grand or meager.

As the carriage approached the port authority building, Margaret tried to collect herself, to plan what she would say and how she would ask about Tom's whereabouts. She was spared from having to go inside, however. Her heart leaped when a man walked out, closing the door swiftly behind him. She knew immediately that it was Tom.

Her cheeks flamed from excitement and embarrassment. She stepped out of the coach, glad for the way the soft snow fell against her cheeks, cooling them.

He paused, spotting her instantly, in that way he had, that awareness of her presence, whether in a crowded room or an empty house, that always made her spine tingle.

The cabbie stood still, watching them both. It was as

if he knew that she and Tom were to meet here, on this night. She was sure he was able to sense the heat and electricity passing between her and Tom at this moment. She half wondered that the very gas lamps around them did not grow brighter. A breeze blew the gently falling snow into small swirls and lifted the sprig of mistletoe hanging on the coachman's top hat.

Margaret took two steps forward, wishing with all her might that he would spread his arms wide in a gesture that would invite her into the comforting warmth of his embrace.

But he made no move at all. He stood, watching her, his expression guarded, but unable to hide the piercing yearning. "What are you doing here, Maggie?"

Margaret's heart did a tiny dance that he could still think of her as his Maggie. "Yes, well, I..." she stammered. *I love you!* she wanted to cry out. *I will thank God to the end of my days if I can only be yours once more.* These thoughts ran riot in her head but could not seem to find their way to her mouth. Instead she stood, helplessly silent, barely able to breathe, much less speak.

Everything within her stilled, however, when he added coldly, "Have you some business for me, then?"

Perhaps the yearning she thought she saw in his eyes had been a mere trick of the gaslight. Snow settled on his hat brim and his lashes, and his face was set hard as stone. Margaret's legs trembled, but she dared not move, not wanting to show her desperate fear that he might be gone from her forever. "Yes, I do have business." Her voice was, happily, not as shaky as her legs.

She gestured back toward the carriage. "I've brought some papers with me that I need you to sign."

He closed his eyes briefly, and Margaret was sure she saw pain shoot across his face. "What do you have for me now?" he said. "Something to do with the estate, I expect. Is it more money you'll be wanting? I thought we were done with this."

"No." As the frost formed around her breath as she exhaled, Margaret hoped it would give a corporeal force to the meaning of her word. "I don't need more money. I need—"

Just Tom.

What if he laughed her to scorn? Told her she was a fool? Refused to take her back? What if her land would slip away from her forever, but without Tom in return? She must risk it. Better to lose all in the attempt than to regret not having taken the chance. She licked her lips, a habitual gesture, but here in the chilly evening it made her lips sting. "I wish to sell the land to Mr. Innes." Tom's eyes widened, but Margaret pressed on, desperate to get the words out before she lost what remained of her courage. "I wish to sell the land—the entire estate, all of Moreton Hall—to Mr. Innes. He has been keen to buy it for some time. But I cannot do it without your signature on the bill of sale."

Tom shook his head in disbelief, as though trying to dislodge cotton wool that had somehow gotten stuck in it. "You wish to sell the land," he repeated flatly. "But why? You love Moreton Hall. It means everything to you." His expression was coolly blank. "As well I know."

Because I love you. I want to be with you, anywhere in the world, rather than alone at Moreton Hall. Why could she not say the words aloud? She licked her lips again, hoping the frost nipping at them as a result could spur her to speak. "He's offered a very good price, you see. Far more than you had paid to get it out of debt. You will come out ahead."

"You are still trying to pay me back. You don't wish to be beholden to me."

"No," Margaret said. She took two faltering steps forward, unable to fight the desire to get closer to him, her entire body sending him an appeal. "I can never repay you. I can only offer you my love, and hope you can love me in return." Her words came out quiet, but sure.

"Maggie," he said softly. His breath seemed to catch on the word. Something flickered in his eyes now— something that this time had nothing to do with the gas lamps, kindling hope in Margaret's heart.

She threw herself against him, wrapping her arms around his neck, her face pressed hard against his broad chest. "I want only to be with you," she sobbed. "Anywhere you are, that's where we will make our home. Please, take me with you to Australia."

"No." The word was not spoken harshly, but with certainty. "You would not like Australia, Maggie. You are better off here."

She clung to him more fiercely, feeling a fool, and yet not caring that every last scrap of her treasured dignity and reserve was now completely gone. "Please," she begged.

Tom did not move, but neither did he attempt to push her away. Margaret remained pressed against him, clinging to him, savoring the feel of his rough wool coat against her cheek and the strength emanating from him. Moments slipped away, fading into the quiet night, as neither one of them moved. Slowly Margaret's panic subsided, and she became aware that his arms were wrapped gently around her, offering comforting warmth. "I cannot allow you to sell the land," he said again. "If we do that, then where would you and I live?"

She lifted her face now, unable to believe the meaning of his words. "You are not going to Australia?"

He reached up, brushing snow and tears from her cheek as he shook his head. "I'm here only to deliver a letter for Sullivan. I wanted to personally make sure it went on the ship along with the business papers I'm sending him." A ghost of a chuckle escaped his lips. "I'd really prefer to avoid ships for the foreseeable future."

"So you are not angry to see me?"

"*Stunned* would perhaps be a better word." He nodded briefly toward the customshouse. "That letter I just sent to Sullivan explains to him why I have decided to remain here in England. I'd made up my mind I was going to do whatever it took to win my wife back." He gave her a wry, self-deprecating smile that sent her heart into giddy flips. "I had no idea it would be so easy."

"But I don't understand."

"Geoffrey pointed out to me, and rightly so, that my highest duty lay right here. As your husband, I am to love you and cherish you. And in truth—" Margaret saw him swallow hard, choking back his emotions. "In truth, I never wanted to do anything else."

Despite his best efforts to wipe them away, Margaret's tears continued to stream down her face as she looked into the eyes of the man she loved with all her heart.

"Cheer up, my love," Tom said. He gently pulled her toward him, bringing her lips mere inches from his. "Living with me won't be so bad as all that."

A laugh—half-strangled with a sob—escaped her. She leaned forward, desperate for his kiss, eager to once more feel his lips on hers. But he pulled back, surprising her. He looked over her shoulder, and she turned to see what had captured his attention.

The cabbie was still standing there, watching and listening to every word of their conversation with complete lack of shame. Grinning at Tom, he said, "Congratulations, govnah!"

Tom laughed, and Margaret thought she had never heard a more satisfying sound. "Mr. Cabman," Tom said deferentially, removing his top hat, "might I trade with you?"

This brought an even wider grin from the cabbie. He removed his mistletoe-garnished hat and held it out to Tom. "With pleasure, govnah!"

Despite the cabbie's wide girth, his hat size was smaller than Tom's. As Tom placed the hat on his head, it perched precariously to one side. He looked ridiculous, and Margaret loved him even more for it. "Oh, look," Tom said, once more pulling Margaret close. "We seem to have found ourselves under the mistletoe."

After five years of exile, Lizzie Poole returns
home while living under an assumed identity.
But when she falls in love with a handsome
clergyman, will her secret cost her true love?

An *eiress at Heart*

Please turn the page for an excerpt.

London, June 1851

"If you've killed her, Geoffrey, we will never hear the end of it from Lady Thornborough."

Geoffrey Somerville threw a sharp glance at his companion. The man's flippancy annoyed him, but he knew James Simpson was never one to take any problem too seriously. Not even the problem of what to do with the young woman they had just accidentally struck down with his carriage.

The girl had been weaving her way across the street, seemingly unaware of their rapid approach until it was too late. The driver had barely succeeded in steering the horses sharply to one side to keep from trampling her under their massive hooves. However, there had not been enough time or space for him to avoid the girl completely, and the front wheel had tossed her onto the walkway as easily as a mislaid wicker basket.

Geoffrey knelt down and raised the woman's head

gently, smoothing the hair from her forehead. Blood flowed freely from a wound at her left temple, marring her fair features and leaving ugly red streaks in her pale yellow hair.

Her eyes were closed, but Geoffrey saw with relief that she was still breathing. Her chest rose and fell in ragged but unmistakable movements. "She's not dead," he said. "But she is badly hurt. We must get help immediately."

James bounded up the steps and rapped at the door with his cane. "First we have to get her inside. People are beginning to gather, and you know how much my aunt hates a scandal."

Geoffrey noted that a few people had indeed stopped to stare, although no one offered to help. One richly dressed young lady turned her head and hurried her escort down the street, as though fearful the poor woman bleeding on the pavement had brought the plague to this fashionable Mayfair neighborhood. At one time Geoffrey might have wondered at the lack of Good Samaritans here. But during the six months he'd been in London, he'd seen similar reactions to human suffering every day. Although it was no longer surprising, it still saddened and sickened him.

Only the coachman seemed to show real concern. He stood holding the horses and watching Geoffrey, his face wrinkled with worry. Or perhaps, Geoffrey realized, it was merely guilt. "I never even seen her, my lord," he said. "She come from out of nowhere."

"It's not your fault," Geoffrey assured him. He pulled out a handkerchief and began to dab the blood that was seeping from the woman's wound. "Go as quickly as you can to Harley Street and fetch Dr. Layton."

"Yes, my lord." The coachman's relief was evident. He scrambled up to the driver's seat and grabbed the reins. "I'm halfway there already."

Geoffrey continued to cautiously check the woman for other injuries. He slowly ran his hands along her delicate neck and shoulders and down her slender arms. He tested only as much as he dared of her torso and legs, torn between concern for her well-being and the need for propriety. Thankfully, nothing appeared to be broken.

James rapped once more on the imposing black door. It finally opened, and the gaunt face of Lady Thornborough's butler peered out.

"Clear the way, Harding," James said. "There has been an accident."

Harding's eyes widened at the sight of a woman bleeding on his mistress's immaculate steps. He quickly sized up the situation and opened the door wide.

Geoffrey lifted the unconscious girl into his arms. She was far too thin, and he was not surprised to find she was light as a feather. Her golden hair contrasted vividly with his black coat. Where was her hat? Geoffrey scanned the area and noted with chagrin the remains of a straw bonnet lying crushed in the street. Something tugged at his heart as her head fell against his chest. Compassion, he supposed it was. But it was curiously profound.

"She is bleeding profusely," James pointed out. "Have one of the servants carry her in, or you will ruin your coat."

"It's no matter," Geoffrey replied. He felt oddly protective of the woman in his arms, although he had no idea who she was. His carriage had struck her, after all, even if her own carelessness had brought about the calamity. He was not about to relinquish her, not for any consideration.

He stepped grimly over the red smears her blood had left on the white marble steps and carried her into the front hall, where James was again addressing the butler. "Is Lady Thornborough at home, Harding?"

"No, sir. But we expect her anytime."

Geoffrey knew from long acquaintance with the Thornborough family that Harding was a practical man who remained calm even in wildly unusual circumstances. The childhood escapades of Lady Thornborough's grand-daughter, Victoria, had developed this ability in him; James's exploits as an adult had honed it to a fine art.

Sure enough, Harding motioned toward the stairs with cool equanimity, as though it were an everyday occurrence for an injured and unknown woman to be brought into the house. "Might I suggest the sofa in the Rose Parlor, sir?"

"Excellent," said James.

As they ascended the stairs, Harding called down to a young parlor maid who was still standing in the front hall. "Mary, fetch us some water and a towel. And tell Jane to clean the front steps immediately." Mary nodded and scurried away.

Another maid met them at the top of the stairs. At Harding's instructions, she quickly found a blanket to spread out on the sofa to shield the expensive fabric.

Geoffrey set his fragile burden down with care. He seated himself on a low stool next to the woman and once again pressed his handkerchief to the gash below her hairline. The flesh around the wound was beginning to turn purple—she had been struck very hard. Alarm assailed him. "What the devil possessed her to step in front of a moving carriage?"

He was not aware that he had spoken aloud until James answered him. "Language, Geoffrey," he said with mock prudishness. "There is a lady present."

Geoffrey looked down at the unconscious woman. "I don't think she can hear me just now." He studied her with interest. Her plain black dress fit her too loosely, and the cuffs appeared to have been turned back more than once. Her sturdy leather shoes were of good quality, but showed signs of heavy wear. Was she a servant, wearing her mistress's cast-off clothing? Or was she a lady in mourning? Was she already sorrowing for the loss of a loved one, only to have this accident add to her woes? "If she is a lady, she has fallen on hard times," Geoffrey said, feeling once again that curious pull at his heart. He knew only too well the wretchedness of having one's life waylaid by one tragedy after another.

A parlor maid entered the room, carrying the items Harding had requested. She set the basin on a nearby table. After dipping the cloth in the water, she timidly approached and gave Geoffrey a small curtsy. "With your permission, my lord."

Something in the way the maid spoke these words chafed at him. He had been entitled to the address of "my lord" for several months, but he could not accustom himself to it. There were plenty who would congratulate him on his recent elevation to the peerage, but for Geoffrey it was a constant reminder of what he had lost. Surely nothing in this world was worth the loss of two brothers. Nor did any position, no matter how lofty, absolve a man from helping another if he could. He held out his hand for the cloth. "Give it to me. I will do it."

The maid hesitated.

"Do you think that is wise?" James asked. "Surely this is a task for one of the servants."

"I do have experience in this. I often attended to the ill in my parish."

"But you were only a clergyman then. Now you are a baron."

Geoffrey hated the position he had been placed in by the loss of his two elder brothers. But he would use it to his advantage if he had to. And he had every intention of tending to this woman. "Since I am a baron," he said curtly, motioning again for the cloth, "you must all do as I command."

James laughed and gave him a small bow. "Touché, *my lord.*"

The maid put the towel into Geoffrey's hand and gave him another small curtsy. She retreated a few steps, but kept her eyes fastened on him. Geoffrey suspected that her diligence stemmed more from his new social position than from the present circumstances. It had not escaped him that he'd become the recipient of all kinds of extra attention—from parlor maids to duchesses—since he'd become a baron. The years he'd spent as a clergyman in a poor village, extending all his efforts to help others who struggled every day just to eke out a meager living, had apparently not been worth anyone's notice.

Geoffrey laid a hand to the woman's forehead. It was too warm against his cool palm. "I'm afraid she may have a fever in addition to her head injury."

James made a show of pulling out his handkerchief and half covering his nose and mouth. "Oh dear, I do hope she has not brought anything catching into the house. That would be terribly inconvenient."

Harding entered the room, carrying a dust-covered carpetbag. He held it in front of him, careful not to let it touch any part of his pristine coat. "We found this near the steps outside. I believe it belongs to"—he threw a disparaging look toward the prostrate figure on the sofa—"the lady."

"Thank you, Harding," James said. He glanced at the worn object with equal distaste, then motioned to the far side of the room. "Set it there for now."

That bag might be all the woman had in the world, Geoffrey thought, and yet James was so casually dismissive of it. The man had a long way to go when it came to finding compassion for those less fortunate.

He turned back to the woman. She stirred and moaned softly. "Easy," Geoffrey murmured, unable to resist the urge to comfort her, although he doubted she could hear him. "You're safe now."

James watched from the other side of the sofa as Geoffrey cleaned the blood from her hair and face. "What a specimen she is," he remarked as her features came into view. He leaned in to scrutinize her. "Look at those high cheekbones. And the delicate arch of her brow. And those full lips—"

"This is a woman, James," Geoffrey remonstrated. "Not some creature in a zoo."

"Well, it's clear she's a woman," James returned lightly, unruffled by Geoffrey's tone. "I'm glad you noticed. Sometimes I wonder if you are aware of these things."

Geoffrey was aware. At the moment, he was *too* aware. He could not deny that, like James, he had been taken by her beauty. Except her lips were too pale, chapped from dryness. He had a wild urge to reach out and gently brush over them with cool water...

"Good heavens," James said, abruptly bringing Geoffrey back to his senses. He dropped his handkerchief from his face. "This is Ria."

Geoffrey froze. "What did you say?"

"I said, the young lady bleeding all over Auntie's sofa is Victoria Thornborough."

No. Surely that was impossible. There were occasions, Geoffrey thought, when James seemed determined to try him to the absolute limit. "James, this is not the time for one of your childish pranks."

James shook his head. "I am absolutely in earnest."

"But that's preposterous."

"I think I should know my own cousin. Even if it has been ten years." He bent closer as the woman mumbled something incoherent. "You see? She heard me. She recognizes her name."

The room suddenly became quite still. Even the servants who had been hovering nearby stopped their tasks. All eyes turned toward the sofa.

Was this really Ria? Geoffrey had to take James's word on it for now; he had never met her. He had been in Europe during her brief, clandestine courtship with his brother. This woman, to whom he had been so curiously drawn—for some reason he could easily believe her to be a lady, despite her dirty clothes and bruises. He had no trouble believing Edward could have fallen in love with her—had he not been taken with her himself? *No,* he told himself again. It had been mere compassion he'd been feeling. And it was utterly incomprehensible that his sister-in-law should appear like this out of nowhere.

"If this is Ria," Geoffrey said, "then surely Edward would be with her?"

"So one would expect," James replied. "I agree that the situation is most unusual."

"Unusual," Geoffrey repeated drily. The word might describe everything about what had happened between Ria and his brother. Their elopement had taken everyone by surprise, causing a scandal that was bad enough without the embarrassing fact that Ria had been engaged to his other brother, William, at the time.

"At least we can surmise that they were not aboard the ill-fated *Sea Venture*," James said. "Where *did* they go, I wonder?"

"That is only one of the many things I'd like to know," Geoffrey said. He'd exhausted himself with searches and inquiries after Edward and Ria had disappeared without a trace. The best they could discover was that the couple may have booked passage on a ship that had sunk on its way to America. And yet all was conjecture; there had never been answers.

Geoffrey took hold of the woman's left hand and began to remove a worn glove that was upon it. He heard the maid behind him gasp, but he was beyond worrying about the possible impropriety of his actions. If this was Ria, he wanted evidence that Edward had made an honest woman of her. He did not think his brother would deliberately trifle with a woman's affections, but he also knew Edward was prone to rash whims and irresponsible actions. Anything might have kept him from carrying out his plans.

With one last gentle tug from Geoffrey, the glove came off, revealing a hand that was rough and calloused.

It was a hand that had done plenty of manual labor. Though she was not wearing a wedding band, she was wearing a gold and onyx ring that Geoffrey recognized as having once belonged to Edward. The sight of it nearly devastated him. He could think of only one reason she would be wearing it instead of his brother.

"Why?" Geoffrey asked roughly, as his concern melted into consternation. "If they were in dire straits, why did they stay away? Why did they not ask us for help?"

"If you were in their shoes," James answered, "would you have wanted to face William's wrath? Or Lady Thornborough's?" He looked at the woman thoughtfully. "Perhaps they were not always so destitute. Look at her, Geoffrey. Look at what she is wearing."

Geoffrey allowed his gaze to travel once more over the slender figure in the plain black dress that seemed to declare her in mourning. "No!" Geoffrey said sharply. How could she have survived, but not Edward?

Geoffrey rose and gave the towel and the glove to the maid. He walked to the window and peered through the lace curtains to the street below. It was filled with carriages moving swiftly in both directions, but he could see no sign of either his coach or the doctor's. He knew it was too soon to expect their return, but he could not quell the anxiety rising in him.

Which was worse: the continual pain of not knowing what had become of his brother, or the final blow of discovering he really was dead? If anyone had asked him that question before this moment, he might have given an entirely different response.

He had to get Ria well again. And he had to get answers.

About the Author

The youngest child of a Navy pilot and a journalist, Jennifer acquired a love of adventure and an excitement for learning that continues to this day. She's lived in three countries and traveled throughout the United States. An avid reader of classics and historical fiction, she also enjoys biographies and histories, which she mines for the vivid details to bring to life the characters and places in her books. She resides with her husband in North Carolina—where, when not writing or dreaming up romantic adventures for her characters, she can be found fantasizing about her next ski trip or European vacation.

You can learn more at:

Twitter, @JenDelamere

http://www.facebook.com/jennifer.delamere

THE DISH

Where Authors Give You the Inside Scoop

♥ ♥ ♥ ♥ ♥ ♥ ♥ ♥ ♥ ♥ ♥ ♥ ♥ ♥ ♥

From the desk of Jennifer Delamere

Dear Reader,

One reason I love writing historical fiction is that I find fascinating facts during my research that I can use to add spice to my novels.

For Tom Poole's story in A LADY MOST LOVELY, I was particularly inspired by an intriguing tidbit I found while researching shipwrecks off the southern coast of Australia. In describing the wreck of a steamer called *Champion* in the 1850s, the article included this one line: "A racehorse aboard *Champion* broke loose, swam seven miles to the shore, and raced again in the Western District." Isn't that amazing!? Not only that the horse could make it to land, but that it remained healthy enough to continue racing.

Although I was unable to find out any more details about the racehorse, as a writer this little piece of information was really all I needed. I knew it would be a wonderful way to introduce the animal that would come to mean so much to Tom Poole. Tom and the stallion are the only survivors of a terrible shipwreck that left them washed up on the coast near Melbourne, Australia, in early 1851. Tom was aboard that ship in the first place because he was chasing after the man who had murdered his best friend. By the time he meets Margaret Vaughn in A LADY MOST LOVELY, Tom has been involved in two other real-life events as well: a massive wildfire near Melbourne, and the gold rush that would ultimately make him a wealthy man.

As you may have guessed by now, Tom Poole is a man of action. This aspect of his nature certainly leads him into some interesting adventures! However, when he arrives in London and meets the beguiling but elusive Miss Margaret Vaughn, he's going to discover that affairs of the heart require an entirely different set of skills, but no less determination.

Jennifer Delamere

♥ ♥ ♥ ♥ ♥ ♥ ♥ ♥ ♥ ♥ ♥ ♥ ♥ ♥ ♥

From the desk of Erin Kern

Dear Reader,

There are two things in this world that I love almost as much as dark chocolate. One of them is a striking pair of blue eyes framed by thick black lashes, with equally dark hair just long enough for a woman's fingers to run through...Excuse me for a moment while I compose myself.

And the other is fried pie.

Okay, I just threw that last part in as an FYI. But what I'm really doing is tucking that useless tidbit away for a future project. That's just how my weird mind works, folks.

But in all seriousness, while I really do love a blue-eyed man, even more than that I love a wounded soul. Because I love to fix things. In my books. In real life I kind of suck at it.

Way back when I first started writing the Trouble series, as was kicked off with *Looking for Trouble*, I had an atypical wounded soul already forming in the cavernous recesses of my mind. I just needed to find a home for her.

Yes, I'm talking about a wounded heroine. I know that sounds kind of strange. Most romance readers love a scarred hero who gets his butt kicked into shape by some head-strong Miss Fix-It. Not that I don't love that also. But I also knew *Looking for Trouble* wasn't the place for her.

Lacy Taylor needed her own story with her own hero. And not only her own hero, but one with an extra tough brand of love that could break through her well-built defense mechanisms.

But make no mistake. Lacy Taylor isn't as much of a tough cookie as she'd like everyone to think. Oh, no. She has a much softer side that only Chase McDermott could bring to the surface. Of course, she tries to keep Chase at arm's length like everyone else in her life. But he's too good for her defenses. Too good-looking. Too loose-hipped. Too quick with his melt-your-bones smile. Not to mention his blue eyes. Gotta have those baby blues.

But Chase underestimates Lacy's power. And I'm not talking about her tough-girl attitude. Never in Chase's years as an adult would he have expected Lacy Taylor to get under his skin so quickly. Not only that, but nothing could have prepared him for his reaction to it.

Or to her.

You see, Chase and Lacy have known each other for a long time. And that's another one of my weaknesses—childhood crushes turned steamy love stories. And Chase and Lacy can cook up steam faster than a drop of water on hot pavement. But it wasn't always like that for these two. You see, Lacy blew out of Trouble years earlier, and after that Chase hardly gave the tough blonde a second thought.

But then she comes back. Now *that's* when things get interesting.

Mostly because Lacy had to all but beg Chase for a job, which, in Lacy's opinion, was almost as painful as a bikini wax. So then they're working together. Seeing each other often. Subtle brushes here and there…you get the picture.

It gets hot. *Real* hot.

But the most fun part is seeing how these two wear each other down. Lacy thinks she's so tough, and Chase thinks he can charm the habit off a nun. Well, actually he probably could.

Needless to say, heads butt, tempers flare, and the clothes, they go a-flying.

But which of these comes first? It's all in HERE COMES TROUBLE. Because every woman needs some Trouble in her life.

Especially the blue-eyed kind.

Steamy readin',

Erin Kern

From the desk of Lily Dalton

Dear Reader,

History has always been my thing.

Boring? Never! I've always viewed the subject as a colorful, dynamic puzzle of moving pieces, fascinating to analyze and relive, in whatever way possible. I used to have a history professor who often raised the question, "What if?"

For example, what if Ragnar Lodbrok and his naughty horde of Vikings had decided that they adored farming, so instead of setting off to maraud the coast of England in search adventure and riches, they had just stayed home? How might that omission from history have changed the face of England?

And jumping forward a few centuries: What if historical bad boy Henry VIII had not had such poor impulse control, and had instead just behaved himself? What if he'd tried harder to be faithful to Catherine? What if he'd never taken a shine to Anne Boleyn? There wouldn't have been an Elizabeth I. How might this have changed the path of history?

At the heart of history, of course, are people and personalities and motivations. *Characters.* They weren't flat, dusty words in black and white on the pages of a textbook. Instead, they lived in a vivid, colorful, and dangerous world. They had hearts and feelings and suffered agonies and joy.

Just like Vane Barwick, the Duke of Claxton, and his

estranged wife, the duchess Sophia, who stand on the precipice of a forever sort of good-bye. Though the earlier days of their marriage were marked by passion and bliss, so much has happened since, and on this cold, dark night, understanding and forgiveness seem impossible.

Of course, in NEVER DESIRE A DUKE, the "what if?" is a much simpler question, in that the outcome will not change the course of nations.

What if there hadn't been a snow storm that night?

Hmm. Now that I've forced that difficult question upon us, I realize I don't want to imagine such an alternate ending to Vane and Sophia's love story. Being snowbound with someone gorgeous and intriguing and desirable and, yes, provoking, is such a delicious fantasy.

If there hadn't been a snow storm that night. . .

Well… thankfully, dear reader, there was!

Hugs and Happy Reading,

Lily Dalton

www.lilydalton.com
Twitter@LilyDalton
Facebook.com

♥ ♥ ♥ ♥ ♥ ♥ ♥ ♥ ♥ ♥ ♥ ♥ ♥ ♥ ♥

From the desk of Debbie Mason

Dear Reader,

So there I was, sitting in my office in the middle of a heat wave, staring at a blank page waiting for inspiration to strike. I typed Chapter One. Nothing. Nada.

And the problem wasn't that I was writing a Christmas story in the middle of July. I had the air conditioner cranked up, holiday music playing in the background, a pine-scented candle burning, and a supply of Hammond's chocolate-filled peppermint candy canes on my desk. FYI, best candy canes ever!

No, the problem was my heroine, Madison Lane. I didn't get her, and honestly, I was afraid I wasn't going to like her very much. Because really, who doesn't love Christmas and small towns? At that point, I was thinking of changing the title from *The Trouble with Christmas* to *The Trouble with Madison Lane.*

It took a couple of hours of staring at her picture on my wall before Madison finally opened up to me. Okay, so I may have thrown a few darts at her, drawn devil horns on her head, and given her an impressive mustache before she did. But she won me over. Once I found out what had happened to her in that small Southern town all those years ago, I fell in love with Madison. She's strong, incredibly smart, and loyal, and after what she suffered as a little girl, she deserves a happily-ever-after more than most.

Now all I needed was a man who was up for the challenge. Enter Gage McBride, the gorgeous small-town sheriff and single father of two young girls. A born protector, Gage is strong enough to deal with Madison and smart enough to see the sweet and vulnerable woman beneath her tough, take-no-prisoners attitude. But just because these two are a perfect match doesn't mean their journey to a happily-ever-after is an easy one. The title of the book is THE TROUBLE WITH CHRISTMAS, after all.

I hope you have as much fun reading Gage and Madison's story as I did writing it. And I hope, like Gage and Madison, that this holiday season finds you surrounded by the love of family and friends.

Wishing you much joy and laughter!